To the Great Author, the Muse of my soul;
To Michael, my own Christopher Lake
To Mamma, my invaluable research assistant;
and to the critters at ChristianWriters.com & Eastside Authors Chat,

Thank you.

SEARCHING FOR SARA | HEART OF THE BLESSED, BOOK 1

This is a work of fiction. Names, characters, places, and events are products of the author's imagination or are used fictitiously. Any resemblance to actual persons, living or dead, locales or events is entirely coincidental.

Searching for Sara © Nona King a.k.a. Nona Johnson
2005 - First Printing
2012 - Second Printing
2013 - Third Printing
2016 – Fourth Printing (Extended Edition)

All rights reserved, including the right to reproduce this book or portions thereof in any form.

ISBN: 1-4404872-0-0 | EAN-13: 978-14404872-0-0

The Library of Congress Copyright Office
Searching for Sara/ Johnson, N.M.
TXu1 - 131 - 355

Cover design by Taria A. Reed.

Printed in the United States of America

HEART OF THE BLESSED

Searching for Sara

Releasing Yesterday

Broken Angel

OTHER BOOKS BY NONA KING

To Save a Soul

My Fair Princess

The Story: A Tale of Redemption and Romance

The *Bookworms and Booya!* Saga

Few Words

A Rose By Any Other Name

The *Terra* Saga

Searching for Sara

Heart of the Blessed

Book One

THE BEATITUDES

Blessed are the poor in spirit,
For theirs is the kingdom of heaven.

Blessed are those who mourn,
For they shall be comforted.

Blessed are the meek,
For they shall inherit the earth.

Blessed are those who hunger and thirst for righteousness,
For they shall be filled.

Blessed are the merciful,
For they shall obtain mercy.

Blessed are the pure in heart,
For they shall see God.

Blessed are the peacemakers,
For they shall be called sons of God.

Blessed are those who are persecuted for righteousness' sake,
For theirs is the kingdom of heaven.

Matthew 5:4-10 (NKJV)

ONE

Freedom's Whisper

February, 1892 | London

Sara's heart thudded in her chest as she crammed her scant possessions into the worn valise. A shout echoed through the hall. She cast a furtive glance over her shoulder. Her trembling hands clutched the black frock to her chest. The door to her cell-sized room remained shut, but the bellowing from the floor below escalated. A door slammed.

Sara latched her valise. The finality rang in her ears and beat in her heart. No more. Tonight would be the last day she cowered. She rushed for the door and peeked out. Reverberating steps hurried her from the room and into the back hall. Would she make it free in time? *Dear Lord, please help me!*

Her friend Beth stepped from the kitchen and beckoned her. The scullery maid's lank black hair escaped in wisps from her white mob cap. Sara rushed through the kitchen and into the chill February air. Big Ben chimed the midnight hour.

Beth tucked an old pair of gloves into Sara's hands. "You get thee gone, Sara. Do no' look back. Do no' even think on us. You be done with the servant's life here and get thee to America like you promised."

Sara clutched the young woman to her, tears burning her dark blue eyes. "Beth... I wish you would come with me."

Beth pushed back, her brown eyes red-rimmed. "I wish too, Sara, but—get thee gone," she cried. Then she fled and bolted the door closed behind her.

Sara stifled a sob and rushed through the cobbled streets toward the old church from her childhood. If the old priest, Amicus, did not remember her, God would provide another way. How could she believe anything less? The first step for freedom would be her responsibility.

All else would rest in the good Lord's hands.

March, 1892

Sara stared beyond the plain teacup. When she ventured to the docks that morning, the fear of being seen by someone from Mr. Brockle's household dogged her every step. But now there rose a much more daunting obstacle. How long would it take to save such a sum as she needed for but a third class fare? There was also spending money she would need in America: food, lodging, cab fare, clothes.... She hid her face in her hands. Why had she not waited to leave? Two more days and she would have secured her past wages.

She forced her back to straightened, clasping hands in

her lap as her cooling tea once more drew her stare. No, she would not give up hope. Despair was not of the Lord. He could be trusted with this as well, and He would fulfill His promises.

A step behind her drew her gaze. An older woman with raven locks and silver eyes stood at the doorway. She exuded regal grace, her satin brocade walking dress immaculate. The hat upon her raven tresses alight with various shades of blue, two doves perched upon the brim and arranged in such a way as to seem the wings of angels shielding her from the sun.

Sara bobbed a curtsy. "Good morning, mum."

The woman inclined her head. "I noticed the light and expected the priest."

"I'm sorry, mum. He stepped away until the morrow." Nervous tension set her knees to trembling. She indicated the tea service. "Would you care to take tea, mum?"

"Thank you, dear. That would be grand."

The woman slipped from her kid gloves and lowered herself with noble poise to the straight-back chair across from her. Sara readied another cup.

"Are you kin, dear?"

"No, mum. He was a close friend of my mum before she passed." He had given her a first Bible, long since lost.

"Will you be visiting long?" She accepted the tea, the tone of her question courtesy rather than interest.

"I... I do no' know, mum."

"Well, regardless, I am certain he is pleased to have the company." She sipped her tea and perused her surroundings with a slight smile. "I also knew him as a child. It will be good to reminisce over better days." The woman focused those silver blue eyes on Sara. "I wonder if you are the young woman he discussed in his letter?"

Sara's teacup chinked upon its saucer.

"Do you journey for America?"

"M-mum?" Did the household know? Why would he betray her?

"My daughter is to be wed in little more than half-a-year. She is in need of a few items yet for her trousseau." The woman paused to sip her tea, those sharp eyes of blue never wandering their scrutiny. "Should you accept the duty of the design and creation, I shall pay handsomely. In addition, I will pass the knowledge of your skill to my friends. You should accumulate wealth enough to pay for your passage before the storms of the next season."

Speechless wonder fogged Sara's mind, her eyes unable to retreat from the older woman's unflinching gaze.

The woman smiled, set aside her cup, and stood. She extended a card. "This is where I can be reached. I will forward my daughter's measurements to you. Should you require anything more, send a note however you wish. Discretion is my intent. Good day, dear."

Sara blinked after her, even after the closure of the sturdy cedar door. Then she lowered her head and whispered a blessing, silent tears wet her clasped hands.

September, 1893

"You have a letter."

Sara's head snapped up, the pencil slipping from her trembling fingers to clatter upon the hardwood floor. Her hands clutched her sketchbook. The priest's smile did nothing to soothe her nerves as he presented her an envelope. "Is it... ? "

"From America? Indeed, Miss Sara. From a Mr. Christopher Lake. Virginia."

Her hands couldn't release their hold on the sketchbook as she stared at the elegant handwriting. How many months slipped away since her letter requesting instructions? Almost long enough to quench her remaining embers of hope. But each day a whisper greeted her in the quiet hours of the morning as she read the scriptures. To be still and trust in her Lord's provision. Now, when faced with the realization of all her dreams.... "I-I can no'. Please, sir. Could you... could you read it to me?"

"Of course, my dear." The elderly priest sat in the straight-back chair across from her in the quiet living quarters behind the small church's main room. He set his spectacles upon his bulbous nose and peered at the writing, his head tilted to allow better focus.

> Miss Sara Little,
>
> I hope this letter finds you well.
>
> In answer to your request for travel instructions, please find the following information. I hope this is helpful to you.
>
> Firstly, find the passenger vessel 'Dawn's Angel' captained by a gentleman by the name of Robert Cowell. Mention the names Carla and Christopher Lake and he will book you passage at a discounted rate. If this letter finds you in time, he will be leaving the port nearest you on September 20th, 1893, at eight in the evening.
>
> Secondly, once the ship arrives in New York, there should be an almost immediate departure of a passenger train for Richmond, Virginia. If Capt. Cowell arrives on time (he is generally a day or so early), you should have plenty of time to purchase a ticket. Should you not have enough to cover the cost of passage, again, explain your situation and mention

my name and the ticket-master will take care of the rest. The train is due to depart on January 3rd, 1894, at one in the afternoon. Depending upon how early Capt. Cowell arrives in port, he will be responsible for arranging your stay in a hotel.

According to the schedule I've enclosed with this letter, the train is due to arrive at or before noon the following day; someone will be waiting for you at the station.

Good luck and safe traveling.

Christopher Lake

The priest lowered the letter. "Well. Now that is fine. What a blessing the Lord has brought upon you, my dear."

Eyes closed and lips trembling, Sara clasped her hands to her chest. A prayer of thanksgiving warmed her heart, the anxiety subsiding to a stronger glow of hope. Tomorrow.... Blessed tomorrow would find her journeying to America!

TWO

Journeys

3 January 1894 | New York

The passenger car of *The New York Central* beckoned Sara with its sharp whistle. Her gloved hand clasped her valise. In London the days bled into months as she scraped and saved for this journey. But each morning the Amicus offered encouragements from the scriptures. Each morning those whispered in the quiet hours as she sat by herself. Be still. Trust the Lord's provision.

Now.... Could she truly be faced with the realization of her dreams? Did freedom from every belittling bark now linger at the next station in Richmond, Virginia?

She squashed down her charcoal bonnet as a sharp breeze tugged the ribbons.

"All aboard, miss?" The conductor's wrinkled face drew her gaze. He broke into a kind smile. "We're about to get underway."

"Oh! Yes, thank you." Her English lilt drew glances from the other passengers as he helped her ascend the steep steps.

Sara paused on the outer platform of the passenger car, eagerness battling with the anxiety of the unknown. *No more fear*, she promised herself. Her chin rose and she clutched the heavy shawl tighter around her before pushing inside. She settled into the first empty seat as the locomotive lurched forward.

She set her valise onto the seat beside her and retrieved a faded journal, a snub-nosed pencil, and a worn leather portfolio of yellowed paper. Together they stood as the compilation of her adventure to date. A visual and verbal representation of every struggle from the time her mother passed until today, her moment of freedom from scorn and cruelty.

The journal rasped in welcome as she revealed its dog-eared pages, skimming those entries leading to the day she penned her first, blessed letter to America. How many years since that communication? Two? Almost three? Sara freed the worn response from the journal's grasp unfolding the pages with care. Her lips trembled upward as she again read those words which invited her to hope.

Dear Sara,

I felt such relief at the receipt of your letter! A mutual friend wrote of you, but she did not feel certain you would respond. For truth, she and her husband are of the mind your employer treats you with a harsh hand. She has insisted, and I agree, that you deserve a place better suited to your sensitive nature.

My husband and I have long held a passion for providing people with opportunities for greatness. I feel the Lord's hand upon my heart and I brim with concern. Please accept my invitation to come and choose your possible future. My husband and I will fully support you, whatever your chosen path.

Please write back with any questions you might have, Sara. We are eager to assist you however you need.

In Christ,

Carla Thiesen Lake

Sara's eyes burned as she returned the letter to its place, smoothing its slight creases with quaking fingers. *Thank You for this blessing.* Tears dripped from her chin to her clasped hands.

"Excuse me, miss?"

She startled and looked up, fumbling for the kerchief at her cuff. "Yes, sir?"

"Ticket?"

"Oh! Yes. It is here in my bag." Her search of the usual pocket for such items resulted in nothing. "This is odd."

"Where are you traveling from, miss?"

"London." Frustration stung in her eyes. "Dear me. It should be just here."

"London you say, miss?" The conductor whistled through his teeth and set his cap back upon his head. "You've been on quite the journey!"

Sara paused in her search to both gather her wits and offer him a smile. "I have, sir, but it has been a dream of mine for such a long time."

"You haven't been this way before?"

"No, sir." But she would not allow herself to worry. Directions were, even now, in her journal waiting for the last leg of her journey.

"Where are you headed to, miss? Washington or Richmond hereafter?"

"Richmond. I... is there a transfer?"

"No, miss. At Washington we wait for a bit to board up and unload, and then we're off the rest of the way. But you seek me out should you have any question. Anything at all."

"Thank you, sir. I will." Sara's focus dove once more into the depths of her valise. "There is a pocket specifically for that ticket—Mercy! Here it is. I must have died a thousand deaths just now," she said, laughing.

He punched the appropriate corner of the ticket. Then he read the specifics of her itinerary, nodding along as if a voice explained their meaning. He offered her back the item and motioned forward. "Come this way, miss, and I'll show you your berth for the night."

Shock and confusion pulled at her smile. "M-my berth?"

"Aye, miss. You will be here in the coach during the day trip, right enough, but you will have a berth for tonight. In the sleeper car, and that be just up here a bit."

Sara mutely rose, following the conductor as he continued on his way, punching tickets from those scattered passengers on his way through the car.

"It's nothing fancy, of course, but you'll have your own space and the people that're above and below usually do a right fine job of keeping themselves quiet."

She didn't trust her voice to offer much more than a quiet acknowledgement. When she stood in the warm and narrow hall of the sleeper car, he pulled aside the heavy curtain to a small compartment with a mattress and pillow within. As mentioned, there were similar compartments above and below.

"There you have it." He stowed her valise into the

compartment. "I don't know much about how they do things across the water, miss, but you should be comfortable enough here, right?"

"I.... Thank you so much, sir. It is certainly more than I expected."

"Miss?"

"I thought I would sleep in the coach. I did not know the price of the ticket meant...."

The conductor chuckled. "Ah no, miss. There will also be coffee and tea in the dining car just through there. Also included in the cost of the ticket." He tipped his cap. "You remember what I said, miss. Let me know if you need anything."

"Thank you, sir."

He continued on.

Sara lowered her gaze to her journal, caressing the front of it as she retrieved her pencil and portfolio from her valise and made her way once more to the coach. The scenes from her adventure played in her imagination, speaking to her with an intense urge to put her gratitude onto paper.

She sat in the seat nearest the door, again turning the pages of her journal with absent deliberation. Her fingers paused and she stared upon the elegant script of the letter within. It fluttered into her fingers, quivering in the slight breeze of the passenger car.

What waited for her in Richmond? A companion position? Seamstress? Nanny? If possibilities were endless, what dream would she seek out first? Mr. and Mrs. Lake wrote of a common goal, to set people less fortunate onto a better destiny. What a blessing to their spirit to help those in need!

A prayer of thanksgiving warmed her heart, the anxiety

subsiding to a stronger glow of hope. She retrieved her small pencil and balanced the journal upon the leather portfolio as she sorted the collection of thoughts flitting through her mind. How could she harness so many wonders and make sense enough to put it down into words?

A smile caressed her rose lips as she lifted her pencil to the journal pages.

> *My mind will not be still for the thinking of all that is left behind. The sorrow. The loneliness. The fear. But I have promised to start over, and You whisper to my heart to look forward. I see now that You used each "yesterday" to ready me for this journey. As this train carries me closer to my destination, I know there is so much more to discover. About myself and what I offer this new place. Please Lord, let this new life be everything I dreamt of having.*

Sara tucked the pencil away, and her fingers drifted yet again to that last letter. Its edges peeked just outside the journal's cover. She had freed herself from the oppressive past known since birth. An open future lay before her, waiting for her first step.

She had come to America!

4 January 1894

"Now disembarking at Richmond, ladies and gentlemen. Fifteen minutes until departure."

Sara stepped from the passenger car, her blue eyes wide as she surveyed the hustle and bustle to and from the platform.

The conductor tipped his cap toward her. "You take care, miss, and remember what I said about needing a place to stay. The missus would love to have you."

"Thank you, sir. In his letter, Mr. Lake said someone would meet me."

"Very good, miss, but I'll keep watch just the same." The conductor touched the brim of his cap and then tended to the other passengers.

Sara smiled after him. The locomotive blasted a warning call, and Sara's breath caught at a sudden tremor of excitement. When in her memory did she experience such an adventure? She laughed and stepped forward, navigating the icy train platform with care.

Once inside, Sara settled herself upon an oak and iron bench in the corner near the door. The warmth of the crowded station served as a pleasant change from the winter's chill. Luggage dollies clacked about, and the shouts of porters offered a comforting sense of similarity with England. That, when paired with the people bustling to and fro, would act as a perfect addition to her collection of sketches.

Sara pulled free her sheaf of papers and half-used pencil. Only a scarce few pages remained for scenes such as this. She hadn't decided yet if she dared sacrifice her last coins to purchase another handful. She guided the bit of pencil across the page with a deft whisper and tried to soothe her anxiety. Both Mr. and Mrs. Lake wrote of an opportunity here. How could she then begrudge the spending of a few meager coins when surrounded with such possibilities? Yet not knowing the details steeled her against the impulsive desire.

Her brows furrowed, her gaze flicking from the

developing sketch to her valise and the letters. *'My husband and I will fully support you whatever your chosen path might be.'* Those words resonated in her heart.

"Miss Sara Little?"

The baritone voice caused a hiccup within as she lifted her gaze. An attractive gentleman in a tailored gray suit drew her attention. His brown curls and straight nose bore an uncanny resemblance to the lady who referred her.

She tucked the portfolio into her valise while whispering a prayer for strength and courage. "I am Sara Little."

He navigated through the crowd with ease, begging their pardon at any jostle. It served as a delightful change from the arrogance of men in past experience.

"A pleasure to meet you, Miss Little. I am Christopher Lake. I wrote in response to your last letter?" He enfolded her hand in a friendly grip.

"Mr. Lake." Sara curtsied. It amazed her the master himself would have come to fetch her, though he did not seem miffed at the duty. "You should no' have troubled yourself with me, sir."

"Nonsense. No trouble. I apologize for my tardiness. Today has been a rash of the unexpected." He motioned to the bench just vacated. "Please."

"Thank you, sir." His brow furrowed and Sara's breath caught. "Something amiss, sir?"

"Miss Little, I...." He cleared his throat, his hazel eyes the dark of a spring storm.

Hope began to mold. Had she misunderstood the invitation? "Y-yes, sir?"

"My wife passed on before I received your request for travel instructions."

A chill tightened her spine.

"Now, I do not tell you in order to send you from whence you came. It is but, well, we did not hear from you for such a space of time that my late wife and I thought perhaps you experienced a change of heart."

"N-no, sir, I am sorry, sir." She bit her lip to prevent a further rush of words.

"Just as I am sorry you were required to seek my help rather than I volunteering it forward. As Carla—as my wife mentioned in her letter, and as the lady who referred you knows, we feel it a call upon our lives to help those who may not necessarily have the ability to help themselves."

Mr. Lake's hazel eyes held her gaze as if awaiting a response. "Th-thank you, sir."

"Hm? Oh. Quite welcome." His regard of her didn't waver. The hairs on her neck stood at attention. "What do you do?"

"Sir?"

"What do you do?"

"I... I do what needs to be done, sir." Servitude had been the way of her life since she could remember. How else could she answer a question like that?

He smiled, and the action lightened the darkness of his eyes. "No, Miss Little, not how are you employed. My mistake. What is it that you do as a creative outlet? Neither Dix nor Paul confessed a knowledge of your interests, so I am at a loss where my focus should begin."

"Oh." She considered the question, her fingers knit together to prevent a nervous flutter. "I sew well enough, selling gowns to pay for my passage."

"That rings with promise." He motioned to her valise and the papers peeking forth. "Do you have a portfolio of the designs?"

"N-no, sir." She tucked the pages deeper within, her gaze downcast. "They were lost."

"Ah. No matter. Considering your presence in America, I believe I will take you at your word. Have you tried your hand at any other type of craft?"

"I can sketch a bit." Her heart raced with the rush of confession. "My mum said I have quite a way with a pencil."

"Ah! Now we come to something I understand." He stood and took up her valise. "Come along. Let us talk more about your 'way with a pencil'."

Sara tightened the shawl around her shoulders as she followed him from the station. Outside, he led her to the waiting carriage. She gaped at the golden lettering, *The Richmond Gallery of Art*.

"Neither of us mentioned the gallery? Odd. I hope it does not pose a problem."

"No, sir. I never...." She never considered herself appropriate staff for a gallery.

"I can see you have questions." He opened the carriage door. "You may ask as many as you like once we escape this wind. Much longer and we'll catch our death."

He steadied Sara's ascent into the carriage and then sat across from her. The carriage lurched forward. "We have always been eager to take someone less fortunate under our wing. It added excitement to our own lives, the adventure of creating an artist's opportunity."

A darkness shadowed his countenance while he spoke. Then he forced a smile. It didn't quite reach the hazel of his eyes. "Now, a question, and that strictly out of curiosity. Please don't think me impertinent, but what delayed your journey?"

Sara blinked at him. "P-pardon?"

Mr. Lake cleared his throat. "Well, I understood from your letter—That is, you first contacted us some time ago, so I wonder now if you experienced difficulties due to family concerns. Would you need me to contact them and set them at ease? They shouldn't believe we take advantage."

She stared at him, baffled. "Y-you would do that, sir?"

"Contact your family? Certainly! I feel it stands as my responsibility since my wife and I set you on this path. Now, tell me what kept you. If there is a lingering doubt, I shall put it to rest."

"B-but there is nothing to tell, sir. I only had to save for my passage. That is why—" Her gaze fell to her white-knuckled hands. They began to throb. "That's why I stitched the gowns."

"An entire wardrobe on your own? It is a wonder you arrived at all." He withdrew a gold pocket-watch from his vest pocket to toy with it in his palm.

A quick examination from beneath her lashes discerned a trace of gauntness to his cheeks. It teased a sense of recollection in the back of Sara's mind. But that fell away when the carriage drew up in front of an immense, single-story brick building.

"Ah! Here we are."

Mr. Lake retrieved Sara's valise and steadied her descent. She whispered her thanks, her cheeks burning as she followed in his wake up the gallery's marble steps.

"Being from England you will find our gallery somewhat modest in size and scope to your own. However, I must assure you it provides an adequate introduction point for local talent."

"It seems quite grand, sir." The charming simplicity to the red brick and white shutters invited entry. The museums of her limited experience loomed with an almost dour outlook. How could one appreciate the wonders of art when overpowered by the expectations of silence and reserve?

He held the door for her, the warmth and brightness inviting her deeper into the front hallway. "We are here to have you sketch my daughter. To her dismay, I would not allow her to tag along with me to the station. My daughter finds the Richmond Station the most adventurous of places, especially for hiding."

Sara laughed, the quiet sound echoing as a whisper of welcome. She flushed and lowered her gaze. The feeling of comfort and safety hadn't been expected.

"This way, Miss Little. Gwyn's favorite room is just down this hall."

At the end of the main hall they came upon a pair of overstuffed green brocade chairs setup beyond a picture window. It encouraged comfort, a place to chat and observe. She felt certain that served its express purpose during art forums.

A cozy library stood beyond the picture window, and a young girl dressed in velvet and satin sprawled upon the floor flipping through the pages of a picture book.

"Such a darling," Sara whispered.

"That she is. Gwynnie is five years young, precocious, and forever brimming with questions." He offered Sara the nearest chair and then presented her a pencil and sketchbook. "Take as much time as you need. While engrossed in a storybook, the dear forgets there is a world outside this room. I will wait in the office, the first door on the left just before the exit."

"Yes, sir."

He inclined his head, cast his daughter a fond glance, and then proceeded from whence they came. Sara stared after him. Mr. Lake bore such a striking contrast to her last employer. He showed compassion, demonstrating a kindness and understanding that seemed a facet of his persona. *I would not mind working for a gentleman like him, Lord.*

Sara lowered her focus to the pencils and paper and began outlining the different parts and positions of the child and objects in the room. Mr. Lake's attitude encouraged conversation while giving her a feeling of welcome. The only welcome received before was that of inappropriate innuendo.

Her eyebrows dipped into a frown as her pencil glided with deft motions across the paper. *Here will be different,* she promised. *This is America. A land of dreams and promises.* While Sara didn't understand yet what that fully meant, she recognized these past months as the first when she hadn't dreaded the morning.

Sara shivered with expectancy, her frown vanishing into a smile. Now she but needed to continue to step forward, daily, and strive for her different future. Hadn't this already presented the most challenge for her heart? She could feel the whisper of her new future lingering on the outer portions of God's page, waiting for His design.

Sara buffed the final touches to the sketch and then held it out for review. "Well enough."

She gathered her things and hastened to Mr. Lake's office. Her hesitant knock received no answer. Sara clutched the front of her brown traveling dress as her troubled gaze drifted to the polished brass of the handle. She repeated again the instructions explained, nodding along as she once more lifted her hand to rap.

This time the door opened. Mr. Lake's gaze met hers, a familiar haunting of grief darkening his features. Her breath caught in her throat.

"Ah. Miss Little." His stiff smile ushered the shadow away. "Please, come in."

Sara cast him a quick scrutiny as she entered the office. But whatever memory caused such poignant melancholy had gone.

"Now then." He leaned against his desk, the light oak enhancing the charcoal of his suit. "What have you drawn for me?"

"I-I suppose I should have taken more time, sir, only my mind ran away with me." She lowered herself into the nearest chair before presenting the sketch with unsteady fingers.

"Nonsense. Let us have a look."

An easel in the corner distracted her from his scrutiny of her sketch. The light of the bay window behind his desk served a stark exclamation to the blank canvas.

"This is quite good. The strokes are sure and steady, and the shading is exceptional."

Her insides clashed between the euphoria of praise and the anxiety of not wanting to say anything foolish. "Thank you, sir."

He lifted his gaze to meet hers. "Is this the only media you use? Have you done much with oils, or watercolor?"

"No, sir. My mum and I did no' have the means to purchase oils or any of that. I only ever learned how to sketch with pencils and charcoal."

Nodding, he set the paper aside and met her gaze. "Lunch?"

"Certainly, sir. What would you like? Are the kitchens just down the hall?" She stood, the familiar question setting her at ease.

"I—" His brows dipped. "Pardon?"

"Oh." Sara's gaze faltered. "N-nothing for me, sir. Thank you."

"No? I have been instructed time and again not to make decisions on an empty stomach. Let us gather Gwyn and make our way to the Manor for a bite." He proceeded to the open doorway.

Sara couldn't force a step toward the door. "You need no' bother with me, sir."

"It is no bother. Come along. I can assure you there is plenty for all."

"No, sir, truly. I have no' yet found a place. I can sup there." She didn't believe her nerves would tolerate eating in front of a prospective employer.

"Miss Little, what type of host would allow a visitor—of my country and my gallery—to fend for herself?"

Sara clicked her mouth shut. *It is only a bit of lunch, Sara Ann.* She worried her lower lip as she escaped to the hall. When he came to walk beside her she uttered a prayer for calm. *Only lunch.*

"How long have you been an active artist?"

She peeked at him. "I have tinkered with charcoals and pencils since before I could write." Again, his gaze shone with genuine interest. Presented with such a difference from the past mantra of 'seen and not heard', she found it a challenge to settle her nerves.

"Why?"

"Why what, sir?"

"Why did you pick up those first pencils and charcoals?

What motivates you?"

Nonplussed, Sara gawked at him.

"Certainly someone has posed such a question before. You exhibit obvious talent—No one? Gads! Are you certain you haven't a collection of sketches? A sketchbook of any kind?"

"N-no, sir." The thought of the portfolio in her valise pricked her conscience.

"Ah. Well, I suppose it matters little. If you are a fraction the artist I believe, you shall fit well."

But how did a body 'fit well' any place? Sara hadn't done much more than pass a gallery in all her years in London.

Mr. Lake opened the door to the sitting room and ducked his head inside. "Gwyn? We are off to the Manor for lunch."

"Yes, Papa." The rustle of papers, satin, and velvet preceded her appearance. In the hall, Gwyn cast Sara an uncertain look, her gaze shadowing to emerald.

"No monsters coming from the art, I hope?" Mr. Lake knelt to greet his daughter with a kiss on the cheek.

The girl giggled and shook her head, her blonde ringlets dancing around her shoulders. "Of course not, silly Papa."

"Good girl." He motioned toward Sara. "Gwyn, this is Sara Little. She will take lunch with us. Is that fine?"

His daughter edged closer. Again, the girl directed only the merest of glances toward Sara. "I suppose so."

"Who is this shy little girl?" Mr. Lake tousled her curls. "Mama and I invited Sara from England as our guest. Certainly you can offer a 'hello'."

Gwyn's eyes softened to the lush green of a spring glade. "Truly, Papa? England?"

"Indeed. As our guest, her comfort is our responsibility. Do you suppose you could make her feel at home? If you could, that would help me a great deal."

The girl nodded, expression adorable in its seriousness. Then she bestowed Sara a bright smile and a curtsy. "My name is Gwyneth Marie. I will take care of you and make sure you don't get lost."

"Thank you, miss." Sara shook the girl's hand, eliciting an endearing giggle.

"Excellent." Mr. Lake smiled, and the years slipped from his face to reveal a man younger than she first thought. "Miss Little, welcome to Richmond."

THREE

Adventure's Introduction

As the carriage lumbered toward Lake Manor, Sara struggled with the reality of Mr. Lake's sincere welcome and his daughter's acceptance. Yet here she sat, the plush velvet of the carriage cushions soothing her tired soul to peaceful contemplation. A deep breath of relief whispered past her lips, and she smiled when Gwyn tightened her handhold.

"How did you find your trip? It has been ages since I ventured to England, so I am curious how you fared."

Sara's eyes rose to meet Mr. Lake's amused expression. "The trip, sir?" She never engaged in lengthy conversations with would-be employers. How much chatter was appropriate? "I... I fared well, sir, thank you."

A dark eyebrow inched upward. "The weather? The Atlantic can be quite rough this time of year."

She couldn't fathom where to begin. For the first time in her life she traveled beyond England's shores in the pursuit of a new life. The storms served as poignant inspiration for the images now tucked away in her valise. "It was fine, sir. Thank you."

"Good. One's first journey from one shore to another should be the best possible adventure."

Gwyn tugged Sara's sleeve, drawing her gaze. "What was the best part?"

"Oh, Miss Gwyn, I could no' possibly list but one. America has been a dream of mine."

The girl's delicate brows furrowed. "Papa, is Sara to be a drawer?"

"Artist." Mr. Lake leaned forward to tap his daughter's knee. "She will not be expected to hold clothes like a piece of bedroom furniture. But yes, that stands as the intention and will be subject for later discussion. At present I am curious to know what she has thought of her adventure to date?"

"I...." Sara pulled her gaze from his. "I could no' say, sir. My arms are pink from pinching to wake from a dream."

"Ah. Then it is safe to assume you are enjoying yourself?"

"Oh yes, sir. So much. America has such a hushed air of expectation. Since coming all I know of tomorrow is the sun will rise and set." He chuckled, setting her cheeks aflame. "I-I am sorry, sir. I am singing like a teapot at full steam."

"Do not feel a need to apologize. Without conversation I doubt I will reason out where your talents are best utilized."

"Yes, sir—"

"Please. I know it is too soon to request you call me Christopher or Chris, but 'sir' is simply too much. Will you attempt to replace the 'sir' with 'Mr. Lake'?"

Hesitation teased her voice, but she gulped it down. "Of course, Mr. Lake."

"That's fine. Now, our next step will be a deeper discussion on what we offer young artists. This can be shared over lunch. Then I will show you the house and allow you time to settle yourself before dinner. These past months have been collections of the unexpected, I am certain."

The carriage lurched to a halt. Sara leaned forward as Mr. Lake and Gwyn disembarked. A hand fluttered to her chest. "So lovely!" Lake Manor reminded her of a particular country cottage she worked as a sixteen-year-old scullery maid.

Mr. Lake cast a glance over his shoulder to the setting of his home, bright against the blue skies. "Thank you. I have always been fond of it myself." He retrieved her valise and steadied her descent from the carriage. Gwyn scampered ahead of them and disappeared behind the manor's cedar doors.

Mr. Lake offered his arm. "Disregard the foolish notions of my daughter. The porch steps are often slick, so exercise caution."

She stared at his arm, her heart threatening to pound from her chest as she accepted. She hadn't been treated with gentlemanly regard since—He tucked her hand into the bend of his elbow and stepped forward with careful confidence. As they reached the top step the door opened to reveal an older man with the recognizable attitude of deference.

Gwyn dashed from around the man's legs, excitement twinkling in her eyes. "Harold, this is Sara. Papa said she is staying with us."

"Yes, Miss Gwyn. The lady's room is prepared, Mr. Christopher. Might I welcome you to Lake Manor, miss? If you need anything, don't hesitate to ask. I am the butler, Harold."

Sara curtsied. Relief at his genuine kindness settled her

heart.

"Mr. Christopher, Mr. Theodore is on the telephone for you. A matter of life or death?"

Telephone? Sara leaned slightly to one side, her gaze scouring the hall for a peek at such an extravagant luxury.

"When does Teddy not believe something is grim? He likely realized Gwyn was to be in his charge while I rescued Miss Sara from the station." Mr. Lake presented Sara's valise to the butler. "I am sorry, but Gwynnie will need to be responsible for your tour. Harold, can you make certain these ladies have lunch? With Teddy there's no telling how long I will be."

"Of course, Mr. Christopher."

He disappeared through the second door of the hall.

"Come on, Sara, I want to show you our house!" Gwyn clasped Sara's hand and pulled her forward into the front hall. Oak hardwood floors, watercolors and oils, antiques, plush carpets of red and gold all melded together in artistic grace and simple complexity.

"It is lovely, miss."

"This is the first house Papa ever owned. When he got it, he did a lot to make it pretty—oh wait!" Gwyn dashed to the front door and indicated a push-button switch to the left. "This makes the lights go on or off. Watch." She clicked it, squealing with glee as darkness fell over them. "There's one in all the rooms. No more drippy candles." She punctuated the statement with another click.

"Goodness!"

"The first room is Papa's studio." Gwyn motioned behind to a door on the immediate right of the front entry. "He has pretty pictures on the walls, and this is where he keeps all his painting stuff." The girl pulled Sara toward a door, beyond which could be heard muffled conversation. "This is Papa's office, where he talks to the other drawers and sells them to people."

Sara stifled a laugh.

"The conservatory is there. It has a gazebo and a pond and flowers. It stays hot all year so we can have flowers whenever we want. We have another garden, but now it's too cold to grow. It stays closed, but I can show it to you when it's not winter."

"That would be grand, miss."

They crested the stairs of the second story, the girl's step continuing forward as she labeled each door they passed. "There's Papa's room, the library, and my room is here by Papa. And this—" Gwyn threw open the door and rushed inside to stand in the center, arms outstretched. "This is my play room."

White papered walls and light wood flooring whispered of fun and excitement, as did the child-art decorating the walls and the shelves of animals and dolls at just the right height. An adorable room, typical of a five-year-old girl.

"You like it?"

"Indeed, miss. I adore it."

The girl slumped into a chair at a nearby table with a content sigh. "Now what?"

"What of the third floor?" Sara couldn't imagine not being shown the staff quarters.

"Papa keeps his stuff there. I don't want to break it, so I stay down here." Gwyn traced a pattern on the tabletop. "Sometimes Papa will take me and show pictures. Or he'll let me play with his toys."

Sara sat herself across from the girl. The child's face beamed with memories. "You like that."

"I do! He gave me some of his toys once." Gwyn pointed to the tall bookshelf behind her and an old wooden dog on wheels with a pull-string, a toy soldier, and a wooden music box. "Papa put them there so I won't break one." She stared up at them for a long moment before plopping her chin onto her hand. The poor dear brimmed with boredom.

"Do you know how to make a picture book?" Sara asked.

Gwyn's eyes sparkled, her little body shooting upright. "A picture book? With colors on all the pages?"

Sara laughed. "Yes, miss. I have this idea for a story, but I need help with the pictures."

Gwyn's jaw dropped open by increments as Sara spoke, wonder widening her gaze. "May I help?"

"I hoped you would."

Gwyn bolted to her feet, scurrying from cubby to nook to table like a cottontail rabbit. How many times did her own mother offer the same diversion? It served an unexpected reminder of a past she thought forever lost.

Lunchtime passed without Mr. Lake. Instead, Harold brought a tray of simple sandwiches. The absence didn't bother Gwyn, preoccupied with the sudden decision to use her colored chalk. The girl accepted her assignments with eagerness and a multitude of questions. They laughed over unexpected plot twists and mistakes both, delving into deeper inspirations before they finished their current task.

Sara didn't remember ever having such fun.

"What an adventure—Goodness, we are dusted from head to toe! We should wash up, poppet. What would your papa think if he were to come and see us in such a state?"

"That fun once again came of chaos, of course," said a male voice.

Sara flinched, her eyes drawn to the figure of Mr. Lake as he leaned against the entryway of the nursery. An almost boyish smirk softened the age of his features.

Gwyn dashed forward. "Papa, you were spying!"

"Guilty as charged." He lifted her up into his arms. "What have you been up to while your papa suffered at the gallery?"

"We made a book, Papa, but now we need a cover!"

"Indeed?"

"The letters. We want the big and fancy ones. Like a big book."

"Ah-ha. I suppose this person to create the cover must have many years of writing practice so they can create those oh-so-wonderful script letters your heart so desires."

Gwyn solemnly nodded. "Do you know one?"

"Not a single soul."

The shock of his response dropped the girl's jaw. A smile whispered across Mr. Lake's lips moments before his daughter squealed.

"Papa, you could do it! Oh Papa, please!"

"I would be honored, Angel Girl."

Gwyn threw her arms around his neck and kissed his cheek.

"Such exuberance. I do believe you understand the worth of your picture book."

She pulled back, her eyes wide. "Is it worth a lot of monies, Papa?"

"With Miss Little contributing, I have no doubt you could sell your storybook for quite a sum." He punctuated the statement with a fond touch to her nose.

"I don't want to sell my storybook."

"Then keep it to yourself, but I hope you will at least show it to me."

"Papa's so silly."

"Well, 'Silly' has come to escort you ladies to dinner, though I believe you should take your cohort's sage advice and wash the dust from your faces and hands." He nudged Gwyn toward Sara. "I will wait for you downstairs."

"Yes, Papa."

Sara did her best to keep her mind distant from the thought of dining with the Lakes as she helped Gwyn wash her face and hands. But the memories of so many lunches and dinners could not be silenced. She set aside the dampened washcloth and followed as Gwyn rushed from the play room.

At the entry of the personal dining room, Sara could do more than stare, her hands white-knuckled in front of her. Staff stood at the ready to serve as Mr. Lake settled Gwyn into her chair to his right. When he turned to seat Sara, surprise launched his eyebrows upward.

His gaze sought hers. "Is something wrong?"

"No, sir. I...." But how did she explain a life of eating with the other servants downstairs?

He pulled out the chair to his left. "Come along, Miss Sara. Decisions are seldom as daunting over the comfort of a meal."

Grappling with her courage proved difficult, but she persuaded the dozen or so steps required to navigate her way from entry to chair. Guilt assaulted her as dinner commenced, and she found it impossible to make eye contact nor do much more than pick at her food. She felt like an imposter dining with the Lakes with such familiarity.

What did a maid know of true civility and genteel manners?

Their plates were cleared from the table and Gwyn escorted upstairs to begin her evening toilette. A heavy silence invaded the room without the girl's effervescent presence. Sara lowered her gaze to the wrinkled twist of her napkin.

"Thank you for the distraction of the storybook." A blank look shadowed Mr. Lake's expression. "My wife would often do such projects with her. She claimed Gwyn inherited her creative spirit from me, but I often wonder if it is simply the nature of children."

"You are an artist, sir?"

"Oils." He straightened a shift in the tablecloth. "Though I worked with watercolor for several years and, as most people do, I began with pencils and charcoals. Life has proven too hectic for artistry the past year." The smile he offered seemed stiff. "So, let us talk possibilities. You should be allowed a day to settle before answering uncomfortable questions, of course. But you should know beyond a shadow of a doubt what we intended when we first contacted you."

Sara blinked at her napkin. A bubble of anxiety hovered in her throat and prevented any response.

"Finding a patron is an extreme challenge," he continued, "especially for artists not yet introduced to the creative community. You display a natural talent and, hopefully, you will agree to my sponsorship."

The word snapped her attention outward to his sincere gaze. "S-sponsorship, sir?"

"Indeed. Much as when a father introduces a debutante into society, a sponsor introduces a young artist using his or her reputation as a... launching point, as it were. I will wait until you have acclimated yourself, of course, but my intention will be to introduce you as our gallery's newest prodigy."

FOUR

Subtle Treasures

Sara stared at him, horror strangling her voice. A hasty refusal could mean the difference between a new life and homelessness. "I-I could no' possibly, sir...." Put her art on display so all could mock her lack of training?

"You are working toward a different future. Under my sponsorship you will have ample opportunity to shine. Your sketches will inspire, a rare opportunity."

"Sir, thank you, but—an artist, sir? You.... Sir, I'm the help." Her voice caught. No one would mistake the daughter of a lady's companion as a woman of society.

His expression softened. "Let us make no final decisions this evening. You will need a day to decide what it is you want for the future. All of this must be overwhelming, especially for one unfamiliar with the way of things here." He motioned toward the dining room's entrance. "Let me show you to your room."

Sara smoothed the skirts of her brown wool traveling

habit. The Lord never before asked her to trust someone with her artistic side. "Thank you, sir." Nor had He asked her to confess anything of her personal life. It kept her safely distant. Did the Lord truly intend her to—

A sudden, light touch at her elbow caused a twitch. Mr. Lake made no comment. "Would you be interested in the lesser enthusiastic tour?"

"I do no' want to trouble you, sir."

"Nonsense. No trouble. I am certain you would find it intriguing, being an artist." His gesture encompassed their surroundings. "Lake Manor was originally built in 1856. During the Civil War she suffered myriad of damage from looters and soldiers, to say nothing of the battles that raged within cannon distance."

Sara gazed with interest at the bright halls, paintings and colorful rugs. "She is a charming home, sir."

"I agree. The more formal dining hall is beyond here. We haven't hosted a party sizable enough to warrant it's use, but I feel certain one day they will... convince me to open the doors and plan one. To be honest, I have enjoyed the peace and quiet."

Mr. Lake opened the double doors to the formal dining hall and pushed a switch on the left side of the entry. Two crystal chandeliers twinkled to life, their reflections casting rainbows upon the walls and hardwood floors. A grand piano and harp stood in the far corner by a stack of folded chairs. Oils, watercolors and charcoal sketches hung along the walls, giving an added flair of sophistication.

"How grand, sir!"

His lips danced with a smile and he pulled the doors closed once more. They continued to the far side of the hall. When he focused on the entry to the conservatory, his expression darkened. He cleared his throat and reached out to open the doors. "The conservatory." He descended three steps to the path winding deeper into the lush flora and fauna.

Sara followed, her gaze unable to cease its examination of his profile. "My wife loved this garden. It blossomed to an uncanny representation of each fact of her character." A quick glance toward Sara drew him back from the memories. "Any time you need a quiet place to relax and gather yourself, I recommend this be your first venture."

Sara nodded, her eyes wide as he ushered her from the conservatory and drew the doors shut with a firm hand.

"There is also a kitchen and staff quarters down the back hall, and entry to our spring garden, which happens to be Gwyn's favorite escape during spring and summer. Let us make our way upstairs to the library and your room. The library is Gwyn's preferred hideaway, besides her play room, so prepare to spend most of your time shared between the two."

"You—" Sara's step halted as she gawked at him "You wouldn't mind me reading your books, sir?"

"Of course not."

"But...." She couldn't stop the rush of her heart at the possibility. "M-mightn't I spoil them?"

"I didn't buy them to gather dust." Mr. Lake crossed his arms, his brows knitting together. "Which of your employers reprimanded you for reading their books?"

Sara lowered her eyes, remembering a shining bald head and a pinched expression. Hard, cold green eyes behind glasses that heightened accusations—Sara bit her lip a little too hard and flinched. "The b-books were never for the likes of me, sir."

"I see."

She peeked at him, unable to read his expression.

"Let us strike a bargain, shall we?"

"A bargain, sir?"

"At Lake Manor you can read any and all books at any time. No permissions needed, no explanations demanded should I find you reading in the wee hours of the morning. You've but to promise to read as many books as you wish each day."

Her breath caught, and her eager nod only just shook free her voice. "Thank you, Mr. Lake, sir. I will, sir."

He chuckled. "Please. You promised to call me 'Mr. Lake', remember?" He escorted her to the foot of the stairs. "I haven't yet asked of your family's wishes. Will your parents be joining you once you are settled?"

Sara's heart faltered, her gaze snapping to his as she nearly tripped up the first step. "P-pardon?"

"I...." He cleared his throat. "Well, I assumed you would want to inform them of your safe arrival. Should you need help with the cost of their passage, it would be my responsibility as your sponsor."

Shame and grief burned her eyes. "My mum p-passed when I was twelve." And how could she admit to never even knowing her father's name?

"Gads—" Mr. Lake's lips pressed into a thin line. "Sara, I apologize."

She offered a tremulous smile. "It was only polite for you to ask after them, sir, and I did no' intend to put you on the spot."

"You are very gracious." Mr. Lake turned again to ascend the stairs. Sara noticed the absent way he tapped the balustrade. Nervousness settled like a stone. The knowledge of her being an orphan usually caused families to hesitate in taking her on staff.

They crested the stairs, Mr. Lake pausing the briefest moment before motioning to the right. "The library." He opened the door and stepped inside, standing opposite the towering bookshelves with lightly crossed his arms. "You are bound to find a book or four to keep you and Gwyn busy. She never tires of hearing them." He withdrew a leather-bound volume. "Shall we see if we can find one for you?"

Sara wrung her hands in the doorway, uncertainty threatening her knees with collapse. The shelves of books continued to draw her gaze back. Could she truly read all of the lovelies found there?

Mr. Lake focused on her, his lips curving upward. "They won't scold, Miss Sara. Come along. I feel certain you will discover a favorite friend."

Sara shuffled forward, each step assaulting her memory with sharp tones from the past. Shoulders hunched, her heart thudded the memories silent. Then those massive shelves loomed before her. Caution flared, but she ignored it as she withdrew one of the leather volumes. An inscription drew her focus.

'To Carla: my passion and inspiration, the woman who has always persuaded me to be the man I am. Love forever, Christopher.'

Tears stung as Sara tucked the volume away again.

"Ah." Mr. Lake's exclamation drew her focus in time to accept a presented book. "You should start with this one."

"*Aesop's Fables*." Sara blinked up at him. "I love folktales, sir."

"I thought you might. What better to unlock the imagination of an artist? Be forewarned, Gwyn will demand you read these aloud more than any other."

She clasped the leather-bound volume to her chest. "Yes, sir."

"Excellent. Your room is last, though certainly not least. We made certain you would have the best view of the surrounding streets. There are some immaculate rose gardens to set your imagination afire, although they are blanketed by snow at present. Come along then." Mr. Lake escorted her to the room adjacent the library. "This will be home."

The door opened in silent welcome to reveal a space alive with color. There were no dour shades, no peeling wallpaper nor cracked paint. Two large windows overlooked the streets of Richmond, the sun reflecting in warmth and brightness from the snow blanketing the streets and carriages. A happy pop of flame and fire drew Sara's misty gaze to an inset marble fireplace.

She choked back a sob, tears escaping before she could brush them aside. "It is more lovely than anything before, sir. Than anything I ever dreamed. Sir, I...." She fumbled with the kerchief tucked into her cuff.

"Miss Sara, did...." Mr. Lake offered her the chair from the oak vanity. "Did Carla know of your situation? I do not recall her mentioning specifics of such a difficulty. Nor Dix, my sister, who referred you."

Sara shook her head.

"Why would you keep such a fact secret? We could have presented more help."

Sara lowered her gaze to the leather volume clasped in white-knuckled hands. "Orphans do no' often find a position like this, sir."

Mr. Lake tapped his lips with a single finger. "Miss

Sara, I have a question for you. Please answer as truthfully as you can."

"O-of course, sir."

"Why did you come to America?"

She blinked at him. His hazel eyes didn't burn with annoyance or anger. They were calm and... kind. "Sir?"

"What did you want from your journey here? Not to be confused with what you might have expected. I want to know what you wanted, then and now."

All the dreams and expectations ever hidden in her heart clashed to the surface of her memory. Sara choked down her hesitation, unable to break his gaze. "I came to America for a second chance at life, sir. A second chance at... myself."

Mr. Lake nodded. "Ah. Now we come to it. Please, go on."

"In England I was no better than a slave, sir, just an orphan. But you made me feel more in one letter. So here I am, two dresses to my name, and not money enough to support myself beyond tomorrow. I...." She tore her gaze from his. "I been taking care of myself with the Lord's blessing since no taller than a stump. Never held a position longer than three months, and no man will marry a servant girl scared of her own shadow. Sir, you and your wife offered me a place to call home and—" Tears robbed her voice.

"That is something you do not wish to lose."

Sara inclined her head, shame keeping her eyes downcast. She didn't want to sound desperate. She could work anywhere if given the chance.

Mr. Lake released a quiet breath, his slow nod drawing back her attention. "Consider today the first in your new home. You are free to wander within these meager halls. Free to come and go as you please. Lake Manor is your home. Understood?"

An intensity of relief and wonder constricted her throat, allowing her only an imperceptible nod.

Mr. Lake's lips tilted upward. "Then I will leave you to your new surroundings." He paused at the door. "Let me know if you need anything, Sara. Agreed?"

He didn't wait for a response, though she would have been hard-pressed to offer one. The door closed and a single tear dripped onto the rug at her feet.

Christopher stared out his office window. He didn't see the bustle of the avenue nor the diamond stars above. He saw Sara Little's tears, and the darkening of fear in her blue gaze. Yet her desperate desire to belong continued to press her forward, with no family to fall back to should she fail. He shook his head.

Trust would be the most important aspect of the woman's character to cultivate. That would require patience. He crossed his arms and returned his focus to the winter landscape. With Carla gone, what if he provided less than what she intended? He could rob Sara of her last ounce of hope.

Did he still understand the meaning of the word?

Christopher exited his office, each step on the stairs requiring more energy than the previous. The eighteen months since Carla's death were a painful blur of forced laughter. With Sara's arrival came again the incessant memories of his wife, their shared desire to help others, a common love for the less fortunate, her laughter and touch.

He jerked open the bedroom door and stumbled inside, his gaze averted from their bed—The sound of voices drew his attention to Gwyn's room.

"Didn't you want to?"

"Of course I did, poppet, but I worked for an evil tyrant of a man named Mr. Brockle. He threatened to tell all the people I was a horrible, lazy person if I left."

Christopher crept to the connecting door between their rooms. Sara tucked Gwyn into bed, the covers up to her chin.

"What did you do?" his daughter asked.

"I was scared, so I thought if I stayed for a bit he would let me come away." Sara searched out a chair and drew it close.

Gwyn watched with wide eyes. "He didn't?"

"No, miss. Though I suppose it foolish of me to hope for that end."

"Papa would have bust him in the nose."

Christopher restrained a chuckle as Sara laughed.

"I wanted to do that, too, poppet, truth be told."

"Then what happened?"

"I kept asking if I could go, and if he could say nice things to your mum and papa about me. But he said 'no' again and again."

Christopher frowned. It was no wonder she cringed from him after such a past as that. He commended her determination to arrive at all.

"One day I snuck myself out the back and made my way to a church."

"A church? Did Mr. Bockle find you?"

"No. The priest wouldn't tell him I hid there." Sara cast

a secretive glance behind her. "He was a friend of my mum."

Christopher watched with interest the interaction between his daughter and Sara. For the first time since their meeting she seemed at ease, comfortable. Perhaps Gwyn was the key? He smirked. He might not have his wife to help him set this woman on her new life's path, but their daughter was more than up to the task of bringing Sara beyond her shell.

His smile drifted as he continued to watch the ease with which the woman soothed his daughter to sleep. Then she placed a kiss upon Gwyn's forehead and turned to leave the room. When she paused outside the door to peek in one last time, Christopher met her in the hall. Fear glittered in her eyes at first, as before, until she recognized him. Her cheeks flushed and she wrung her hands. Christopher wasn't certain if she did so out of fright or simple nervousness.

"I know it's late, sir, and I did no' mean to bother you." Her words rushed together. "The poppet could no' sleep and asked if I would tell her a tale."

He tried to offer her an encouraging smile. "Curfew only applies to Gwyn."

Sara blinked. Then her features softened into a hesitant smile. She was lovely when she didn't cower, and that realization made him understand why Paul and Dix urged her to write. There was a welcoming spirit about her. Something that would be of great benefit to the gallery and their dreams for others. The challenge would be to find the best way to draw her beyond the fear to trust.

FIVE

First Daze

5 January 1894

Sara stared at the reflection of the morning sun dancing across the ceiling of her room—Her room. It wasn't a cell or closet, nor even servant's quarters. She woke in a room all her own. She rolled onto her side and cuddled the down pillow. At any moment she expected the explosion of Mr. Brockle's bellow. But she heard only the occasional rumble of conversation.

Her eyes focused to the bedside table and a miniature representation of the Lake family. They were a bit of wholeness Sara dreamed of having herself. *It is still possible, Sara Ann. Now is your time to stop listening to the "do this" and the "do not do this" and listen for what God has waiting for you.* Maybe that was a family?

"Amen," she whispered, all her hopes and dreams carried on the breath heavenward.

She sat up to kick her feet over the side of the bed and stare at her toes. This morning would be the first where the only expectation would be her own. No mending, no cleaning, no scrubbing or buffing. *What am I to do with myself?* After twenty-four years of being a servant forever bustling and chaotic, the never-ending peace seemed surreal.

It invited a sense of guilt for being idle.

A smile caressed the edges of Sara's rose lips, and when she succumbed to a childish impulse and wriggled her toes within the plush rug at her feet, she giggled. At Lake Manor there were soft covers and a warm bed in a room which felt more like a home should. Even more than all she shared with her mother. *Lord, might I stay in this dream a bit longer?*

With the sun filtering in through the great windows, she could feel a definite *Yes* shine in her soul. Was her previous life but a dream?

Sara released a fast breath as she stood, padding to an adjoining door to search out her bath room. The sight on the other side of the door brought tears. A claw-foot ceramic tub, another large fireplace crackling in greeting, a vanity and chair, full-body mirror, and all the luxurious provisions she could have imagined. Running water. A lavatory in the corner with a pull flush-handle—Sara reached over and pinched herself, sounding a hiss and giggle at the sudden pain.

She knelt at the tub and spun the appropriate white handle. A few minutes later, hot and cold water began to broil and foam within the tub in a giggle of welcome. Sara rested her forehead upon the coolness of the tub rim, her fingers playing in the roaring water—

A knock roused her from her prayers. "Yes?"

The door to the bath cracked open and a pretty face

peeked around. "Miss Sara?"

Sara offered a smile to the young maid. "I am Sara."

"Good morning, miss." She bobbed a curtsy and brushed a few wisps of reddish-brown hair back under her mob cap. "I'm to help you get prepared for breakfast. I'm Amy. Your maid, miss."

Sara blinked.

Amy scurried forward. "Oh, bother, miss. You shouldn't be drawing your bath! Let me do that."

Sara sat back, worrying her lip as she watched Amy test the temperature of the water and make minute adjustments to the ratio. "Please, Amy. I can manage my bath."

"Oh no, miss. It will just take a moment to finish and then we'll get you all dolled up and everything. Mr. Lake is going—drat that rotten bar of soap!" It splashed into the bath water and slunk to the far corner of the tub.

Sara laughed. "Soap is the worst to hold fast."

"I'm sorry, miss. I never been a lady's maid." Amy came around the tub to help Sara from her robe, all the while glaring at the reclusive soap. "It's plain, ain't it?"

"You are doing fine, Amy. How long have you been a chambermaid?"

"This's only my second week." Amy groaned. "Mother would box my ears if she saw me slip up like this at home."

"At least you have the blessing of running water. Once I used a coal bucket - Was I nervous! - There was coal dust all over the tub and the missus."

Amy settled Sara into the tub. "You look more a lady than a maid!"

"Oh, Amy, do no' fib. I have no' the wits to be a lady, and have only been a servant. Learned the trade from my mum."

"You've got the carriage for a lady, miss, and that's no lie. But I don't mind that you've seen my side of the serving tray." Amy giggled as she once again fought with her hold on the soap.

"Am I no' still there?"

"Still where, miss?"

"I.... Mr. Lake says Lake Manor is my home now, but...." The confession still made Sara's breath catch. "I do no' know what to do with a blessing like that, Amy. How does a maid view a place like this a home without tripping over her own hem?"

"That's a good question, miss—"

"Call me Sara."

"As you please, m—" Amy flushed and Sara laughed. "Don't be laughing at me! I was in the kitchens for two years before, and so I never did much talking."

"The kitchens...." Sara bit her lip and cast Amy a sidelong glance. "Is the cook... grumpy?"

"Oy! Grumpy doesn't describe it, miss. If you trudge into his kitchen in the middle of a meal because the smell has got you craving a taste, you might as well prepare your ears for a tug!" She winked. "But give up enough compliments and he'll grant you a feast."

Sara laughed.

Amy helped Sara dress before Cook summoned her away, leaving Sara to stare at her freshly cleaned face in the mirror. A lady with silver hair and kind eyes appeared at the doorway. Her uniform of charcoal dress, sturdy belt and key-loop defined her role as Housekeeper.

"Pardon, Miss Sara. Mr. Christopher wants to see you in his office once you've had breakfast. Harold can show you in."

Sara dipped in a curtsy. "Thank you, mum."

"Call me Emily, dear."

Sara stared after them for a long moment before lowering her gaze to her craft basket. Then she adjusted her dress and exited the bedroom to make her way downstairs.

Harold met her at the bottom step. "Breakfast is through here, Miss Sara."

"I am no' a bit hungry, sir. I m-mean H-Harold. Could I...."

"Of course. Mr. Christopher is waiting for you in his office."

She followed his direction, not noticing her hands fidgeting with the front of her dress. She only heard the staccato of her footsteps on the hardwood floor, the knock against the office door and the muffled "Come in," followed by a near silent purr.

Mr. Lake stood near the bookshelves to the left skimming through the pages of a particularly thick book. Silence fell over the room, heightening the clink and clatter of dishes from the kitchens. Mr. Lake's brow furrowed as Sara opened her mouth to speak, sending her thoughts scattering.

He raised his gaze. "Ah. Sara." He tucked the book back upon the shelf and motioned to a chair across from his desk. "Please. Have a seat."

Sara settled onto the edge of the chair, her cold fingers knit together to still their trembling.

"Did you sleep well? I know how excitement can keep one up through the night."

"I slept fine, Mr. Lake. Thank you." Only an hour here and there, but even that didn't squelch her deeper sense of... peace.

"Good. Have you had a moment to decide regarding your art? Will you allow me to act as your sponsor?"

Sara felt thankful she hadn't eaten breakfast. "S-sir, I...."

He retrieved a thick album from his desk and sat in the chair beside her. "Here is a glimpse at what we do, so you may see a possible future."

Opening the album revealed photographs of a gathering at the gallery. Ladies in fine gowns, gentlemen in suits, a rainbow of sophistication. Mr. Lake turned the pages with deliberate slowness, allowing her the time to view and understand the story the pictures told.

"Some of the gentlemen we sponsor setup their own galleries with a modicum of success," he said, occasionally scrutinizing her profile. "The ladies most commonly become wives, but a few have become instructors at respected universities. A small number of artists decide to focus on a more lucrative career than that of painting, but they will occasionally orchestrate another display of new and old work."

Sara accepted the album to stare at the large photograph of him, his wife, and a grinning young man. Could taking such a risk lead to such an ending for her? Sara lifted her head to meet his hazel gaze. "I...."

Mr. Lake nodded. "I understand your hesitation, Sara. Let me be quite clear. As sponsor your protection is my first priority. Meaning, I shelter you from all unhealthy interaction. Your audience, screened. The responses you read, censored. The images you display, selected with the utmost regard to your opinion. I will even withhold your identity. You must only hazard the first, frightening risk and trust me."

Sara's hands clutched the album. Could she trust the Lord to give Mr. Lake wisdom in even this? Could this truly be why the Lord led her to America? "Y-yes, sir."

"Your courage is commendable." He stood, and Sara's gaze retreated to the dark leather photo album in her hands. "If you should change your mind, don't hesitate to discuss options with me. Yes, I believe this is the path Carla intended, but there is the matter of discovering your other talents, and I am certain they are many."

Sara couldn't risk a glance for fear of losing hold of her tears. Instead, she curtsied and left the room with another whispered statement of thanks and retreat. How many more secrets would the Lord ask her to reveal to others? How many more doors would He ask her to open, exposing herself to possible ridicule and mockery? How many more tests would He lead her through?

The challenge of a new way of life loomed as frightful as it had that first day three years ago. That day she determined to leave it all behind and start anew in America. Now she began to see that changing her life would involve more than simply her journey to a different land—

Sara's step faltered at the entry to her room. A tower of hatboxes and trunks assaulted her vision, and Amy worked at the task of unpacking.

The young maid glanced toward the doorway and smiled. She lifted up a formal of dark navy. "Aren't these the loveliest gowns you've ever seen?"

Horror pushed Sara back a step, ugly memories propelling her into a run back downstairs. She threw wide Mr. Lake's office door and rushed inside. "Please, sir, you cannot!"

He sat back in his chair, nonplussed. "What in heaven's name is the matter?"

"Please, sir, I...." Sara wrung her hands until they throbbed. "The clothes.... I can manage on my own, sir. You need no'—"

"Ah. Yes. I quite forgot." He motioned to the chair across from his desk. "Please, Sara. Have a seat and calm yourself."

Her knees trembled as she lowered herself onto the chair edge. *Please, Lord. I do no' want to believe him the kind....*

"Let me assure you there is nothing inappropriate in the giving nor your acceptance of the wardrobe. I apologize for any impertinence, but it must be done. You said you haven't money enough to support yourself and it is in my power to end this specific need. In fact, I consider it my responsibility because of our role in your journey here."

"B-but—" Shame set her cheeks afire. "Thank you, sir."

Mr. Lake released a quick breath. "I apologize if I seem to tread over you like a pig in a field of flowers. Carla warned of my tendency to badger. 'Chris,' she would say, 'you shove instead of nudge. It isn't very diplomatic.' " He shrugged. "Ah well. What is done is done. Next time I will allow Gwyn's charm to work its magic before asking you to mend my shirts."

Sara laughed, her hand lifting too late to muffle the sound.

"Much better. Now, please do what you need to anything you find acceptable. They are yours to do with as you see fit, remnants from a benefit we held a season ago. Ladies and gentlemen ventured from all over creation, or so it seemed, to donate fashions to that evening." Mr. Lake flipped to a page in the great album. "In fact, I have a photograph."

Blurred vision prevented Sara from discerning much more than a vast array of shapes and sizes. "It sounds lovely, sir. Thank you, sir."

"Mr. Lake."

"Y-yes, Mr. Lake."

He smiled. "I will see you for lunch then."

Sara pulled the office door closed behind her. He didn't seem to understand that, to her, the trunks held more than simple frocks and gowns. They commanded her to follow a different set of rules, to entertain an opposite mind-set. Possibilities and fancies lay within those trunks. Sara wasn't certain she wanted to free them. If she released one, she could set loose those bits of her own heart tucked away. Did she have courage enough to step into this new life?

Her eyes drifted from the shine of the hardwood at her feet to the second story. If she wanted a change, she needed to embrace the journey with her whole heart. Sara released a deep breath and stepped forward, preparing her heart for the feel of the first satiny folds of her future.

SIX

Memories of a Lost Passion

"Blast it."

Christopher scowled at the album cover. While he expected Sara's refusal of the supplement to her wardrobe, the initial refusal of his sponsorship caught him by surprise. Her attitude thus far reflected meek deference, so he anticipated an immediate acceptance of his professional experience. He hadn't intended to press her into a decision. How would he encourage trust if he continue to badger her into terrifying situations?

"Papa? Why are you mad?"

Gwyn's appearance melted his frown to a smile. He helped her into one of the wingback chairs. "I acted more than a tad bossy toward Miss Sara. Mama would be furious." He would have given almost anything to hear her irritation as long as it meant her warmth beside him—

"Not Sara! I like her."

"I know." Christopher kissed her forehead. "I will

apologize again at lunch."

"You should say sorry now, Papa." She wriggled from the chair and pulled him from the room.

He laughed, allowing her to drag him down the hall. "Gwyn, Angel, I believe it would be prudent to leave well enough alone at the moment. At least until lunch."

She didn't release his hand until they stood outside the French doors leading into the conservatory. All emotion vanished from his countenance as he stared at the polished handles.

"You get flowers for Sara now, Papa, and I will get her." She scampered away.

Christopher blinked, slowly, and fisted his hands at the swell of dread and misery. He tried to shake free of the memories, but he knew it wouldn't deny the nightmares access... and he needed to fetch a flower. He shuddered as he pushed into her garden.

Sara set aside the ivory gown of lace and satin brocade and opened her bedroom door. Gwyn smiled up at her. "Hello, Miss Gwyn—"

"Look at the pretty dresses!" She scurried past Sara to caress the gowns and frocks strewn across the bed. "Are these yours? Are you going to wear one?"

Sara laughed. "Not just yet, poppet."

"We need to separate them into seasons before she can do anything," Amy said.

"Can I help?"

Amy and Sara exchanged amused glances. "It won't be very exciting."

"But... but I want to help." Her green eyes shimmered.

"Of course you can help." Sara knelt in front of a trunk and drew the girl close. "We but wanted you to know how dull this adventure will be."

"I don't care."

"Just remember that when you're bawling to be let out." Amy pulled aside the layer of tissue paper on the second trunk. "Lord have mercy!"

Sara withdrew the gown of rich mahogany velvet to the accompaniment of a symphony of rustles. "Has there ever been such a gown?"

"Sara, try it on!"

She flushed. She wasn't ready for that step into this unknown realm. "Not yet, Amy. Let's hang the rest before we start."

"You would be beautiful. Like Mama." Gwyn's curls bobbed in unanimous agreement.

"Thank you, poppet." Sara peeked at the girl. "What do you remember about your mum?" At her age, even one year from the care of a mother equated most of her lifetime.

"I remember her laugh. When Mama laughed, Papa did too." Gwyn leaned her arms against the trunk. "I miss her at Christmas most."

"Goodness gracious what a time that would be." Amy clasped her hands to her chest, memories dancing in her expression. "The mister and missus would throw the grandest parties. Such lovely voices they had, singing the hymns like angels."

Sara touched the girl on the nose. "Those are good memories, Gwyn."

"Mama says we'll be happy, but...." Gwyn hid her face against Sara's chest. The girl's shoulders trembled.

"Oh, poppet. I know it's hard, but it takes a little bit to let the pain go." Sara brushed the tears from the girl's cheeks. "You keep loving your papa and, one day, happiness will find you again."

"Will you stay to help?" Gwyn's eyes twinkled with her sudden smile. "Maybe Papa will laugh like he used to?"

Sara caressed more of the wetness from the cherub face. "Of course, poppet." It would be a daily prayer, for a kind man like Mr. Lake deserved happiness.

"Goodness gracious me, look at the time!" Amy bolted to her feet. "We've got to get you dressed for lunch or it's my head!"

Amy helped Sara into a frock of orchid and ivory and then hurried to the kitchens to help serve. Sara only just finished lacing her boots when Harold announced lunch. When Gwyn and Sara arrived, Mr. Lake wasn't to be found.

"Where's Papa?"

Harold entered the room from the kitchen before Sara could hazard a guess. "Your father is in the conservatory, Miss Gwyn."

"Oh! I forgot!" Gwin tightened her grasp on Sara's hand and tugged her from the room through the kitchen. "We'll be right back, Harold!"

"Why, Gwyn, what is it?"

"We need to go!" The girl shoved through the etched glass doors of the conservatory, Sara tugged along in her wake. "Papa! Papa, I forgot!"

"Gwyn!" Sara laughed. "Gwyn, Poppet, what is the—" They turned the path corner and Sara drew the girl up. Her father sat upon the steps of the vine-trellised gazebo, his shoulders stooped and his expression forlorn. He held a rosebud in a gentle clasp.

Gwyn tugged at Sara's hand. "But, Sara," she complained, tone hushed as if even she could sense the melancholy taint.

Sara drew the girl back a step. "Your papa needs a bit of time to himself." Though even she could discern the grief that settled over him. How could she leave him to himself?

Gwyn pulled at Sara's arm. "He was getting you a flower."

A flower from the garden of his beloved wife. A journey into a painful memory. Hesitation trembled in her knees, but she struggled toward the gazebo.

"Papa!"

Mr. Lake straightened, drawing a ragged breath. "Ah. I forgot the time. My apologies." He forced a stiff smile and stood, tossing the rosebud into the pond. The splash caused a flinch. "Come along, Gwynnie." Mr. Lake enfolded the girl's hand in his. "Lunch is waiting, and you know how Cook fusses if we run tardy."

The pair disappeared around a bend in the walk, their figures lost from sight by the lush greenery. Sara pressed a trembling hand to her forehead, her eyes burning. Now she understood why the Lord called her to this beautiful family. Mr. Lake hadn't yet grieved his wife, and now an untold agony grew to an oppressive burden. Who better than she could understand how he suffered?

Sara choked out a prayer for guidance.

"Mr. Christopher?"

Christopher looked up from his examination of Sara and Gwyn's combined effort of the picture-book. Harold stood in his office doorway. "Yes?"

"Jeffrey Stillwell is here to see you. He has no appointment, but asked to wait for your earliest convenience."

"Show him in, Harold. It doesn't appear I will make it to the gallery today." Christopher set the sketch aside. "Interrupt me when that call from Paul comes through."

"Yes, Mr. Christopher."

A moment later a gentleman of short stature entered his office. Jeffrey Stillwell's silver eyes twinkled with his easy smile. Christopher shook the man's hand and urged him to sit. "What can I do for you, Jeff? And don't ask for more of Sean's work. I haven't any."

"No, no, Chris. I know I wrangled it all. I am on a mission for a friend of mine."

"Oh?"

"Yes, it seems he wishes to invest into some art or artist." He chuckled. "He saw my charcoal collection, I believe they were your firsts, and offered me quite a sum."

"Odd. Charcoals aren't normally seen as an investment."

"But everyone knows you are not an active artist. That increases their worth, especially in consideration of your talent."

"Enough honey," Christopher said, smiling. "What did you want?"

Jeff laughed. "Do you know of another artist of your caliber? All for my friend, of course."

"Of course." Christopher glanced to Sara's sketch of his daughter, hidden near his file tray. "Charcoals?"

"Why yes. Do you know—"

"Mr. La—Oh. P-Pardon me."

Both Christopher and Jeff turned. Sara Little stood in the doorway the embodiment of uncertainty. She wore a skirt of powder blue with an ivory chiffon blouse that heightened her delicate physique and slender form.

"Ah. Miss Sara. Come in and meet an acquaintance of mine. This is Jeffrey Stillwell, a regular patron of the gallery here. This is Miss Sara Little, recently of England."

Sara bobbed a graceful curtsy. When Jeffrey stepped forward to offer his hand in greeting, her cheeks flushed crimson.

"Miss Little." He bowed over her hand. "A pleasure."

She glanced toward Christopher. He smiled. "Did you have a question?"

"Y-yes, Mr. Lake. I wanted to.... I m-mean—" She lightly bit her lower lip.

"Why, my dear!" Jeff urged her to sit. "There's no need to tear up. Come now. Tell us what has happened."

"I... I used my last bit of paper." Sara hid the charcoal stains of her fingers, clasping her hands in her lap.

"No paper! That is a tragedy for certain. Chris, certainly you will allow her to raid your treasure-trove of supplies?"

"Certainly. There is a portfolio overflowing with paper on my desk in my studio. Take the entire sheaf."

"There now, my dear. Problem solved." Jeff gave her clenched hands a fatherly squeeze.

"Thank you, sir."

"I would love the opportunity to come again and see what you have sketched. How long will you be staying in America, Miss Little? And with whom are you staying?"

Christopher blinked at a sudden, sickening realization. "Jeff, let us allow Sa—Miss Little to return to her sketching. Shall we?"

"Thank you, s-sir." Sara stood and curtsied, once to each gentleman before retreating from the office.

"What a charming young woman. Lovely—Chris, are you well?"

"I experienced an epiphany that is a bit of an embarrassment, Jeff." Christopher slumped into the chair Sara just vacated. "She is a guest in my house. Why did I not think of this before?" He focused on the older man. Perplexity furrowed the man's brow. "She has no chaperone."

"Dear me. When did she arrive?"

"Yesterday morning." Christopher scrubbed at his scalp. "We invited her before Carla.... Unfortunately, complications delayed Miss Little's arrival. I did not think of arranging her lodging elsewhere. Why would I?"

"Could Miss Little stay with your sister? She enjoys guests for extended periods."

"Dix and Paul are still in New York." Christopher scrubbed at his scalp. "Here I am responsible for her welfare and I could have damaged her reputation!"

"Nonsense. Do not surrender yourself to melodramatics."

"Melodramatics, Jeff?" Christopher chuckled. "Yes, of course you are right. It has simply been too long since...."

Jeff waved the comment aside. "Indeed it has. I certainly will keep this challenge to myself. Might I suggest you call Dixon and make arrangements? Gregory, which is the Donovan Houseman, correct? Gregory will be more than able to care for her until they arrive.

"I appreciate your secrecy, Jeff. I will keep you apprised of my search for an artist appropriate for your friend."

"Thank you, Chris. And do let me know if you need anything. You know the misses and I would love to have company, even should they stay a single night."

Christopher gave the man's extended hand a firm clasp. "Thank you. I will."

Jeff exited. Harold appeared a few moments later. "Excuse me, but Mr. Paul is on the line from New York."

Christopher made his way to the adjacent studio and picked up the line. "Paul, you have an idiot for a brother-in-law."

"Chris, what on earth is the trouble?"

"I need you and Dix to come out right away."

"What has happened?"

"Do you remember the English woman you referred?"

"English wom—Dear Lord! She only just arrived?"

"There were complications. Now I have been a fool and did not arrange separate accommodations for her, though goodness knows she mentioned it more than once." Christopher grumbled. "She stayed the night here at Lake Manor, Paul."

"Understood. Dix and I will leave on the first train available this evening. We should be there by Saturday. Send her on over to our place with her maid, if she has one. You have the key?"

"Yes."

"Fine then. We will see you in two days."

"Thank you, Paul."

Christopher slammed down the receiver, cursing his stupidity as he exited his studio. Emily passed to the kitchen. "Emily."

"Yes, Mr. Christopher?"

"Miss Little will be staying with Paul and Dixon until further notice."

Emily blinked. "Now?"

"Yes. Straightaway. Can you have Amy pack her things? Let Harold know to have Brian and Thomas ferry them over. I have the key, so I will go along with them."

"Certainly, Mr. Christopher."

"Ah, and have Gwyn go along after dinner. Have her things packed and sent as well."

"Yes, Mr. Christopher." After another glance, she hurried upstairs.

The scratch of pencil against paper teased Sara's rose lips with a content smile. In the east corner of the conservatory she found a nook with a wrought-iron bench surrounded by fragrant bushes. Lilacs, Harold called them. The small hideaway whispered visions of fairytales. Such fun to have sketching her only responsibility! To listen for the murmur of inspiration and explore herself with the act.

She surveyed her sketch at multiple angles and laughed. Most of the scenes were silly nothings, an allowance of fun she hadn't experienced before. Her eyes and cheeks glowed with it.

"Ah. You have found it then."

Sara's pencil tumbled from her fingers. Her gaze met Mr. Lake's and her fingers clenched the sheaf of remaining paper. A stab of fear quickened her heartbeat. *Silly girl! He urged you to come here, yes?* "M-Mr. Lake. How are you?"

He retrieved the pencil, gathering also those sketches beside her. Sara watched him in mild horror.

"Miss Sara...." He motioned deeper into the conservatory. "Walk with me."

"O-of course, sir."

The silence pressed at her as they walked along the path, the flora and fauna doing little to soothe the troubled expression from his brow.

Mr. Lake shot her a lengthy glance. The look preyed on her heart so she feared she would tremble from her skin. But what could she do? Starting conversation hadn't been expected of her in the past. She willed her voice to remain calm. "Did you have a good visit with your friend?"

"Yes."

His absent response voided her smile. She noticed another glance her direction, and his ears darkened to scarlet.

"My friend made an innocent comment, as a matter of fact. I am quite embarrassed. I, er, you are a single lady and I a widower—" Sara gasped, fighting a sudden swell of nausea. "Yes. I believe I had a similar reaction. Since your protection and care are my responsibility, I arranged a safer place for you to stay. With Paul and Dixon Donovan. We are neighbors, for the most part."

"Mr. Lake...." Sara's step faltered and stopped; her hands clasped, white-knuckled. "Sir, I am t-too much of a bother. I-I can stay at a church or—"

"Nonsense! Your presence has been nothing but a blessing, especially to Gwyn. Everyone has commented on her raised spirits. Even you seem less tired after a good rest."

"B-but I am naught but a girl off the street to you, sir. What if I were lying about your wife and the friends from England? What if it's but a tale?" Her voice cracked. Sara looked away.

She didn't understand why he would do something like this for someone like her. What did a servant girl know about a reputation? More than one of her acquaintances gave into the temptation of a trip to the master's bed. That he would think to save her reputation! Tears tickled her cheeks.

"You have shown yourself kind-hearted and compassionate, so I will not believe your situation a lie. Gwyn will enjoy having you to herself, and I...." He smiled and gave her arm a gentle pressure. "Well, perhaps I will be better able to work at the gallery when I know Gwyn is in such capable hands."

"But, sir—"

"No." Mr. Lake chuckled. "You should enjoy this adventure. Gwyn will."

Sara looked down. "Y-Yes, sir."

"I will allow your escape to your artistry now, and Harold will fetch you before dinner so you may have the time to change. Is that well enough?"

"Yes, sir. Thank you, s-sir."

Mr. Lake remained quiet for a long moment. Then he turned and made his way back to the Manor. Sara lowered herself onto the bench seat with a slow sigh.

Christopher reached out for in the darkness when the coldness of loneliness began to creep. But he was alone. He sat up. "Carla?"

Silence.

Throwing back the coverlet, Christopher slipped from the large bed to wrap a plush navy-blue robe around him. He proceeded across the floor of their room and out into the hallway. Empty and cold. Silent.

Panic began to flare. "Carla? Where are you?"

There was no laughter. Only silence. Dead silence. He moved down the hall and began descending the stairs. No scent of flowers. No warmth. He heard a soft sigh. Relief flooded over him as he reached the bottom step and turned toward the hall to his left--

Christopher blinked. "Miss Little?"

She turned and flushed, lowering her blue gaze to her clasped hands. She still wore the powder blue dress with the white blouse she wore that evening, her mahogany-brunette waves gathered on the crown of her head and glistening with streaks of red. The moonlight shining through the conservatory doors and the glass on each side of the front entrance glowed on her clear skin and in her eyes.

Confusion lowered Christopher's brows. Especially when, looking to his own attire, he now wore the dinner suit from earlier at dinner. As a matter of fact, he remembered escorting her and Gwyn to Paul and Dix's afterward.

He looked up. "Is something wrong?"

"No, sir," she said softly. "I was listening."

Christopher came to stand near her, again noticing the dramatic scent of lilacs. "Listening? To what?"

She glanced toward him, dark eyes glimmering. "To the sounds of your home."

The conversation rang eerily familiar. "The sounds of my home?"

As if a cue were spoken, brightness, laughter, and lively activity burst forth around them. Brian and Thomas were heard exchanging encouragements while hauling filled buckets of ash to the conservatory. Amy laughed along with one of Emily's stories. Harold gave kind instruction to a new steward in the kitchen.

Christopher shifted his attention to Miss Little's profile. She had closed her eyes, tipping her head back as she once again absorbed the sounds. The enrapture of her expression heightened the delicate loveliness of her face, just as the action of intense listening enhanced the curve of her neck and jaw. The same pose she had taken that evening, the night of her departure to the Donovans' home.

"Laughter," she whispered. "Acceptance. The joy in their work." A tear escaped, and she quickly wiped it away as she opened her eyes and cast him a peek. "Your home fairly sings with a feeling of belonging, Mr. Lake. I have never heard it so strong before."

Christopher stared at her in carefully controlled silence as he felt--He cleared his throat and looked away. "Thank you for taking the time to listen. Usually it's neither heard nor appreciated."

Giving a slight nod, she confessed, "I will miss it so."

He allowed his gaze to be drawn back to the gentle lines of her face, noticing that her eyes had again closed. Her extreme appreciation for something so often taken for granted reminded him of the harshness of her life before America. Christopher swallowed hard before reaching out to gently clasp her hand. She twitched, another poignant reminder of her harsh history, and opened her eyes to meet his.

"I will have you over for coffee," he promised.

Her natural color flushed as she timidly smiled. "Thank you, sir."

He gave the softness of her hand a brief caress. "Call me Christopher, Sara," he corrected.

"Chris–"

Christopher bolted upright with a strangled call of "Carla!" But when he looked to his left, again, there was no one. He reached out to stroke the bare pillow with trembling fingers, tears burning in his throat and eyes. "The voice was yours, Carla." But she was not beside him. There rang only chilled silence.

White-knuckled hands clutched the blankets as Sara

listened again for the pained shout. But only the wind howled against the windows. She took in a calming breath--there sounded a child's cry and she scrambled from under the covers, snatching up her robe as she rushed to the door. Hurrying across the hall, she found Gwyn standing in the center of her room crying, arms searching the darkness. Sara knelt and gathered the weeping girl into her arms.

"Papa? Where's Papa? He's going away. Why's he going away, Sara? Why's he leaving?"

Sara kissed Gwyn's temple, smoothing her blonde hair as the little girl hiccupped and sniffed, body trembling. "Your papa is no' leaving. You had but a bad dream."

Gwyn still sobbing against her shoulder, Sara scooped her up and carried her to the bed. Once she tucked the girl under the covers, Gwyn clutched at her hand. "Sara, don't go away," the little girl sniffed.

"I will stay right here," Sara whispered as she laid down beside her. The little girl scooted closer, wrapping her arms around her as she snuggled her head against her bosom. "Do no' fret, poppet."

"Don't let Papa go, Sara," she mumbled sleepily. "He's gonna get lost if he goes."

"I will no', poppet. I will no'." But Sara wondered how far he had wandered already.

SEVEN

Revealing Heroes

6 January 1894

Christopher stared at the tombstone. His hand trembled as he clutched two rings strung on a chain of fine gold. 'You must keep living,' Carla had whispered, her hand clasping his with her last moment of strength. 'Hold to your passion.' Then she slipped into eternity. His wife, his love, his reason for living—dead, and their son with her. *Why?* But there were no answers. There never would be.

A breeze ruffled his dark curls, the bite of winter stinging his face. He turned away, girding himself for yet another day without the melody of her laughter. Eighteen months seemed an eternity, and while his soul yearned for comfort, he couldn't find his way beyond the silence. He could still feel her breath upon his face. The fragrance of her teased his senses when he passed the library. In the midst of his loneliness he could feel her skin against his—

A moan ravaged his throat, and his hands fisted at his sides. *You lied.* His head fell back, the blackness of his hazel eyes staring heavenward. *You asked for trust and I gave it to You. I believed You would heal her, but You did nothing.*

Thunder grumbled a warning of the coming winter storm. Christopher clambered into the carriage. It lurched forward. Without Carla, what did life offer? Christopher dropped his head in his hands. Reliving their moments together wouldn't make that fact any less true, any less painful, or any less... forever.

The front doors of the gallery thudded closed. "Teddy?"

Sculptor and friend Theodore 'Teddy' Parker partnered with Christopher to open the gallery out of college. Together, their connections with the artistic community set them up as the gallery of Richmond's younger set.

"Top! Where are you?"

"Main hall." Christopher frowned as he studied the layout of the main reception area.

The staccato of Teddy's shoes on the marble flooring signaled his approach. "What has you by the scruff?"

"A new artist to unveil but I have not the faintest of notions how we should exhibit them, unless we use one of the smaller rooms. Of course, if we hold a reception for a secondary artist at the same time that might be key to a larger audience."

"Who's the artist?"

"Hm?" Christopher looked up. As usual, Teddy's straight red hair needed a comb, and stone dust plagued his once nice suit. "What was that?"

A smirk teased Teddy's lips. "The artist? Who is it? I don't recall signing anyone to a contract."

"Ah. A new talent from England." A talent he couldn't wait to unveil. People would flock to her. Would it bolster her confidence?

"And what little bird did you eat?"

"Hm?"

"Nothing. What style?"

"Charcoals and pencils." Christopher frowned at the wall across from him that displayed a modest collection of watercolors. Could her images be described so simply? They were extraordinary sketches of life. Captured bits of innocence. Scenes from a feminine heart somehow undamaged by a harsh life. "Charcoals and pencils."

"Yes, you said that. It has been a while since we received a display of those. Oils have been the rage of late. How many?"

"Only four or five."

"Excuse me? I don't believe I heard aright. Fourteen?"

"No. I said four, and you know I did. This is a teaser, Teddy. Once we gauge the response, then I will ask the artist to release more." Hopefully Sara would allow a second and third display. Amy and Emily both reported Sara had produced a sheaf full of images. Eagerness to see them bit at his patience.

"If displayed here, you know they are going to clamor—Why the timidity?"

Christopher shot Teddy a glance. "The artist had to be gently"—or not so gently—"urged to agree to any display at all. So, in respect of that hesitation, we will wait."

Teddy inclined his head. "You want them to see their own success."

"Something like that. Yes." The enthusiasm would be an instant bolster to Sara's confidence.

"Might I see what we plan to cause a spectacle with?"

"Of course." Teddy followed Christopher to the office. "I have chosen my favorites, but I refuse to make a final choice until I have a chance to speak with the artist."

"Fine. When will they be coming by?"

"I hope sometime tomorrow afternoon." He only had to reason out the best way to coax her.

Teddy cast him a probing glance. "Will they remain anonymous from everyone? Or will you deign to let me meet them?"

"I haven't decided."

Teddy cuffed Christopher on the arm. "What's that supposed to mean?"

"That I have known you long enough to encourage prudence."

"Wha—" A knowing smile heightened Teddy's usual expression of mischief. "Now it all makes sense."

Christopher withheld a groan. "What are you talking about?"

"Does she have a name?"

"Who?" The heat spread to Christopher's face.

"Don't give me that, Top. The artist from England, what's her name?"

"Don't be an ass." Christopher stalked into his office.

"I'm not being an ass. Did I say it was a horrible bit of truth the artist is a woman? I only want to know her name—"

"I am warning you, Ted." Christopher snatched up Sara's sketches. The action created a smudge in one corner. He flinched.

"Of what? I haven't said a word these past eighteen

months," Teddy complained. "I let you bury yourself, though I knew what would come of it. But what did I know about losing a wife? Especially someone like Carla."

"Drop it, Teddy."

"Chris—" He intercepted Christopher's sharp look and frowned. "Fine. Are these the charcoals—These are spectacular!"

The sketch in Teddy's hands drew his attention. As with all Sara's sketches, an intensity in the image spoke to the viewer's soul. An intensity of innocence. Of purity untouched.

"Who is this woman?"

"Sara Little." Christopher leaned against his desk and crossed his arms. "Hardship is woven in her life, Teddy, which is why Paul and Dix encouraged her to contact us. As a rescue."

Teddy blinked. "You.... Why did you not tell me?"

"It has been two years since we made the arrangements for her."

His friend nodded. "Thought she experienced a change of heart?"

"Something to that effect, yes. It broke Carla's heart, as I recall." Now, to think back on the prayers she lifted for Sara.... "Something has protected her these two years." He motioned to the sketches in Teddy's hand. "You hold the proof, as is her very persona when you meet her."

Teddy thumbed through the sketches once again. "You want me to order those invitations we use?" He shot Christopher a sidelong glance as he set the sketches aside. "We may as well set things to motion."

"I would appreciate that." Christopher met his friend's gaze. "I am not up to the trip."

Teddy smirked. "You haven't been up for much of anything. Thank God you've finally got yourself an artist to display. I didn't want to do something drastic."

"I arranged a showing of Sean's art. Remember?"

"Sure, and you started that five months ago. It took you, what? Nearly two months just to get the little thing planned? Sean wondered if you would ever set the date for the display."

Christopher sat at his desk. "Yes, well, this is not the only gallery I own." But the excuse rang hollow.

"Don't pull that one. You haven't set foot out of Virginia—" Christopher frowned. Teddy backed toward the door, arms raised. "I will talk to the printers and give the final approval for—Wait. I can't do that until we know a date. Any idea?"

"Pick a date."

Teddy blinked. "Pardon?"

"Go away. I have work to do."

Teddy smirked. "I know. It's called 'Ignore'." The staccato clicks of his shoes receded down the hall and out of the gallery.

A small smile tickled the corners of Christopher's lips. Sara's sketches drew his gaze and he gathered them from the corner of his desk. His smile faded. 'Something has protected her these two years.' A sharp pain behind his right eye elicited a hiss. He lifted a hand to rub at his forehead.

A whisper drew his attention. "Hello?" Another whisper. He stood from his desk and opened the door. "Gwyn!"

His daughter smiled up at him. She stood in front of a lunch cart. "Sara and I made lunch!"

Sara hovered on the opposite end of the cart, her cheeks

flushed and her eyes downcast. "Why the excitement? Were you and Miss Little bored?"

Gwyn shook her head, expression serious. "I missed you."

Christopher smoothed her curls. "I appreciate it, Angel Girl. To tell the truth, I fought with boredom myself. Come along." He urged her inside, holding the door for Sara who followed with the lunch cart. The ivory of her dress enhanced the richness of her mahogany waves and the soft blush of her cheeks.

Gwyn grabbed his hand and tugged him to a chair. As Sara prepared the cart with grace and quiet, he attempted to hear his daughter's excited chatter regarding their adventure that morning.

"You had yourself a busy day. I am glad I wasn't missed too terribly."

His daughter gasped, emerald gaze shimmering. "Oh, Papa! We missed you terribly!"

"As I missed you, Angel Girl. Not once did I hear a giggle."

Gwyn squealed, as he knew she would, and threw herself into his arms. Sara laughed. The feminine sound of joy grabbed Christopher by the throat, draining all blood from his face. He forced a smile. How long since he heard laughter – feminine, adult laughter?

He cleared his throat and shot the young woman a quick glance. Her cheeks burned crimson, blue eyes intent upon her clasped hands. "Thank you, Miss Litt—"

"Papa?"

"Gwyn. What have I told you of interrupting?"

"I didn't mean to, Papa."

"I know, Angel. Ask your question."

"Why do you call Sara 'Miss Little'?"

"Only in certain public situations. It would be unfair to demand she call me Chris and not return the courtesy."

"Did your papa call you a special name?" Gwyn asked.

Sara paled, her expression stricken as she stared at his daughter.

He hissed. "Gwyneth Marie!" The reaction turned yet another page of confession into her past. An absent father? An abusive one?

Gwyn's chin trembled. "I-I'm sorry, Papa."

"Sir, please. " Sara's voice quivered, her shoulders slumped. "She couldn't know, sir."

His daughter leaned against Sara, her little hands caressing the young woman's tear-stained face. Sara forced a tremulous smile.

"Don't cry, Sara," Gwyn pleaded. "Please don't cry."

She gathered Gwyn into her arms.

Christopher couldn't look from the embrace. Though it brought to mind vivid memories of Carla, he sat mesmerized by the ache in his soul. A thirst for a similar embrace. For a remembered warmth. For a revisit to a fragrance of femininity and compassion. Tenderness. Softness—

Something collapsed within his hand. He set aside the mangled spoon and covered it with his napkin.

"Sara...." He met Sara's glimmering blue gaze. The grief of her father's loss could be seen so clear. "Please forgive me, but, do you know your father?"

Sara swiped away a tear. "No, sir. Barely a name. It hurt my mum to ask. And, the truth of it is I did no' want to know of him. If he loved us, why did he leave? W-why did he no come home when I needed him? Was I no' enough—" Her voice cracked, tears choking any further words as she shook her head.

He didn't blame her decision, this fight against the hope her father could be alive. After all, if such were the case, why did he allow her to struggle on her own? The lack of her father's presence contributed to the harshness of her past. Christopher covered her hand with his. He did not know how to comfort her, but he understood the agony of betrayal and loss. Perhaps that would be enough?

EIGHT

A Collection of Firsts

8 January 1894

The observation room became Sara's favorite of the Donovan home. The windows overlooked the rear gardens, now blanketed by snow dancing with the brightness of the early morning sun. She lowered her gaze to the tatting shuttle in her hand. Time never before passed so quiet and calm. Instead of a constant rush and mere moments to herself, she completed a needlework cushion for Gwyn's room, tatted edgings for Mr. Lake's kerchief, and uncounted sketches tucked away in her leather portfolio.

"Sara?"

Mr. Lake entered, a dashing figure in his pin stripe suit and light gray tie. She stood to bob a nervous curtsy. His sister and brother-in-law arrived that afternoon, and Sara fully expected the early morning to herself. "G-good morning, sir."

"Good morning to you. I hope today finds you well." He motioned for her to sit and settled himself into the wingback chair across from her. The lush jade heightened the darker tones of his skin.

"I slept well, sir. Thank you."

"And Gwyn? She did not keep you up too late watching the snow, did she?" Mr. Lake retrieved one of Sara's new crocheted doilies from the oak side-table. "She will want to play in the snow this morning. I recommend having one of the younger boys indulge her with a snowball fight. She has impressive aim with... a.... This is extraordinary!"

Sara flushed, unable to look from his handsome face as he scrutinized the stitches. "Crocheting, sir?"

"This must have taken months!"

Sara laughed. "Not so long as that, sir. You won't let me do naught but my crafts."

"You mean to say this took but a few days?" Mr. Lake set to a more extensive examination. He seemed to study each knot and loop.

Sara stole glimpses as she worked the tatting shuttle. His brow creased, concentration evident while his mind planned the process of creating a doily. Sara hadn't before met a gentleman interested in her crafts. They spoke only of hunting or cards. While she did her best to seem interested, some still accused her of slow-wit. Sara lifted her shoulders in an absent shrug and counted the knots for the kerchief edging.

"What is that there? Such grace."

Mr. Lake's question drew her gaze. "This, sir? Tatting." She showed him the ivory thread looped around her fingers. "I use a fine thread to create knots in a specific pattern. These knots form loops and rings combined into a type of lace for edgings. Or I can make doilies, baby bonnets, dress collars, and boutonniere."

"With such simple motions of that tool?"

"Yes, sir. A shuttle." Sara showed him the shell shuttle pinched between her thumb and index finger. "This was my mother's."

"Such an intriguing art. Is it a common pastime for maids in England?"

"No, sir. But my mum served as a lady's maid for the aristocracy."

"Ah. A rare opportunity then?"

Sara nodded. Her gaze settled on the shuttle. Memories of laughter and scolding alike hovered in its luminescence. Whenever she took up the shuttle she felt her mother there beside her, offering encouragement, strength, love. Hours spent learning and laughing.

"Carla would have envied this skill."

Sara met Mr. Lake's gaze, startled. "Sir?"

His hazel eyes darkened with an unsettling visage of haunting. "You have shown the grace in the creation of something many of us take for granted. The patience such a delicate art requires would attract her respect."

"Thank you, sir." Sara never thought of tatting in such a way. As a child it became a way to spend more time with her mother. As a young woman, it served an entrance to memories.

"Your mother taught you?"

"Yes, sir."

"You must have enjoyed that time with her."

Sara peeked at him. He continued to watch her hands while his fingers tapped a rhythm on the chair arm. "I did, sir." She treasured those short hours together, remembering them with fond distinction.

"You and she were close."

Sara nodded, tears brimming. "She was all I had, sir."

"What of the children of the families where you were employed?"

She counted the knots three times before she could continue. "They did no' care for me."

"Ah." Mr. Lake adjusted the crocheted doily in his fingers. "You were likely the quiet one. Carla was so different."

A stab of pain marred his face, and he set the doily aside to again meet her gaze. This time his expression was guarded. *Dear Lord, why do his memories cause pain –*

"I need your opinion on how to display your work."

Sara lost count. When she tried to pick it up again, she could no longer remember the pattern. "Y-yes, sir?"

"To save—"

The door opened. Gregory entered with a tea-cart.

Mr. Lake directed the cart from the butler's care. The tall, balding man bowed and exited, closing the door behind him. More prim and proper than Harold at Lake Manor, his emotional distance reminded Sara of the many houses she worked throughout her life. She missed Harold and the bright welcome of Lake Manor.

Mr. Lake halted the cart between their chairs and began the task of preparing two cups before Sara could offer. "Do you prefer sugar or honey in your coffee?" he asked as he poured. "Will you want cream?"

Sara stared, bewildered. "I...."

He set down the carafe. "You have never tried coffee, have you?"

Sara gave a slight shake to her head, humiliation

tightening her throat.

"Ah. A first."

"Sir?"

Mr. Lake presented her the cup and saucer. "It is hot, so take care."

She gazed down into the deep richness. The strong aroma reminding her of home, but a different side of the memory. Sara gingerly tilted the cup to draw in a tiny sip. The flavor was full and powerful, though a hint of bitterness caused a wrinkle of nose.

"Never have I witnessed such a complete exploration." He chuckled. "The verdict?"

"Sir?"

"Your first experience? How did coffee fare?"

"It is wonderful, sir. It only needs a bit of cream and honey to soften it."

"So I have won you over." Mr. Lake added the cream and honey and returned her cup. "Believe it or not, coffee is either liked or disliked. Though, some enjoy the aroma. The way of opinions, I suppose. Teddy once commented coffee is like a punch in the mouth."

She took another sip. The sweetness of the honey and the silky smoothness of the cream enhanced the richness brought a smile. "I love it."

"To coffee." Mr. Lake lifted his cup toward her. "Quick may it grow, rich may it brew, and dark may it pour."

Sara laughed, her cheeks burning at the unexpected emotion of ease. It felt unlike anything she remembered. Simple. Comfortable. Another separation from her old life.

"Do you realize you called me 'sir' at least twelve times in this brief conversation? I do believe you only said 'Mr. Lake' twice."

Sara blinked at him.

He sipped his coffee, his examination of her launching her into a mild panic. His expression seemed a mixture of seriousness and that hint of mischief. "Not once did you even attempt to stumble over 'Mr. Christopher'. You could say it once, couldn't you? If only to prove you consider the possibility."

"I...." Sara's eyes strayed to the doorway. "I do try to remember, Mr.—"

"Mr. Christopher."

"M-M-Mister...." To her shame, her cup rattled against the saucer.

"Oh dear." He set aside his coffee. "Sara, I apologize. As you can see, I am a pest. More so than usual this morning. Dix would banish me from the house if she were present."

Sara gawked at him. She could count on one hand the times she received an apology.

"I am sorry," he said again.

A clear tone of regret rang in his voice. Sara offered a small smile. "It is fine... Mr. C-Christopher."

He blinked. Then his handsome face relaxed. "That wasn't so difficult, was it? The world has not ended. You are still there. I am still here."

Sara found herself laughing.

"Now, about your art display. Would you like to be present anonymously, so that you can hear viewer reactions?"

Sara's smile vanished. "I...." She fingered her cup with trembling fingers.

"Sara, I do not intend to force an attendance upon you. We made an arrangement that I would screen responses. I am more than willing to do so. This is only an opportunity to change your mind."

"You... you do no' mind, Mr. Lake?"

"Of course not. I will mingle on your behalf; as your sponsor it gives me the right. Though I doubt I look as good in that burgundy gown I saw Amy working on earlier."

Sara flushed and lowered her eyes.

"Oh. I decided not to display all your work. Did I tell you? This shall serve a tease to their palate, drawing them back for more. I plan to also speak with Paul and Dix regarding a minor showing at the gallery in New York."

"N-New York?"

Mr. Lake smiled. "You would not need to attend, Sara. Proxy is perfectly acceptable, and I am certain Dix and Paul would be happy to act in your stead." He drew out his pocket watch. "I better trudge to the gallery. If you can stop by sometime today, we will begin plotting the best layout to enhance your work's intense simplicity. I will also want your final opinion on which art to display and which to save for future."

Sara mutely nodded, her eyes wide as he stood.

"Have a good morning, and give Gwyn my love."

She squeaked out, "Yes, Mr. Lake."

When the door closed behind him, she lowered her gaze to her coffee, her thoughts jumbled. Mr. Lake acted kind, but in a way that didn't rouse her suspicious. He behaved thoughtful and compassionate. He urged her beyond what she knew, so she could try for what she dreamed of most: A second chance at life. But.

Sara set aside her cup. Growing up, emotions became dangerous for her. So, she taught herself to feel nothing for her employers or fellow employees other than mild gratefulness or respect. No matter how handsome or charming, Sara kept her distance.

Now she didn't know how to build up that distance. Mr. Lake wasn't her employer. He wasn't a fellow employee. He was the husband of the woman who offered her an opportunity for a new future. He was the director of a gallery of such beautiful things. He was... her introduction to a world she and her mother only whispered about.

Sighing, Sara lowered her gaze—she lifted her hands. 'God gave you these hands,' her mother often said to her, 'and He gave you the gift of creating beautiful things with them. Pictures of dreams. Scenes of innocence so many people cannot see. Pretties designed with your mind and crafted with care.' But they were calloused, dry and somewhat wrinkled. They were mature hands belonging to an older 'Sara'.

"Here you are."

"Amy?"

Amy came to stand beside her. "Yes, miss?"

Sara raised her hands, her heart catching in her throat. "Can I get pretty hands?"

The young woman smiled. "I'll get my things."

NINE

Timid Ventures

Sara's blue eyes didn't waver from their regard of the front door. Mr. Lake's invitation to the gallery pulled at her, but each moment she reached for the latch, terror rose. Venturing to the gallery would mean welcoming commentary on her art, and that from those of an artistic profession!

She turned aside but couldn't retreat. A whisper in her soul coaxed a first fateful step outside her area of comfort. To experience another waiting adventure. It only required a step beyond all she knew.

The fear continued to press, overwhelming her imagination with irrational possibilities. She lowered her head. The Lord protected her, His provision a constant. Forever had He led her to a next position for food and clothing, shelter, something to learn. Sara sighed deep and once again faced the massive wooden door.

Gregory exited the parlor. "Oh. Miss Little."

"Mr. Gregory." She curtsied.

"Do you require something, Miss Little?"

Hesitancy tightened Sara's throat, but she pressed onward. "Mr. Lake asked me to stop by the gallery. Miss Gwyn is down for a nap, and so I thought...."

"Will you need a carriage then, miss?"

Sara nodded, silent for fear of voicing a protest.

Gregory bowed. "I will see to it immediately." He made his way outside, closing the sturdy door behind him.

Again, she stared at the door—

"Here's your coat and gloves, Sara."

Sara gave a startled jump. "Th-thank you, Amy."

"I found a nice warm scarf you can wrap up in so as to keep yourself warm. I think it's angora—Here now. What's the matter?"

Sara's cheeks burned. "I am such a goose."

Amy set the scarf and gloves aside on the hall table to help Sara into the dark-blue wool coat. "Don't be so hard on yourself. You think you're going to take to America the first days here? It'll come."

She sent the young woman a timid smile. She reminded her so much of Beth in moments such as these. "Thank you, Amy. Days like this I forget to trust God with the keeping, though He's never turned from me before. I have no reason to be in a fright."

Amy buttoned Sara's coat. "Well then, you better hold tight to that or everyone'll think you're scared of your own shadow. That would never do. Teddy'll likely pick you out to prove how funny he supposedly is. Believe me, you don't want that."

"Teddy?"

"Mr. Christopher's friend." Amy adjusted Sara's coat over the skirt of her blue dress before turning for the scarf. "They went together on the gallery out of college. He does the clay and stone works, and Mr. Christopher the paintings and sketches." Amy adjusted the scarf over Sara's thick waves and tucked it into the wool coat. "He's right handsome, but a bit on the—" The young woman shot Sara a glance before finishing with the scarf and turning to retrieve the gloves. "Just take what he says with a grain of salt and sand and you'll be fine."

Sara's eyes widened. "Is he–"

"Oh he's no rogue, or whatever you call 'em, but he twists a word just the way he wants." Amy presented Sara the gloves. "I just heard the carriage come 'round. You have fun there at the gallery, and make sure Mr. Christopher shows you 'round and tells you all the stories of the receptions he and the missus used to throw."

Then Gregory ushered Sara outside and into the carriage. "The gallery, straightaway," he said, matter-of-fact.

Sara closed her eyes, whispering a prayer as the carriage lurched forward. Over and again she reminded herself of Mr. Lake's kindness. Why would his associates be different? Certainly he wouldn't partner with a bully such as Mr. Brockle?

The carriage creaked to a halt, the door opening moments later to the smiling face of the driver, Patrick. "You need help to the door, miss? The streets be slick."

She accepted his help down, only just keeping her feet from tangling in the fullness of her skirt. "N-no, Patrick. Thank you. I do no' want to keep you."

"No trouble, miss. That's what I'm here for."

Sara sent the lanky, middle-aged driver a timid smile.

Gathering the front of her coat in trembling hands, Sara

ascended the stairs. The gallery loomed as impressive now as when she first arrived. An artist at a gallery such as this? Dare she believe it? She stared at the gallery doors, biting her lip as her hands worried the front of her coat. *Push them open. You can do this. He asked you to come by.* She reached out—

"Of course, Top. No prob—Well, hello! Who might you be?"

Sara startled back as she stared into the silver gaze of a tall, attractive redhead. "I am sorry, sir. I did no' mean—"

"What's the ma—Oh! Sara. You made it after all."

Sara's gaze retreated to Mr. Lake's familiar face. "I... Miss Gwyn went down for a nap, and so I... I thought this would be the best time."

Mr. Lake stepped back to usher her inside. "Perfect timing. Come in before you catch your death. Teddy, don't stand there gawking. Close the door before you die of exposure."

She lowered her focus to the floor. The gallery doors closed behind her as she followed Mr. Lake. "Let us have some hot cider. You are trembling."

"Yes, sir—I mean, Mr. Lake."

Another figure came to walk beside her. Sara cast a frightened look to the redhead. He smiled. "S-sir."

"Ah. Yes. Er, this is Theodore Parker. Teddy. My partner and friend. He helps me plan the events. Teddy, this is Miss Sara Little. The artist I told you about."

"A pleasure to finally put a face to the art, Sara."

Sara curtsied. "Sir."

"None of that," Teddy said, chuckling. "Call me Ted, Teddy, or something the like. You can even call me Parker if you want. Top over here knows as well as anyone I don't deserve respect."

Top? Sara peeked at Mr. Lake. He frowned at his friend, his hands clasped behind his back. "I will try, sir... I mean...." Teddy winked at her. Sara flushed and looked away. "Mr. Parker." She heard Mr. Lake chuckle.

"Mr. Parker? That sounds horrible. Like I'm a partner of some respectable establishment."

Sara halted. "But are you no'...."

"The partner of some respectable establishment?" His silver eyes twinkled. "Yes, but I don't care for the sound of it at all."

She blinked at him, then she smiled. *Americans.*

"Lo and behold she smiles, Top. Something I said must have struck a funny bone."

"Teddy, Sara smiles on a regular basis. You haven't a special talent for bringing it about."

"Did I say I did? I just commented. Less coffee for you, I think. You get cranky—Of course, your sister is due later and we both know how she can be. Nor have we lunched yet, and the layout of the display has not cooperated."

The two sounded like bickering brothers. Another peek at Mr. Lake revealed a boyish smirk.

"I had lunch," he said. "You were too engrossed to notice."

"And you didn't offer me anything?" Teddy scoffed.

"I offered. You grunted and continued on about the layout. Then you promptly pushed me aside and moved everything around again." Mr. Lake intercepted Sara's scrutiny and smiled.

"I don't believe it," Teddy said. "You always insist I think with my stomach. So why didn't I smell the food you offered?"

"How should I know? Your mind never does seem to work the same twice in one day. I'm forever believing you've lost what little sense you had."

Sara laughed—both men focused on her, inciting a wave of crimson to her cheeks.

"Well, well. She laughs as pretty as she looks."

"Teddy." Mr. Lake's eyes narrowed.

"Oh. I apologize, Sara."

Her gaze darted from his.

"Teddy, pour Sara a mug of cider." Mr. Lake held open the door to the kitchen. "I will show her what we have in mind for the display."

"Why do I—"

"Ted."

"Fine, fine. Cider." He disappeared into the kitchen.

Mr. Lake gestured toward the main hall. "The testament to my lacking as a sponsor is this way."

"Sir, layouts are a challenge for all things." How many times did she herself receive brow-beatings for failing to please the Housekeeper?

Mr. Lake clasped his hands behind his back, a quick glance sending her heart into her throat. "It is as you say, but considering my past experience, and my enthusiasm for this particular display, I do not believe that a feasible excuse."

Considering her sketches would be the topic, Sara felt an immensity of humility in any type of exhibit, poor or otherwise.

"Oh, you should know that my sister and her husband arrive in about an hour. Would you care to join me?"

"Oh no, Mr. Lake. Gwyn will be terribly put out if I do no' help her finish the picture-book we started. And she asked me to show her some needlepoint on a pillo—Oh bother! That was to be a surprise."

Christopher chuckled. "My performance of surprise is quite accomplished. Just ask Carla—Ah. I...." His countenance tightened, the color of his face retreating to ash.

Concern caught her breath. "Mr. Christopher?"

He cleared his throat while tugging a golden pocket-watch from his vest. "It was nothing. Simple slip."

"A-are you well, sir?"

"Fine."

But Sara could read the agony in the pallor of his face. For almost two years he had borne life without his dear wife. She knew well the chill of that misery.

A gentle touch on his right arm invoked a violent shudder. Sara nearly cried aloud at the haunted expression in his eyes. Then he tore his gaze away.

"Mr. C-Christopher, the ache goes away. Truly. It does."

He shook his head, his throat working hard at swallowing the grief. The ache of loss seemed to overwhelm him. Did it twist the view of his daughter? Haunt his dreams with whispers of a dead wife? Did it even pervert the joy that should have been warm in the memories?

Sara blinked away the tears and stepped close, forcing her hand into the grip of his fist. He clutched at it, his gaze never wavering from the blank wall before him. *Dear Lord, please help him find peace.* The chaos of grief tarnished everything.

Sara watched the carriage rumble away toward the train station, the tickle of a falling tear drawing a quick swipe. *Sweet Jesus, please.* Mr. Lake's heart broke under the weight of the agony, and reminiscing his wife didn't offer him the comfort that it did for Gwyn, Emily, or Harold. The memories didn't bring him a smile, as Sara's did for her mother. But why? Why would happy memories hurt?

Yet Sara remembered her own fight against the memories. Accepting them would have meant accepting his wife's death, and a forever separation from everything he had shared with her. "You did no' want that either, Sara-Ann. Remember? You wanted your mum, not the dreams of things that would no' happen again. You wanted her voice, not a whisper."

The memories had softened the grief eventually, but only after weeks and months of allowing herself to relive those treasured moments spent with her mother before and after her sickness. Sara lowered her gaze to her hands as they clenched the gloves still unworn. The Lord had gentled their touch to her mind and heart, too, knowing she needed the time.

Lord, how do I tell him You helped me say 'good-bye'? Sara released a deep breath. If he had suffered this way the entire time she had been gone.... Mr. Lake's separation from God must have been that deeper torture she sensed. His faith and security had toppled in so many more ways than just the death of his wife. Hadn't Sara also felt lost and betrayed when her mother died?

Sara absently nodded as she turned to climb the steps of the Donovan home, wiping away more tears. *Sweet Jesus, You give me the words to say.* It was a promise that Sara would fight every warning in her head and history to do. She couldn't let him keep God on the outside. It was his only hope of peace.

God was the only key to life past the grief.

Christopher absently rubbed the face of the golden pocket-watch as he stared out onto the distant rolling white hills of Virginia. Silence. Insulated stillness. Stark whiteness. Once, snow and winter had been romantic. Fun. Warm. Welcoming. A time of family and togetherness. Adventures and trips elsewhere. Singing—Christopher drew in a ragged breath and closed his eyes, his soul rocking in time with the sway of the carriage, trying to heal. To recoup. To slink past the memories.

"Chris." Poke. "Christopher Andrew, do stop falling asleep. Mother and Father will think you don't want them here."

Christopher opened his eyes and looked to his left, down into the vibrant green eyes of his wife and lover. He smiled, and a shadow seemed to melt from an aching heart. "I'm sorry, Carla. I was up late last night finishing that landscape."

Carla's eyes brightened with the smile of her expression. "Oh how wonderful! I had promised to show it to Mother when we went to the gallery this evening before dinner. She wants to put a landscape in the sitting room over the mantle. I thought that winter scene would be perfect, and such a wonderful contrast to the roaring fire."

The loveliness of her face, the dimple on the right side of her mouth. He lightly stroked the line of her jaw. "Perfect," he whispered.

Carla's expression softened, and she drew his hand away from her face to press her lips against the palm. Then she snuggled against him. "Chris, can we plan a trip to England? I miss Dix and Paul's faces."

"Of course."

"We could visit the gallery there that first gave you your start. And we could meet Paul and Dix's new friends, they wrote of a young woman they specifically want me to meet, and I've always wanted to visit the cathedrals and museums there. So that I could see where you were first inspired."

"It sounds as if you have it all planned."

Carla laughed. "No, no, Chris. I only thought of it a few days ago. I meant to talk to you about it yesterday, but I was distracted by Mother's letter asking to come for a visit."

"All right. Just as long as you hadn't planned on leaving me behind."

Carla laughed again. "Of course not."

Christopher groaned and sat up to cradle his face in his hands. It wasn't fair. They made so many plans for their future. A future ripped from him as surely as a newborn son stolen from a waiting family. Wiping roughly at the wetness on his cheeks, he pulled Carla's gift to him from his pocket—and stared down at the unfamiliar kerchief with a frown of confusion. It lightened to a very slight smile.

"M-Mr. Lake?"

Christopher looked from the passing winter scenery to Sara sitting across from him. "Hm?"

She hesitantly stretched out a hand, in which she held a bit of cloth. Christopher accepted it, looking down to a handkerchief having a finely worked monogram of 'C. A. L.' in one corner. It was also edged with tatting similar to what she had done that morning.

"I asked Mrs. Emily for your initials so that I could make this for you," she said in a somewhat rushed whisper. "For everything done for me." She motioned to it. "I have meant to give it to you

since day before yesterday." She ducked her head a bit and sent him a timid glance as she softly confessed, "I am a silly goose when it comes to giving things. I never know what to say."

Christopher lifted his eyes to meet hers, and he offered her a reassuring smile. "Thank you, Sara. Thank you very much."

She flushed and smiled as she clasped her hands tightly in her lap. "You're welcome, sir."

Christopher fingered the monogram, the stitching fine and delicate. The almost earthy colors giving a soft, masculine feel the same as the tatted edges gave an effect of elegance and care. Great thought had gone into the creation and design of it.

Retrieving Carla's gift from the same pocket, he held each side by side as he recalled the care and compassion behind each offering. He released a deep breath and tucked them both away to look again out the window to the silence of the winter scenery. The insulated stillness. The stark whiteness.

He closed his eyes as he tried to remember when he loved it. That time seemed forever ago. A year for each month she had been gone. An age and a day— *"It has been forever and a day since seeing a winter like this." Sara slid down the glass of the carriage and hesitantly poked her head out.*

Christopher watched her with a slight smile. "Certainly they have snow in England."

Sara's lips danced with a genuine smile before sliding the glass back into place and sitting back. "Of course they do, only not like this. I suppose it is... brighter here." She pointed out toward the hills. "And those? They look like piles of baker's sugar ready for a bit of a fresh-baked cookie."

Christopher's lips twitched upward. "Gwyn would love that visualization."

Sara giggled. "I will be certain to tell her. She will likely want a picture of a big baker missing the baking sheet."

He chuckled.

Then Sara leaned her head back against the plush upholstery and released a soft sigh, nestling her hands into the lined pockets of her coat as she still looked out the window. "I love the white here. It is so utterly white. It reminds me of a Psalm about being washed as white as snow." Sara sighed again, and her blue eyes glimmered. "I love the white."

Christopher watched her as she absorbed the brisk and natural loveliness of his Virginia. The line of her throat and neck, the caress of an errant curl against her temple and cheek, the softness of the misty gray scarf as it heightened her natural beauty and color of life....

"Did your wife like the winter, Mr. Lake?" Sara asked softly.

Christopher's hands fisted as his chest tightened, and he looked from her face to the coldness outside. "She did," he recalled, voice tight. "She said it made her appreciate more the waiting warmth of fire and family. Cider. Hot chocolate. Soup in mugs around the fire. Knitted socks and scarves."

Sara sighed again. "I am so glad Gwyn had a mum like her," she whispered. "Those happy memories will lift her when she's down. They will keep her. Like mine of my own mum."

Christopher clenched his jaw, fighting back the sharp retort and the wave of agony-driven rage as the carriage lurched to a stop outside the Donovan home. The driver scrambled down and opened the door, offering Sara a hand when Christopher made no move to do so. At the bottom of the carriage step, she turned and sent him a tremulous smile.

Christopher looked away. "We'll return as soon as we can."

Sara stepped back from the arc of the door as it closed. "Yes, Mr. Lake," she said softly. "I will have Gwyn prim and proper."

"Thank you." The driver climbed back aboard. "Drive on."

The carriage lurched forward, and Christopher looked back outside to see her staring after the carriage... and still... and longer still....

Now, Christopher opened his eyes and reached up to scrub at his scalp. "I'm sorry, Sara."

She was right. Gwyn was lucky to have happy memories of her mother. Christopher only wished memories were not all she had. Gwyn and he deserved their family. He clenched his jaw and straightened in his seat, tightly crossing his arms. "What glory could He possibly have received from the death of you and our son? What good will go to others? What good to me? Or to Gwyn?" Christopher felt a press and urgency, but he fought it violently back. It would take a miracle to prove a death could be a blessing.

"Chris!"

Christopher raised his gaze from Carla's picture within his golden pocket-watch. A man several years his senior approached, an elegant woman beside him. Tow-head and raven-haired beauty, Paul and Dixon Donovan were a striking couple.

"Paul. Dix. How was the trip?"

"Harried and rushed, but thrilling." Dix drew him into an embrace. She kissed his cheek and then held him out at arm's length, clucking her tongue. "Chris, aren't you eating? You look positively scrawny."

He kissed his elder sister on the forehead. "I missed you too, dearest."

She laughed.

Paul Donovan pulled his brother-in-law into a tight hug. "Topper. How's Gwyn?"

"Talking more than ever. Sara has an endless supply of questions on her hands."

"Was she troubled by the sudden move?" Dix's chocolate-brown eyes darkened.

"Sara or Gwyn?"

"Don't be daft. How was Sara?"

"Dix, I made certain to explain everything."

"It must have been a shock for the poor dear. Did you discover why so long passed before she could come?"

Christopher motioned to the exit. "I will answer your questions in the carriage. Is your luggage being forwarded?"

"Yes. Everything is arranged. Dix and I have enough at the house to hold us until it arrives. But we aren't concerning ourselves with that just now. How is Sara acclimating?"

"She is fine, Paul. Gwyn is absolutely smitten." Christopher began to think his daughter the only reason Sara remained. After all, how many times did he browbeat the girl in order to have his way with her art?

The trio exited the station into the crisp briskness of the winter afternoon. They scurried into the carriage.

"How are you?" Paul asked. His gray eyes scrutinized Christopher's profile. "This must have been a shock."

"Stop your clucking. Both of you."

"Cluck-cluck," Dix retorted. "Will you at least tell us what has been decided for her?"

"She has an exceptional talent with pencils and charcoal."

Dix smiled at her husband. "You were right, Paul. Charcoal dust on her fingers."

"Playing detective again?"

"Everyone needs a hobby. You had one, too. Remember?"

Christopher flinched. "Paul, I do not paint any longer. Leave it alone."

"Carla would be heart-broken."

Paul squeezed Dix's hand. "Leave him be, my love." Her expression protested, but she remained silent. "How long will you need us to stay, Chris? Will Sara be attending any showings in New York? I assume you will arrange some."

"Yes, but I believe Sara would feel more at ease if either you or Dix acted as her representative."

"I don't doubt she declined. The showings in New York would be too extreme for someone such as her. I will do my best to act on her behalf, but we won't arrange an exhibit there for a little while, correct? Not until a few here have met with success?"

"Correct. I want her to see how well received she is before asking her to take another step forward. I have warned her of the possibility."

"Oh, Paul, I can hardly wait to meet her again. She was such a dear at the party. Very attentive and sincere." Dix frowned. "I only wish her employer—do you recall his name, Paul? Brockle?—I only wish he would have left her alone. Shouting and harassing the poor dear. What a brute! I am only glad she esca—He didn't happen to be the one causing the complications?"

"Yes. It seems he made untoward advances and then threatened to dismiss her without pay or references if she left his employ." Christopher did his best not to chuckle when Dix sputtered with rage.

"What happened?" Paul asked.

"She left his employ without pay or references. She stayed with a friend of her mother's until she could save up enough to purchase her ticket." If she had but written him sooner the cost of her passage would have been provided.

"The poor dear." Dix shook her head.

"Indeed. She is a courageous young woman."

"Yes, she is." Christopher stared out at the passing winter scenery. "She reminds me of Carla, in that respect."

"Gwyn has likely done wonders in helping Sara acclimate. She is so much her mother's daughter," Dix offered carefully.

Christopher nodded, his gaze lowering to the pocket-watch in his hand. Then he cleared his throat and tucked it away. "Yes, and that is the reason I had Gwyn stay with her."

"I hoped you might." Paul chuckled. "You know how Gwyn loves adventure."

Dix laughed. "Paul, do you remember the last time she came to stay? You and Chris had a showing in the City and Carla and Gwyn came to spend the week."

Paul frowned, tapping his lips with a finger—he snapped. "The three of you designed a play, sets and costumes included, and performed it on our return. Pirates?"

"Female pirates, to Gwyn's pleasure."

Christopher smiled. "Gwyn was just three and played an admiral, didn't she?"

"Yes, and we had to keep prompting her with her lines and said most of them ourselves."

"My favorite part was your capture and Gwyn trying to wrestle around that wooden sword!" Paul laughed.

"Oh...." Dix wiped tears from the corners of her eyes. "Dear me, such fun. I wonder if we have the costumes yet?"

"Seems to me we tucked those away in the attic, along with the other projects you three devised while Topper and

I were away."

"Oh it would be great fun to bring them down, Paul. Sara would make a wonderful damsel in distress."

Paul shot Christopher a glance. "Let's be sure to talk to Sara. With her talent, she is likely to have wonderful ideas for rejuvenating the sets and costumes."

"Think of the plays Gwyn has likely imagined while we've been away!" She clapped her hands. "Oh, I can hardly wait!"

"Don't volunteer Sara until she is given the opportunity to warm up to us, Sweet. Otherwise, you're liable to undo those miracles Topper and Gwyn have done."

"Don't be ridiculous, darling! Sara and I will get along famously. Isn't that right, Chris?"

Christopher looked from the winter scenery. "Hm?"

"Sara and I," Dix prodded. "We'll become fast friends, which I am determined to prove this evening at dinner."

"Only if you are gentle with her."

"Chris, don't be ridiculous! Certainly I know Sara is timid. I met her long before she knew the safety of Lake Manor."

"I am only offering a reminder, dearest. She has already been submitted to Teddy's playful flirtation. I do not believe she could emotionally handle your instant affection without a little warning."

Dix scoffed. "As I say, brother mine, just you watch my dear Sara Little in the comfort of Lake Manor as we dine this evening."

TEN

Bittersweet Reminders of Nothing

Gwyn leaned across the arm of the chair, paddling her feet as she watched Sara guide the charcoal across the page. "That is pretty. Is it me?" She pointed to the child on a log.

"Yes it is. Your papa is there, and God in the clouds... and do you see that face right there? That's your mama looking over you."

"So pretty...." Gwyn's face puckered. "Where are you?"

"Not in this picture. This is your family."

"But you are in our family now! Papa said so."

"Gwyn...."

"If you're not in it, it's not done."

Sara worried her lower lip as she hesitantly lifted her pencil–

"Excuse me, miss." Gregory stood in the doorway of the observatory. "The Donovans have arrived."

"Uncle Paul!" Gwyn scampered from the room, squeals and laughter followed in her wake.

Sara set the paper and pencils aside, but her fingers lingered. She couldn't ignore what the sketch already whispered, though it made her heart jump—Gwyn's squeal of welcome drew Sara back to reality. She shook the image from her mind and hurried outside.

Paul Donovan set Gwyn upon his hip. As was her custom with anyone, Gwyn cupped his handsome face in her hands and grinned. Paul, Dixon, and Christopher all laughed, the sincerity of it setting Sara's heart at ease.

Paul Donovan's sandy-blond hair and gray eyes added a certain depth to his clean-shaven face and kind tone. His gangly appearance brought with it the memory of their first meeting at a dinner party in England. Expecting his height and excessive amount of limb and leg to become a detriment to his dance, Sara had watched in awe as he guided Dixon Donovan around the floor with the grace of a nobleman. Even now the recollection of surrounding shocked whispers brought a smile.

"Hello, Angel Girl. How is our favorite niece?" Dixon Donovan rested a hand on her niece's shoulder. The smile on her rose lips shone in her brown eyes, heightening the beauty of her heart-shaped face.

"Silly, Aunt! I'm your only one."

Dixon Donovan pinched Gwyn's nose. "True. I wonder if that is why your Uncle and I only brought one of these." She drew a gold bracelet from the inside of her glove.

"Oh!" The afternoon sunshine twinkled off the golden charms, dancing in Gwyn's wide eyes. "Thank you, Uncle. Thank you, Aunt."

"Do you see the charms?" Mr. Donovan reached out to touch one. It looked to be an almost horseshoe-like arch. "That is the Arc de Triomphe in Paris. This is Big Ben, in

England—"

"England?" Gwyn peeked over her right shoulder to Sara. "Have you seen Big Ben?"

Sara nodded, desperate to be calm even as everyone focused upon her. "I did, miss. I worked for a family who lived in just the right place for me to see it every morning." The only blessing of the position.

"Truly?" Gwyn offered up the bracelet. "What are these others? Have you seen them, too?"

Sara peeked at Mr. Lake as she cradled the bracelet. "I am not the one to ask after these lovelies, Gwyn."

The girl pointed to another charm: A ship. "You don't know what this is from?"

"No, miss, but your Uncle and Aunt do."

"You could pretend, Sara? We could get close to what is real."

Sara laughed, her smile fading when she heard the crisp sound of Mr. Lake's retreating steps. Dixon squeezed Paul's shoulder and followed her brother. Concern fluttered and made Sara's throat tighten, but she forced a smile.

Christopher slumped against the door, his breathing rough. Stories compared with real life. Games of imagination to bring laughter. He fisted his hands, fighting against the memories no longer enough—

The door clicked and pulled away. "Chris?"

Christopher straightened. "I am fine, Dix."

"So it finally begins."

"What are you talking about?"

"The realization you have no idea how to continue. The

need to move beyond the shock of her death. Moving on."

"Moving on?" Christopher gaped at her. "To what?"

"To the life put on hold since Carla's passing."

He scoffed. "And what life would that be? Tell me, Dix. What life has been 'put on hold' but the one stolen from me?"

"That is enough!" Dix slammed down her gloves. "Christopher Andrew, stop feeling sorry for yourself! You lost a wife and newborn babe, yes. It was horribly unfair, yes. But what gives you the right to keep Gwyn separated from a woman's care?"

"Oh? So I am to be a good lad and compare pedigrees and histories, choosing the prettiest face to satisfy a man's needs and a daughter's grief?"

"Gwyn deserves a mother, and you need a wife."

"I had one!"

"Yes, and God freed her from the pain of a baby too soon coming." Christopher turned away. Dix released a slow breath. "You can no longer exist on memories. How long will you separate yourself from what you both want? What you crave?"

"Carla is my wife, Dix. My lover. My friend. My passion." Christopher buried his hands in his hair. "Do you know what it is like to lose that? She took me with her when she died, leaving nothing."

"Chris...." She gripped his arm. "This loyalty to Carla is misplaced."

"She is my wife!"

"And she is dead." Christopher flinched. "She is gone, Chris. Move forward with your life. Carla would never want you to suffer like this."

"I told you. There is nothing left." He strode down the

hall into the shadows.

Dix stared after him.

"I hope you have found everything satisfactory here at the house." Paul Donovan adjusted Gwyn in his arms. "I suppose it seems more reserved than Lake Manor, but we are fond."

Sara struggled with her attention. Mrs. Donovan and Mr. Lake had been gone such a long time. "It is a lovely home. My favorite rooms are the library and the observatory. At least, that is what I call the room by the garden."

Paul chuckled. "I spend quite a bit of time there myself. Reading. Pondering. Or listening to Dix read *Harper's Weekly*. It's especially enjoyable in the spring. There is a family of—"

Dix Donovan exited the house.

Sara's heart twittered at the troubled expression on the woman's countenance. "Is something wrong, mum?"

"Where's Papa?"

Dix offered Gwyn a reassuring smile. "Don't you worry about your papa, dear. He needed some time to stretch his legs after a long carriage ride." Dix cast Sara a direct look. "Could you find out from Chris when he would care to leave for Lake Manor for dinner this evening? I believe I saw him heading for the back garden."

Sara hurried forward into the townhouse, her steps echoing the patter of her heart. Mr. Lake stood a few yards down the garden's main path, both hands clenched behind his back as he stared forward. She stepped toward him, hesitant. What could she say? Words meant nothing in the face of grief. All she knew to offer was what God offered her, a listening ear and an understanding heart.

The breeze pinched her face, coloring her breath white as it danced and mingled with his. *If he's searching, can You help him take the right path? I know how lonely a place it is to be without the people you count on most. Like drowning when you see your freedom just out of reach.* Sara blinked away the tears. *But You helped me get back each time. Can you help him, too? Use me.*

"They tell me to move on."

Sara met his gaze, his hazel eyes obsidian.

"How do I forget someone like Carla? The mother of my child. The inspiration to my art. The passion of my gallery.... Sara, how do I simply 'move on'?"

She gave a slight shake of her head. "You canno'." He looked away. "No' the way you think they mean for you to do it. Your Carla will always be with you. Just like my mum is always with me. I know that's not nearly good enough, because even I find myself wishing for her. When I am lonely. When I am confused and scared.... But I have my memories. Of the way she touched my cheek. A whisper of a song she used to sing. The times we talked together.... I remember those and feel better. Like she stands with me again."

"But Gwyn needs a mother, and I...." He released a ragged breath. "Some days I believe I will go mad from missing her. Others, hearing her laughter is a dagger. I am as afraid to lose those memories as to relive them."

"But you loved her, sir. You should no' forget that."

"It is hell to remember."

Sara laid her hand upon his arm, the touch drawing his pained gaze. "Do no' try to remember her alone, sir. You have an angel of a daughter, a best friend at the gallery, your sister and her husband.... They all loved her. They miss her. You need to let people help you."

"But, Sara, I do not want her to be gone."

"I know, sir, and that be fine."

Mr. Lake stared down at her for such a long time. Then he gave a slight nod and reached across to cover her hand, his grip tight. "Thank you, Sara." He turned toward the house, shoulders slumped.

"Mr. Christopher?" Sara rushed to stand beside him, gazing up at his taut profile with wide eyes. "May I... may I pray for you, sir?"

His persona changed at that question, and narrowed eyes snapped to meet hers. She cringed back. "If He answered prayer, my family would still be whole, your mother would live, and your father would never have abandoned you. But if you still wish to believe in His munificence, who am I to stop you?"

Then he stalked away, Sara left to stare after him as hot tears streaked winter-flushed cheeks.

ELEVEN

Seeking

The aroma of Sara's meal did nothing against the leaden weight of her stomach. Most of the conversation throughout dinner faded into the background, blotted by the thundering reminder of Mr. Lake's last words in the garden. Even the joy of being at Lake Manor for dinner held no glow. Instead, his tone of hatred rang in her memory.

He despised the One truly responsible for her survival.

Sara twisted her burgundy napkin. *Lord, how do I explain when he has such an aching heart? How do I make him see that You have been my all when the seeing is the pain?* She couldn't bear to think how much more agony his admittance created. Now a heavy mood muted the conversation, and Sara could only blame herself. If she had remembered her own rage at the Lord.... A tear dripped from her nose. She wiped the wetness away.

Someone voiced an offering of something. Sara refused with a slight shake of her head, appetite long since faded.

Prayer. That remained the only thing left to her now. She didn't know how God would heal a sore soul like Mr. Lake's and—

A feminine hand covered hers. Sara flinched and met Dixon Donovan's brown gaze, dark pools of concern.

"Sorry?" She flushed. "Did you ask me something, mum?"

"I asked if you were well, love."

Sara peeked toward Mr. Lake. He stared at his partially touched meal, his countenance guarded and his jaw clenched. Sara shook her head and returned her gaze to the napkin clenched in her hands. "Fine, mum."

Dix shot her brother a glare.

Panic fluttered. "Did you have fun on your trip? Mine was one adventure after another." The words tumbled out before Sara could think otherwise.

"Before or after the long journey via ship?"

"I-I suppose the whole trip was an adventure." Sara forced a smile. Mr. Lake hadn't lifted his gaze from his plate. "I have done nothing like that before. That is why I was so blessed to have your brother send me instructions in his letter."

Paul's not-so-typical American good looks brightened with his smirk. Sara suspected he had quite a bit of Irish blood—"If our dear brother hadn't responded, how would you have found your way?"

She paled. "Oh... I-I...." She would have prayed and trusted the Lord to guide her steps. Her eyes darted toward Mr. Lake's stoic countenance.

Dix followed Sara's glance. "Yes, love?"

Sara's shoulders wilted. "God would have found me a way, sir." Mr. Lake fisted his hand at her soft confession.

But Sara couldn't deny the truth, no matter the rage he felt toward her Lord. "He has been with me each step of the way. I count on Him. I suppose some would say my life has been rough. But each place was worth more than the few shillings in my pocket. They gave me a roof over my head, and food on the table. I always met someone who taught me something of myself, too."

Sara tried not to think about the fact she rushed over like an overflowing tub. The press to show Mr. Lake why she believed in prayer was like a hand on her heart. If he could understand why she believed God cared.... "With Mr. Piffle I met another Sarah who taught me patience. She was the governess of the master's children." Sara wrinkled her nose. "Little beasts, they were. Never happy unless they pranked someone. The master went after me with the switch for breaking a dish in the hall—"

Dix and Mr. Lake both grunted.

Sara-Ann! She grabbed at a tattered bit of tranquility and held her breath for a moment. "She said I have a natural voice for reading, so she taught me how to read poetry and literature. She helped me speak more calmly, too." Sara cheeks flushed, and she sent Dix and Paul a timid smile. "When I get nervous I slip back into the bad habits."

"Don't fret, love. We, all of us, have some form of bad habit or other."

"Yes, indeed." Paul cast Dix a mischief smile. "Sweet here snorts when she finds something particularly amusing."

"Paul Michael Donovan! I do not." She punctuated the assertion with the tossing of her napkin.

Paul tucked the napkin into the front pocket of his suit coat. "Yes, dear."

"You fool. Can you not see Sara is attempting to bare her

soul. My word." Paul feigned a dutiful expression, though it didn't mask the twinkle. "Now, Sara love, what else did you learn from your adventures?"

"Well...." A glimpse at Mr. Lake revealed nothing. "When I was sixteen I worked in Cornwall—that was my only other position outside the city. I met a pleasant young man by the name of George." The thought of him still invited a skip to her heart. "He taught me how to fish, how to clean them, and he taught me how to speak to... to people without sounding like a spitting cat."

"And he likely attempted to steal a first kiss."

Sara's cheeks flushed molten.

"Paul, leave the dear alone."

"I am not causing harm, Sweet. I am simply stating what I did when you were sixteen."

"Keep any further comments to yourself. It is terrifying enough for the poor dear to be telling all. She certainly is not in need of help from you, you little dickens."

Paul smiled at Sara. "I apologize. I will do better at behaving myself." He leaned forward and pointed to Mr. Lake. "He told me to say it."

"Paul." Dix turned more toward Sara. "It must have been hard to leave such a friend behind."

"Yes, mum. But... but I would not have wished it not to happen. The experience, I mean. Life is like that, having to say good-bye to people we care for. I reasoned God waited with something better down the road a ways. I but needed to get from this little adventure what I could. Since I never had a.... Since I never had a beau before, I thought He wanted to teach me something through it. Maybe He wanted me to see it was fine to want that. That He wanted it for me, and that I should pray for what I wanted in a... a husband."

Dix smiled. "You are so adorably mature, Sara love."

Sara's laugh trembled. "I still have my fits about what I will and will no' do, mum."

"Even I can list a few times where I myself flew into a tantrum." Paul offered Sara wine, which she refused.

"Some more than others." Dix shot a look toward her brother. Then she touched Sara's shoulder. "You have us on the edge of our seats, love."

Sara noticed a shadow settled over Mr. Lake's face, and he picked at a section of the tablecloth. *Please, Lord. Please help him understand why I trust You.* She blinked away a hint of tears.

"What about Mr. Brockle?" Dix prompted.

Sara heard the clink of silverware from Mr. Lake. "M-Mr. Brockle?"

"Indeed." Paul leaned forward. "What in heaven's name could you learn in such a place?"

"Oh. I-I...." At times she felt working for Mr. Brockle tested her very belief God answered prayers. After all, she worked for him longer than any other position, despite what she had to endure. But God asked her to wait. To trust Him. Even when Mr. Brockle threatened so many things—

"Why, Sara, you're trembling!" Dix took Sara's hands in hers. "What's the matter, love?"

"That's enough!" Mr. Lake shot to his feet. His chair grunted against the hardwood floor and clattered behind him. All present stared at him, open-mouthed. Sara paled, staring at his reddened face with burning eyes. "You've pressed her too far. Can you give no thought to how heart-wrenching these stories might be? Are you so concerned with your own thrill?"

"Chris!" Dix sputtered.

Mr. Lake strode around the table to grab Sara's arm. He lifted her to her feet. "Find another source of amusement and adventure for this evening." His gaze snapped to Sara's ashen countenance. She shrank back from him. "I am walking you home. Where's your coat?"

"H-h-hall."

"I expected better of you, Dix. Come along, Sara."

Sara accepted his rough help into her coat, and his firm push of her scarf and gloves. Then he took hold of her arm once more and hustled her out of Lake Manor and back toward the Donovan home. She fell into step beside him, pacing two steps for every one of his.

The brisk walk felt glorious, especially the sharp tang of the wind that hinted at a coming snow. It reminded her of winters walking to church with her mother. It even brought back a memory of one crisp evening with George. However, the most precious memories were those overcome by the presence of God beside her. Giving comfort. Giving peace. Letting her know He held her future.

She tucked her hands deeper into the satin softness of her overcoat pockets. Mr. Lake's hold loosened to a gentler clasp, and his quick pace slowed. Sara peeked at his profile. The rage had gone, leaving his cheeks red from the bite of the winter wind. It bothered her how he had flown at his sister for such an innocent question. Dix couldn't have known all the trouble that came under Mr. Brockle's roof, and Sara didn't mind—

"I apologize." Mr. Lake's jaw muscle convulsed. "For myself. For my sister. For many things."

"But you did no' do anything, Mr. Lake."

He pulled her to a stop. Sara blinked up at him. "Sara, I attacked your faith. My sister and her husband bombarded you with questions on a personal life that is none of their business. I have been rude and argumentative throughout dinner.... How can you say that and believe it?"

"B-b-b—" Sara couldn't focus on the next syllable for the haunting that marred his handsome face.

"But what? You offer understanding and patience yet we return harshness, a sick sense of curiosity, and an arrogant belief we deserve to know all of your experiences." He held her gaze for such a long time that Sara found it difficult to breathe. Then he sighed and shook his head, releasing his hold of her arm. "Again. I apologize."

"For what, sir? I... I do no' mind talking about what's passed. I'd be the pot calling the kettle black if I told you that we should never blame God for the bad. I felt hell's fury at Him for taking my mum. It happens. He knows. It breaks His heart, but He works through the rage. Otherwise, I would no' be standing here. I'd likely be at the bottom of the Thames."

Mr. Lake's gaze snapped to her face. "What did you say?"

"I told you. I've been on my own since twelve. Twelve years old, Mr. Lake. What kind of life is that for a young mite without her mum and no memory of her pop? I had to grow up in one day what should have taken me another five years at least. What else could I do but trust the Lord above? Drop myself into the Thames? I could no' do that, not when I felt there was something yet to come. I had to keep looking at the one day and let God keep the 'tomorrow's in His hand."

A tear escaped. She swiped it away while Mr. Lake offered a comforting grip to her arm. "So you be angry at God. He can bear it, and He will find the way to get at you through it. Likely settin' you on your bum with the wonder of it. That's what He did for me, and I do no' think you deserve less, not with the heart He gave you to help people who did no' have no one else to care one way or the other. So you go ahead and rant. He listens. He always does. It does no' matter if we be right or not. He listens."

Mr. Lake didn't respond. He only presented her with a handkerchief, his dark eyes watchful as she dried her face and eyes. When Sara handed the kerchief back, he continued to hold her gloved hand in his, staring down at their grip with a blank expression. Sara didn't like that look on his face. He shouldn't be afraid to think things. He shouldn't be haunted by memories of a loving wife. Another tear dripped onto their gloved hands.

"Sara... you offer more understanding than I deserve."

"No. I give you more than what you give yourself. I give you a bit of what God wants to give you."

He pulled his hand from hers. "I can't accept it from Him."

"I know. So does He. Like I said before, if you be angry you tell Him. He can take it."

"He takes many things."

The vehemence with which he spoke tore at Sara's very soul, reminding her of her own rage at being left alone. She took his hand. "If you want to say God took her, then I guess that's so. He took her from all the pain to a heaven she dreamt about. Yes, it would have been a miracle to heal her, but... He sees a bigger canvas."

Mr. Lake's hold of her hand tightened. "Why couldn't He see my wife and son within my landscape?"

"I do no' know, sir. But I know God loves us too much to leave pain like yours alone." Sara pressed a handkerchief into his hand. "Please, Mr. Christopher. You be sad she's gone. You miss her. You be angry, guilty for being angry. Please let it go."

He stared at the handkerchief, his face a slight shade of green.

"The ache goes away," she whispered. "I promise."

He inclined his head, his gaze never wavering from their clasped hands. When a single tear escaped his eye, Sara began to pray for him with more fervor than she ever prayed in her life.

Christopher stared up at the ceiling of his room, unable to sleep for the whisper on the wind and in his mind. A name? He couldn't hear it. A phrase? He couldn't understand it. All he could hear was the hiss of a soft tone.

He gave an exasperated breath and tossed back the covers, snatching up his robe and jerking his arms into the sleeves as he strode to the exit and the hallway beyond. The whisper quieted, and all he saw in the dimness was a collection of grays and blackness. Muted tones without color. Harsh lines and angles smoothed only by shadows.

Like a charcoal.

Hesitation slowed Christopher's step from the room, but the whispers.... He looked sharply to his left, toward the doorway leading to the third story stairwell. It drew him forward, palms sweaty as he clenched and unclenched his hands. The whisper could be heard and yet not, but maybe the voice would be brighter if he opened the door…?

When Christopher stood outside the third story door, his reach for the handle hesitated. Again, there were no colors. Only muted blacks, shades of gray and shadowed white. While the whisper urged him forward, the lack of color kept him back. Afraid to touch it lest it bleed color from his own life. Taking away that which made him who he was.

"Christopher...."

Color and muted shadows swirled around the handle, inviting hope that something more waited beyond the black and gray. That all he had to do was open a simple door.

Christopher clenched his jaw and reached out, shutting his eyes tight as he twisted the handle and jerked the door open. Releasing it with a quick motion, he wiped his hand on the softness of his robe as he stepped into the inky blackness.

Yet there appeared something different about it. Light blues of moonlight swirled and twisted within the grays and blacks, tainting the shadows with color and light. Offering a promise of what could be. Showing a glimpse of what waited beyond the charcoal. Yet he couldn't step forward. The stairs led to a place where color waited. Color he had, once. In fact, he could see it there, beginning to creep down the stairs toward him. Whispering his name. Whispering phrases he couldn't bear to hear. Scattering the grays and blackness of a safer existence. One without risk of pain. One without color of life or living –

"Christopher?"

He shook his head. "I'm afraid."

"I know, and that's fine."

That whisper of promise and safety beckoned him forward, through the shadows of gray and black and up into the softening to blue and brown. Steps hesitant. Mouth dry. Chest tight. Hand gripping the rail... and then the last step loomed.

Christopher stared down at it, unable to move to the soft colors that waited just beyond. Unable to leave behind the grays and blacks of his safer muteness. The numbness. He shook his head again. "I can't."

"He knows it. It breaks His heart, but He works through it."

Christopher's grip tightened on the rail and he took a step down. "After all I've done? After all I've blamed Him for?"

"He can bear it."

Christopher moved down another step. "Why?"

"He has something waiting for you."

Christopher bolted upright, the sweat dripping from his chin. Then he fell back, mopping the wetness from his face with shaking hands.

TWELVE

Fancies

9 January 1894

"Sara?"

Dix and Paul stepped into the parlor dressed in such finery Sara wondered if they set off to a party. "Yes, mum?"

"Paul and I need to go out for a time. Some dear friends have invited us for an impromptu luncheon. I wish we could take you along, but Paul is certain I may ruin the mystery of your identity."

"It's fine, mum." Though she cherished the luxury of being alone in the house, she missed the sounds of Lake Manor. Sara's lips drooped.

"Don't fret, dear. Nothing said at dinner did any harm."

Paul caressed his wife's arm. "We'll be late."

"Coming." She kissed Sara on the cheek. "Pray for him, love, though I know you do so more than he realizes anyway. You should have Gregory arrange a carriage to

Lake Manor. Chris promised to breakfast with us, but he's likely enthralled with the planning of your unveiling. If you don't go yourself, you won't see him until the night of the event." Dix blew Sara a kiss. "Good day, love. Enjoy yourself."

"Have a nice luncheon."

Then Paul urged Dix out to the waiting carriage. Sara stared at the parlor entry, voices from the night before ringing in her memory. Mr. Lake's sister worried about him. Last night Dix confided that at times she believed he may come to harm... at his own hand.

Sara lowered herself onto the couch with deliberate care. Concern chilled her soul. She didn't want to believe he would harm himself. To damn his soul for the missing of his wife? When she felt a gentle press in her heart, she stood.

Gregory passed.

"Gregory?" She hurried to the parlor entry as he turned.

"Yes, miss?"

"May I have a carriage p-please?"

"Right away, miss. I will need but a moment."

She gathered her things, trembling fingers rebelling against fastening the coat buttons. The sharp clatter of the carriage horses matched her heartbeat as she hurried down the steps. The driver helped her up, commenting on the weather as he secured the door behind her.

The carriage surged forward and Sara bowed her head. She didn't want to be a detriment to Mr. Lake's healing. What if she acted too hasty? What if she caused more pain? Sara breathed deep, willing herself to leave the worry to God. *Lord, please keep him safe. Let Him feel... peace.* But would he allow himself such a thing?

The carriage rumbled to a stop and Sara swung wide

the door. The moment her feet touched the ground she gathered her skirts and rushed up the front walk.

Harold opened the door as she crested the top stair. "Why, Miss Sara. Good morning."

"Good morning, Harold, sir." She passed him into the hall. "Is Mr. C-Christopher?"

"He's in his studio, miss."

Sara bit her lip, her hands still clenched upon the fabric of her dress. Why did she come?

Harold regarded her a moment. "Might I take your coat, miss?"

"Oh. Y-Yes."

"Did you wish me to announce you? I'm certain Mr. Christopher will want to know that you've arrived. It won't take but a moment."

"I...."

Harold ushered her toward the studio. "Wait right here, Miss Sara."

Harold knocked and entered, closing the door behind him. Her heart skipped a beat when she recognized Christopher's baritone voice. If Harold didn't show concern, did that mean all was well? Sara crossed herself and whispered a prayer of thanks.

The butler stepped out. "You may go in, Miss Sara."

"Thank you, sir." She passed into the studio, unable to lift her gaze from the hardwood floor. The door clicked shut behind her.

"Hello." Christopher's voice rang different than she remembered. Calm.

Sara curtsied, swallowing the sudden lump in her throat. "Hello, sir." She risked a peek. "We expected you for breakfast—"

"Breakfast! I completely forgot." He chuckled. "Has Dix convinced herself I am pouting?"

Relief swelled to a smile. "No, sir. She thought you might be busy with the display." He looked at ease in his beige slacks and shirtsleeves, and those rolled up to his elbows.

"As you can see, I am fine. I made the mistake of plotting your display more in-depth over coffee." He motioned toward an easel and corkboard displaying an arrangement of five pieces of her work. "I had an epiphany of how I want your art specifically displayed, using your initial ideas of course. What do you think?"

"Me, sir?"

"Indeed you. Who better? Come along." He escorted her closer to the easel. "Out with it. What say you?"

Each picture served a progression of the one before. The first depicted a night laden with storms, a single candle shining in the parapet of a mammoth castle. The second, a spring day in the garden of a small church. The third, a seaport with vessels waiting for their journey beginnings. The fourth, a massive wrought-iron gate, stoic walls on each side. The hint of a garden portrayed by vines creeping over the boundary. Finally, the fifth, and her favorite. A child peeked over the walls of the garden to that which beckoned beyond its borders.

"Why, it seems to tell a bit of a story, does it no'?"

"Good." He studied the display, his hazel eyes glittering with approval. "Such being my intent, but have I the correct chronology?"

"Oh it's perfect. I can hardly believe all this hid in that bunch of sketches I gave you. No wonder you have such a lovely gallery, Christopher. You see things we others miss."

"I wasn't expecting high praise for doing my duty— Where are my manners?" He motioned toward the door. "Would you care for some lunch? My stomach reminds me of the time."

"I—" Her eyes darted behind him to the door. "Should I not get back?"

"Is Dix expecting you at a specific time?" He pulled his watch from his vest pocket. "Of course I wouldn't want her to worry after you. I can have Harold bring the carriage back around."

"Christopher, I...." Sara's cheeks flushed molten as she held his gaze. "I would like to stay for lunch, and since the Donovans are out.... But only if it would no' be trouble for you, sir."

"No trouble at all, my dear. Come along with me and say 'Hello' to Gwyn. She has missed you terribly." He slowed his pace to ascend the stairs beside her. "I am surprised Dix did not invite you along with them. This would have been a prime opportunity to see the face of Richmond."

"I know, sir, but...." She enjoyed the peace of a life without duties. Relished the calm. To have no expectations but the fitting of her own wardrobe? She still viewed the time with suspicion.

"But?"

She peeked at him from under her lashes. "Is it wrong of me to like doing nothing but the fancies?"

Christopher laughed. "Of course not, Sara. It is, by far, a better opportunity than bouncing about in a cramped carriage. As long as Dix does not fuss at you, I say take as many days as possible to do 'nothing but the fancies'. I hope that includes more sketches for a future display." He opened the library door and peeked his head in before Sara could respond. “Gwyn. We have a guest.”

“Sara!”

Sara returned Gwyn’s tight embrace. “Good day to you, poppet.”

The girl pulled back, her eyes wide. “I wanted to tell Papa about breakfast, but I am to stay outside his studio when the door is shut.”

“Do no’ fret. You were here to serve the guests their tea or coffee, and what a gift to your father.” Sara smoothed the girl’s soft cheeks. “You were their little hostess if your papa needed the help.”

“Hostess?” Gwyn whispered, her emerald eyes agleam. “Papa, I could be hostess?”

“Of course, Angel Girl.” Christopher dropped to one knee and took her hands in his. “But I fell into my hermit habits this morning. No guests to be charmed; no tea to be served. I dare say you couldn’t have missed me too greatly, though.”

Gwyn wrapped her arms around her father’s neck and pressed her lips against his cheek for a wet smack. Sara’s heart swelled with relief when his aspect softened. His devotion to Gwyn acted as a door beyond the torture... and yet, something different brightened his look when the three planned her display. A warmer tone in his voice. Had he not painted since his wife’s passing? Sara tilted her head in silent study. Could art be the key?

“I sat outside the door and listened to you talk to yourself.” Gwyn giggled. “I had your picture, too.”

“Picture?”

The girl nodded, her curls dancing upon the collar Sara crocheted for her. “Sara made a picture. I borrowed it.”

Christopher shifted his attention to Sara as she hid a

smile. She had wondered where it vanished to.

"A picture, is it? Sara, are you keeping things from your sponsor?" He crossed his arms in feigned displeasure... an expression Sara still found gave her a fright. "This will never do. Gwyn, may I see it?"

Gwyn led them into the library. Sara hovered in the doorway, uncertain. Any image of his late wife could shepherd a return of the agony. Hadn't she seen the hurt after his sister's urgency to let her go? Sara watched Christopher as Gwyn pointed out the different portions of the picture. He examined it in silence, unreadable.

"Can you finish it today, Sara?" Gwyn drew Sara into the room toward her father. "I want to show everyone. Can we put it in a frame so I can have it in my room?"

Sara forced a smile. "I will try to finish it today, but I do no' know about a frame. You should ask your papa."

"Papa?" Gwyn tugged on his sleeve. "Do we have a frame?"

Christopher smoothed her blonde curls, his gaze drawn from the sketch to his daughter's expectant scrutiny. "Of course we can frame it, Gwyn. I am sure we have one hiding upstairs. I will go in search after lunch while you wait for the finish." Then he set the image aside and gathered the squirming girl into his arms. "In the meantime, let us not keep our guest waiting."

Christopher listened with rapt attention to the melody of his home, his lips tilted upward in a half smile. Thomas told a joke to Harold of two men in a boat. A young kitchen maid wove the tale of her Christmas experience to the cook.

There could also be heard the sound of feminine laughter mixed with a child's joy—

A fresh medley of flowers flared Christopher's nostrils. He gripped the baluster, his heart suffering a momentary convulse. Memories resurfaced on the fading breeze of that aroma. Christopher turned aside, his steps instinctual. The conservatory. Her favorite refuge.

"Gwyn has not laughed as often as she does now, Carla." He closed the double doors behind him and slipped his hands into his trouser pockets. He kicked an errant pebble. "Dix is right, again, in saying Gwyn needs the comfort of a woman's heart. There is a definite change in her. More stories and sketches. More chatter. More laughter. Since Sara's arrival, Gwyn has not suffered from nightmares."

He groaned and lowered himself onto the top-most step of the gazebo. "Carla, I do not know what to do. Dix presses me to marry so Gwyn will once more have the blessing of a woman's care. But."

Grumbling, he tossed a pebble into the pond. Gwyn craved the love of a mother, and Christopher could feel his own need rising. The thirst for support... and he recalled again Sara's soft and broken voice encouraging him to lean on others. Her press to talk of his grief while seeking the companionship of his family and friends.

Christopher shook his head and stood, though he felt a definite reluctance to leave the conservatory in search of the promised frame. The search would take him to the third floor, a rustling of the dust and images from his past. As he rummaged through those crates for the sake of his daughter's happiness, the need would yet again rise from the depths.

He pushed through the conservatory doors and

navigated the short distance to the main staircase. Though he told Dix there remained nothing to offer a new wife, he knew that as a bald-faced lie. Regardless of how passionate he argued against the desires, they remained, and now they beat at him. The night dreams of his life with Carla were no longer enough. Remembering the devotion did nothing more than keep him teetering on the brink of sanity.

The base of the narrow third-story stairs paused his step. He stared up into the muted light of the third floor. Would he truly be able to face the canvas, so bright with life he no longer saw—He clenched his jaw, his hand clutching the railing as he ascended.

The same fourth step from the top creaked an echoing refrain. The railing still threatened splinters with its spiky touch, needing sandpaper and a coat or two of stain. The trunks, boxes, old furniture and toys beckoned him to remember images and memories long since tucked away. Those whispers of past stories halted his step, resurging the guilt. Had his faith been stronger, he could have saved the one person he would have died for—

Christopher shook the memories free and shuffled forward, reluctant to approach the crates which encased his oils and supplies. He unpacked one, unveiling the canvas beneath the protective sheet. A watercolor landscape of a stream and church. The beauty of nature and the peaceful existence of man with its Creator.

The frame creaked under his grasp, jerking him back to the present. The next canvas represented a similar scene, but with the hint of a fatherly visage within the clouds. Similar to the sketched countenance in Sara's rendering, but hers alongside the image of his wife—Christopher set the frame aside.

A bulky portfolio drew his focus, the last item within the first crate. His furrowed brow relaxed as shaky fingers groped to untie the leather string. With dreaded sluggishness he revealed those first images created during his studies at Richmond College. Charcoals, pencil sketches, even some small watercolors. The most prominent, the silhouette of a woman's back as she gazed out a window.

Though he titled them doodles, Carla declared them a key to his inspiration. He still recalled her reaction when he revealed them to her that first time, her emerald eyes bright and shining. 'Doodles? These? Certainly you jest! Look at the wonderful lines. This young woman seems as if she's about to turn and give you a smile. Who is she?'

Christopher slapped the portfolio closed. "Nothing but a faceless visage. Once I married you, you were the finish to my images. How can I consider a different face? How can I draw a different silhouette when it is yours I feel?"

Yet they wanted him to love another.

He hurled the portfolio away and fled downstairs, each page whispering 'gone' across the hardwood floor.

"Mr. Christopher?"

Christopher straightened, lowering his hand from his face to the vision of Sara's concern. He forced a smile and indicated the sketch in her hand. "I see you have finished. Let us have a look."

She presented him the drawing accompanied by her usual timorous smile.

The intensity of each stroke whispered to his soul of wistfulness. The poignant image of family stole his breath.

"Magnificent."

"Did I... did I get the likeness of your wife right, sir? I meant to ask before."

Christopher only just prevented himself from touching his wife's lips. "She smiled like that when... when she said 'good-bye' that last morning." Agony burned behind his eyes. He cleared his throat and stared out across the pond. A gentle and warm touch covered his hand, accompanied by the whisper of prayer. It brought a memory of better days. How long since he experienced simple pleasures?

"We loved to sit here, listening," he admitted. "Shortly after Gwyn's birth we spent most of our mornings here with her. Carla and Gwyn were meant for canvas."

He lowered his gaze, his focus drawn to the warmth covering his—He withdrew his hand but the warmth lingered.

"I-I am sorry, sir."

"For what?" The gruffness of his voice surprised him.

"Taking... taking liberties. I thought it would be a comfort."

"You did not take liberties, Sara. I—It was a comfort." A comfort he hadn't experienced for ages. "Do not trouble yourself."

"But I do, sir." She stole a look from under her lashes. "I do no' want you to think poorly of me."

Christopher gaped down at her. Think poorly of a woman so tenacious in her concern for others? "I do not. How could I?"

"N-no?"

A reluctant smile loosened the strain behind his eyes. "You do not need me to prove my character is more than your Mr. Brockle, do you?"

Sara wrinkled her nose. “I know you be nothing like him, sir. I could hardly be polite without making him think he could take liberties he should no’ even thought. Mr. Brockle being engaged, too.”

“Gasp and horror.”

“You would no’ poke fun if you had ever met Mr. Brockle.”

Christopher laughed. “No. I guess I would not. I believe Paul called him an ‘old sod’. Though I feel quite certain Mr. Brockle has earned more colorful titles than that.”

“Yes, sir, but I did no’ think Mr. Paul would have come to hear them.”

“Our Mr. Paul fancies himself a detective.” Christopher motioned ahead and offered her his arm. “In fact, he will at times call the Police Department to request files of unsolved cases.”

“Truly?” Sara asked, her voice hushed. “Has he...?”

“Solved any cases?”

Sara nodded. She listened with baited breath, and for the first time in a year he felt himself relax. “No, Paul has not solved any cases that I know of, but that doesn’t mean he hasn’t been a help. Actually, I heard him tout that the Police Department gave him an honorary title of Detective. In appreciation for some new information on one of their older cases.”

“How exciting!”

“Paul would deny that. He states most of a policeman’s day is surrounded by paperwork and investigating... leads, I believe is what he called them.”

She smiled, her blue eyes like sapphires. “What a dear he is. He and your sister both. When did you first meet Mr. Paul?”

"Dear Lord. I have known him since I can remember, or close to. Hm. Eight years? Seven? Yes, I believe I was seven when I first met Paul."

"Goodness!"

"If I remember correctly, Paul and Dix met at a church function about that time. His family had newly arrived in the area, and so Dix did her neighborly duty of showing him about Richmond." He chuckled. "I still remember the look on her face after the afore-mentioned 'stolen kiss' on, or very near, her sixteenth birthday."

Sara laughed. To Christopher's surprise, the joyous melody erupted a wave of pain. He looked away. "Soon thereafter, Paul came by on a regular basis to court her before asking Father for her hand at seventeen. They married just after her eighteenth birthday."

"What a blessing to marry your friend," Sara whispered.

A blessing? He clenched his jaw. But what of the cursed after? The life without their support. The absolute silence. Christopher sensed Sara's sidelong scrutiny and cleared his mind before meeting her gaze. "Question?"

She flushed and shook her head.

"I suppose we should head to the gallery to work on the display." The comment drew her gaze of disappointment, unexpected. "If I keep you longer, I will be late getting you home and Dix will believe it is done deliberately."

"Will you come to the dinner party this Monday?"

A reluctance to say a definite denial rose up. He shifted his feet. "Well, I still have a lot of paperwork to do. To finalize Sean's sale to Jeffrey."

"Oh. Of course you would be busy."

Guilt nagged at him. "Teddy keeps pressing me to hire an assistant to help, but one never knows the passions of a stranger. What if they are not an adequate fit with the gallery?"

"Could I, perhaps?"

Christopher relaxed into a smile. "Has life become too dull with only your crafts?"

"Oh no. I dreamt so long of working in a gallery. I would no' forgive myself if I did no' ask."

A smirk tilted his lips upward. "Well, I must confess I would be delighted to have your assistance. We should discuss your wage this evening at dinner."

"Oh no, sir! You taking me on would be pay enough."

"Such is a statement from a true artist."

Cheeks crimson, she lowered her gaze. "No, sir. I but love the thought of helping with all the lovelies. To make a struggling artist's dream come true?" Sara peeked at him from under her lashes. "That could be seen as a true miracle for some of them, and what a blessing that would be. For me and for them."

The telltale glint of tears glistened upon the fringe of her lashes. The tautness of Christopher's heart eased. *In this woman you would have found a lifelong friend, Carla.* For her heart rang with the same passion for others.

THIRTEEN

Comfort of Liberty

15 January 1894

Christopher stared out at the newly fallen layer of snow. The insulating white matched the numbness within him. The carriage door opened against the gusts of biting wind. Laughter could be heard from within the Donovan townhome, giving rise to another wave of reluctance. He fought it back, remembering again the disappointment in Sara's eyes. She looked to him for protection and guidance. If he took his responsibility with a grain of seriousness....

He clutched his woolen coat against the blustery weather as he rushed into the front hallway. Gregory helped him from his overcoat and accepted his scarf and gloves. "Dining hall or parlor?"

"Parlor, sir. Mr. Parker arrived before you, so they decided to warm up with cider and tea."

Paul, Dix, and Teddy gathered around the parlor's

marble fireplace.

"Blow the trumpets, he's come after all," Teddy said. He gestured Paul and Dix's attention to the doorway, watching his friend with a knowing smirk.

"Pipe down, Parker." Christopher's gaze swept the room for any sight of Sara. "Since this is Paul and Dix's first visit in a year, I thought it would be rude to stay away."

Dix kissed his cheek. "Likely story. You only want to eat my food."

"Believe what you want, dearest. You will anyway."

Sara stood at the farthest window, her attention captured by the dance of falling snow. Burgundy satin set off the red highlights of her hair. She glanced from the scenery, smiling when their gazes met.

"Excuse me while I offer my greetings to your houseguest."

"Of course, dearest. Go on with you."

Sara's cheeks flushed as he came to stand beside her. "Miss Little."

"Mr. Lake." She motioned outside. "Is it no' lovely, sir?"

"Snow seems to fall heaviest on party days, I've found." Christopher shifted his scrutiny from Sara's expression to the drifting flakes of the outside garden. "Carla loved snow. She called it 'a fresh start for beauty.'"

"How very true." Sara eyes widened. "Mr. Christopher, have you ever ridden on a sleigh? With... with bells and carols?"

He nodded, memories becoming poignant and clear.

"Oh my." Sara looked again to the drifts of snow that beckoned for a toboggan. "I so often dreamt of those. What a wonderful way to celebrate such a beautiful time! The laughter and the songs. The cheerful jingle of bells."

"Carla loved those," he admitted gruffly. He leaned a hand against the windowsill, white-knuckled.

Sara faced him, her smile drawing his focus. "Gwyn said as how you and your sweet would sing duets at parties. I imagine it to be so lovely and beautiful, people smiling and singing along when they know the words."

The whisper of those times drifted in and out of his memory, somewhat rudely interrupted by a more amusing one of a less-than-beautiful sound. Christopher chuckled. "Be certain to never sit beside Paul."

Sara cast a stealthy glance toward his brother-in-law. Paul seemed too engrossed in conversation to notice. "He canno' sing?"

"Not a note." Christopher feigned horror. "It's horrible. Dogs bark and howl for miles."

"He must no' be very popular at caroling parties," she observed.

Christopher laughed outright. "No, but that doesn't seem to affect how many invitations he and Dix receive." He turned and leaned back against the sill. "Of course, I think his personality has something to do with that. That and Dix would call them to the carpet with hellfire and brimstone."

"Mr. Christopher," she scolded. Then she laughed.

Teddy somehow manipulated Sara to have a seat beside him during dinner.

Carla, why does Teddy enjoy seeing just how quickly he can annoy, irritate, or even insult young ladies? Christopher clenched his jaw. *I wonder if Paul will help keep Teddy off*

Sara's arm this evening?

"Christopher!"

"Hm?"

Dix threw up her hands. "For goodness sake! Will you stop glaring at your salad and answer my question?"

Heat flared from neck to ears as he gathered up his salad fork. "What question?"

Teddy laughed and gave Sara's arm a nudge. "Top is always distracted just before an unveiling. A person can say just about anything and not get a single reaction."

Christopher noticed Sara sent him an extended glance, but those blue eyes darkened with concern and not laughter. "It wasn't purposeful, Dix." He shot Teddy a brief glare. "I suppose the week has caught up with me. Addressing and mailing invitations, organizing responses, organizing the display itself, and then accepting phone calls for Sara's evening next Friday."

"Paul, isn't it a thrill? It seems forever since the last unveiling."

Paul motioned toward Christopher with his fork, greens attached. "It will seem a bit of fresh air for you, Topper. Don't you think?"

"How so?" He toyed with a yellowish leaf.

"Talking about art again; mingling with fellow artists and remembering a favorite thing. Opening yourself to inspiration." Paul turned his attention to Sara, who focused on him only after a pause on Christopher's expression. "Artists feed off the passion of others, building up their own intensity with it. Most of the time even using the energy to push themselves over a creative slump or"—Paul waved his fork—"or block, as it were."

"We're attention gluttons," Teddy observed, winking.

"Attention gluttons my eye." Dix scoffed. "Everyone needs a comment or two from someone other than family to let them know they're talented. After all, a man is just a little boy in a larger frame, and doesn't Paul like being complimented the same as a woman?"

Paul chuckled as he refilled Dix's wine glass. "No one is arguing your point, Sweet."

"As well they shouldn't. It's the truth." Dix motioned to Sara. "Don't you like hearing compliments on your stitchery? Oh, Chris! You should see the needlework pillow she did for me! Absolutely breathtaking. I feel guilty for accepting the gift."

Sara shyly smiled, Teddy watching her reaction with a smirk. Christopher frowned.

"And the dresses and gowns?" Dix threw up her arms. "Dear Lord! She's adjusted hers and begun adding unique touches of tatting, crocheting, or ribbon work. She's begun the same with mine as well, though I didn't ask her to do it. She's marvelous!"

"It was my pleasure to do," Sara whispered. "No one said much about my crafts before."

Dix scoffed.

"Why haven't I been given any fancy stitched thing?" Teddy's gaze still focused on Sara.

All four looked to Teddy. Sara paled. "P-Pardon?"

"Well, everyone else has something made by you. Can't I get something?"

Christopher frowned. "Teddy, you know as well as I do that you wouldn't know what to do with any 'fancy stitched thing'."

"I keep a kerchief in my pocket, don't I?"

"If you can call that scrap of shirt a kerchief."

"All the more reason for me to get one."

Christopher thrust his plate away. "Oh for God's sake."

"O-of course I can make you a kerchief, Mr. Parker." Sara peeked at Christopher. "It will just take a day or so."

Teddy grinned. "Wonderful. I'm looking forward to it."

Christopher scoffed.

"Chris, let him have his way. You know he'll pout and whine if he doesn't."

"Dix, I'm not a child!"

"Oh really now? I've yet to see the proof." She paused long enough to allow the kitchen staff to take away the salad plates and place the soup. "You know better than anyone that you pout."

"No, I protest. That's different."

Dix waved it aside. "Has Chris told you who he's inviting to the unveiling?" Sara shook her head. "What? Chris, why haven't you told her?"

"And have her fret the entire evening about who thought what? Not likely."

"You're being over-enthusiastic, Top. Sara can handle the knowing."

"It's a simple teaser," Christopher reminded his friend, "and I'm taking my role as sponsor to heart. Unless she tells me otherwise, I won't say who I've invited."

Sara peeked up at him. "I do no' need to know."

"But—"

Christopher set down his spoon. It clinked against his soup plate. "Dix."

"Very well. I surrender. I'll find out when I arrive and then tell her later anyway."

Teddy smirked. "I don't doubt it."

"And what is that supposed to mean?"

"You know what it means. You talk too much."

Dix's eyebrow arched. She set her soup spoon down with deliberate calm, her napkin beside the utensils. "You base this assumption on what?"

"Only saying the truth as I see it," Teddy said. His focus hadn't yet shifted from the duty of eating his soup. Christopher found it interesting that his friend couldn't hear the irritation in his sister's tone.

"Theodore, if not for company, my bowl of soup would be in your lap."

Sara watched the exchange through wide eyes, as if she expected the two to come to blows.

"Here now!" Paul waved his napkin. "You two would do well to call a truce."

"Don't be ridiculous," Teddy said. "She knows I'm pulling her leg."

"Oh?" Paul motioned toward his wife. "Does that seem to be the expression of a woman enjoying a good joke? Does she know not to kick you out on your ear the next chance she has?"

Teddy laughed, until he caught Dix's hard brown gaze. "Gads, Dix!" His ears and face flushed crimson. "I know you don't talk any more than I do. Why do you think I said something?"

"I am not amused."

"Come along, Sweet. Let him off easy tonight. There's always tomorrow."

"Very well. Mark my words, Theodore, your day is coming, and when Paul will be unavailable to rescue you from your own quick tongue."

The remaining portion of dinner was eaten to the accompanying stories of Paul and Dix's recent adventures in New York, including art displays at other galleries, excursions to museums, and the never-ending visits to the elder Lake's. Sara listened with her usual rapt attention. Christopher couldn't help but watch her. She reminded him of Gwyn.

After dinner they moved to the sitting room to visit over coffee and tea.

"Chris, I wondered if you might consider the idea of teaching Sara to use watercolors."

Christopher frowned as Teddy approached Sara with an accompanying gesture toward the hall. "Hm?"

Paul glanced toward the pair as Sara accepted Teddy's offer and set aside her teacup. "After the excitement of the display, naturally," Paul said, smirking, "as I don't believe you should juggle both at the same time."

Christopher rubbed at the face of his golden pocket-watch as Teddy lead Sara out of sight. He wrestled his attention back to his brother-in-law. "Did she mention something?"

"Not in so many words. Though I do believe she would enjoy the opportunity. You know she wouldn't muster the courage to ask you herself."

"Fine idea. I'll ask her now." Christopher brushed past the two to exit the sitting room to the hallway—A sharp smack echoed through the hallway and propelled Christopher around the corner. As he feared, Sara stared up at his friend with wide eyes, shielding her mouth in surprise. Teddy stood across from her, slack-jawed.

Christopher strode forward and caught Teddy by the arm. "I think you need some air." He dragged his red faced and stammering friend to the back garden. "What are you doing? She's under my protection, Parker, and you take advantage of her?"

"I-It's not what you think!"

"Not what I think?" Christopher wanted to shake the man. "Sara Little is by far the gentlest of God's creatures and she slapped your face! What should I think?"

"I don't know," Teddy stammered, "but it—"

"This is your final warning, Parker. Behaviors such as these will stop immediately!" Christopher stalked back inside, slamming the garden door behind him.

Sara hurried forward. "M-Mr. Christopher, he did no' mea—"

"I know all too well what Parker meant." He took her hands in his. "I apologize, Sara. I've warned him time and again that he's to be on his best behavior. It seems he doesn't take me seriously."

"He is not as awful as you believe."

Christopher held her gaze. "You have a lot of patience for the undeserving."

She flushed and looked away.

FOURTEEN

Unveiling

26 January 1894

Christopher straightened the lapels of his jacket, observing his reflection in the mirror and ignoring Teddy's sidelong glances.

"I don't understand why you didn't ask her again," his friend finally admitted.

"I told you, Teddy, when I asked her earlier she said 'no'." He adjusted his black bow-tie and suit-coat.

"Yes, but she had hardly been here long enough to make a footprint!" Teddy nudged Christopher out of the way and adjusted his own charcoal suit-coat and tie, smoothing down an errant lock of red hair. "You didn't ask her again since."

"I have no intention of putting her at your mercy tonight. Just remember how much of a fool you made of yourself after dinner that Monday, and Dix without another invitation for your return, I notice." Christopher turned away to the tables of refreshments. Everything stood in order.

"Don't be a stick in the mud," Teddy protested. "Sara took it all in fun."

"Ted, she slapped your face without pause. How is that 'all in fun'?"

Teddy's ears reddened. "I did not mean the kiss."

"There was none, Ted." Christopher pushed past him toward the gallery entrance. "If it hadn't been for her standing there, I would have thrashed you. I warned you about your behavior."

"I know! I apologized, Top. Too much wine and watching her laugh most of the evening."

"I attended the same dinner party, Teddy." He unlocked the wooden double doors to keep from back handing his friend. At times he could be more dense than his marble sculptures. "I don't recall needing to dodge a sharp strike."

"Stop rubbing it in. How could you survive the entire evening without even a touch of lip on hand—Have you noticed she smells of lilacs?"

"Teddy, please." Christopher passed to the small room displaying Sara's story cycle. He had noticed a recent fragrance of lilacs and vanilla, to be honest. He adjusted the angle of a sketch, double-checked the note cards with the artwork and gave a slight nod.

When he faced the doorway, Teddy leaned against it with arms crossed. "What?"

"Top, how can you be so casual about her? You visit practically every morning for coffee?"

"In case you forgot, I happen to be her sponsor. Would you rather I ignore her? Besides, I want to encourage a friendship, and I would like to think I have done so."

Teddy grimaced. "Who wants to be friends with a goddess like her?"

"Parker, there is more to women than the curve of a supple hip and velvet softness of rose lips. The sooner you realize that, the sooner a lady will accept your proposal and put you out of your misery." He shoved through as the first group of guests entered the gallery.

"And the doors have been opened."

Sara lifted her gaze from the intricate needlepoint design. She smiled. Dressed in crimson brocade with inset roses of black, Dixon Donovan presented a picture of romantic elegance. "You are beautiful, mum."

Dix's smile softened as she entered the observatory. "Sara, I cannot thank you enough for your diligence all this week stitching these lovely ribbon-worked flowers along the hem and bodice. I will be the envy of every woman there."

"The least I could do, mum, for your graciousness."

"Yes, love, I know. But I'm still of the mind I don't deserve your talent rained upon me." She sat on the edge of the chair across from her. "I've come to persuade you to join us. This will be my last attempt before I admit defeat. We can call you something other than 'Sara Little'. No one will know you're the artist. Come along. It will be great fun."

"Thank you for the invitation, mum, but I'll wait here." Sara returned her gaze to the design and began again. "In my life there have been parties aplenty. This is the first when I have leave to stay home. Your brother said I should do as many firsts as I can, so I will stay home and finish this project. Maybe read a bit?"

Laughing, Dix gave Sara's knee a gentle squeeze just as Paul came to the doorway. "Ready, Sweet?"

"Coming, darling." She stood. "You cannot stay distant from all the parties, love."

"Oh no, mum. I have a whole closet of gowns to wear."

"Very well then. With that assurance given, I shall leave you in peace."

Dix accepted Paul's kiss. Sara watched the pair with a wistful smile.

"See you this evening, my dear," Paul called.

Then the door closed behind them and Sara heard the carriage rumble away. She released a sigh and focused on the needlepoint project in her lap, her smile fading. "You goose."

Sara's art caused a sensation, much as Christopher knew it would. All evening his guests bombarded him with questions about the unknown artist. No one voiced a single negative comment, except there were too few on display and those not for sale.

A hiss directed his focus to Teddy. His friend beckoned. "What is it?"

"You won't believe who just arrived." Teddy motioned behind to the main lobby.

Christopher passed to the main entrance—Sara doffed her satin-lined wool coat to reveal a gown of navy velvet the rich blue of a winter's night.

"My God," Teddy whispered just behind him.

Christopher swallowed a firm lump. Her mahogany tresses, gathered upon the crown of her head, had been woven through with blue and silver ribbons that sparkled in the light of the hall. Her shoulders and neck were bare save a necklace of fine silver, a simple pearl suspended at its center.

Moving forward on silver slippers, Sara's sapphire eyes explored the milling crowd. Several men attempted to dissuade her progress, but she only offered them a kind smile and a "Have you seen Mr. Lake?"

"I thought you said she wouldn't be here!"

"That is what she told me." Christopher frowned, thinking back.

Then Sara's gaze met his and her smile dazzled the room. She curtsied to the man still attempting conversation. "I found him. Thank you." Then she stood in front of him amidst the distinct aroma of lilacs and vanilla.

Sara curtsied and offered a merry, "Good evening, Mr. Lake," as she presented a silver-gloved hand.

Christopher enfolded her hand in his, returning her gentle clasp. "I'm delighted you decided to attend—"

"Miss Kreyssler," she finished with a hesitant smile. "Curiosity won the battle, sir." Her English accent lilted in perfect harmony with the music in the background.

The sharpness of an elbow struck his side. He motioned to Teddy. "You remember Mr. Parker?"

"Yes, I believe I do." Sara accepted his clasp, but her eyes remained lowered. "Mr. Parker. How are you?"

Teddy grimaced. "Well. And you?"

Sara tugged her hand free. Christopher pitied the man. He offered her his arm. "Come along, Miss Kreyssler. Let me give you the tour." Once he guided Sara to one of the more secluded rooms of watercolors and free-form art, he halted and lifted an accusatory finger. "You've been practicing that entrance this entire week, haven't you?"

"No, sir. I promise."

"I'm not so sure I believe you. But in any case, I'm glad you're here." Christopher gathered her hands in his, drawing her gaze from a scrutiny of the hardwood floor. "You're a success, my dear."

Her lower lip trembled. "Truly?"

A tear escaped to caress her cheek. She swiped it away, but another followed.

"Sara." Christopher tucked his kerchief into her hand. "Didn't you believe me when I said your art would be loved?" It still amazed him that she could be so unaware of her innate talent.

She dabbed the tears from her eyes. "Thank you for pressing me to do this, sir."

"Thank you for allowing me to do so. You should have hooked me under the chin."

Sara's eyes crinkled at the corners with her smile.

"Come along." Christopher guided her hand to the nook of his arm. "We don't have much time before midnight."

"I do no' think your sister's carriage will turn into a pumpkin," she said, laughing. "She'd be madder than a wet cat if it did."

"Yes, well, I would rather not risk it. You must admit your life to this point resembles a fairy tale."

"I know. I should have stopped pinching myself days ago, but...." She revealed a red mark just above her elbow. "See?" She nervously laughed, her cheeks warming to a romantic shade of rose.

Christopher smiled. *Carla, what a dear woman we've*

rescued. He wished she could have met her, for he knew Carla would have fallen madly in love with her, as Dix and Gwyn had done.

"Watercolors are so different from charcoals and oils," Sara observed, her soft comment drawing his focus to the watercolors to their left. "They are... a whisper of a dream rather than the telling of a story." She sighed. "I wish I could paint like that."

"If you're serious about that comment...."

Sara's sapphire eyes brightened. "Sir?"

"Paul and Dix instructed me to inquire whether you wanted me to have a hand at instructing you."

She offered a tremulous smile. "I would count that a great blessing, sir."

"Good. I would have offered earlier, but they charged me to wait until after the display. Taking on too much and whatnot. Dix always chews my ears about it. She says that I take on too many projects and that's why I practically never finish any of them."

"You canno' help but be excited about your gallery here. Not if that's your passion."

His smile vanished, the word lancing a brand of ice and fire across his mind and heart. He lowered his hand from her arm.

"Mr. Christopher?" Sara's scrutiny darkened her eyes to the tortured blue of a stormy sea.

"I am well, my dear. I have neither seen nor painted an image since Carla's death." What passion remained for him now? At times, the gallery seemed more a torture than a triumph.

Sara's gaze didn't waver in its study of his features, setting his teeth on edge. "You miss it."

The safe vision of the watercolor drew Christopher's gaze. "As much as I miss her."

She faced the same landscape, what seemed a sneering testament to a once peaceful existence. Sara experienced a greater blessing in her life. She used her artistry and passion even through a death and a struggle of survival. Her passion became the art now on display around him. Yet his ardor faded in the face of struggle, swallowed by the void of grief.

Sara suddenly looped her arm through his, the simple action of support drawing his gaze.

"It is still there," she whispered. "You have but to listen."

His chest tightened at the promise he desperately wanted to believe. She sounded so certain, how could he not?

FIFTEEN

The Other Side of the Platter

Sara fingered the lip of her crystal tumbler of punch, staring wide-eyed at the art before her. An oil mountain-scape, it gave life to a part of America she hadn't yet seen. Sara read the note card. *Crater Lake, Oregon; E. C. White.*

"Oh how lovely," she whispered.

"I understand from a friend this happens to be Mr. Lake's favorite."

Startled, she turned. An older gentleman stood behind her. He looked about the same age as Mr. Stillwell with blue eyes, gray hair, and a somewhat slender physique. He stood about as tall as Mr. Lake.

"Good evening, sir."

"Good evening, my dear." He presented a hand. "My name is Joseph Conklin. Whom do I have the honor of meeting?"

"Ann K-Kreyssler." It sounded odd to voice the last name of her father in relation to her identity.

"Very pleased to make your acquaintance." Mr. Conklin motioned to the landscape. "Do you paint?"

"Oh no, but I wish I could. It seems as if it might come off the very page."

"Yes. Eva has quite a talent with the brush."

"You know her?"

Mr. Conklin chuckled. "I know quite a few artists, being as I do my best to support them. We must stick together, you know."

"You paint, sir?"

"No," he said, quiet. "Not for a long time." He glanced toward her. "Well, at least not as often as I would have liked."

"But why ever not?"

"Too much control given to what should not have had it." Mr. Conklin adjusted the hanging of the frame. "So, have you come to mingle? Or have you come to do your best to persuade Mr. Lake to sell you one of the forbidden sketches?"

Sara's nervous laugh twittered through the room. "I came because I had no' ever been to an artist unveiling before—You truly like them?"

"Yes, indeed. I haven't seen a hand like that for years. Not since returning from England, where I believe I happened upon one of Mr. Lake's first displays." He motioned toward her. "Where do you hail from?"

"London. I was born in a borough there."

"Richmond-Upon-Thames?"

Sara's eyes widened. "You know it?"

"In passing." Mr. Conklin focused beyond Sara to the crowd in the main room, nodded, and then offered her his hand. "I must away. A pleasure to meet you, my dear. I hope to see you again."

Sara curtsied. "Thank you, sir. Have a pleasant evening."

The warmth of Mr. Conklin's hand lingered even after he passed to meet an associate in the crowd. All Mr. Lake's acquaintances seemed kind and thoughtful.

A hiss from the side entrance drew her attention. Teddy Parker leaned around the doorframe, his handsome features taut with pleading. Sara almost wrinkled her nose. She didn't know what to believe about him. He didn't seem a bad sort, but the way he flirted and carried on brought to hand so many memories of broken hearts.

"Hello, Mr. Parker."

Teddy hesitated before entering the small room. "Are you enjoying yourself? No one bothering you?"

She only shook her head as she regarded him and his sidelong glances.

"This is Top's favorite. It is a lake in Oregon made by a volcanic eruption. Top wants to go there someday. To prove it as lovely as the picture, I suppose—" Teddy faced her, hands outstretched. "Sara, I feel horrible about the other night. Too much wine. It goes to my head every time."

She continued to examine the landscape. Before coming to America, nobody had apologized to her about their behavior. It made her feel... more.

"Top said that if I didn't apologize, and make doubly sure you knew I wouldn't do it again, he would forbid me from visiting the house."

Sara blinked at him, unprepared for the confession of Mr. Christopher's ultimatum. "Mr. Parker, are you promising to be better behaved?"

"I don't know if I can. My bad habit seems to be talking first and thinking only after I feel the sting of the slap."

A reluctant laugh bubbled up. "Well, if you do better, I will help you."

Teddy grinned. "No fooling?"

" 'No fooling.' You have likely only not had the chance to learn about ladies, being a sculptor. And you did no' have sisters, did you?"

Teddy shook his head. "Three brothers. And Dix never did have the patience to put up with me longer than a dinner, and that only because Top came between us. Or Paul."

"See? You only need a bit of practice."

"One problem. All the practice will likely get me into trouble."

"Trouble? With who?"

Teddy chuckled. "With you or Top, or both."

"As long as you try, I will no' get upset with you. And Mr. Lake will no' be angry. I will explain what happened, if he does."

Teddy's smile remained as he reached out to give her hand a squeeze. "No. That's fine. I will be a big boy and face him myself. We have been friends since college, so I think I understand most of his quirks."

"Is that why you call him 'Top'?" She tugged her hand from his.

Teddy tucked his hands into his trouser pockets. "Top? I call him that because he stood at the top of our graduating class, and almost everything else. Especially popular with the ladies, although he focused more on his collegiate studies than studies of other... more gentle things."

"Mr. Parker."

Teddy's gaze glittered with curiosity. "What?"

"You should no' talk about things like that with a lady."

"Things like what?"

"Anything personal about Mr. Lake. It is no' your place."

Teddy raised an eyebrow. "Hm. I will need to remember that one. Might save the two of us some arguments."

Someone called Teddy's name. He winked and then disappeared back into the crowd. No, he wasn't a bad sort, only very... free-spirited. Sara restrained a laugh.

The sound of approaching steps behind her drew her attention. She smiled. "Oh, Mr. Christopher! All these people and the conversations—So wonderful!"

His hazel eyes twinkled. "Then why are you hiding?"

"Because I love watching them when they do no' know it. You can learn so much more about people by watching."

"Yes, I have found myself trapped in the same habit."

A pastime Sara completely understood, especially with his gift of art. "Will you invite different people for the next reception?"

"I had not yet decided. Most likely, but there are a few local patrons I should invite as well. I also hoped to invite a few directors from New York galleries."

Sara took in a quick breath, and her fingers tightened on her crystal punch glass.

"Here now." He took her glass from her and set it on the tray of a passing waiter. He directed her hand to his arm. "No frowns this evening, Miss Kreyssler. This is your night." She flushed. "Now, let us have a stare at the newest group 'ooo'ing and 'ahh'ing over a mysterious artist's first display. Unfortunately, that is all we will have time for before I will need to escort you to your carriage and send you on your way."

Sara's smile faded. "Could I no' stay longer?"

"I am afraid I promised Dix to have you home before one o'clock. She's of the mind too much excitement wouldn't be... wise. I will be certain to keep quiet next time."

Sara laughed.

Christopher held Sara's overcoat for her. She slipped her arms into the sleeves as the clock chimed the three-quarter hour. Almost two o'clock, Dix had been giving him the reproachful-eye every moment she could spare. But the conversations had been a relief, Sara's presence a tie to his beloved wife, and the laughter satiating a previously unchecked hunger. Reluctance was plain in Sara's expression, so he ignored both his sister and the time with pleasure.

He adjusted the coat over Sara's shoulders. "Dix will chew my ears for delaying you."

"I hope not, sir. I had such fun, and so different from the parties in England!"

"Oh?"

"The laughter. It sounded... more real. And the people? They were all so charming."

Christopher chuckled and motioned her toward the front doors. "They believe you to be the mysterious new artist, Sara. Could you not tell they were attempting to winkle it out of you?"

Sara laughed. "A fairytale party. I am glad you forgot the time."

He signaled for her carriage before closing the outer doors against the chill of the early morning. "I confess my intent was selfish. No one else laughs at my jokes." Her eyes gleamed. "But in all seriousness, I am glad you decided to come. You altered the tone of the party."

The carriage rumbled to a stop outside. Christopher escorted her out, and held the carriage door open as he steadied her ascent. "Good evening, Sara. I will see you tomorrow." He secured the door and stepped back.

Sara lowered the glass. "Christopher." Her choked voice drew him forward. She clasped his hand. "Thank you so much."

"It was my pleasure, Sara."

The carriage lurched forward, pulling her hand from his. She leaned out, errant curls of mahogany dancing in the wind as she watched him. Then the carriage disappeared into the mists of snow and early morning fog, leaving Christopher alone on the gallery steps. His smile waned, and he lowered his gaze to his hands before turning away. His shoulders wilted.

Dix met him just inside. "You must have meant you would have her home before two."

He shrugged out of his overcoat and handed it off to Harold. "No, I meant one."

"Lost track of the time, did you?"

"I purposefully ignored it."

"I see."

"Dix, you would have done the same if you had seen the expression in her eyes. She did not want to go, and I do not blame her. You did not truly wish me to force her away before she was ready, did you?"

His sister laughed. "Heavens, no! Why do you think I suggested one o'clock? You never listen to me, and you go against any suggestions I make, as a general rule."

"Of all the—You conniver." He grinned. "Good for you. I deserved that."

She wrapped his arm in hers and drew him forward.

"Come now. Tell me what had you two sniggering all evening. It was wonderful to watch."

"We weren't sniggering," he protested.

"Oh please. You and Carla would do the same thing; sneak up on groups of inexperienced art-watchers and then make them embarrass themselves by asking their opinion on the art. I've seen you do it a hundred times."

"They deserve it, Dix, and you know it. Instead of repeating what they've heard throughout the Gallery, they should do their best to answer from their self. Until they realize that their interpretation on art is just as relevant and important as someone like myself, I will–"

"All right, all right," she laughed. "Just tell me what happened."

"Sara came to their rescue." Christopher fought back a smile at the memory.

"What? How so?"

"She offered something quite innocent yet valid about one of the other paintings in the gallery, one of the oils I believe, and then pointedly asked what they thought."

Dix laughed. "The dear girl. Good for her."

"You should have seen the look of relief on their faces. Apparently they had thought much the same." Christopher chuckled. "Then she stepped up to her favorite of the sketches--the one with the little girl trying to peek over the wall into the garden?--and confessed she didn't know what to think about it. She only knew she liked it. They, of course, were all too willing to offer what they thought about it, and most of the impressions were insightful into the type of artists they are, or soon will be. It was great fun to watch."

"I imagine so." Dix gave a shake of her head. "That girl. She's such an angel. Tries so hard to appreciate and accept everyone. I even saw her laughing with Teddy earlier."

Christopher frowned. "Yes. I had words with him before that conversation. Made it clear to him that if he didn't begin to watch his behavior a bit more closely, he'd be banned from the house."

"Chris, Teddy didn't mean anything by the kiss. You know that's how he is."

"Yes, I know, but Sara doesn't. She shouldn't be required to protect herself from flirts who have nothing better to do."

"He did it to spite that you asked him not to."

"I wouldn't be a bit surprised."

She gave his arm a pinch. "Well, don't be such an old fuddy-duddy! The experience with people like Teddy will do Sara some good. Loosen her up a bit. And she looked as if she enjoyed herself with him. Handled him nicely, even if I do say so myself."

"Sara's experience with people in England is responsible for that," Christopher reminded.

"Oh? And you making her feel safe and welcome didn't matter at all?"

Christopher smirked. "Fine, fine. I'm a hero. Hurrah to me."

Dix pointed at him. "And as such, I had best see you and Gwyn day after tomorrow bright and early for church services."

"Yes, yes, Dix. I apologized for missing last Sunday, and I promise to be there this week."

"Good. Now come along with you. We've a few more guests to mingle with while encouraging them to leave so that I can go to sleep. I'm getting too old for this."

"Too old? Dix, you're not even thirty-eight."

"Yes, well thirty-eight is making its presence known,

and I want to get some sleep."

Christopher laughed.

Dix pushed at him, eyes twinkling even as she forced a frown. "Don't laugh. You'll be complaining soon enough of these late nights when you have a few more years under your belt."

A smirk continued to tilt his lips upward. "Yes, dearest."

"Oh, you're impossible." But she laughed just the same.

Sara adjusted her position on one of the steamer trunks near the window. The snow began again, and its lazy drifting reminded her of the many dances seen as a child peeking through the railing.

She lowered her chin to her knees, hugging her legs to her chest. *Sweet Jesus, please help him. There's so much joy waiting on the other side of the grief.* He only needed to struggle through the sorrow and accept the Lord's help to the other side. But to say that to him? She felt afraid he would react with as much rage as before. *Lord, please take the little joy he has and make it more. Maybe then he will see You wait to give him back his art.* Maybe then the haunting she saw in his hazel eyes would disappear?

Sara's heart ached as she lifted tear-filled blue eyes to an absent viewing of the snow's winter dance. He had lost so many parts of himself. How would she show him the Lord wanted to give them back?

"Sara?"

Sara offered a smile to Amy as she entered the room dressed in her nightgown, robe, and slippers. "Hello, Amy."

The young woman scurried to Sara's position on the

trunk and sat across from her, also tucking her knees up to her chest. "How was the party? Was it everything and more?"

"It was. Thank you so for pressing."

Amy softly clapped her hands and scooted a bit closer. "Tell me what happened."

The telling of the artists and the images, the guests and the compliments, the surprise of her coming and the disappointment of leaving was as exciting as the entire night had been. When the telling was finished, Amy sighed deep and cast a wistful expression out the window to the falling snow. Sara's eyes crinkled at the corners before she, too, looked out to the winter wonderland of Virginia. Her new home. She hadn't ever suspected that she would come to see this place as that. But she felt safe here.

"Is Mister Christopher going to plan another party soon?" Amy asked.

Sara very slightly shook her head, resting her cheek again on her knees. "I don't know."

"Oh I hope so. It's so nice to know the gallery's full of people again. He hasn't done that for a while. Not since Sean's display, and that took longer than the ones he and the missus would plan." Amy sighed. "Those were so wonderful. I loved listening to the people talking. They were so nice and thoughtful, too! They'd always ask my opinion, even though I were dressed in a maid's apron!" Amy giggled.

Smiling, Sara's eyes focused on the larger snowflakes dancing past her window. "All of Mister Christopher's friends are like that," she said, absent-minded, remembering the eager conversations and the acceptance that had made her feel giddy and... new. She sighed and then meeting

Amy's gaze to offer a smile. "I better off to bed."

Amy nodded, following behind as she made her way to her bedside. "Will you be having yourself a lesson tomorrow?"

Sara shrugged, a somewhat silly smile on her face as she scrambled into bed and pulled the covers to her chin. "I do no' know," she yawned, "and it do no' matter. I have taken myself to a party. I wore a lovely gown. And they love my sketches." She snuggled into the covers and closed her eyes, lips caressed with a sleepy expression of happiness. "They love me."

Amy smiled down at Sara a moment before leaning forward to adjust the covers around her mistress and then sneak softly out.

SIXTEEN

A New Canvas

29 January 1894

"Sara love, you are positively aglow with rhapsody."

Sara's cheeks blazed. "He's teaching me to paint, mum. No one understood what that meant for me before. My art, I mean. I taught myself. To read and practice, and then practice again. My mum encouraged me, but she did no' have the wherewithal to teach me. Your brother...." She blinked away the tears and watched the blur of passing scenery.

"I know, love, and you are sweet in that you don't have the words to say for the glory of it all. Makes it worth a bit more to everyone."

The carriage lumbered to a stop outside Lake Manor. Sara rushed out before the driver dismounted his perch. Dix followed in her usual sedate grace.

"Good morning, Harold." Sara's fingers trembled as

she fussed with her coat, scarf, and gloves.

"Good morning to you, Miss Sara. Mr. Christopher is in his studio setting up. Good morning, Mrs. Donovan."

"Harold, for heaven sake," Dix scolded. "Stop calling me that. You make me feel like a grandmother."

"Will you be having coffee?"

"That sounds lovely, Harold."

Sara squeezed Dix's hands. "It feels like a first Christmas, when my mum bought me my pencils."

Christopher's baritone chuckle sounded from behind. "Eagerness borne from excitement is a good motivator for the first days of learning."

Anticipation burned Sara's cheeks as she faced him. The comfortable beige trousers and painter's apron suited him. "Good morning, Mr. Christopher."

He nodded to both. "Good day, ladies. I hope you had a pleasant ride."

"As much as one can in the winter."

"Dix, why don't you warm your attitude with a cup of Emily's special roast while I introduce Sara to her work-station."

"That is a capital idea."

Christopher laughed. "Go on, Dix. Take your time. I'm sure my student won't miss you."

Something different shined in his expression, something Sara didn't remember seeing before.

"Come along, O student of mine." He ushered her to his studio.

"I canno' thank you enough for offering." Each word tumbled over itself, her insides fluttering with nervous exhilaration. "I do no' care how difficult, I will do my best, and do all my studies, and read whatever you want for me to read. I just want to paint as well as you do."

A smile teased his lips. "I see."

"Your sister had herself a miniature you painted of yourself for one of your classes at the college. And Mr. Paul? He had a watercolor of Monument Avenue you done and did no' care for. They showed them to me yesterday when I balked whether or not I wanted to come."

Christopher's hazel eyes twinkled down at her, arms crossed as he nodded along with her statements.

"Not that I did no' think you wonderfully talented. I know you are—I have a feeling on things like that—but will I be a very good student? I have no' been a student before, and I did no' want to annoy you with silly mistakes that even Gwyn would no' do. But then your sister and Mr. Paul said that it's fine for students to make mistakes."

He laughed. "Your enthusiasm is appreciated. Let us put it to good use."

"Yes, sir."

"Ah ah. I might be your instructor, but rules remain the same." He motioned to the easel and paper, directing her focus with a hand on her shoulder. "This is an experimental area for right now. I only need you to do simple brush strokes with the different styles of brushes so that you can get your fingers, hands, and wrists familiar with their feel. Then we'll add some paints so you can get accustomed to the friction of paint, brush, and paper."

Sara nodded, eyes wide.

"Now." He retrieved one of the small brushes from the easel's tray. "These are made of horse hair, so they're a bit firm, but not so much as to give you much of a fight. The larger ones are of the more coarse hair, for texture and backgrounds and the like. Here. Try this."

Sara took it from him, hesitant, her eyes focused on the dark brown of the bristles.

Christopher chuckled. "No need to be fearful, my dear. Tickle the paper a few times."

Her uncertain expression melted to a smile as she focused to the blank piece of paper. Once she felt and heard the first cautious swish, she retreated.

"No fear, Sara." Christopher covered her hand with his and guided a few more certain strokes across the paper. When his hand enveloped hers yet again, Sara blinked at the touch. "Note how the grain of the paper effects the bristles? Let us try another brush. One more firm." He released her long enough to gather one of the larger brushes.

"Do you feel the added resistance?"

Sara nodded, wide eyes unable to look away from their shared touch. It felt different than any other purposeful touch experienced. Even George, when he taught her how to clean a fish, hadn't felt the same. Gentle, yes, and warm, but not—Sara tilted her head as she stared at their hands.

"Question?" Christopher released his hold, leaving a lingering warmth and impression of a gentle grip.

"Not just yet." Her eyebrows furrowed as she thought back....

"Then let's give something a try."

Sara blinked and turned to look at him. His handsome face seemed brighter as he gathered a watercolor palette. Then he adjusted a small cup of water in the tray of the easel and met her gaze, his hazel eyes clear of any shadow. He helped position the palette within her hands, directing fingers and holds alike, and turned her again to face the easel.

"Now." Christopher directed her brush to the cup of

water. "The trick with watercolors, in my opinion, is to use the water itself to manipulate the clarity or vagueness of the paint. If you want an impression of color, then you use more water. If you want something brighter or more brilliant, you use less. It all depends upon the mood you wish to convey."

Sara watched his hold guide her hand from water-cup to palette.

"Even the flair of the strokes used effects the painting, most often in how the color is spread about the paper or how it seems to absorb the colors into its grain. If more water is used later, you can often achieve a bit more of a streak or... mysterious quality, I suppose." He guided Sara's hand and the brush along the paper with gentle strokes, the sound much like a whisper for attention.

"Oo. I like that." Sara continued with the gentle strokes until very little color transferred from brush to paper.

"You like which? The feel or the sound?"

Sara beamed over her left shoulder at him. "Yes."

He chuckled. "That's fine then. Now, take stock of what you have there. Only a bit of blue. Is that enough for what you want? Or do you think it needs more?"

Sara looked to the soft and dreamy strokes of blue against white. "I... I do no' know."

"Well, let's continue on." His warm hold surrounded her hand to direct it to water and then paint. "Then we'll see what comes about."

Sara's eyes danced with her smile.

But the picture didn't become much more than blues and greens, an experiment with a new media and the different types of strokes it offered. Sara allowed herself to be taught, enjoying it more than anything in her life.

Christopher's patience reminded her of her mother, encouraging her with new things and allowing a retreat to the familiar to make a habit. Neither took notice that Dix never arrived from her retrieval of coffee.

1 February 1894

Christopher heard the pitter-patter of Gwyn's steps toward his studio. "Good morning, Papa." She rubbed sleep from her eyes with the backs of her hands, her blonde curls dancing around her head.

He turned from the set-up of easel and paint to greet her. "Good morning, Angel Girl. What brings you down so early?"

Gwyn wrapped her arms around Christopher's neck. "I missed you," could barely be deciphered between yawns.

He scooped her up and ascended the stairs to the second story. "I apologize for not spending more time with you, Angel."

She released a slow and deep breath as she snuggled against him. "You're helping Sara not be homesick."

Christopher kissed her forehead, her blonde curls tickling his nose. "You are a help in that."

Gwyn sleepily smiled. "I am?"

He lay her down and tucked the covers up to her chin, placing another kiss on her forehead. "You and I will both keep helping Sara. Yes?"

Gwyn nodded, another yawn making her squeeze her eyes shut. Then she rolled to her side and hugged her pillow close. "I'm helping, Mamma," she whispered, her breathing deepening as sleep embraced her.

Christopher sat upon the edge of the bed as he watched her sleep, smoothing her blonde curls from her face. Carla would sit on the edge of their daughter's bed for hours, watching her breathe. Other mornings the two would laugh over stories of fantasy and fairy tale. Days and evenings of watching them together. Hearing their laughter. Watching their games. Enjoying the picture of motherhood and devotion—

Christopher's throat convulsed. The temptation to fight back the memories gripped him.... Then he heard Sara's timid voice. Her urgency to remember the woman he loved so he could once again be the man who had loved her. The laughter. The music. The poetry of life and living. The peace. The joy. The celebration of family. Christopher raised a hand to his burning eyes and wiped it hard down his face, feeling the wetness on his cheeks and somehow acknowledging a slight release within.

He stood, his mind overwhelmed by the fog of remembered scenes. "I miss you, Carla," he whispered, gruff.

'And that's fine.'

Such a simple statement, yet it gave him permission to allow the ache and release it.

Sara hurried up the steps and into Lake Manor. Dix chuckled, her pace serene. Harold waited in the hall and accepted Sara's coat, scarf, and gloves before letting her know that Christopher waited in his studio. As per usual, Dix could not be immediately present, but she urged Sara on without her.

Christopher straightened. As tradition dictated, he dressed in a simple shirt and well-used trousers. Paint-stains colored both. "Good morning."

Sara's cheeks stung from the fervor of her smile. "Good morning."

"How did you sleep?"

"I could no' for all the pictures flying around in my head and the excitement of what's down the road."

"We had a full week, haven't we? Though I will be easier on you today. Fewer hours cooped up in here. The rest of the day is yours to use as you see fit."

"Oh I do no' mind, Mr. Christopher. All the busyness is wonderful." She nervously laughed. "I canno' sit around all day just tatting and crocheting."

"You may regret those words when you don't know which way is up for all your projects."

"I do no' think you can get me as busy as in England, sir. But you are welcome to try."

"A spoken challenge. My, my." He motioned to the blank page on the easel. "Here is your newest bit of nothing waiting for your inspiration. What do you feel should be done first?"

Sara stepped up to the easel, searching the white for the waiting scene. Christopher stood beside her. "I do no' know. It's the same as before: Blank."

"It is different when you sketch?"

"Yes, sir. There have always been pictures in my mind. Almost in my fingertips."

"Ah. Well, let us try something new and different." Christopher searched his desk-drawers. A moment later he returned to present her a small tin of charcoals. "When you take these in hand?"

Sara accepted a charcoal from the tin and focused once more on the page—she blinked.

"You see an image, do you?"

She nodded, her blue eyes wide. "Why would it come with the charcoals and not the brush?"

"Inspiration often does not appreciate explanation. Your creative spirit is comfortable with the charcoal, so it allows you to see what awaits. This does not mean you stop use of the brush. No. Only continue teaching your spirit to see with other eyes." He directed her toward the easel, guiding the charcoal toward the paper's stark whiteness. "I did not always paint with watercolors or oils."

Sara whispered the charcoal against the paper. "Did you see the images first? Like I do with my charcoals?"

"No. With each media a period of instruction became necessary."

Sara bit her lip as she drew the silhouette of the peeking image. "Should I watercolor the images I sketch out? Do you suppose that might help?"

"Possibly. In fact, let's try that and see what happens. Although I believe it would serve better to begin with pencils rather than charcoals."

Sara's lips quivered with a smile as she continued to bring out the image of family, welcome, and acceptance.

He chuckled. "I seem to take advantage of your apparent eagerness to study."

"Oh no, Mr. Christopher. This is such fun! Not a chore with the house, or the mister or missus."

"What of the 'something good' you mentioned? Another Sarah teaching you to read prose and public speaking, et cetera."

"But not a thing with art, sir. My mum tried, but she could no' teach what she could no' do. And reading books or looking at pictures and paintings is no' the same as having a breathing person explain how something is done and why." She pointed at him with her charcoal pencil. "You are the first who ever thought about teaching me something."

"A first? For me and for you, it seems."

"For you?"

"You, my dear, are my first student."

Sara gaped at him. "But what about your Carla?"

He cleared his throat and lowered his focus to the floor. "She loved the arts, yes, but she didn't have the talent for its creation. She once attributed it to a lack of patience." Christopher straightened the charcoals within the metal tin. "We, both of us, attempted those interests to the other." He closed the tin and set it aside to hide a slight cringe. "A common sharing of interest couples partake in, I imagine."

A sorrowful expression darkened his handsome face, and Sara noted how his gaze could not rise from the charcoal tin. *Lord....* But how did she pray away his discomfiture? Sara turned back to the easel—the image gone. Sara sighed and lowered the charcoal.

"My apologies, Sara. I distracted you."

"Mr. Christopher, it was all myself." She offered forward the charcoal, still holding his gaze. "I should try again with the watercolors. Is that fine?"

His expression softened to a smile as he took the charcoal. "Fine."

Sara focused on the white as she heard him gather up the palette and brush. *Please, Lord. Can I see a little thing?* But she didn't know why she thought seeing an image on a bit of paper would help anyone.

"Sara."

She met his gaze. "Yes, sir?"

"Do not try so hard to see or feel anything. The watercolors won't come as eager as your charcoal images do now. Instead of expecting that, you must remember when you first began sketching."

"Could I see your paintings? Maybe it would help?"

Christopher's focus jerked away. "I set aside my art long ago."

"Oh." Sara worried her lower lip, questions hounding her until frustration burned. She cast it heavenward and spoke. "Mr. Christopher, did... did your wife help you decide just where to display your paintings? Did she design the reception for them at the gallery?"

The shadow of memories crashed across his face. She could almost hear the parties and laughter from those receptions hosted so long ago. His wife likely took such great care with each one.

"Yes," he admitted. "She did."

"Would...." Sara bolstered her courage. "Would no' those be good, happy memories to have around you? So you do no' feel she's all that far away?"

Although, when he put them away, the reminder of her absence must have felt akin to a knife hacking his soul. *Was no' my mum's crafts the same?* But after weeks and months of no longer having her voice, the presence of the crafts and the basket soothed and comforted. They were all that remained, and the memories were welcome.

"Do you no' think your Carla would want them out?" Sara whispered.

Christopher released a deep and slow breath as he nodded.

"I know unveiling those memories is a bittersweet duty, sir, but...." Sara rest her hand upon his arm, the action drawing his gaze. "But they deserve an unveiling to the light. A celebration of her life, sir."

A light of hope, and a reminder of his own inspiration.

SEVENTEEN

A Conflicted Truth

"Chris, we've got a problem."

Christopher didn't bother looking up from three of Sara's newest sketches laid out on his desk as Teddy entered his office at the gallery. "Problem? What problem?" The sketches were her best yet. They seemed aglow with a newfound acceptance.

Teddy presented a folded newspaper. "Here."

Raising an eyebrow, Christopher took the offered paper and sought out the main article.

> New artist and new beauty take Richmond by storm at the unveiling held at the 'Richmond Gallery of Modern Art' the previous Friday. Not many details were given of the mysterious talent of S. A. L.. Yet at the appearance of English lady Miss Ann Kreyssler, even the reclusive Mr. Christopher Lake was in immediate and constant attendance.
>
> Reliable sources say that another unveiling has been scheduled for the unknown S. A. L., with invitations limited as previously. Will the lovely Miss Ann Kreyssler

be in attendance? And is Miss Ann Kreyssler soon to be the newest Mrs. Christopher Lake?

He slammed it aside. "How did a reporter get that information? We restricted invitations!"

Teddy crossed his arms. "Yes, but a starving artist could say a few words all too eagerly for a little extra wealth."

Sara. Christopher gathered up the sketches and tucked them safely into his desk.

"What's the line of attack?"

"None." Christopher grabbed his overcoat from the back of the office chair and shrugged into it. "No comments. No interviews."

"And Sara?"

"I will make certain she does not blame herself if she has seen this. If she has been spared, I will make certain that continues."

"See you later?"

"Perhaps."

Christopher strode from the gallery and down the walk toward Monument Avenue. "She will likely attempt to protect my reputation, even should that put her own future at risk." He shook his head and jerked at his gloves. "Well, Carla? What do you suggest? If I grant an interview and answer the questions truthfully, he—or she—could take things out of context. But what options do I have? Say 'No comment' when asked about our friendship? That will lead them to a false conclusion worse than their interpretation of the truth. Blast!"

An ideal compromise did not present itself.

But, as of yet, no harm had been done, since blind suppositions had only been tossed about to get a reaction. If those suppositions grew into whispers of something deeper, he had no idea how to counteract the repercussions.

"Carla, I wish you were here." Then Sara's future would be safe.

Dix and Paul opened the door of their townhouse as Christopher reached the bottom step. He hurried inside and shed his overcoat. "Has she seen it?"

"No, but how do we keep her from it?" Dix cast a furtive glance upstairs. "She enjoys reading the paper in the morning—*Harper's Weekly* wouldn't publish something like that, would they?"

Dread settled in the pit of Christopher's stomach. "Why do you ask?"

She motioned upstairs. "She's reading it right now. With Gwyn."

"Blast." He rushed upstairs.

The door of Sara's room stood open. When he heard laughter and cheerful chatter, Christopher released a relieved sigh. Inside, Sara and Gwyn lay on the floor coloring pictures. The scene rang of innocence, fun, and family, and it caused Christopher's chest to tighten as he fisted his scarf.

"Mamma said she wanted a masked ball, but they were too busy," Gwyn was saying.

"Masquerades are a lot of work, Gwyn, and so is a gallery. Your mamma likely did no' want to stress your papa. Not with all the hard work he does already."

"But it would be fun, Sara." Gwyn sighed. "I want one like this." She pushed the picture toward Sara. "See? There's Papa and you and Auntie Dix and Uncle Paul and Teddy—Oh! I forgot Mamma!"

Christopher cringed as Gwyn took the picture back to add the image of her mother. Sara glanced toward the doorway—Her cheeks flushed and she sat up. Unable to force a smile, Christopher brought a finger to his lips.

Sara lowered her gaze to the task of arranging her skirts. "You should show that picture to your papa, Gwyn. Maybe he will be persuaded to have a ball for your next birthday?"

"Truly?" Gwyn asked, eyes still intensely focused on her project.

"It never hurts to ask." Sara cast Christopher a questioning glance. "I will ask when I next see him.

"You will ask who what when you see them?" Christopher stepped forward.

"Papa!" Gwyn scrambled to her feet and over to his waiting arms.

"Hello, Angel Girl."

"Papa, may I have a masked ball for my birthday please?"

"Oh." Christopher feigned seriousness. "I didn't know you actually wanted a birthday."

Gwyn's mouth dropped open. "Papa!"

"You've had so much fun as a five-year-old, I thought you didn't want a birthday. I cancelled it."

"But you can't! I want to turn six!"

Sara laughed and gracefully stood. "She has been quite enthralled with the idea, sir."

"Oh? I don't want to un-cancel your birthday and then have you change your mind."

"Please, Papa. I want my birthday."

"All right then. I'll see a man tomorrow about your birthday. But I haven't any idea how to arrange a masquerade, Gwyn. I'm afraid all I can manage is a party."

Gwyn's lower lip trembled. "Oh."

"I know how to plan a masquerade, Gwyn," Sara offered. She rested a hand on his daughter's head. "May I be responsible for it? It's been ever so long since I had one to do."

"Please, Papa?"

"Of course, but we don't need to worry about it now. Your birthday isn't until July, and it's only just February."

Gwyn sniggered. "I forgot."

Christopher laughed. "And, Sara, you're only to agree if it isn't a bother. I don't want you taking on too many projects."

"Oh no, sir. It will be fun." The twinkle in her eyes made him believe it.

"All right then. You're welcome to the duty, but you must promise to ask for help. Harold, Emily, all of them will be more than willing to offer their expertise. Especially myself. I imagine Dix and Paul will likely want to be involved as well."

Sara nodded.

"Very good." Christopher was about to turn from the room when he noticed the opened *Harper's Weekly* on the foot of Gwyn's bed. "Ah. Anything on the unveiling the other night?"

"Pardon? Oh!" Sara's face gleamed. "There was such a lovely article. Did you want me to read it for you?"

"Certainly." Christopher lifted Gwyn into his arms and sat on the edge of the chest at the foot of her bed. The fact that she showed such excitement soothed his nerves.

> Mr. Christopher Lake of 'The Richmond Gallery of Modern Art' held one of the most successful displays of the new year. Though little information was provided on the artist, S. A. L., the works shown were a refreshing breeze of inspiration and innocence seldom seen since the civil war.
>
> Mr. Joseph Conklin, long-time patron and sponsor of the arts, was quoted as saying "The artist has an

> instant following. A talent only very few, of which Mr. Christopher Lake is included, can attest to. When he or she is ready to accept their deserved attention, I will certainly be the first to offer them a sponsorship. In the meantime, I voice praises to Mr. Lake for protecting their identity and what is likely a sensitive soul."
>
> These are encouraging words for artist and gallery alike, and this reporter hopes that another display will be arranged forthwith.

Sara lowered the paper and offered Christopher a brilliant smile. "Was that no' wonderful? And all those nice things Mr. Conklin said. I knew I liked him, and now I think he's smashing."

Intrigue arched his eyebrow. "Did you meet him at the unveiling? I don't recall ever meeting a Mr. Conklin."

Sara's eyes widened. "I thought he knew you."

"People know me simply by reputation. Ah well. He was likely there upon invitation of a friend." Christopher motioned to the article. "I'm eager to meet him after that bit of praise. And the offering of a sponsorship? You should take that as a compliment, definitely."

"What's sponsorship, Papa?" Gwyn asked. "Is it good?"

"Extremely good. It means this gentleman is willing to pay for Sara's work to be displayed at galleries all over the country. Perhaps even own them all himself."

Gwyn squealed and threw her arms around Christopher's neck. "Oh goodie!"

Christopher laughed and intercepted Sara's smile. She flushed and looked away. "It seems your future is set," he offered. "Would you like me to contact Mr. Conklin and pass off the responsibility of the second showing to him?"

"Oh no—I mean.... Can I no' have you as my sponsor still?"

"Of course, I only ask that you give it some thought. After all, if Mr. Conklin has the 'in' to more galleries than I, it would be a shame to pass up the opportunity."

"Oh." Sara lowered her gaze to her fidgeting fingers. "Well, I suppose...."

"Sara." She peeked up at him, and he offered her a reassuring smile. "It's fine. You don't need to make a decision right now. If he offers the sponsorship at the next showing, you can tell him then. Or you can ask more questions about what a sponsorship would entail. For right now, if you're more comfortable with my gallery, then I'm certainly not going to usher you somewhere else."

Sara's timid smile returned as she nodded.

"I better get myself back to the gallery, Gwyn. I'll come by a little later this afternoon. Fair enough?" Gwyn nodded. He kissed her cheek, accepted her return, and then turned to exit. He met Dix and Paul at the foot of the stairs. Their expressions were hopeful and curious.

"Well?" Paul pressed.

"*Harper's Weekly* held a glowing review of the unveiling, which Sara read to me."

Dix released a deep breath. "Praise the Lord."

Christopher took his overcoat from Paul. "I need to get back." He motioned to the front entrance with a movement of his head. "Don't be surprised if you have reporters coming 'round. Everyone knows you're my sister."

"Let them come. I'll rout them out of the county," she warned.

Paul chuckled. "We'll be fine, Chris. You just watch yourself and Teddy."

Christopher reluctantly made his way out and down the front steps, experiencing a challenge in wrestling himself into his overcoat as he did so.

"Mr. Christopher Lake?"

Hackles rose as Christopher lifted his focus to the young-faced man waiting at the bottom steps of the Donovan home. "May I help you?"

"I'm Roger Whitaker, sir. With *The Virginia Chronicle*?"

"Mr. Whitaker," Christopher said with forced civility. "Before you proceed, you will need to make an appointment for any type of interview. Come by the gallery at a later date and we'll see what's available." Christopher finished wrestling into his coat and passed the man on the lower step. "If you'll excuse me."

"Have you courted Miss Kreyssler since your mourning officially ended?"

Christopher halted, body tense. "Pardon?"

Mr. Whitaker cleared his throat. "Is it true that you're courting Miss Kreyssler?"

"Mr. Whitaker, I refuse to answer your question on principle. Questions regarding my personal life are none of your concern. Understood?"

Mr. Whitaker gave a slight nod.

"I'm glad we understand each other. Good day." Christopher turned and strode away.

Christopher scoffed and jammed his hands deeper into his overcoat pockets. He should have known the sudden activity would draw attention. He hissed with annoyance. Christopher didn't know how to protect Sara from speculation.

"What happened?"

Christopher had just closed the front door of the gallery when Teddy strode forward from a side-room.

"Paul caught the article before she had a chance to read it, handing off an edition of *Harper's* instead."

"And they didn't have the same version?" Teddy asked, cautious.

"No, thank God. Only praises and a quote from a Mr. Joseph Conklin."

"The art critic?"

Christopher smirked. "I'm glad someone knew who he was. Sara apparently met him at the unveiling."

"Holy Hannah! Joseph Conklin at the unveiling?" Teddy grinned. "We're on the map, now."

"When were we not?"

Teddy laughed. "With the extra attention, you're going to bring out your art, right?"

Christopher's smirk vanished. He passed to the coat-rack. "With what the *Chronicle* supposes? I don't know if it's wise to go ahead with it. Especially if Sara decides to reveal her identity."

"What? Since when do you let anyone influence you?"

"Since my late wife asked me to take care of this woman," Christopher barked. "To give her the choice. To protect her as I protected the others. If I reveal my art and the fact that S. A. L. is Miss Ann Kreyssler, an invitee of me and my late wife as well as an acquaintance of my sister, they will suppose the worst and make Sara's life miserable. Do you really want me to do that just so that our gallery can display my art and make a lot of money from the sale of it?"

Teddy frowned. "I didn't say it like that."

Christopher released a deep breath and rubbed at his scalp. "I know. I'm sorry."

"It's fine. So when are we going to get this mess with the *Chronicle* straightened out?"

"If you're implying I should give an interview, I don't trust they won't twist what I say for a wanted impression."

"So? Have *Harper's* get the interview."

"But why should I give any response at all? It will only make them believe there is something to their supposition, and that would only compound the issue."

Teddy grumbled under his breath. "Blasted reporters."

Christopher smirked. "Yes, but they have their good qualities, such as free advertising and name-dropping."

"At a price, admit."

"Admitted."

"So what do we do about the whole Sara Ann Little-Kreyssler mystery? They'll pounce on that whether we reveal her at the next unveiling or not. Well, *Harper's* might not, but *Chronicle* will." Teddy chortled. "We should reveal her anyway, as a spit in the eye to whatever they might say as the truth. You've got enough of a fan-following that I doubt they'll believe anything bad about you. And what's so bad about supposedly courting Sara these months out of mourning anyway, even if you did just meet her? She's a sweet thing, and you two are friends."

Christopher balled his hands into fists before stepping again toward the main hall. "Friends. Exactly. The last thing she needs is for everyone to be convinced there's more to our relationship. It would keep any prospective beaus out of contact with her, and she doesn't need that problem."

EIGHTEEN

Perspectives

6 February 1894

"I still believe we should use the main hall," Teddy said.

Christopher frowned. "Ted, she's not ready for the main hall. You saw her expression yourself when you asked."

"But if we use the main hall, we can have her sketches displayed to the left and a display of her watercolors over on the opposite wall. A type of tribute. A featured artist, anyway. Don't you agree?"

"There won't be any watercolors," he said, and he saw again her sad expression at the realization she didn't progress as she thought she should. "She's having problems seeing the image. I'm sure it's nothing, but she's understandably disheartened. Try not to mention it."

"Of course."

Christopher motioned to the main display. "That's a good idea, though. Maybe if we displayed another artist?"

"Oh? Like who?"

"She continues to suggest I bring out my watercolors and oils again."

Teddy reeled to face him, his eyes wide and blinking. "You—you're considering it?"

"I am."

Teddy grinned. "It's about time someone pushed you the right direction." He rubbed his hands together. "We should arrange it so that both oils and watercolors can be displayed at once. No, we should have them in separate rooms. Watercolors with the others, only with a focus on yours because of the re-introduction.... Am I boring you?"

Christopher focused on Teddy, frown disappearing. "Hm?"

Teddy pointed to the entrance. "Go home, Top."

"I'm not going home. We have too much to do."

His friend took up Christopher's overcoat, hat, and scarf. "You're distracted, and you're no good to me that way. Go start choosing which you want displayed. Have Sara help you if you have problems choosing. Maybe she'll keep you on task." Teddy shoved Christopher's things at him and then directed him toward the exit. "I'll try and remember the old layouts and do something with it. Thank God we sold all of Sean's art. We have more room for the new ones coming in."

Christopher shrugged into his overcoat. "I don't know why I even bothered to come in this morning. You don't listen to anything I say. I could stay at home and play with Gwyn."

Teddy laughed. "So do it, then. Maybe I'll get some work done on my own projects." He pointed to the exit. "Now go, and I don't want to see you until you have at least five pieces of each media chosen."

Christopher exited the gallery, breathing in deep of the chilled air before striking out toward home. When he arrived, the house was silent. Gwyn hadn't yet woken, the time being only a little past eight in the morning, and the lack of her laughter made the hairs on his neck rise. Though silence had been the norm for more than a year, Christopher still didn't care for the sound of it, nor the lack of feeling inside. It reminded him too much of the silence the day Carla lost the baby. The silence following her death. The silence broken only by Gwyn's tears and calls for her mother.

His step hesitated down the front hall—Harold stepped from his office. "Good morning, Harold. I've been 'shooed' home earlier than I thought."

"Mr. Theodore practicing his role as partner with more gusto?"

"Something like that, yes."

"Would you care for coffee in the studio before Miss Sara arrives?"

He glanced toward the open studio door as he handed over his overcoat, scarf, and gloves. "That would be... good, Harold. Thank you." Harold went to see to it, leaving Christopher in the hall staring at his studio doorway. He could still hear the whispers of Sara's happy voice, excitement brimming at the prospect of artistic learning. *Her eyes. They sparkled so bright, Carla.* He hadn't seen an expression like that for... for ages.

Eagerness to paint.

To stretch out beyond something she knew.

Christopher cleared his throat and forced himself forward into the studio, unable to do anything but stare at the blank canvas set up for Sara's lesson. Nothing came. No image. No tickle of inspiration. He dragged his gaze away and fisted his hands. He hadn't seen an image in—A sharp pang made him close his eyes, running his hands down his face to rub inspiration alive within. When he focused again on the canvas, the starkness remained.

He lowered himself into the wingback chair and hid his face in his hands. Again he tried to force aside the burning need to create an image of loveliness and family. The desire to have again the thirst to paint. The feel of the pencil on paper. The brush. The paint on canvas.... *Why, God? Why did You take everything?*

Art had always been his passion, a release to create beautiful things. To inspire those trapped in an ugly world. To give hope to those who didn't have it....

A year.

The passion had laid stagnant since the death of his wife, and even his love and devotion for Gwyn hadn't brought it to life. Now.... Christopher fisted his hands before standing to his feet in exhausted slowness, his eyes and mind riveted on the canvas. He smoothed a hand across it, remembering. Reliving....

His focus shifted to the paints and pencils, those brushes forgotten for so long. His throat tightened at the memories as he reached for the palette—He flinched away and turned, striding from the studio even as the memory of Sara's voice and laughter whispered.

Christopher tapped on the lip of his coffee cup while waiting for Sara in his office. His focus continued to drift to the closed door between his office and studio. That blank bit of paper waited for her inspired hand, it wouldn't give up its image to his touch. A frown furrowed his brows as he forced his gaze to his cold coffee.

Then he heard the quick sound of Sara's steps up the front stairs. The whisper of the front door opening followed by Harold's greeting. Sara's reply rang with excitement and eagerness, the same as every morning. As usual, Harold would barely have hold of her heavy wool coat before she would hurry toward the studio—

"Oh...."

Christopher heard the confusion in that single, breathy word when she stepped into the doorway of the empty studio. He released a slow breath but didn't stand. He didn't call out. Something about the expectation and dread of seeing the eagerness in her expression wouldn't allow him. It was too much of a reminder to so many visions of the same.

Then he heard the rustle of her skirts as she stepped down the hall.

"M-Mr. Lake?"

Christopher continued to stare down at his coffee as she came to stand in the doorway, his finger still tapping the lip of the cup.

"Oh." The word was tainted with concern. "G-Good morning, Mr. Lake."

He forced himself to smile and look up as she entered, hesitant. She wore royal blue with a softening of cream at the collar and cuffs. "Good morning. Where's Dix?"

Sara motioned behind. "She's talking with Harold. Did you want me to fetch her?"

And have her prod and badger? "No."

Again, a simple, "Oh," after which she began worrying her lower lip. Debating. Arguing. Praying. Then she took another hesitant step forward. "Are you well, sir?" Her tone so unobtrusive, respectful, and steeped in concern that he wondered how any of her employers' wives or mothers could have believed her to be anything but a charming and caring woman.

Christopher set aside his coffee cup, forgoing the forced smile. "I'm not much in the mood for lessons, Sara. I apologize."

The expected disappointment didn't appear. "That's fine, sir. It was selfish of me to suppose we would do them daily. I did no' mean to cause hardship."

"You didn't." Not intentionally. Christopher lowered his gaze. She never hurt anyone intentionally. With her it was always an offer, a suggestion that would make something about their life easier. Carla would have respected that of her.

"Oh." Thoughtful silence. "Then, I suppose I'll have your sister take me home again. Would you and Gwyn care to come for tea this afternoon? I've thought of making scones."

Christopher met her gaze, and he again noticed the reluctance. It mirrored his own to be left alone with the blank piece of white which remained so silent. It reflected his dread of being left to the duty of unpacking the images upstairs that would only remind him of a past passion.

"Actually, since I have you here, we may as well make our way upstairs and choose the first pictures for my...." Christopher forced a smile. "My re-introduction into artistic society."

"I would love to help," she said, her voice breathless

with excitement. "Are you choosing oils or watercolors?"

To his surprise, that enthusiasm lessened the dread. "I hadn't decided yet. Teddy believes I should choose five of each media, but I'm not so sure I should. Wouldn't it be better to keep it simple?"

"But you've been painting for so long! Everyone will be so eager to see how you've grown over the years. You should have a bit of a time-line almost. Don't you think? That way it would give encouragement to the different depths of artists that come."

"That isn't a bad idea." Christopher chuckled. "Who's sponsoring whom?"

Sara's smile blossomed to laughter. "I suppose I have a few more opinions than I should."

"Nonsense." Christopher ushered her toward the hall with a light touch at her elbow. "Teddy specifically instructed me to have you keep me on task. He doesn't believe I'm seriously considering it."

"But why would you no'?"

"I don't know. Maybe he's hoping to have them on display with yours. Although that's not only ambitious but cruel. I wouldn't want to rob you of attention."

"I would no' mind, sir. You deserve as much."

Christopher steadied her step up the stairs to the second story. "Don't be ridiculous. I've already a fan-following. Yours is the reputation that needs a lift. Explaining that to Teddy will be the challenge."

Sara smiled. "You need no' tell him."

Christopher halted his final step to the second story and faced her with an expression of shock. "What?"

A flush colored her cheeks, but her blue eyes still twinkled with a surprising bit of mischief. "Do no' tell him you'd rather wait. He canno' do much about it if he finds out the evening of the party."

The expression of shock melted to a smile. "Teddy, she's plotting against you. I don't have the heart to warn him. His view of you will be crushed."

Sara laughed.

Christopher motioned her toward the doorway of the third-story stairway, a return of the reluctance slogging his step. "I won't tell him you put me up to it. He has a tendency of being a prankster."

The two arrived at the door to the third-story stairwell. He cleared his throat and opened the entry to click on the light. "Forgive the dust and clutter. I, uh—" He scrubbed at the back of his neck. "I haven't been here in... a while."

Her smile overflowed with assurance, but Christopher's reluctance and dread didn't retreat. He ascended the stairs before her. Each step caused a shift within.

"The fourth step from the top creaks." He partially turned, offering a hand to steady her up the narrow staircase.

Sara gathered the front of her skirts and accepted his hand to follow his careful ascent. Once the two crested the stairs, he released the warmth of her clasp and motioned toward the far wall. He tried to ignore the knot in the pit of his stomach.

"The crates are here, although I believe I unpacked one looking for a frame for Gwyn."

They crossed the room toward the dozen or so crates stacked neatly parallel one to the other. Sara's steps matched his for hesitation. Christopher fought back the rising dread as he gathered the sketches and images loosed from the abused portfolio. Then he set the portfolio onto the floor by the far wall with a soft thump.

The packed crates drew his focus. He noticed Sara's occasional glances to his profile. He couldn't remember how many images and silhouettes of a previous passion lay hidden within the crates. Just as he wasn't sure that viewing them wouldn't give him a shock. What would that do to Sara? She would blame herself for the suggestion.

"I do no'. You only just...."

"I'm fine." Christopher met her gaze. "I only don't know what to expect as a reaction."

"Mr. Christopher.... Sir, we do no' need to do this today. Just the thought of bringing them out again is likely enough. It's never wise to force one's heart when it's not ready."

The crates whispered at him, and the reluctance twisted into a firmer emotion of dread—He shook his head and allowed himself to take a step back. "I can't. Not yet."

"And that's fine," she said, her voice gentle and... warm with understanding.

He lowered his gaze. "Maybe tomorrow?" Already hidden for what seemed a lifetime, what was another day?

7 February 1894

"Chris."

"Hm?" Christopher looked up from his letter from Joseph Conklin. Teddy approached. "Don't tell me. You have another idea for Sara's display."

Teddy smirked. "You don't have to sound as if I don't have one worth a moment's thought, Top."

Chuckling, Christopher folded the letter and tucked it into his jacket coat's inner pocket. "Sorry, Ted. Habit."

"Mr. Christopher Lake?"

Christopher recognized the same young man seen outside Paul and Dix's two days before. His hackles rose, and he gathered his temper. "Mr. Whitaker, was it?"

The young man nodded and slowed his approach, noticing the guarded hostility on Teddy's expression. "Yes," the young man said. "That's right."

"What can I do for you?"

Mr. Whitaker swiped the hat from his head and worried it between his fingers. The action revealed straight blond hair combed back from a young face and an attempt to grow the style of beard currently popular. "I think you might have made a wrong assumption the other day," he began hesitantly, his blue eyes cautious.

Christopher sent Teddy a warning quick glance. Teddy clenched his jaw. "If I did, I apologize."

Mr. Whitaker cleared his throat. "I guess I can understand why you would. You likely thought I was the one who wrote the article. But I'm just an intern. I actually came to find out the truth. I don't like the fact the *Chronicle* published an article that is mostly hearsay and gossip."

"Try getting an internship with a different paper," Teddy quipped.

Mr. Whitaker nodded, fingers still worrying his hat. "I'm trying to do just that, but there's a waiting list for *Harper's*, and none of the others will grant an interview. Not until I've more experience."

Christopher felt an itch in the back of his mind and thoughtfully crossed his arms.

"It's a type of paradox, actually," Mr. Whitaker continued. "I need a little more experience in order to get accepted as an intern. But I need to become an intern in order to get experience."

Christopher motioned to the young man, directing his attention away from Teddy. "Why did you come here today, Mr. Whitaker?"

"I—" The young man shot Teddy a quick look. "I wanted to try and explain why I asked that personal question."

"Fair enough."

Mr. Whitaker cleared his throat. "I hoped to prove blatant slander published by the *Chronicle*. Then, I could manipulate the new manager out of the position, or prove to another newspaper I have what it takes to be an intern."

Teddy smirked. "Revealing all that would definitely get you a higher position."

"I'm not in it for fame or glory," Mr. Whitaker countered. "For me it's about the news. The excitement of uncovering a mystery and reporting on it. Traveling to other places and opening people's eyes to what goes on there, whether it be politics or customs."

Christopher nodded, gauging Mr. Whitaker's young face and his expressions as he spoke.

"When I read the pre-post article, I did my best to keep them from publishing it. I knew we didn't have the facts to support it. But the manager said the public had a right to know due to the fact that both you and the gallery are high-profile."

"I see."

"When I proposed an alternate article...."

"He didn't take well to the suggestion." Mr. Whitaker shook his head. Christopher nodded, regarding the young man a moment before asking, "Would you like a position as our media liaison?"

"Chris," Teddy spluttered, "we don't know anything

about him or his politics! We can't simply offer him a job in hopes that he won't blast our reputation a bit later down the road!"

Christopher ignored Teddy's protest. "I need representation by a trustworthy individual, Mr. Whitaker. While we haven't yet arrived to the 'trust' aspect, I'm willing to take a risk in order to prove myself right."

Teddy threw up his hands and stalked away.

Mr. Whitaker stared at Christopher in shock and disbelief. Finally, he swallowed hard and presented a hand. "Thank you. I'll do my best."

"I know you will. In fact, I have just the traveling adventure into a mystery that I would like you to investigate."

NINETEEN

Forever Moments of Sweetness

"I will cover the cost of the journey." Christopher escorted young Roger Whitaker to the gallery entrance. "If you need a place to stay while you're there, check the names and addresses of my acquaintances."

"I will be fine. Like I said, I have friends there."

"Fair enough. Your ticket will be waiting at the station for you. Captain Cowell will have further instructions once you board." Christopher produced his hand. "Good luck, Roger."

"Thank you, for everything." Then he exited the gallery.

Christopher stared at the door a moment after, his brows drawing together before he turned away.

"And?"

Teddy emerged from a side display of sculptures. His friend looked less than pleased, by the twist of his frown. "Pardon?"

"Don't give me that," Teddy grumbled. "I am talking

about your sudden insane impulse to give the man some undeserved attention."

"Insane?" Christopher smirked. "Maybe."

"I don't see what's amusing." Teddy regarded Christopher through a narrowed gaze. "How insane did you go?"

Christopher's attention swung to the bare wall reserved for Sara's display. "I sent him to England." Guilt kicked at his head for the direct disobedience of her wishes.

Teddy's jaw dropped. "You did what? Why?"

"Because the young man deserves an opportunity." Christopher turned on his friend. "Because I refuse to believe that Sara Little has no living relative concerned for her well-being." The intensity in Christopher's voice echoed back at him as he glared at his friend. Then he dropped his gaze to his absent rub of the face of his pocket-watch. He didn't remember pulling it from his vest.... He tucked it back again. "Because... because it seemed the next step."

"But we don't know if we can trust him!" Teddy pressed. "He just walked off the street with some story about—"

"And that's why I've given him no information other than what is necessary. A name. An occupation. A time frame. That's all, Teddy." He thudded his open hand against his chest. "Do you really believe that I would openly give this man the opportunity to hurt her? She's under my protection, and now I have the means to open a door into her past. In order to do that, I need to utilize whatever I can. This man has a passion for mysteries and discoveries. He needs an opportunity to prove himself to others in his field. He seems to have ethics and high-moral character. Why shouldn't I use that?"

Teddy leaned back, eyes blinking in surprise. "You've

changed, Top, and I'm not so sure it's for the better."

Then he turned away, shaking his head. Christopher stared after him.

Sara's hands paused stitching the ribbon work for the purple-velvet gown when she heard voices in the hall. It sounded like Amy and Thomas. Amy had invited him for tea.

"I'm glad you told me," Thomas could be heard to say, voice quiet. "I wouldn't even have thought to try if you hadn't said something. I thought it were all in fun."

"All in fun?" Amy asked, surprised. Then she giggled. "Did you see me acting that way with Brian or any of the others?"

"Well, no, but—"

"But nothing. I like you, Thomas," Amy confessed, her voice tender. "I suppose I'm being more forward than I should by telling you, but I don't care."

Sara's smile faded. She fidgeted with the needle.

Thomas chuckled. "I like a girl who's not afraid to be open about different things. How else am I supposed to know the difference between anything?"

Silence again settled over the two; a silence full of meaning, futures, and tender exchanges. Sara's throat tightened, and her eyes burned. *I could have had that with George.* But she shouldn't look back at the 'could have's. It hadn't come, which meant it hadn't been time for her. Sara sighed. *But I surely want a special someone, sweet Jesus.* And He knew it.

Laughter sounded in the hall. Then Thomas promised

to escort Amy home that night. Amy walked him to the door, where they shared a meaningful pause, and offered him a gentle good-bye before closing the door behind him. Sara heard the sigh after the click of the closing door, and then the giddy giggle before Amy again entered the sitting room.

The young woman flopped down onto the couch beside Sara. "I did it. Six months of holding my tongue and I finally told Thomas how I feel about him."

Sara blinked back the burning of tears. "Good for you." Amy picked up her own needlework project on another evening gown. "Was it very difficult?"

"Not really. I was nervous at first, but only because my Ma had been telling me to keep it to myself." Amy giggled. "If Ma finds out I said something first, she'll go to an early grave."

Sara's wide blue eyes didn't look away from Amy's bright face, and the girl's smile faded. "How do you know you like him as more than just a friend?"

"There's just something different in how I feel when he's around. I can't help but smile, and my insides get all feathery, and I think about him all the time."

"It's different for the others?"

Amy nodded. "I'm comfortable around them, too, but I don't feel nearly the same. With Thomas...." She flushed. "It's just different."

"Are you no' scared you might make a mistake and hurt his feelings? And what if he does no' care the same for you? Are you no' afraid he might leave you? Or hurt you?"

Amy set the gown aside. "Of course. But I know I like him enough to find out. Nothing good ever comes about without a little risk and heartache."

Sara lowered her gaze to her trembling fingers. "Yes. I suppose that is true."

"Actually, the little fear is something like a rush," Amy admitted. "Anticipation, happiness, the risk. It's all wonderfully glorious because something deep inside is pushing me forward even when something bad could happen. He's been such a great friend, I know that I can trust him, and I'm willing to make something come out of that. He's wonderful," Amy sighed.

Uneasiness flittered away at the giddiness on Amy's expression. "I am happy for you, and I pray blessings for both of you."

"Thank you, Sara." A clock in the hall chimed the half hour. Amy bolted to her feet. "Goodness! I've got to get you your afternoon tray!" She scurried from the room.

Sara laughed and focused yet again on her ribbon-work. But then their conversation filtered back through her mind. She hadn't ever been in the same position before, not even with George. She wasn't sure how to know when she was sweet on a man enough to say 'I love you.' Seeing a look of love and adoration in a smile? Sara released a wistful sigh, her lips caressed upward. *Yes. I want that very much –*

The front door slammed open. Sara flinched around to face the front entrance. She couldn't see face nor figure. "Hello?"

There came no answer, only the firm bang of the closing door.

Sara set aside her needlework and made her way to the doorway of the parlor. Christopher Lake looked sharply toward her, hazel eyes dark and brown curls disheveled.

"Why, Mr. Christopher, what has happened?" She had never seen him so irritated.

"Don't worry about it. It's my own issue." His tone was so near a roar that Sara took a step back. He fisted his hat in his hands. "I'm sorry, Sara. I didn't mean to bark at you."

Sara hurried forward to help him wrestle free of his coat. "I been bit and barked at before," she assured. "I do no' pay it mind." She draped his coat over her arm and accepted his shed gloves. She motioned behind her into the parlor. "Did you want some coffee? Maybe some tea?"

"Agitation and coffee don't mix well." He glanced toward her. Nodding, he released a quick breath. "But I will have some tea."

"Certainly. You have yourself a seat. I'll put these up and be in to pour in a moment."

He lowered himself into the chair as though he fought against the press of a crushing weight. Exhaustion was plain in the slump of his shoulders as he leaned back and closed his eyes. *Lord*... But she didn't know what to pray or how to help.

When she returned to the parlor after hanging his overcoat, Christopher's eyes remained closed, his countenance taut. There was pain and confusion marring his handsome face, similar to when she first met him, though certainly not as severe.

Sara whispered a prayer for guidance and stepped forward. Sitting onto the couch to his left, she poured and sweetened his tea. When she turned to offer it, the memories twisting his features halted her. Those visions flickered as plain as if she saw them within her own mind. Memories of his wife and the sounds she used to make; remembrances of a time when an ache didn't mute the happiness.

Sara covered his hand with hers, causing a twitch from him as he opened his eyes. He pushed himself up and attempted a smile of thanks. It only served a confession to his hurt. She blinked back the burning of her eyes and prepared her own cup.

"The servant's life is a hard one?"

Sara looked up, and he glanced in time to catch her curious gaze. "Yes, sir, I suppose it is."

"How did you manage as you have? Through such challenges no one would fault you an attitude of bitterness."

"God never asked me to go through a challenge I couldn't handle with Him beside me." She peeked at him, unable to label his overly calm expression as he stared into his teacup. "It seemed to work for the best in the end. I only had to make sure I looked for what that blessing was."

"Being treated unfairly can't offer too many blessings."

"I suppose that's true. But I did no' think on that. I remembered the other things. The Sarah's and George's, and Emma's and Beth's." Her smile widened. "And the Mr. Brockle's, believe it or not." He scoffed. "Oh no, Mr. Christopher. Do no' jeer."

"And why not? From what I've heard from Paul and Dix, the man was—"

"Yes, he was, but Mr. Brockle did something for me no one else had. He tested my faith. I had no' ever been asked to trust God as much as I did back then. I nearly fell out of faith more than once, but you know what? If I had no' been put to the test, I would no' been ready to trust Him through this new life. I would no' truly known, deep, that God could... could...." Sara's hand fluttered for the answer. "I would no' put all that's happened into His hands."

Christopher regarded her a moment before lowering his gaze. "I trusted Him that much once."

"And then you lost your wife," she whispered, fingering

the edge of her cup. "I know it's not what you want to hear, and I'm sorry, but this is where the trust comes in. He truly does have something waiting, Mr. Christopher. Maybe it's the happy ending you want so dreadfully?"

His jaw muscle twitched, and the teacup clinked.

"I know," she said, the words rushed. "You want Him to prove that He can be trusted, because He seemed to promise one thing and another came about." Sara hesitated. "He can give as many proofs as you need."

Christopher set down his mug with a firm clatter of china, angry hazel eyes sparking as they met her blue ones. "Then He better start now, Miss Little, because it will take more than a few to prove He cares one way or the other." He stood.

As did Sara, ignoring the burning of her cheeks as she blocked the exit. "Please do no' go. I... I do no' mean to nag at you."

He fisted his hands and frowned down into her wide blue gaze. Then he skulked back to his chair, slumping into it much like a pouting child, his chin in his hand.

"I suppose America and your sister are bad influences," Sara confessed. She sat across from him. "I never would have said word one about anything before coming here."

He shifted in his seat while stealing a look.

She moved her gaze to her tea. "I am sorry, sir."

"Don't apologize to me, Sara," he said suddenly, contrite. "It's I who should beg your forgiveness. I bark at you because I know you listen to my ranting."

"I do no' mind so much." She sent him a fleeting look.

"So you say, but your expression tells a different story." He accepted his tea from her with an attempted smile, but Sara could still see the pain. Christopher broke their gaze.

"How are you with your studies?"

"I...." *Please, Lord. Help me help him.* "I am painting on smaller bits of paper, in case the size was what gave me the fright."

"Has it helped?"

"It seems to, a little." She peeked at him, and his distant expression pulled at her heart. *I truly am trying to help, Mr. Christopher.* "I love combining the watercolors with pencils. It gives an added little bit that you canno' find on the watercolors in the books."

This time Christopher didn't answer at all; he only fingered his cup while staring beyond it. Expression blank. Sara lowered her cup to the tray and swallowed hard, sitting there still and silent as she continued to watch his face while praying. She didn't know what else to do. What to say. How to help. How to comfort—

"Carla, do y—" Horror washed all color from Christopher's face, and his cup and saucer clinked to the tray. "Sara, forgive me."

Sara forced a smile, his wife's name still ringing in her ears. "What do you need to be forgiven for?"

"I...." He scrubbed a hand through his brown curls.

A wave of compassion and concern propelled her from her seat to kneel at his feet. She held his dark gaze. "Do no' fret, sir. You said her name for years. Why no' fall into the habit again?"

"Because she's gone. Dead. Buried." Each word resonated with gruff agony. "Because she's not here to comfort, to assure, to reassure, to—" He shook his head. "She's not here. She won't be. Ever."

"Mr. Christopher, I might not be your sweet Carla, but I can listen if you need to talk about something." She would do all within her power to help him beyond the grief. Hadn't he been the key to the blessing at the end of her own rough journey?

"Something?" He sneered. "Everything. Nothing. I don't know." He pulled his arm from her touch and leaned back. "I don't know," he repeated, quiet, lost. Then he faced her, his hazel eyes searching her face for any answer. "Teddy says I've changed, and I must say I agree. I don't like who I've become, but when did I change? I don't remember. I didn't think I had until Teddy said something." He moved his focus to the tea service. "Carla would have noticed. She would have said something."

Sara's mind and heart scrambled, but words continued to stick in the lump in her throat. *Dear God, what do I say?* But all she felt was a press to listen and hear.

"I never used someone before—plotting always made me angry—yet here I am, using one to help another. Manipulating a situation so that...." He shook his head. "No. I never did that before... did I?" He met her gaze. "Did I?"

Tears burned, but she could only wordlessly shake her head. Unable to even voice the simple 'I don't know' she knew wouldn't have helped.

"Giving one an opportunity isn't manipulating, though... is it? He wants a chance and I'm giving that to him. If it helps... shouldn't I? I'm not harming his career or his life by having him do it, so how is it wrong?"

Helplessness robbed her of the words she knew he needed to hear. She didn't like feeling helpless. It was too much like in England, surrounded by condescending people—"Mr. Christopher?"

"Hm?" was all he said, his tone and expression vacant of emotion.

Sara's throat tightened. Dix was right; he missed his wife. Understandably so, with such a sensitive soul. How else would he react at the face of such loss. Out of reach. Out of sight. Lost. Of course he would pine. Much like the hero from a tragic love-story.

Sara lowered her gaze to her clasped hands—Her eyes focused on a carefully folded letter peeking from a hidden pocket stitched at her waist. "Mr. Christopher?" She pulled the letter free and offered it to him. The action caught his attention, pulling his focus from where it teetered between present and past.

"What's this?" he asked. His tone didn't hold the interest expected. As before, it sounded distant.

"A letter from your wife to me."

"From—" He reached out with a trembling hand. "From Carla?"

"Yes, sir. She hid a gift for me, too. A 'Merry Christmas'. She said she woke one morning and could no' set aside the feeling of making a gift for me, even when she was no' certain I'd like them. There were sachets and creams and oils... lilac and vanilla—" Sara's voice caught. "Never had such care been taken with a gift to me, and such a collection of fancies and frills."

Christopher opened the letter as Sara spoke, his dark eyes devouring each word like a man who knew it to be his last meal. He swallowed hard, blinking away the wetness as he read her letter again and yet again.

"Do you see, sir? She will no' ever be far away." Sara's voice struggled through the tightness of tears. "I have her letters. Gwyn has your pictures and her imagination. You have her very self with you." Christopher lifted his eyes to meet hers. Sara held it, enveloping his hand as it held the letter. "Please try to remember that. For the help to Gwyn and your own grieving heart."

He seized her hand, desperation evident in the tight clasp. And as he continued to read the words crafted by his sweet wife, the misery in his expression overwhelmed Sara's heart. *Please, Lord, help me guide him to a safer viewing of the memories.* It was the only way she knew to help him to the other side of the loneliness.

Christopher sat up. A whisper seemed to tickle his neck at the same time it beckoned his spirit. But dread settled at the return of the grays and blacks, the shadows and muted white of his charcoal dream. Robbing his color of life and living.

Throat tightening, he threw back the covers and slipped from the bed, grabbing up his robe with shaking hands as he stepped toward the door of his room. There he halted, staring at the handle while unable to open it. Knowing the voice would whisper his name, beckoning him to tread through the gray to the muted color which waited.

All he must do was admit the grays weren't enough.

The thirst for color pulled him to the foot of the narrow stairs, again looking up into the swirling of gray and black which met the hint of blue and brown. He wanted an end to the gray, but what if the color wasn't enough? What if the gray came again? What if the black stole his color, plunging his passion and art again into the void.

"I—" Christopher tightened his hold on the railing. "I can't. Not again."

"He knows it. It breaks His heart, but He works through

it...."

Christopher clenched his jaw and took a hesitant step up. "How? I've blamed Him for every hardship and loss! I've made myself hate Him."

"He knows your heart."

Christopher blinked back the burning and stepped forward again. "Why?"

"He... has something waiting. The happy ending you want."

Hope pushed him up to the crest of the stairs, standing within the shadows of the grays of fear while being pulled by the promise of soft shades of color and laughter. Then his gaze was drawn to the form on the far side of the room, sitting upon a box while sifting through one of his portfolios... Carla.

Swallowing the grief and loss, Christopher stepped forward. He remembered the scene as if it were yesterday, finding Carla here and wondering why.... He released a deep breath as he came to stand behind her, resting a hand on her shoulder and closing his eyes at the remembered warmth.

Carla looked up, her green eyes and delicate features brightening with her "Oh, Chris. Did I worry you? I'm sorry."

Throat tightening, Christopher leaned down to place a kiss on her lips... *Oh God*. He forced himself to straighten and motioned to the sketches and watercolors within the portfolio balanced so carefully on her lap, eyes hungrily taking in the loveliness of her face. "What are you looking for?"

"Nothing," she said, her gaze once again drawn by the images. "I was only looking. I love looking at your art. It's so lovely. So alive."

Christopher moved his hand from her shoulder to her hair, the softness of the curls heightening the loss and the– He lowered his hand to his side, hiding the warmth in a fist. "These are only old dabbles, Carla."

"I...." Carla bit a fingernail as she retrieved a sketch with her other hand, balancing the portfolio more securely on her lap. "I was looking for... her."

Eyes darkening, Christopher focused on the pencils, charcoals and watercolors, memory focused on the sketch of a simple room and a single lady facing out a solitary window. Nothing seen of her but the back of her silhouette and the grace of her carriage.

Carla lifted her focus from the sketch to Christopher's blank expression. "Chris, who is she? Where did you meet her? Why don't you ever talk about her?"

Christopher slightly shook his head. "She doesn't exist, Carla. Only a figment." But there came a whisper of familiarity when he allowed his gaze to stray. *She can't be real.* He shook free of the thought. *I've been alone too long.* Forcing his gaze from the images, he met her serious expression. "Come down for lunch, Carla. You've been up here since breakfast."

But when he attempted to take the image and the portfolio away, Carla kept it from his grasp.

"A figment couldn't possibly feel this real," she protested, looking again to the woman's profile. "I can almost hear her breathing, Chris. Everything about her is so... vivid."

Again drawing Christopher's pained focus, the brightness and compelling image caused a twisting within. Especially when the Lady seemed more apt to step from the gray to the color of life. But he knew it impossible, she being a romantic imagining. A dream for paper alone.

Christopher cleared his throat. "Carla," he assured as he took the sketch carefully from her grasp. She looked up. "Carla, it's a sketch, nothing more. You're my reality." Now that too had gone.

"But what if she's looking for you?" Carla pressed. "You can't just leave her alone."

Christopher's expression softened, even amidst the grief and loss to never again have her intense concern and compassion beside him... "I'll sketch her a beau. Fine?"

Carla stood from the box to embrace him, causing Christopher to close his eyes as he held her.

"I knew you would understand." She pulled back, emerald gaze aglow. "I will bring your charcoals."

She turned and made her way downstairs. Christopher lowered his gaze to the sketches and colors... and the Lady. It pained him to change the simplicity of the silhouette and her content. Her calm waiting. Her patient understanding....

TWENTY

Inspiration's Subtle Whisper

8 February 1894

"Chris."

Teddy crested the second story as Christopher closed the third-floor doorway. "Ted."

"Top, I was out of line yesterday. What is it to me what you do with a newspaper intern?"

"You weren't completely in the wrong, Teddy. A warning now and again keeps me deliberate." How else could he be brought face-to-face with changes needed? Christopher motioned down the hall. "Would you like some coffee? I'm expecting Sara for our lesson. We could plan the display instead."

"Only if that means planning a joint one."

"Teddy."

"I know. You don't want to do that until the mess is sorted out with the *Chronicle*." Teddy followed Christopher downstairs. "But I don't see any retractions being printed, and I don't see you stomping down there with threats of suits. So, that said, I think it should be a joint display, thereby being a spit in the eye to what they reported."

"I don't think they would see it as that, Ted. Something tells me that it won't be the first time they've used these tactics to get a story to increase circulation."

"Because they did it so well?"

Christopher chuckled. "Something like that."

"Yes, well, if it were up to me—which it isn't, blast it—I would stomp down there and mess up some office papers and shirtfronts until they agreed to my demands. You and Sara deserve better than what they've alluded to. Blast it! The gallery deserves better."

"I know, Teddy, but let's offer them another chance. Who's to say they won't be on their best behavior for the next unveiling?"

Teddy scoffed, but further comment was interrupted by the sound of quick steps. Then the door opened and Sara rushed inside before Harold could approach. Teddy and Christopher both watched in amusement as she chatted to Harold about the morning and that past Sunday's service while he helped her from scarf and coat. Then she cast him a bright smile and turned toward the studio.

When she saw Teddy and Christopher, her eyes sparkled like stars. "Good morning, Mr. Lake. Mr. Parker. How are you? Is it no' a lovely morning? The sun fairly sparkles off the snow."

Teddy laughed, but Christopher swallowed his own amusement to offer a calm, "Good morning, Sara. I'm fine, thank you. And, yes, it is a lovely morning. Makes me miss spring." He motioned toward her. "How are you?"

"Oh I am lovely, Mr. Lake. Thank you."

Teddy sniggered, and Christopher elbowed him while never shifting from Sara's gemlike gaze. "Where's Dix?"

"Mr. Paul brought me today as your sister has company coming for a late breakfast." She motioned behind her. "He will be right in. He wanted to have a word with Patrick."

Paul entered a few moments thereafter, looking toward the trio to offer a smile and a "Morning, all," as he passed his hat, gloves, and coat to Harold. "Good morning, Harold."

"Good morning, sir. I will have coffee in but a few moments."

"Outstanding. Thank you." Paul stood beside Sara. "Teddy. Topper. I hope you don't mind the change. Sweet has company coming."

"So I heard. Unfortunately, we have a bit of a change ourselves. Sara, I hope you weren't set on having a lesson this morning. I volunteered the two of us for a meeting with Teddy to plan your second display. At least on paper. Perhaps we can shift your lesson to afterward?"

"What a grand idea!" Sara focused on Teddy with that same bright expression. "But I am afraid you canno' stay for the lesson after, Mr. Parker. I am no' good at the watercolors yet, and do no' want an audience." She giggled. "A silly goose."

Teddy cleared his throat, forcing away the smirk while sending Christopher a sidelong glance. Then, with as much decorum as was possible for Teddy Parker, he said, "Nah. When I started out with the stone-works, I broke all my not-so-wonderfuls. I didn't want anyone to see how bad I was." Teddy motioned to Christopher. "Top's the only one with a sadistic streak. He keeps everything. Doodles. Mess-ups. Roughs. Finals. Things that would be better off burnt.

He says he wants to keep himself humble. I think he only wants to dig for compliments."

Paul chuckled.

"Mr. Parker." Sara put hands on hips and actually sent Teddy a playful frown. "You are to poke fun when he is no' in the room."

Christopher and Paul laughed. Teddy, ever the character, snapped his fingers and cast Sara a wink. "Right. I forgot that."

Sara wrinkled her nose at both of them. Christopher tore his gaze away, clearing of his throat at a sudden flare of heat and a rising ache. Teddy accepted the look with a full grin, of course.

"Come along then." Christopher gestured for his office, drawing Sara's smile. "Why don't we see what everyone thinks, firstly? Then we can see which artwork we believe will receive the highest praise, although I'm of the mind all should be shown. I don't remember seeing a mediocre one in the lot."

Sara fell into step beside Christopher as he moved toward his office, Teddy and Paul following behind. "Could you find another story-cycle?" She paused at the doorway. "It was such a wonderful surprise when you did before, and I rather think everyone would love to see another."

"Not a bad idea," Paul said. "You should have heard some of the verbal renditions of the story-cycle I heard at the party. Inventive, every single one."

Christopher smiled down at her. "Of course I can try, but are you so certain another display like that is what you want? Don't you want to try something new?"

"But it would be new."

"Yes, I guess it would," he admitted, chuckling. He

motioned inside. "After you." Christopher caught Teddy's amused smirk. "Shut up, Parker."

Laughing, Teddy moved to sit in the chair beside Sara as Christopher retrieved the collection of sketches from their locked location of his desk.

"Could we keep the first story-cycle up?" Sara offered. "You put so much thought and care into it. I would hate to have it missed by those who were no' able to come to the first unveiling."

"That isn't a bad idea," Paul agreed. "And there's no reason we should move it, either. The lighting in that room is perfect for its simplicity."

"Should we have more drama in the second?" Christopher pulled out the sketches. "I seem to remember several with a bit more flair for that."

Teddy nodded. "Drama in the main room would be great. The openness of the hall would invite louder discussion. The smaller room is more confined, and people have a tendency of whispering there."

Sara looked from each person with wide eyes, listening with awe and wonder as they discussed options. Christopher's attention continued to stray to the rapt expression in her dark blue eyes. Her lips would tilt upward in a smile, and then slightly part as either Teddy or Paul made an observation on one of her sketches which caught her by surprise.

The flush remained on her cheeks as well, making him certain she never before held the center of positive attention. Yet, of her own confession, she always chose to remember the good in each one of her experiences. The sunshine in a rainy afternoon. The laughter from children after a snow. The possibilities of a new life after leaving a familiar, old one.

Christopher lowered his attention to the sketch in his hands; A woman sitting at a vanity regarding herself in the mirror while a child peeked around the woman's shoulders.

"A great many of these have a certain feeling of... family and safety," Paul noted, lifting his held sketch. He attracted Sara's attention. "Why don't we have that the focus of this display?"

"Not bad." Teddy pointed to Christopher. "It seems to me we haven't had the same amount of families come. Maybe we could use this display to get into that again? Remember the fun we used to have with the kiddies coming over to do clay-works with me, or drawing with you and reading with Carla?"

Christopher's insides twitched, but he forced a smile as he lifted his gaze. "Yes. It's been a while, hasn't it?"

"Say. Why don't we have this unveiling earlier in the day? Then families could come and see that we're getting back to the same-old, same-old. We could even have children's activities in some of the side-rooms," Teddy continued.

Excitement shone in Sara's eyes, her hands clasped tight in her lap. It would be fun to have children in the gallery again, reminding him of a past of laughter and play that seemed to now only vaguely echo in the halls. Christopher lowered his focus to the sketch. The woman and the child. Family. A completion previously broken.

"Teddy, we shouldn't get too carried away," Paul was saying. "Maybe an art contest, but nothing much more than that. Not until we remember how to keep them occupied and satisfied and not screaming for their parents."

Teddy laughed. "I guess you're right. It would be just

my luck to have a clay fight break out five minutes after starting the class."

Christopher caught Sara's glance of concern and offered her a small smile. She flushed and lowered her gaze. "Fair enough," he said. He cleared his throat and dragged his focus back from regrets and too-soon endings. "So it's agreed then. Family will be the focus. Which pieces should we have out?" He set the one with the woman and the child aside. "This one, most definitely. Maybe even as the finale. Paul? What do you have?"

The remainder of the morning was invested in choosing ten pieces of art for the second display, agreeing upon a time-line for the story-cycle, and then laughing at possible children activities over coffee and cookies. The lesson was forgotten, especially when Gwyn ambled down sometime before lunch to say "Hello" and "Look what I drew." She then robbed all attention, especially Sara's, who drew the girl up onto her lap and shared awed commentary for each image.

Teddy retreated soon after, deciding to make his way to the gallery to begin the set-up of the display. He wrangled a promise from Christopher to come by after the lesson.

"That's right," Paul said suddenly. He laughed and came around to take Gwyn up into his arms. "Come along, Angel. Your papa needs to give Miss Sara a lesson, and he won't be able to do that with the two of us causing distraction."

"But can't I watch?" Gwyn asked as Paul carried her from the room.

Paul's answer and the reason for it was lost as the two proceeded down the hall to one of the other rooms.

Christopher straightened from the desk, looking this way and that for something to focus on to hide the dread.

The initial lessons the previous week hadn't been any type of challenge, simply an introduction to the media. But now, as he knew she needed to begin actually painting objects and specifics, he didn't know how to... inspire her when he couldn't see or feel the images himself.

"Well then." He cleared his throat. "Lesson." His eyes were drawn to the closed studio door. The blank paper waited just beyond. Pencils, colors, palette. All waiting for her touch of inspiration.

A soft contact on his arm caused an internal jolt as he glanced to his right. Sara stood beside him, hesitancy darkening her blue eyes as she worried her lower lip. Dread dried his throat. She only ever looked like that when about to speak directly to a need. Pushed by Someone Christopher tried desperately to ignore. Someone who wouldn't be ignored. Sara displayed courage in that; speaking in a way that didn't accuse or belittle. She simply offered.

"Mr. Christopher, I...." Sara sent a fleeting look to the studio door before again meeting his gaze.

He noticed something different in her expression, and the hesitancy didn't seem to be for him. "What's the matter?"

She flushed but didn't look away. "I know you have no' painted since—" Sara's cheeks paled. Christopher cleared his throat and looked away. "But could you... could you help me? I try so hard," she confessed, her blue eyes wide as the recognizable glimmer of frustration appeared. "Even using my charcoals before the paints I still do no' see an image. I thought...." She finally lowered her gaze, clasping her hands in front of her. "I thought, perhaps, if you could help me as before, something might come of it. You are such a natural hand with the brush."

His chest tightened with the overwhelming desire to

do what she asked. To paint. To create. But when he again focused on the studio door and remembered how large the white—"The blind leading the blind," he mumbled.

"Mr. Christopher, you are no' blind." Sara's tender tone drew his gaze. Her eyes glowed. "You have but closed your eyes to what's there, perhaps a bit frightened of what you might see."

"Or what I won't."

"But that is no' what you want." She rested her hand on his arm, and the warmth of it burned. "Do you no' want to see the images again?"

Christopher clenched his jaw and slightly nodded.

"Then believe you will and move to the doing of it. God's whispers never stop. We only stop listening."

Christopher frowned and pulled his arm from her touch. "He stopped listening a long time—"

"No, Mr. Christopher. No, He did no' stop."

He moved his glare to the studio door.

"You are hurt and angry, and wanting to know a 'why' that your heart and mind likely canno' accept. He chooses no' to answer, and you hate it. I did, too. But He's still there. Listening. Watching. Doing what needs to be done to keep you moving forward. That little bit of strength coming when you had no' left. That little bit of silence when a laugh would have been too much."

Christopher swallowed hard at the words and what they meant, even as he fought against them. "If He cared, why did she die? Why am I blind? Empty—"

"Do no' ask for the answer to the 'why'," Sara pleaded. "There's no answer to be had until we face God at the hereafter. Ask the 'what' and the 'how' and the 'when'. 'What can I do to go on?', 'How can God make it better?', 'When will God bring the blessing from this?'" Sara wrapped a hand around Christopher's arm and gently but firmly squeezed. "Look for it, sir. It be there. It is always there."

"I—" And the cacophony of desires, to see the blessing, to have the release, to have that security back; they bombarded him. Pushing. Pulling. Tearing at something deep that hid a terrible agony. A mountain of loss, his wife, his faith, his passion. Desperation to have it back clawed at him, but the betrayal fought it back.

Christopher shook his head and tried to pull his arm from her hold. "I... I can't."

Her hold didn't loosen, which drew Christopher's gaze. Tear trails glistened on her face as her blue eyes shone with her own memories.

"You must," she whispered. "For Gwyn. For yourself. For everything waiting to give to everyone else. You canno' stay in this black place, sir. Yours is a good heart. One that hungers after God's whisper. You canno' ignore that. You die each day you do. Your Carla—" Sara's voice broke, but she swallowed the tears and began again. "Your Carla dies each day you let the grief keep you from the blessings waiting."

Christopher wrenched his arm from her hold. "What blessing can come from a death?"

Sara shook her head, more tears flowing as she stretched her arms toward him. "I do no' know. That's what you must pray for God to make come to light. Even I forget the blessings. My mum dying. My childhood gone. My George gone. No friends. No family. No father."

She grabbed his hand, not releasing it even when he tried to jerk it free. The intensity of her expression held Christopher's attention.

"I canno' say whether or not my life would be better if she had no' passed. But I would no' have reason to come and find myself a new me if it were another way. Finding the true Sara-Ann Little. A different kind of family than what I had before. Friends who give more than a passing thought to what I might want or need. Would I give it all up to have my mum and pop? I do no' know, and I do no' ask myself that question because it hurts too much. I just keep looking ahead to the blessings waiting 'round the corner. Canno' you do that, sir?" Sara gave his hand another squeeze. "Please?"

Christopher lowered his gaze to the cling of their hands, his insides void as desperation for hope and betrayal fought against each other. Finally, he reached over with his free hand and pulled each of hers from his, silence settling within and without while a very slight and hushed whisper tickled a portion of his soul that hadn't heard anything for what seemed longer than an age.

"Try to listen," Sara whispered, hands immediately clasped together, white-knuckled. "Try to hear it."

He slowly looked to the studio door, reluctance tightening his throat. Though he wanted to hear the inspiration, what if he didn't? He didn't want to find a lie in what she said. The desire to trust someone again rose like a wave, and it was easier than trusting a cold truth: That his wife was dead and he had nothing else.

A hand blindly reached behind to grab hold of Sara's as he stepped toward the door. Clenching his jaw, he opened the door and entered the studio, attention accosted by the stark whiteness of the paper. He halted, and his hand tightened its grip on Sara's the same moment she did the same on his.

"It be fine if there is nothing," she whispered. "You but need to try."

"But why would He whisper when I've come to hate Him." Christopher moved his focus to her pale and tear-stained face. "Why would He?"

"Because He does no' hate you, Christopher. He knows your heart. He knows your rage. He knows you hurt. And He knows how to get through it. You have but to take the first step." She motioned to the white. "If it is there, do it. Scratch out the image or the blot of red or black that shows how angry you are. If it is stomping through the gardens fuming to raise the dead, do it. He can take it because He sees past to the deeper heart." Sara pressed a single finger to his chest. "He sees what we hide here, and that is where He works."

Again Christopher felt the fight. He clenched his jaw and focused on the white, his hold on Sara's hand tightening and loosening and tightening again—She stepped toward the paper and pulled him along after, purposefully positioning him by the easel and pushing a charcoal into his hand. The action blackened his fingers the same as her own.

"Show it," she pressed, pushing his hand toward the stark whiteness as he had done for her the week before.

Sara then dragged his hand roughly over the white, causing a vicious and rage-filled black streak to mar the page.

Christopher blinked and stepped back, but Sara tugged at his arm to draw him back again.

"No," she said, firm. "You must no' keep it inside. Not any longer. Your heart is good, and the black canno' have it. You put it here. You put it on this bit of white." She forced his hand against the paper for a second time, holding it there as she focused on his blank expression. "Here." She pressed his hand harder into the paper, causing the charcoal to snap and a piece to clatter to the floor.

Christopher twitched.

"Here," she insisted, voice cracking.

But where to begin showing and expressing more than a year of rage and loss and confusion? Christopher tugged at her hold, the action causing another streak and another twitch at the sound.

"You canno' run from it," Sara told him, shaking her head. "I know. I tried. But it chases you. Follows you to your dreams and taints your memories into nightmares and horrible faces...." She pushed and dragged his hand across the paper. "Put it here. Let God have it! He knows more what to do with the rage and the ache than we do. It kills us. Bit by bit stealing what God has given."

And she continued the firm strokes of his hand until the white was mostly shadow and blackness. Then Sara released her hold on his hand and tore the paper free with a full motion of her body. Christopher cringed, backing away from her when she presented it to him.

"Here." She pressed it against his chest. Christopher stared blankly down, insides convulsing. "Tear it. Rip it. Burn it. Anything!"

Christopher reached up to hold the paper, hesitant. When Sara's hands grabbed hold of his and guided the tearing action, he retreated away from the sound and the feel of it, causing the papers to fall to the floor.

Again Sara took him by the arm and pulled him to the easel, pressing his hand against the new white as she choked on tears and pleadings to "put it here" and "leave it." To give God those things he had kept far too long. To put it all onto a bit of paper they then ripped into pieces and let tumble to the floor, a little bit of hardness escaping each time they fell.

"Leave them there. Do no' take them back. You do no' want it, so do no' keep it—" Her voice choked on the sobs, gathering Christopher's dazed eyes to hers, glimmering as rich as the midnight after a storm. "Please, Christopher." She stepped closer, resting her hands on his chest. "Do no' keep it."

Christopher gave a slight shake of his head as he drew her close, staring at the whiteness which didn't seem so terrifying. It didn't seem so stark and empty. It looked more like it waited, whispering while waiting for him to hear its voice.

TWENTY-ONE

Displays of Fancy

23 February 1894

Christopher adjusted his tie and suit-coat, his insides in turmoil at a surprising sense of nervousness. This particular display and reception was more... ambitious than any previous.

In side rooms throughout were preliminary displays pertaining to the gallery's past history working with children. Near each introductory exhibit hung a sign-up sheet for those families interested in participating future activities. But amidst the excitement was a fear that, somehow, the *Chronicle* would find a way to taint the project. Making some portion of it questionable, focused on the non-existent 'what if' rather than on the children.

Yet another threat to Sara's reputation.

Christopher's nervous tremble of fingers succeeded only in knotting his tie. "Blast it!" He struggled with the untying as the front doors opened, drawing his attention.

He smiled as Paul, Dix, and Sara entered the gallery, Gwyn scampering forward ahead of them.

Gwyn vaulted herself into his waiting arms. He kissed her cheek. "You look pretty in emerald and white today. I wasn't expecting you until later." Christopher focused toward the entry where Dix and Paul held back.

Sara continued up to him and Gwyn. "I made them come early. I could no' wait longer. It is such a treat to watch everyone arrive, with their smiles and laughter. But so much better to see from the first, instead of when everything is so busy." The excited words tumbled from her rose lips with hardly a pause.

"I'm glad the first unveiling didn't spoil you to the future ones." Christopher set Gwyn down and then stepped forward to help Sara from her usual wool coat. Lilacs and vanilla drifted from her hair. "Most timid individuals, in my experience, don't care for the noise and commotion."

"Oh no, sir." Sara cast him a glance over her shoulder. "I have witnessed parties grander than this since Gwyn's age."

Gwyn giggled, drawing a wink from Christopher as he pulled Sara's coat free. "Well, I'm glad of that. It... has...."

Christopher's smile died away as he drew the coat away to reveal the velvet gown of rich indigo beneath. He swallowed hard. White ribbon roses trailed from right shoulder to left hip, ending in a delicate bouquet of orchid and lilac. Interwoven throughout were smatterings of faux pearls and green ribbon leaves. The effect was elegance personified, the flow of the gown augmenting her statuesque figure.

"Oh Sara," Gwyn breathed. "You look like a princess."

"Thank you, Gwyn." Sara looked to Christopher with an eager and bright expression. She reached for his tie. "Mr.

Christopher, you knotted yourself in."

A laugh cleared the boulder of fire and stone from his throat. "Yes, I suppose I have. Distraction is to blame, proving I can't do too many things at once."

Gwyn gathered his right hand, her laughter echoing through the halls. "Mamma used to do your ties, Papa. You always knotted them."

"Yes, well, that's the way of life sometimes." Christopher watched Sara while she unknot the mess and deftly performed the duty he attempted himself. She peeked at him and smiled. His ears burned, and he shifted his attention to Dix and Paul. Paul helped Dix from her coat while sending Christopher a sidelong glance of amusement. Dix seemed to ignore them altogether.

"There." She gave the tie one last straightening movement with a graceful hand before once more smiling up at him.

"Now, Gwyn." Nonplussed at a sudden churning within, he dropped to one knee and gathered his daughter's hands. "You stay with Auntie Dix and Uncle Paul this afternoon. Just like you used to. Understood?" Gwyn nodded. "Good girl." He kissed her cheek and watched as she dutifully moved toward her Aunt and Uncle. Christopher offered his arm to Sara. "Miss Kreyssler."

"This is so exciting," she said, voice hushed.

"Does that mean you might be open to the possibility of introducing yourself?"

"Your sister seemed to think you may not want to do so tonight, but she would no' tell me why."

"Oh." Christopher cleared his throat. "I had forgotten about that...." He sent her a glance, and noticed her curious expression.

"Well, hello. Look who's early." Teddy approached, smiling.

"Hello, Mr. Parker." Sara actually offered him a hand, which he accepted to give a slight and quick grip. "I could no' stay away nearly so long this time."

Teddy laughed and then motioned toward her. "You look lovely."

Sara flushed. "Thank you."

Christopher scolded himself for not saying it first.

"Seems to me something about her is beginning to itch at the back of my mind. You notice that at all, Top?"

"Teddy," Christopher complained, "don't start the age-old lines now. She knows you too well to fall for them."

Sara restrained a giggle.

Teddy frowned. "I was being serious. Give me some credit." He focused on Sara again, his frown disappearing. "You want some punch and sandwiches? We have cookies this time, too. Em outdid herself."

"No, thank you."

"You certain?"

"I am too excited to eat or drink a thing."

"You'll get tired of these things eventually." Teddy passed to greet Dix and Paul. "Let me know if you change your mind about the punch," he called over his shoulder.

Smiling after him, Sara shook her head.

"Sara."

Sara turned. "Yes, Mr. Christopher?"

"I have a confession."

Her smile dropped away as she blinked up at him. "A c-confession, sir?"

"I won't be able to spend as much time with you tonight as I did before." He forced a smile. "Teddy and Paul have sworn to make certain you're not preyed upon by the more desperate single artists."

"Oh." Sara lowered her gaze to her clasped hands.

The dejection in the single utterance tore at his conscience, but how could he tell her the distance was to protect her reputation against a false report to the *Chronicle*? "I should have told you earlier—"

The front doors opened as the first of their guests arrived. A cluster of regulars, they were distracted to a further entrance by Dix and Paul's greeting. Christopher took up Sara's cold hands to give a collection of squeezes. He cursed himself. "Sara, don't convince yourself you've done something wrong. Your enthusiasm is gratifying, and my distance isn't a punishment. I'm simply taking my role as sponsor one step further."

Sara passed a quick look to him from beneath her lashes.

He willed himself to offer a more convincing smile and gave her hands another gentle pressure. "I want you to enjoy yourself this evening. Mingle. Laugh. Listen to their inspirations brought about by the viewing of your sketches. Relish the freedom to be yourself." Christopher brought each of her hands to his lips—He blinked at the soft warmth of lip and hand, and both their faces burned crimson. "I...." He met her wide-eyed gaze and forced a release of her hands. "Slap my face if I do that again."

Sara laughed.

"That's better." Christopher gathered Paul's attention from the entry. "I won't be absent all evening. I promise. What kind of host would I be if I didn't mingle with everyone, boring and charming?"

Christopher stared after her and Paul for only a moment before more guests arrived. Then he had no chance to gauge or examine anything.

"Ah. You've come again."

Sara beamed. "Mr. Conklin. Good evening."

"I've seen you in here quite a few times this afternoon, Miss Kreyssler." Mr. Conklin motioned toward the watercolors. "I don't suppose one will find its way home with you?"

"Oh no, Mr. Conklin. I am studying."

"You've begun attempting to lift a brush yourself?"

"Mr. Lake has been kind enough to teach me," Sara admitted. "Though I canno' seem to see the picture in my head as I do when I sketch." Her lips drooped. "I am afraid I am no' as good a pupil as I wish to be."

"Now, now, my dear. That you're willing to try something new is a testament to how good a pupil you are. I'm certain Mr. Lake doesn't hold the difficulties against you."

"Oh no! He's more patient than anyone I ever knew before." Sara focused a wistful smile on the watercolor. "Except for my mum, I suppose. There never was a more patient teacher. Though she could no' help me with my sketching, she tried something fierce to do what she could."

"She sounds charming." Mr. Conklin followed Sara's scrutiny of the watercolor. "Did she accompany you this evening? It would be an honor to meet her."

"No. My mum . . . she passed on." Silence followed, and Sara looked up to catch a dark expression of regret on his face. "It is fine, Mr. Conklin. She watches all the excitement from Heaven while giving a cheer. She always encouraged me to go for what was on my heart."

A reluctant smile softened his expression. "And what, my dear, is on your heart?"

"Truthfully, sir, I do no' know. Since coming to America everything's changed, and Mister Christopher and Mister Paul and Dix . . . they press me forward to try new things. Would you like to meet them? I feel certain they would love to meet you." Sara searched the main hall. "There they are." She took gentle hold of his arm. "Come along then. I will introduce you."

"They won't mind the interruption?"

"Oh no. They adore meeting new people." Sara caught Christopher's glance. One of his eyebrows twitched before he returned his attention to the conversation and alerted Dix and Paul to Mr. Conklin's approach. The two arrived just as their current subject finished.

"Mr. Lake? This is Mr. Joseph Conklin, the nice gentleman I met at the last unveiling who said all those kind things in *Harper's Weekly*. Remember?" Sara smiled at Mr. Conklin. "Mr. Conklin? This is Mr. Christopher Lake, director of The Richmond Gallery of Art."

Christopher produced a hand, a smile enhancing his good-looks and compassionate hazel gaze. "Mr. Conklin. It's nice to put a face to the name. This is Mr. Paul Donovan, and his wife Dixon."

Mr. Conklin greeted each before smiling at Gwyn's cherub face peeking from around Dix's skirts of navy and black. "And who do we have here?"

Sara knelt and motioned for Gwyn to come out. "This sweet little miss is Miss Gwyneth Marie. Mr. Lake's daughter." She gathered the girl into her arms and lifted her up, settling her onto her right hip. "Miss Gwyneth, meet Mr. Joseph Conklin. He's the nice man who said those wonderful things of your father. Remember?"

Mr. Conklin bowed. "A pleasure to make your acquaintance, Miss."

Gwyn giggled into her hands. "I like him," she whispered.

Sara kissed Gwyn's flushing cheek.

"I see you've been keeping Miss Kreyssler occupied in my stead," Christopher observed, motioning to Sara. "Thank you."

"It has been my pleasure." Mr. Conklin made a sweeping gesture of the newest display. "Quite impressive, Mr. Lake. You have us all waiting with bated breath in hopes that the mysterious S. A. L. hides somewhere within this ocean of faces. I, for one of many, would like to extend my congratulations. Quite a refreshing array of intensity and innocence."

Sara flushed as she adjusted her arms under Gwyn.

"Thank you, Mr. Conklin, from myself and the artist, though I've decided to wait on their unveiling. Situations beyond my control, you understand."

Sara looked to Christopher, her smile vanishing. 'Situations beyond'...?

"Ah. Yes. I believe I understand. Quite unfortunate that, but good for you at not giving comment. They don't deserve the attention."

Alternating her glance between the two, confusion darkened Sara's blue eyes. What would keep Christopher from confessing her as the artist? Sara forced a smile for Gwyn and then carefully lowered the girl to the floor. She gathered her small hand in hers and stared at Christopher's polished leather shoes.

Why would Christopher need to protect her identity? Sara paled. Mr. Brockle—He wouldn't hound her to America, would he? Why? What could he want from her? She didn't have money, so blackmail— Dizziness threatened a spill, if not for Gwyn's arms wrapped tight around her leg. Oh dear Lord. He wouldn't do that to Christopher, would he? He's not that black of heart... is he?

Sara closed her eyes, whispering a prayer for Christopher's protection and the protection of all the people she had come to know and—She felt a gentle hand enfold her forearm and intercepted Dix's reassuring gaze. Sara tried to offer a smile, but it wavered at best.

"It was nice to have this time to talk with you," Mr. Conklin said. He extended his hand. "I will have my secretary send my contact information so that we might keep in touch. I'm interested in tightening relationships between our galleries."

"An honor, Mr. Conklin. Thank you again for coming. I wanted the opportunity to thank you in person for your kind words in the article."

Mr. Conklin clasped Christopher's hand yet again. "Mr. and Mrs. Donovan. It was a pleasure, to meet you. When you return to New York, I'll be sure to have you over for dinner."

"Thank you, Mr. Conklin," Paul acknowledged. "Hopefully we can discuss a joint display between galleries." He motioned to Dix. "And I know Sweet would love to show you the house. Recently remodeled, understand."

Mr. Conklin chuckled. "I look forward to it, madam. I'm certain it will be as elegant as its designer."

Dix smiled and clasped his hand in both of hers. "Oh, I like you."

Then Mr. Conklin dropped to one knee while presenting a hand to Gwyn. She took it. "Miss Gwyneth, I count it an honor to have met you, and I hope to see you again."

Gwyn sent him a timid smile. Then, after casting a sidelong peek to Sara and Christopher, she gave Mr. Conklin a hug and a kiss on the cheek. "Thank you for saying those nice things about Papa."

"It was my honor." Finally, Mr. Conklin turned to Sara. "Miss Kreyssler, a pleasure."

"I wish you could stay longer," she confessed.

He gave her hand a gentle squeeze. "Yes, well, unfortunately I made other plans. If I were to cancel, it would be the second time this month. I doubt they would forgive me."

"If you're ever in Richmond again, you're more than welcome to tea or coffee. I'm only ever busy in the morning with my lessons, and I'd be more than happy to have you after."

"Thank you. I will remember that." He gave her hand another squeeze before nodding to each and then turning to make his way to Harold and the retrieving of his overcoat.

Sara released a sigh once the door closed behind him. "What a nice gentleman."

"Indeed." Christopher gestured toward her. "Are you well, Sara? You paled a little during the conversation."

"Oh. I am fine. I did no' mean to worry you."

"It's no worry. I noticed Teddy wasn't with you and wanted to make sure he hadn't said or done something."

Sara shielded her mouth. "Oh dear! I forgot he went to fetch me a tumbler of punch!" She searched the faces for Teddy and then hurried off.

Christopher stared after her with a growing smile. "She

gives him too much leeway. I'm afraid he'll take it and run."

"No more than what she gives you," Dix reprimanded, brows drawn.

"What did I do?"

Paul chuckled and turned to Gwyn. "Angel Girl, I think now is the time for us to go look at those bits of clay you wanted to play with." He gathered her into his care and disappeared into the milling crowd of connoisseurs, artists, and families.

"Passing her off to Paul and Teddy."

Christopher blinked at her. "Pardon?"

She pointed at him. "You should be ashamed of yourself for handing Sara off to Paul and Teddy. She's your protégé."

"Dix, you know as well as I do why I did."

"And you don't think anyone will find it suspicious in the least that you've barely spent any time with her at all? After being her escort the previous unveiling?" Dix scoffed. "Please."

Christopher crossed his arms. "What would you have suggested, then? I certainly didn't hear you offering any alternatives when we discussed it earlier."

"I held my tongue so that I wouldn't give you a lashing."

Christopher lowered his voice when he noticed a few glances cast their direction. "I guarantee here isn't the place to speak your mind."

She pressed her lips together. "Fine, but you had better decide which is more important, appearances or feelings."

"Dix, I made the decision I did due to the repercussions to both. I thought I explained that."

"But it's the principle of the whole situation I protest, Chris. They've no right to report something that deliberately and negatively effects a tentative friendship. You shouldn't allow them the satisfaction." She crossed her arms. "I know Carla wouldn't."

"But Carla isn't here," he hissed, "that being the reason for the whole issue in the first place." He sought Sara's form, focusing back on Dix when he didn't see her. "You know what Sa–she would do if they published a false supposition that put a questionable light on the future of our friendship." He glanced around again. People had migrated to different rooms of the gallery, leaving very few within ear-shot. "Knowing her as well as you do, you know that she would try to protect me from slander, even if it meant giving up her own future."

"Don't be absurd. If protecting you from slander is what God puts on her heart to do, then who are we to say otherwise? Certainly it's honorable for you to keep her from that position in the first place, but at such a sacrifice? That's not like you, Chris, and I don't like the fact this article and the possibility of others pushes you to it."

Christopher released a quick breath.

"I'm not saying you're doing wrong in not revealing who she is this evening; I honestly don't believe she's ready. But holding her at arm's length will only prove that in private you treat her one way and in public another. Do you want her believing you're embarrassed by her?"

He flinched.

Dix reached out to enfold his upper arm in a tight clasp. "I'm not saying that is at all what she thinks, Chris. I'm only giving you a warning to the possibility. She's a sensitive soul, and I would hate for all the good changes in her life to be sabotaged."

Christopher scrubbed at his scalp. "I'm an idiot."

Dix smiled and gave his arm another tight grip. "No,

dear. I just have a different perspective on things." She chuckled. "Now let's go save our residing English angel from Teddy's over-eager attempts to win her heart."

"I don't think we have anything to worry about in that respect, Dix."

"Oh? And why's that? He has been more attentive to her this evening than certain other gentleman."

"Teddy shies from commitment like a horse from fire. You know that."

"Yes, and I also know that our charming lady visitor is one of those types men commonly give up their roaming for."

Christopher looked down at his sister, his eyebrow raised. "Teddy? Give up flirting to marry? You're joking."

"Joking, am I? Hm." She motioned ahead. "If I'm joking, what do you call that?"

Christopher followed her gesture to see Teddy and Sara standing close together while examining one of the other artists' displays. Teddy motioned here and there while giving a dialogue or narrative that apparently held some interest for her, as she intensely listened and only occasionally interrupted with either a comment or question.

Something within twitched and roared in protest, causing a very brief frown. Christopher pushed it aside. "That? Friendship is all I see, Dix. Don't commit Teddy to anything more. He'll be horrified."

"With an angel like her showing interest in his opinions, offering encouragement to go further, and doing her best to let him know what's acceptable in talking with a lady? Not likely."

"Believe what you want, Dix. I've known Teddy too many years. He's not ready to see a woman as anything but a bit of curve and sweetness."

"Christopher Andrew," she protested.

He smirked. "Sorry."

"Likely story." She removed her hand from his arm and shoved him forward. "Now go do your duty and behave yourself."

Chuckling, Christopher continued toward the duet. But as he drew closer and began to hear the murmur of their conversation mold into words, he suddenly felt very uncomfortable. The thought of Teddy growing fond of someone like Sara wasn't at all impossible. But would he be able to provide her the security she needed? Would he understand her history and adjust himself accordingly?

Christopher cleared his throat, noticed the sound drew Sara's attention, and offered her a somewhat uncertain smile. "I don't suppose I could interrupt this experience of bonding and camaraderie to take over the duty of escort?"

Sara's smile vanished as she looked toward him, eyes wide. Teddy frowned. "No fair, Top. I thought she was my responsibility."

"She was, for the first half. Now it's my turn to be charmed and charming."

Teddy read the hall clock. "First half, my eye. You don't want me to have any fun."

"Don't be ridiculous!" Sara continued to regard him as he did his best to soothe Teddy's rumpled temper. "I never said you had to leave."

"To be the third wheel who doesn't understand a single word of what you artists find funny?" Teddy scoffed. "No thank you. I'll find my own amusement." He stalked into the crowd.

Christopher stared after him, aware of Sara's curious

gaze still examining his profile. Forcing what he hoped to be an easy smile, he felt a bit of surprise when she held his gaze.

"He was no' happy with you," she observed.

A smirk tilted his lips as he offered her his arm. She accepted. "I think you're right. I wonder why?"

"You took away all his responsibilities."

"Me?" Christopher asked, feigning shock. "How could I have possibly done that? I only took back mine."

"Yes, but I do believe you might have embarrassed him."

Christopher blinked down at her. Again, she held his gaze. "Theodore Parker doesn't embarrass. Believe me. We've all tried our hardest to make it happen at one time or other."

"Oh I do no' doubt that. He seems to be an imp of sorts, but...." Her expression softened, altering the loveliness of her face. "Mr. Christopher, did you not see his face? He likely thought you might no' trust he can do what you asked, which might have hurt."

Christopher halted to stare down at her, nonplussed. "You... You're serious?"

The soft smile didn't fade as she rested a hand on his arm. "I know you did no' mean to, as you do nothing mean or spiteful, but he was trying so hard to be gentlemanly and responsible—"

"I can't believe this," he protested. "Dix chastises me for sloughing you off onto Teddy and Paul—done for your own protection, I might add—and then you chastise me for taking you back from Teddy when you were disappointed that I had passed you off as his responsibility in the first place."

Sara laughed, her blue eyes crinkling at the corners.

"Christopher."

"So what do you want me to do then? Avoid you as I did before and get my ears chewed by Dix? Track down Teddy and hand you off again? Or... or what?" This time Sara lowered her gaze. He scrubbed at his scalp. "I'm sorry."

"I did no' mean to chastise."

He released another quick breath, guiding Sara's hand back to the nook of his arm. "Speaking the truth and being honest is never nagging. The people who need to hear it are the ones who have the tendency of labeling it such."

Sara made no response.

Christopher did his best to gauge the expression on her down-turned face, he couldn't label it. "Maybe I should have left you in Teddy's care. I seem to have ruined your evening."

"Oh no. I was but thinking." Her gaze lifted to his, her features relaxing into a smile. "He will likely complain I confessed, but he was off to find you soon anyway. Said that he had to talk to some sculptors who had come and did no' want to bore me with the conversation." She giggled. "You two are so silly."

Tension melted and he chuckled. "Yes, I guess we are."

"It is fun to watch," she admitted. "I never had brothers and sisters, and I feel as if you and your friends and family are as close as I'll ever come. It is a miracle of a blessing."

"Well, I'm glad you think so."

She wrinkled her nose at him, immediately widening her eyes as she began to comment on the different feel of the party. Christopher gave her hand a gentle squeeze.

"I'm going home, Chris," Teddy said, shrugging into his overcoat.

Christopher balanced another collection of dirtied glasses in his hands and looked up toward his friend. "Go ahead. I can finish cleaning up here. It's not as cluttered as I thought it would be."

Teddy nodded, still not meeting Christopher's eyes while he wrapped his plain gray scarf around his neck and pulled on his gloves. "I'll be a bit late tomorrow. Another meeting with a new sculptor interested in consigning some pieces."

An eyebrow twitched upward as Christopher regarded his friend's face. "Certainly." He motioned toward Teddy with a handful of glasses. "Let me know how it goes."

Teddy grunted and moved toward the exit.

Christopher stared after him, floored silent. Teddy had kept his distance most of the afternoon. Thinking it due to the sudden retrieval of Sara from Teddy's care, Christopher tried to apologize for any insult. His friend simply grunted an acceptance and again disappeared to a mysterious meeting with an unnamed sculptor, much as he did now.

Christopher set the glasses with a firm clink and rubbed at his forehead. The display of Sara's colored charcoals drew his attention. He smiled. Her habit of viewing life through rose-colored glasses began to change things for him. He could sense himself beginning to see and feel something beyond what his wife's death had left. A part of him began to see life as she did. How could he have known that a simple friendship would be the key to that?

He sighed and bent to retrieve a cloth napkin from the floor. When he straightened, his gaze was drawn once again to her art and the dreams and futures it held—He gasped, for at last he saw an image—the charcoal's translation from the whisper of fantasy to the heightened reality of oil.

TWENTY-TWO

Interpretations

24 February 1894

Noon the following day had nearly come before Teddy's familiar steps were heard in the main hall. Christopher scooped up a paint-soiled rag to wipe the oils from his hands as he made his way to the hall.

Their gazes met and Teddy halted, giving an uncomfortable clearing of his throat as he also scrubbed at the back of his neck. Then he wordlessly continued on as he slipped from his well-worn overcoat.

"Teddy," Christopher called. His friend halted. "Ted, what's going on?"

He shot Christopher a sidelong glance before continuing forward. "Nothing. Forget it."

Christopher followed. "Ted, I told you I didn't mean anything by taking over as Sara's escort last night. Dix gave me an earful, tha—"

"It's fine." Teddy attempted to continue on again.

Christopher took hold of his arm. "It isn't." He noticed a muscle twitch in Teddy's jaw and released his grip. "I wouldn't have asked you to be responsible for Sara if I didn't think you could be trusted. It's only—"

"I know." Teddy sent Christopher a sharp glare. "Dix chewed your ears. You said that. Last night twice. Now again. I get it."

"Then what's the problem? I've never seen you like this before."

Teddy momentarily clenched his teeth. "Don't worry about it. I just need to deal with something."

Christopher raised an eyebrow. "You certain?"

His friend's hand momentarily tightened its hold on the overcoat. Then he looked up to meet Christopher's gaze and smirked. "You know my sick need to win everything."

"Ted—"

"Chris," Teddy pressed. "I'm fine. Seriously." He motioned to Christopher. "Except that a certain collection of art isn't here."

"Teddy, I told you—"

"Don't give me excuses. You said you were considering it, and then you come out of your office with paint stains on your shirt and a paint-stained cloth in your hands? I bet if I were to go into your office right now I would find—gasp and shock—an oil painting either in the beginning stages or completed, depending on how much of an inspiration you received."

An eyebrow twitched.

"The itch has you, doesn't it?" Teddy pressed.

Christopher looked away.

"I was right," Teddy muttered. Then he gave Christopher

a slight shove, drawing his attention. "Don't question it, Top. Don't ask where it came from or why it's here or when it might go away again. Just go with it. It's been too long since you've seen something, and I've seen what that's been doing to you. Your life and passion are art, and not creating it was hell." He again gripped Christopher's arm. "Inspiration missed you, Top. Now that she's back, you better listen to her sweet whisper. I don't think you could survive another separation."

Christopher rubbed at the back of his neck. "No. I don't think I could."

Teddy grinned and gave Christopher another shove. "Welcome back."

"Thanks, Ted,"

"You're welcome. Now let me see it."

"It's not finished."

"I don't care. I want to see it anyway." Teddy headed toward Christopher's office. "Did Sara see it at her lesson this mor—Oh wait. You cancel those the day after."

Christopher wiped his hands. He wasn't sure he wanted to show her this one. After all, he hadn't asked permission. While he doubted her reaction would be altogether negative, he knew how protective artists could be of their inspirations.

"Holy Hannah!"

Christopher looked up. Teddy gaped at the canvas. "What?"

"This is one of Sara's sketches!"

"Yes," Christopher admitted slowly. "Why?"

"You never interpret other artists. You say it shows a lack of creativity... or was it originality? Oh who cares! You interpreted one of Sara's sketches!"

Christopher's ears burned. "Yes, I interpreted one of

Sara's sketches. I'm a hypocrite. So stone me to death.

"Are you kidding? When you do something like this?" Teddy stared at the oil canvas, partially complete as it was, and gave a slight shake of his head. "We could sell this for quite a sum, Top. You mark my words. Your innate talent for the vivid and Sara's intensity and innocence together? My. God."

Christopher smirked. "Don't embellish."

" 'Embellish'?" Teddy focused on Christopher, eyes wide. He motioned to the painting. "You create something like this and you tell me not to 'embellish'?"

Gaze drawn to the painting, Christopher's countenance relaxed as the entwining of styles grabbed his focus. The brilliance of the oils paired with the poetic intensity of the simple scene, a foreboding castle holding a promise of escape. Hope within the brightness of a single light.

"This is gold, Chris," Teddy said, voice quiet. "Gold, I tell you."

Christopher cleared his throat, his gaze instead shifting to the paint not wanting to transfer from hands to cloth. "I'm glad you approve."

Teddy gave a slight scoff. "Now who's being an ass?"

Christopher laughed. "I've as much right to it as you do. Stress has been higher than usual the past week or so."

"A truer statement I haven't heard—I've a dangerous idea. Why don't we close the gallery today and declare a mini-vacation? You could use the time to show Sara your art hidden away in the attic—while you're picking out the ones to display," he pressed meaningfully. "Besides, it might inspire her."

"Fine, fine. I'll get my art."

Teddy gestured to the main hall. "I have some things to

finish up here, so I'll lock up. You go ahead."

A smile twitched as Christopher shrugged into his overcoat and buttoned it up. Then he caught Teddy's gaze. "Why don't you come over for dinner this evening? We can talk more about which to display."

Teddy nodded. "Sure. Bring Dix and the whole party. Maybe they can persuade you and Sara to do a concurrent display in New York."

Christopher raised an eyebrow. "Hm. Not a bad idea."

Teddy laughed. "I do have a few, you know."

"Agreed. You do have your occasional uses."

Teddy laughed.

The front door opened and closed.

Sara looked up from her current tatting project, a surprise carnation boutonniere for Christopher. Gwyn continued with her picture-book of an adventure in Africa, but when a recognizable baritone voice called "Gwyn? Sara? Anyone home," both girls scurried for the front hallway.

Sara caught herself, slowing her step to allow the father/daughter their private greeting. She also gave herself the moment or two she needed to quiet the thump of her heart and a surprising full-body tingle when his baritone chuckle caressed her ears.

When Sara arrived at the observatory's doorway, Gwyn had settled onto her father's arm while doing her best to tell him all the things the two had brain-stormed that morning. This included an impromptu performance of a small section of the skit she and Sara created after breakfast.

Pirates and admirals were Gwyn's favorite character-type.

Christopher met Sara's gaze as she appeared in the doorway, offering her a 'hello' smile before returning his focus to his daughter. Sara tightened her clasped hands in front of her as she watched the pair.

Gwyn bestowed a kiss on his cheek once the confession of the day's adventures ended. "Why are you home early, Papa? Lunch?"

"Actually, no. Teddy offered the suggestion of a mini-vacation today." He momentarily met Sara's gaze. "Considering how exciting the past weeks have been, I thought it would be a good idea. Besides, it will give me more time to play with you and Sara."

Gwyn giggled and bestowed another kiss, giving him a moment to send Sara another slight smile. Sara flushed but couldn't look away.

"So, what's first on the agenda?"

Gwyn pulled back, her green eyes wide. "Oh Papa," she breathed. "Can we do a picture-book today? Please?"

"Of course, Gwyn. As I said, the day is yours. You've but to tell me what to draw."

Gwyn squealed, wriggling from his arms to drag him back to the observatory, chattering the entire time of the current project and what other images still needed to be done. He chuckled, eyes bright and twinkling as they met Sara's.

"I hope you don't mind," he said as Gwyn pulled him past.

Sara shook her head, smiling. The opportunity to watch him and his daughter together? No. She didn't mind at all. She made her way back to the wingback chair as Gwyn pulled her father down to the floor with her. He didn't protest nor object, making Sara all the more certain he had been in this type of situation before. He simply did his best to shed his overcoat, scarf, and suit-coat while sitting cross-legged across from his daughter.

The scene continued to draw Sara's attention as she took up a different project from her craft box, tucking the secretive boutonniere away from view. What especially drew her attention were the paint stains on his shirt.

She smiled and lowered her focus to the monogrammed sample in her hands. *Christopher is painting again, Lord.* The thought brought a sigh of happiness and relief. He had so missed that passion, and to have the Lord again giving him the visions of images and lovelies to re-create onto canvas.... *Thank you, Lord. Thank you so much.* She hoped it would be one of the next steps to the healing of his hurting soul.

Maybe an important one.

"Where have Dix and Paul got off to?" Christopher balanced a piece of paper onto the sketch-board and cast her a sidelong glance. "They don't abandon you often, do they?"

"They are off to tea some place. They asked if I cared to go, but I would rather stay with Gwyn."

Christopher sent her a longer glance. "But you accept invitations to teas and luncheons every once and a while?" Another glance.

Sara's smile vanished as she lowered her gaze to her needlework. "Um, no, I... I have no' felt... I...." His scrutiny flamed her cheeks. "I do no' feel ready yet, sir."

"I don't doubt it. After being on the serving side of the tray for so long, I'm certain it's a challenge to get yourself mentally ready for the opposite side."

Sara looked up, not prepared for his insightful

explanation, and not knowing how to offer any kind of appreciation at his understanding.

Christopher offered her a smile. “I had the same challenge when I opened the gallery,” he confessed. “I had been an artist for years, but a director and therefore a person responsible for starting or stopping a young artist’s career?” He gave a shudder. “No. I didn’t take to that at all.”

He focused again on his current picture-book page project assigned by Gwyn. “I wasn’t very sociable when the gallery first opened,” he admitted, absently sketching a scene of tall grasslands and a pride of lions. “Teddy and I sent invitations and ‘Grand Opening’ notices to those students, professors, and galleries we knew, even some of those we didn’t, but that was mostly all. Teddy, he has always been more comfortable in crowds than I, he accepted teas and luncheon dates and dinner parties and more. I always made the excuse of having an inspiration for a story-cycle of my art, which wasn’t necessarily a truth or a lie, only easier for him to believe.”

Offering Gwyn the finished sketch, he received his next assignment and set to work. Sara watched him, throat constricted around any words of thanks or understanding. She had never met someone who understood her like he did. When he didn’t, he did his best to try. Her gaze drifted to the monogram on the needlework sample.

“The only advice I can offer,” Christopher continued without looking up, “is that you should take it slowly while doing your best to actually take steps outside your comfort areas. For myself, with a push and shove from Teddy and later from Carla herself, I was able to get past the initial reluctance of interacting with people I didn’t know. Eventually, it became easier and even something I rather enjoy. So, be sure to come to myself or Dix and Paul if you need help, or even should you have a particularly negative feeling about some invitation. After all, we don't want you to do anything that might just be more of a reminder of those things you left behind."

He pointed out to Gwyn something of benefit to another sketch, not noticing Sara's expressions as she watched him.

"And if anyone, and I do mean anyone," he continued, "treats you with disrespect or with even a hint of condescension, you're to tell Dix and me immediately. There's no reason for you to be bullied and whatnot simply because your history is different. I doubt you'll meet anyone who will give you problems, but I thought I should mention it just the same."

Sara nodded while voicing a surprisingly clear, "I appreciate it," while daubing the warm wetness from her cheeks.

Christopher glanced toward her then, catching the motion and her expression. His smile vanished. "Sara? Are you well?"

She offered him a genuine smile. "Fine." Though this time her voice trembled.

"I didn't mean to upset you."

Gwyn looked up from her sketches at that comment, peeking at Sara with a wide-eyed expression. She giggled. "Oh. Those are happy tears, Papa. Don't you know the difference?"

Christopher's lips twitched. "Apparently not. I'll take better care next time, Gwyn."

Gwyn giggled again. "You so silly, Papa."

He chuckled, watching his daughter continue her artistry before returning his focus to Sara. His expression almost seemed to beg the question of before.

Sara offered a smile before lowering her gaze to the needlework sample. She could still feel his gaze as she worked on perfecting the design on the bit of material, but she didn't mind. Her cheeks burned, but she didn't mind that either. Then he released a breath and focused again on Gwyn and the project, allowing Sara a collection of peeks and glances to watch his own expressions and smiles.

"Speaking of being silly…" Christopher held up his sketch, hazel eyes twinkling with impish mischief as he focused on his daughter. "I don't think I portrayed the elephant very well at all. What do you think, Gwyn?"

His daughter looked up from her struggle with a giraffe and sounded a bright giggle. "It looks like a hippopapomus!"

"Yes. I suppose it does. Maybe we'll call it a hippophant?"

Sara laughed.

Christopher cast Sara a wink before directing his focus to Gwyn and the sketch, the girl enthralled with designing the perfect description. Sara rested her chin into her hand as she watched.

"Gwyn, sweetness," Christopher protested, "I can't fit all that on the page. You won't see the 'hippophant' for the explanation."

"But I want for everyone to know what it is."

"I understand that, but how will they know if they can't see it?"

Sara motioned to the paper. "Why do you no' put the 'how come' on a bit of colored paper and paste it on the back, explanation faced outward?"

Gwyn blinked at Sara a moment before squealing and clapping her hands, jumping to her feet and dashing away in search of the paper.

Christopher chuckled and set aside the image. To Sara's mild surprise, he didn't move to a chair. He simply leaned back onto his hands as he looked over at her, not even stretching his legs out in front of him. The position of ease melted the years from his features.

"There will be a dinner party this evening at Lake Manor," he offered. A smile twinkled in his hazel eyes. "I don't suppose you would be interested in attending?"

Sara's eyes brightened. "Oh could I?"

"Most definitely. All three of you are invited, and if you could come before Gwyn's bed-time, I'm certain she would appreciate it."

"Of course. I will tell your sister and Mr. Paul when they return."

"Actually..." He motioned toward Sara. "You could just come home with us, bring Amy of course, and leave a note here with Gregory for Dix and Paul and have them follow you afterward. Would that be acceptable?"

Sara nodded, eagerness warming her cheeks and setting her heart to thump nearly from her chest.

"Wonderful." Christopher adjusted his position. "Oh, and you'll want to know Teddy and I 'had it out' when he finally arrived." He hesitated. "Well, I attempted to have it out. He didn't offer much by way of explanation, though. Said something I didn't really understand, assured me it wasn't my fault, and then deftly changed the subject. Making me swear to have you and me put together a collection of my art from which to choose a display, in fact."

"So... so he was no' angry for last night?"

Christopher lifted his shoulders. "He says he isn't, so I suppose we should take him at his word. If he is, it's his own fault for not letting us know so that we could solve the issue." He smiled. "But don't worry about it. Ted's one of those who tells you to your face there's a problem. That's why I was surprised he wouldn't talk."

Her expression relaxed. "I am glad. I would hate to be the cause of a falling out."

"Come now, Sara. Be honest. Two men vying for your attention isn't a little thrilling?"

Cheeks flushed and nose wrinkled, she giggled.

"That's what I thought. Speaking of men and your attention, you should invite Mr. Conklin for tea. I know Dix and Paul would love the chance to show you off."

"Would you like me to invite you when he's here?"

Christopher smirked. "I'm sure you'll be safe, Sara."

"Oh, no, I do no' want to say anything out of turn if he were to ask about my sketches once I tell him I am the artist. You are my sponsor."

"I appreciate it, but they are your sketches. You can tell him anything you like. You don't need my permission for anything said or done with them."

"I know," she confessed, surprised she hadn't let the subject drop. Astonished she continued to hold his gaze. Bewildered by how much she enjoyed the conversation. "I would feel better if you were there because... because you said you wanted them. I do no' want to promise them to someone else without meaning to. I know I am a fraidy-cat sometimes. I might do it."

Christopher blinked at her. "You... you're thinking of giving me your sketches?"

"I did once. I only will no' take them back again. You can do whatever you wish with them. Oh." She retrieved her old leather portfolio and handed it to him. He accepted it with an air of deliberation and awe. "I wanted to give you these, too. They're the sketches I had no' given you yet. The ones telling a better story of my trip here from England."

He hesitated a moment before opening it. Sara watched his expression as he sifted through the sketches, not able to tell what he felt or thought about them. Then he carefully placed the pictures back into the portfolio, tying it closed before lifting his gaze to meet hers.

"Thank you, Sara. Thank you very much." He gave a slight shake of his head and handed the portfolio back. "But I can't accept them."

She blinked down at the offered portfolio, her hands clasped in her lap. "Wh-why not?"

"This artwork is your opportunity for greater things."

"But I want to give them to you," she pressed, a panic and desperation to have him understand making her voice tight. Sara shook her head. "I have nothing else to give to repay what you and your sister have done for me." She pushed the portfolio back toward him. "Please. This is all I have."

"And that's why I can't take them." He reached out to take her hand and gently but firmly place the portfolio within her grasp. "Accepting this wouldn't be right, Sara. I would be taking away any chance for you to become financially independent, and I don't want you to feel beholden to me or my gallery."

"B-but—" She blinked back the tears as she again tried to push the portfolio back. He didn't release his hold of her hand or its hold of the folder. "B-but, Mr. Christopher, please. It... it is what I wish to do with them."

Christopher released a deep breath, his gaze drawn again to the portfolio and her white-knuckled grasp under his hand. Then he slightly nodded while giving her hand a gentle squeeze. "Fair enough." He met her eyes. "But no more gifts. These are more than enough to repay me for doing what I've felt it my duty to do. The rest are for your future. Understood?"

Sara wordlessly nodded, doing her best to wipe tears from her cheeks and blink others from her eyes as she lowered her gaze. She had resolved herself to let him refuse, so her press for his acceptance of the gift dropped her spirit into a haze of confusion. After such wonderful blessings at his hand, he never asked for anything in return. No innuendo. No stolen caresses.

At his continued regard, she forced a smile and set the memories away, trying hard to live in the new moment and the promise of tomorrow.

TWENTY-THREE

Sweet Sighs

"It seems Gwyn has tumbled into distraction. Perhaps it's best." Christopher set the collection of sketches aside. "I don't know if I can... I don't think I want her there when I unpack my art. Not yet."

Sara could only watch his dark expression, her heart thudding a prayer heavenward for peace and wisdom.

Finally, he met her gaze. "I'll leave a note for Gregory as to where we've gone, but, Sara, if we don't do it now, I'm afraid I won't have the courage to try again. There are a lot of memories in those crates, and Gwyn.... She won't understand."

Sara gave a slight shake of her head, immediately followed by a nod. "I will help however I can."

A small smile lightened his features, and he reached forward to give her a hand a brief squeeze. "Thank you." Then he stood to his feet, hand still covering hers, and offered her the portfolio. "I'll speak with Gregory. Will you meet me by the front door? I believe I need to walk."

Sara nodded, mute as she accepted the portfolio from him. Once he left the room, Sara lowered her gaze, thoughts jumbled as she set the portfolio aside and forced herself toward the entry hall. *Please give me the words to say to help him.* But as she slipped into her heavy wool coat and gloves, her mind continued to be strangely silent. Hesitation even began to soar, and her head to pound.

Then she heard his quiet step in the hall and released a soft and long breath, offering up all the fears and uncertainties before lifting her gaze from her gloves and meeting his.

Hazel eyes as dark as before, he asked "Ready?" in a reserved tone that lifted the hairs on the nape of her neck.

Sara mutely nodded, preceding him through the door and then waiting for him on the top step. The two didn't speak as they made their way to Lake Manor. She used the time to pray for guidance and wisdom regarding the upcoming, and more personal unveiling. Remembering her own duty of finally unpacking her mom's crafts, Sara had a hint at what pains were waiting, but she knew facing it would be the best way to step beyond.

When the two finally arrived at Lake Manor, Christopher's features congealed into a mask of dread. But as he helped her out of her coat and gloves, he continued to offer her a somewhat forced smile that did nothing to hide his growing struggle. Once more Sara felt no press to offer anything but a small smile of her own while lifting more prayers for his peace.

On the third floor, Sara scrutinized Christopher's expressions while unpacking the crates of canvases, frames, and portfolios. She continued to pray through the entire duty. For wisdom, for him to have peace, for the right words to say.... After a time, Christopher seemed less troubled. He also began talking more, about the histories of some of the art—though they were yet uncovered—or a funny anecdote connected with the painting of one.

Finally, the crates were unpacked and set aside and Sara and Christopher stood side by side looking at the covered canvases, hesitancy looming in the dusty air. Somehow Sara could tell he didn't want to uncover them. It was as if he were afraid to see a happy collection of memories while thirsting for it at the same time.

Sara faced him, resting a hand on his arm. "I will uncover the first one."

Christopher said nothing, dark hazel eyes still intensely focused on the covered canvases. When she turned to step toward the canvases, a sudden and gentle clasp on her upper arm stopped her. She turned.

His focus remained on the covered canvases. "Wait."

So she clasped her hands in front of her. Praying. Waiting. Not knowing what to say or do other than what he requested of her.

Then Christopher's hand released her arm and lightly touched her back, drawing her focus. He nodded, still not looking at her, and whispered, "Go ahead."

Sara stepped forward, kneeling in front of the first available canvas and cautiously reaching out for the cover hiding its face from view. *Dear Lord....* She lifted the cover to reveal an oil of a massive building. "Oh my," she breathed moments before sending a bright smile over her shoulder to Christopher. "Richmond College?" She stood, hearing his hesitant approach. "What a grand building it is."

His lips relaxed into a smile as he took the painting

from her. "Yes. It definitely is that."

Sara watched him a moment more before focusing on the other covered canvases. *Lord, please show me which to choose.* A smaller canvas captured her attention, so she lifted it carefully up and pulled back the cover. Tears sprung to the surface at the sketched image of young mother and newborn baby resting comfortably within a rocking chair near a window.

"Oh how lovely." Sara turned and moved toward Christopher. "Is this Carla and Gwyn?"

He set aside Richmond College and accepted the pencil sketch, expression softening to a pained remembrance. "Yes."

"She is beautiful."

"Yes, she was."

Sara watched his reaction to the image and lifted a prayer. While it was the first time she had seen more of a softening to his face than a shock and twist of agony, there was still a presence of intense grief. *Please, Lord.*

"I remember when I sketched this one." He brushed dust from the frame. "The sun on her hair and the smile on her face. I had never seen her so beautiful as that day. Holding our Gwyn. Our dreams of family fulfilled." Christopher gave a slight twitch, his hand tightening on the frame moments before he set it aside.

When he continued to stare down at it, Sara's heart ached. "M-Mr. Christopher?"

Clearing his throat, he fisted his hands. "I—" He twitched again, even giving his head a slight shake. "Sara, I... I can't do more," he confessed in a gruff voice.

"That's fine, Mr. Christopher, and we've yet to get ourselves ready for the dinner party."

Nodding, Christopher touched her elbow as he gestured toward the stairs, walking along beside her in silence. He then preceded her while holding one hand to steady her down each narrow stair. "Watch your step. This board is loose. There you are." And each comment sounded distant and distracted. As if his attention still focused on an image of family somehow lost. One he regretted.

Lord, give him peace from the loss. Please. He tries so hard to step past it, but... it's so hard for him.

They passed through the narrow door just as Harold crested the stairs.

"Harold. I forgot to mention to Em we're having a small dinner party this evening. Can you let her know and get everything started?"

"Certainly, Mr. Christopher." And he turned to descend the stairs again.

Christopher motioned Sara forward, her eyes intercepting his sidelong glance. "While I could only unveil two, it was easier than I thought it would be," he admitted. "Thank you for offering your help. I appreciate the care."

She forced a smile.

He again offered her a steadying hand as they descended the stairs to the main floor. Then he helped her into her coat and offered forward her scarf and gloves while quietly asking if she minded walking. Sara shook her head. So, once he shrugged into his own overcoat, he opened the door and escorted her out and down to the sidewalk.

Tucking his hands into the pockets of his coat, he breathed in deeply of the late-afternoon air and released it slowly. Sara watched his profile as he did so, noticing that even though the lines didn't seem as haggard as before, there was still the tautness of sorrow. But the realization it wasn't as great eased her heart more than anything else could have, and she found herself sighing as she moved her gaze to an absent examination of the sidewalk.

"Teddy will want to discuss which to show." He looked over at her, holding her gaze. "I doubt he will let me get away with only two pieces, and if I put this off for another day, Ted will hang me by my thumbs."

"At least you made an act of good faith. I do no' believe he would be too upset if you were to wait until after my revelation."

A slight twitch of Christopher's lips caused Sara to release another breath of relief. "Ah. You don't want to share the attention?"

"Oh no. I only thought it would be so much better if you were able to have the evening to yourself." She offered a small smile. "It's been such a dreadfully long time since you had that."

"And I don't need it again," he said. "I'd much rather share, if it's all the same with you."

"But your fans!" Sara protested, eyes wide. "Do you no' want the attention?"

"Hundreds of people 'ooh'ing and 'ahh'ing when they don't truly understand the symbolism?" Christopher scoffed, albeit with a surprising hint of playfulness. "No, thank you. Besides, all those people milling about wanting to offer congratulations and suggestions and handshakes and conversations...." He shuddered and sent Sara a minute wink. "I'll pass."

Sara laughed. "Do no' be ridiculous, Christopher," she said, cheeks burning at the ease with which she said his name the same moment she scolded herself for it. "You've a talent."

"A talent to paint, yes. A talent to entertain, no. At least not when the focus will be *moi*. I would rather watch someone else gather the praise."

"Oh. You would rather my face redden than yours," Sara offered innocently.

"Something like that, though I'll deny it."

"But it's such a happy occasion. Your art has no' been seen for such a time. It should be a celebration to itself, not shared with me. I have gathered enough attention and praise the past weeks."

Surprisingly, Christopher moved his gaze to a scrutiny of the sidewalk, his hands shoved a bit deeper into his pockets. Sara watched him, smile softening at his expression of embarrassment and uncertainty.

"Yes, well, it's been too long since I've had the focus. I don't think I'm up to it. All the compliments and the well-intentioned criticisms...." He bent to retrieve a pebble and gave it a somewhat furious chuck down the walk. "I never was one to accept anything gracefully. Things said on my art are a little too... personal."

"Oh how I understand that."

The smile returned. "Yes. I guess you do." He sent her a sidelong glance. "I'm still amazed you let me push you into that first display."

"I amazed myself with that bit of courage," she confessed.

"Did you actually trust me that much? Even then?"

"I... I wanted to trust someone." She peeked at him, meeting his thoughtful scrutiny. "I did no' have such in so long I suppose... I suppose I missed it."

"But your art? It's such an intense aspect of your persona, Sara. What a terrifying thing to open to strangers, and yet you let me push you into it when you barely knew who I was. Even still you barely know me, yet you allow me to reveal you to who knows how many people."

"But I love people! I was only too much the fraidy-cat to look up and see them before. Since coming here, I have a different way of looking at who I am and what I can offer." She motioned toward him. "You are such a gentleman, and your daughter a sweet bit of heaven, your sister one I never had, Mister Paul and Mister Teddy a way to have me laugh at myself and others, your friends so accepting and encouraging.... I feel safe."

Christopher watched her for a long moment before again focusing ahead, adjusting his hands within his pockets. "I would have said the same about you."

Her eyes widened. "Me, sir?"

The replying nod seemed almost absent-minded. "I've always felt comfortable around you.... Like Carla."

Sara lowered her gaze, worrying her lower lip as she blinked a hint of wetness from her eyes.

He touched her elbow with a kerchief, drawing her gaze back again. "I'm sorry."

"Whatever for, sir?"

"For talking of things that are better left alone. It only upsets you."

"You need no' apologize. I am only upset because I canno' do much more than listen. I know as how that's seldom enough when the pain pushes at a person's heart."

"Truth be told," he confessed in a low voice, "I don't know how to... to talk about it. Since her passing everyone has always kept clear of even mentioning her name. Myself included." He shook his head. "I don't know how to grieve her, Sara."

She watched his profile, how his jaw clenched as he continued to stare at the sidewalk beneath their feet. He didn't seem to understand he already began the journey.

Christopher released a deep breath. "Does it never end?"

Lord. "It is a daily struggle, sir. Some days harder than others." Sara's blue eyes darkened as she watched the twist of the haunting return to his expression. "The difficult part is past; the first, long step beyond the grieving. But we always miss them."

"Always?" He focused on her. "Sara, I am tired. Of missing her. Of remembering a favorite place and seeing her. Or smelling a favorite cologne and remembering how she looked when she gave it to me. Or wearing a favorite suit and remembering a party that went with it.... I guess the ache is less than before, but... I am tired beyond bearing."

The quiet intensity weighed down her lips. "I know, sir."

"I knew ignoring the past would be one of the problems later, but... I just couldn't face it. Not then, and maybe not even now."

"But you canno' move ahead if you live behind." When he didn't answer, Sara halted him with a gentle pull to his arm. "If you keep remembering the death instead of the life, your Carla will no' live. She will only have died."

He cringed. Sara's throat tightened as she held his gaze and offered up a silent prayer for his aching heart that so often seemed to drown with the grief.

Finally, he lowered his gaze before whispering, "I know."

"So do no' keep that image. Let God take that, too. You keep her smile. You keep her laugh. You keep the sweetness that was her life with you and Gwyn. Do no' keep the death."

"I don't know how to let go of that one moment, Sara. It's always right there." He met her gaze. "It's burned into my mind."

"I know, but because you will no' let God take it. You think He put it there, so you think He will no' take it back again. Christopher, do no' choose to keep it there," she instructed, caressing his temple with a single finger. "Keep your age of memories and leave that one to a corner. When it comes, push it away. You know she passed on, and missing her is the only hurt you should face."

He swallowed hard and looked away, reaching to give her hand a tight and lengthy pressure. "I will."

Sara watched his almost gaunt expression before tucking her hand into the nook of his arm and guiding him slowly forward. "Only do no' try by yourself. Your friends want to lighten the burden. They but wait for you to ask, 'Can you help?' "

A moment of silence preceded Christopher's sidelong scrutiny of her profile. Then she heard his whispered, "Can you help?"

Sara's lips curved upward, and she gave his arm a press. "Yes, sir."

TWENTY-FOUR

Fact and Fiction

Teddy slammed a newspaper onto Christopher's desk. "You said something about suing to acquire ownership?"

Dread settled in the pit of Christopher's stomach as he snatched up the paper.

> Clamoring for the identity of art sensation S. A. L. has revealed nothing, and Mr. Christopher Lake of the 'Richmond Gallery of Art' is less than willing to grant interviews that deal specifically with their identity. No known date has been given as to when we might expect a revelation, a granting of an interview, or even a moment to offer congratulations.
>
> In addition, reliable sources have observed a lady matching Miss Ann Kreyssler's description leaving the Donovan's residence on a fairly regular basis and taken to Lake Manor via carriage. Visits there begin early in the morning and sometimes span through lunch until dinner. Mr. Lake is also seen to arrive at the Donovan home on regular occasions, with and without his young daughter, Gwyneth Marie Lake.
>
> These facts, again, present very specific questions: 1) Is art sensation S. A. L. and Miss Ann Kreyssler one and

> the same? 2) Will Mr. Christopher Lake soon be taking on a new bride and mother for he and his daughter, thereby giving Lake Manor an intriguing air of English sophistication for hostess?
>
> When attempting to contact Mr. Lake regarding these questions, this reporter is put off with claims of 'no comment.' Mr. Lake's refusal to grant interviews to this reporter begs another question: Is matrimony to the lovely Miss Ann Kreyssler not a viable option?

Rage burned from neck to hairline. "Not once did they mention the propriety of a chaperone—"

A timid knock interrupted any further tirade. Christopher and Teddy's attentions snapped to the door.

"Gads! She wouldn't...." Teddy hissed. "Sara wouldn't have been able to read that trash, would she?"

"Paul cancelled his *Chronicle* subscription."

"Maybe *Harper's* posted a reply? Haven't they before about a slanderous article on one of their sponsors? Maybe someone phoned for comment?"

"Oh my God."

The knock sounded again, followed by a timid "M-Mr. Christopher?"

"Sara," they whispered in unison.

"What am I to do?" Christopher skirted his desk, shuffling his feet to the door. "Just a moment, Sara," he called.

"How should I know? I'm the one with the big mouth." Teddy's silver eyes clouded, conflicted.

"Don't mention the article." He gestured to the folded newspaper on his desk. "Get rid of that."

Teddy plunked it into a nearby wastebasket. "Now what?"

"Act... nonchalant." Christopher opened the door to offer

Sara a smile—it vanished. Her sapphire eyes glimmered, pale face streaked with tears. Her hands trembled while holding an edition of *Harper's Weekly*. He released a quick breath and accepted the paper. "I know. I read it. Come in, my dear." He clasped her hand to give it a gentle squeeze, her fingers reddened from cold.

"It's not f-fair." Her voice broke.

Christopher guided her to a chair across from his desk. Teddy retreated, mumbling something about actions against reporters as Christopher sat beside her. He gathered up her trembling hands while struggling against the chill of helplessness.

"M-Mr. Christopher, I-I did no' mean for...." Any remaining words were strangled by a sob. She shook her head, gaze never rising from their clasped hands.

"Of course you didn't. Reports like this are expected." *Blast it.* "It will pass. Trust me."

"But if I go to the next reception they will print more of the same," she choked out. "Now we canno' even celebrate your birthday, and your party was to be such a grand affair. A surprise." She shook her head again. "It's not fair. Not fair!"

Christopher rubbed at her icy fingers. "Sara, it's fine."

"No, it is no' fine," she cried. "You were but trying to help, and me to be someone other than what I was—Now they print things that are no' so and make you...." Sara lowered her head, and her shoulders quivered.

Rage broiled anew. "This is my fault. If I hadn't pressured you into displaying your art, you would have been ready to have your name displayed—"

She lifted her eyes, her lower lip trembled. "It's no' your fault, Christopher. It's them. They that printed those half-truths and twisted tellings just so they could sell a few more papers to line their pockets! After all the good you done, they do this! It's no' right. They should be ashamed—of—themselves—" Sobs robbed the remaining words, and she tugged her hands free to cover her face.

"Sara." Christopher brought a hand up to rub her back. His fingers and palm tingled. "Sara, people in my position are under constant scrutiny. People shouldn't pry into the personal lives of others, it's true, but unfortunately it's seen as a necessary evil. Of course Teddy and I will complain to the editor, but in the end it's about what our friends and family know is true rather than what a paper reports."

Sara met his gaze. "But you are an example to others. Young artists. New artists. Authors and poets. Girls like Amy and me. Children like Gwyn. You must no' let them say such things about you, Christopher. It's no' right. God wants you to be an example of all the good and honorable things. So people know they can help others, just as you do. If a newspaper says you do it to—" She shook her head, brows furrowed.

"You are better than what they say you are. You took people in when you did no' have any need to do it. You gave me a chance to make something of myself; something no one else ever took time to do!"

Her chin tilted upward, eyes flashing. Christopher stared, his breath trapped in his chest and battered by a hammering heart.

"I will no' have them say such dreadful things. If they want an interview, I will tell them what I think of them, spouting nonsense like a horde of mewling babes to try and have their way. They should be ashamed of themselves!"

Then Sara set her jaw, the determination filling the

melody of her tone and sparkling in the depth of her eyes. The passion glowed upon her face, the flush of warmth in her cheeks and her parted lips crashing over him with a desire to take her face in his hands and—Christopher wrenched his hands free and stood, stumbling back before realization dawned.

Color drained from her face. She bolted, her path to the door keeping the chairs between them. "I... I'll go," she choked out.

"Oh God. Sara—" Christopher stepped after her, hand extended as she opened the door and rushed out. "Sara, wait."

Her step faltered but didn't stop. Instead, she picked up the front of her skirts and ran.

"Sara!" Christopher scrambled after her. "Sara, stop!" He collided with Teddy exiting from a side-room and Sara made good her escape. Christopher arrived at the front steps of the gallery as the carriage lumbered away.

"Was Sara crying? What did you do?" Teddy demanded.

Christopher turned back, scrubbing at his scalp. "I... I didn't," he mumbled, nonplussed. But there was no arguing with the dejection that marred the fervor. He grabbed up his hat, squashing it onto his head before wrestling into his overcoat.

Teddy turned from his perplexed examination of the retreating carriage. "Where are you going?"

"Are you daft? I'm going to talk to her."

"What the devil happened?"

"Don't ask." He buttoned up his coat as he hurried down the walk toward the Donovan's townhouse.

Sara dried another wave of tears from her face as she stared down at the men's leather gloves in her trembling clasp. She had finished the embroidered monogram of C.A.L. before reading the article in *Harper's*—

A tap sounded.

Sara flinched. "Y-Yes? Who is it?" She swiped any remaining wetness from her cheeks.

"It's Dix, love. May I come in?"

Sara stood, setting the gloves aside. "Y-yes."

Dix entered, closing the door gingerly behind her. "Chris is downstairs. He wants to speak with you."

Sara could feel the tears begin to burn again. "I... I canno', mum."

"Why? What happened?"

"N-nothing happened, mum," she whispered.

"Then why are you so upset?" Dix pressed. "Why haven't you come from your room since flying back from the gallery? Why are you pale as a ghost?" Sara shook her head. The older woman sighed. "Sara love, you need to go downstairs and talk with him. If you're angry with him, he should know why."

"Angry?" Sara choked out as she lifted her gaze. "Angry, mum? I could no' be angry with him. He's done more than what I ever expected him to do for me. Giving me more than a place to stay. More than a new start. More than... more than anyone. I'm only...." Her lips trembled downward as she shook her head. "I'm only sorry I canno' do more than what I have. I canno' give him back the wife he loves. I canno' give him the year he's lost without her." Sara covered her face and wept.

Dix pulled Sara close. "I know, dearest," she soothed. "I know."

Christopher pitched his hat onto the nearest chair within the observatory and dropped onto the seat edge—he stood when Dix entered. "Well?"

"She'll be down in a minute or two."

Relief flooded over him. He scrubbed a hand through his hair.

Dix calmly sat. "Chris, what happened?"

"An unexpected reaction." He swiped up his hat and flopped into the chair.

"Hers?"

"Mine."

"To what?"

"To her."

"Christopher...." She pressed her lips into a thin line, her brows furrowing. "I'm responsible for the girl, and I cannot help her when I cannot understand the problem. Now, forego the vague answers and tell me—"

"I wanted to kiss her." Christopher's face and ears flamed.

"You what?"

"I was trying to comfort her about the blasted article in the *Chronicle* while enjoying her spark of temper and I wanted to kiss her!" He stalked to the fireplace. "Do you need a blasted demonstration?"

"If you don't stop snarling at me, I'll toss you out on your ear."

Christopher gripped the mantle, white-knuckled.

"What do you plan on telling her?"

"I don't know."

"Why don't you tell her the truth?"

He scowled at her. "Oh, yes. Let me tell her I wanted to ravage her there on the spot, immediately chasing her to the nearest man safer than her sponsor. Yes, let's do that."

"Oh dear Lord, Chris. Cease the dramatics." Dix stood beside him, her expression candid. "You are a man living without the comfort and caress of a woman longer than any widowed man should. I've admired your control these last several months. Now you've met a woman whom you treat as a friend. Considering Sara's history, her reaction proves that in the past she was trained to believe fond treatment on her part was viewed as... repulsive."

"Blast it—What must I do to prove her friendship is more a comfort than pain?"

"Tell her the truth. You aren't the first man to have those thoughts, Chris. Or do you forget her reasons for escaping Mr. Brockle?" Dix gripped his arm, her gaze unyielding. "Mark my words, she will be honored you kept yourself from giving into the temptation. That shows just how much you respect her."

"And risk her no longer trusting me?" Christopher slumped into the chair, head in his hands.

"It's your decision." She left the room.

Christopher heard her offer Sara a quiet phrase of encouragement on her way upstairs.

He stood. Sara entered slowly, her face pale and eyes refusing to meet his. The scent of lilacs tickled his senses as he stepped forward to meet her. "Sara, I... I don't know what to say."

"There's no need, sir. I was forward."

The tone of the 'sir' was aloof, reserved. He reached for her hand, but she shrunk from his touch. *Blast it.* "Sara, you were not forward."

"I took a liberty I should no' have taken." This time she glanced toward him. Hurt glistened in their cobalt depths. "It will no' happen again."

"Sara, you're a friend, a close friend, and as such you have the right to—"

"But you pulled away!" Her lower lip trembled. "I... I am sorry, sir."

He steeled himself against the flinch. "Yes, I did pull away." This time he pulled her hands from their tight grip of her skirt. "But because I didn't want to act inappropriately toward you."

"Y-You never do. You are a gentleman." Tears blossomed to mild sobs.

A multitude of emotions crashed as Christopher gathered her into a comforting embrace. The action welcomed a diverse collection of memories. Those images of embraces and tears, and softness of curves—*A friend. A friend,* he repeated. A friend who treated his daughter as if she were her very own. A friend who shared a passion for art—Christopher cut off the thoughts and pushed back from Sara with a gentle nudge. She kept her gaze down. He tucked a kerchief into her hand and watched with rapt attention as she dried the tears. "Sara, I need to confess something."

She peered at him through glistening lashes. "C-confess?"

He averted his gaze. The intensity of the desire for intimacy utterly floored him. Especially in conjunction with the possibility that such a confession would rob him of what he so desperately craved, her friendship. If he confessed to the needs developing for the first time in a year, would she still trust him? If he confessed her friendship made him remember what he lost, would she offer her comfort so freely?

Yet if he recoiled again, would she accept his apology a second time?

He drew a ragged breath. "My recoil was an extreme reaction to an unexpected desire. Acting on it would have caused you to no longer trust me."

She didn't look away, to his surprise. "What?"

He offered her a slightly more certain smile. "You're a beautiful woman, Sara," and his face blazed at the admittance, "and when you offer such understanding, compassion, friendship.... It propelled me to a place beyond the numbness, fighting back a desire for... a kiss."

This time Sara's eyes lowered, and she nervously smoothed her skirts. Christopher couldn't keep from watching her, almost desperate to see if she took offense, or if it caused her fear. She escaped from a history of masters and employees whom took advantage of her sensitive nature. He didn't wish her to perceive the same from him.

"I was married for six years," he explained, "and engaged for nine months before that. Those experiences give rise to instantaneous... surrender, I suppose, to the desire to kiss, or touch, or some other action reserved for a fiancée or wife. That is the only cause for my recoil, Sara. Your trust is precious." Indeed, theirs was a type of friendship he missed. One he would tenaciously protect. "Forgiven?"

Sara lifted her gaze, her blue eyes no longer pained, nor confused and hesitant. She smiled and seemed... at ease. "Forgiven," she said.

Relief softened the growing lump of his stomach. "I don't fault you your conclusions, Sara. What else were you to expect, considering your history?"

"You have been a gentleman, sir. It was wrong of me to suppose otherwise."

Christopher gave her hands a succession of gentle pressures. "It is that standing I want to preserve most."

"How...." She bit her lip and tightened her clasp of his hands. "Mr. Christopher, how may I help?"

"With what, my dear?"

Her cheeks flushed, but she didn't look away. "With your struggle. When I was in England, I but did my best to avoid the master.... I-I could no' come for art lessons but maybe twice a week?"

His insides recoiled against the separation. "I would hate to slow your progress."

"I... I will practice more on my own. If you send Gwyn, she could help. She's a natural teacher." Sara lowered her gaze. "She takes after you."

Christopher clenched his jaw, his muscles tensing as he fought what he knew to be the right thing. After the article. The growing suppositions.... "You're right." He dropped his hands from her arms and rubbed them upon his trousers. The thought of losing the time to share his enjoyment of creation chilled him to the core. *Blast it.*

"Perhaps... you could use the time for more painting?" Those blue eyes peeked at him.

He inclined his head, reluctant. She seemed the key to the desire to struggle through the blankness to inspiration, and now he would need to suffer alone? He forced a smile. Sara's return served as an encouragement he came to expect from her. An offering his aching spirit hungrily accepted. Something that made him cautiously step past a wall of his own making.

Christopher's smile faded, and he saw the reaction to

her expression: Concern. "I better get back to the gallery," he said in a low voice. The tug-of-war with the decision to leave or stay continued, building as he watched the tumult of emotions in her eyes. He gulped down an urge. "I need to talk to Teddy about that letter to send to the *Chronicle's* editor."

Though he wanted to talk more about his wife and the grief which nearly swept him asunder. About the hope he began to sense in the distance. About the deeper insight to his rage against God, and why He kept pushing to be closer. Any release to the confusion would have been a Godsend, and she so eagerly presented tidbits from her own experiences.

But a man talking to a woman about such things was too intimate; not appropriate for friendship. If society had known how intimately their discussions had grown... but she was the first to understand.

Sara's hand gave his a gentle squeeze. Then she deftly wrapped her arm around his and guided him to the front hall Christopher seemed trapped within a bubble of staggered thoughts as he stared down at her, remembering so many other occurrences of a lady taking similar soft actions of care. To have it again—to feel anything at all—was a whisper of freshness.

Sara buttoned his still-worn overcoat and straightened the lapels. She met and held his gaze as she handed him his scarf and gloves from the side-table. Then she smiled and presented him his hat. Christopher took it with an absent motion, fingering the lip as he held her sapphire gaze while remembering a green one and feeling it begin to fade along with the ache.

"Thank you," he whispered.

Sara's blue eyes sang with her smile, even through her continued silence. Then she guided him to the opened door, where Christopher paused. She didn't expect anything in return. Nothing. Ever. Instead, she always gave. And offered. And supported. And forgave—

The desire to embrace her rose as a drowning wave, pushing him beneath images and memories of similar intimacies. He gulped it down, noticing how her smile faded with his struggle. Who else other than Carla was so sensitive to his tortures. He had been right to confess. How else would she understand that these desires were a welcome return of feeling?

Sara gave his arm a gentle pressure. "I will pray for you, sir," she whispered.

Christopher nodded, giving her hand a squeeze. Then he squashed his hat onto his head and forced himself to turn and walk away. He swallowed hard, and again, and still again as the chill wind buffeted his face and eyes. But the yearning to feel, again, the softness of a woman in his arms— Christopher groaned and shook his head, but the image was ablaze in his mind.

He flung a glare heavenward. "I can't do this. I had You before, giving me strength to resist Carla's innocent charm. Sara deserves the same respect." His step faltered. "Yes, I'm asking for Your help, begrudgingly. Take it how You want—"

A sharp feeling of reproach drew him up.

Talking to God as if He were an annoying acquaintance felt odd for Christopher. Previously, his prayer time with the Lord was intense and quiet. A time of reading the Bible searching for clues and hints at how he could use it to inspire and change his own life. Listening for the whisper of

God to reveal something within or without that was either worthy of notice or change. But death changed things of his character... and then there was Sara.

"I'm sorry. Being an ass isn't the way to acquire Your help, is it? I'm still angry at You for letting her die. For taking my son. For taking my art when it would have been the one thing to help me through it." He scrubbed at his scalp. "Sara says I'm looking at it wrong. Perhaps I am. Regardless, I am arrogantly offering You another chance. Do with it what You will. For Sara. For Gwyn. For whoever You want. All I know is...."

A tightness in his throat warped the words to nothing. He clenched his jaw, glaring at the sidewalk as he once again envisioned Sara's tear-stained cheeks. The agony in her strangled voice. "Sara deserves far more than what I can do on my own. She says You have protected her all this time. Help me do the same." And with a final look toward heaven, he said, "Just help me. Fair enough?"

TWENTY-FIVE

Ruffles

26 February 1894

A soft knock drew Christopher to his feet and toward the door. Sara straightened from retrieving a tea service from the bench outside his office. Dressed in pastels of lavender and cream, the twinkle in her blue eyes and the flush on her cheeks encouraged his smile.

"I brought coffee," she said, her tone soft and timid. "Fresh scones, too."

"Is that Sara's voice I hear?" Teddy scurried over. "Coffee!"

"Gregory was kind enough to arrange a carriage this morning, so I brewed it here."

Teddy accepted the tray from her and returned to Christopher's desk. The clink and clang of silver and china immediately followed.

Sara's cheeks flushed rose when she met Christopher's

gaze. "Good morning."

"Good morning." The initial instinct to take her hands to his lips overwhelmed his senses and nearly prevailed. To feel the tender pressure, the gentle warmth, the soft caress—He averted his gaze, his ears burning. "Come in and have a seat, Sara. I need a few minutes before I will be ready to go."

Sara passed to the chair beside Teddy.

"Go?" Teddy paused mid-bite of a steaming scone. "Go where?"

"We're off to the *Chronicle* to have a... discussion about the articles."

Teddy blinked at them as Sara prepared Christopher's cup. "You're going to the *Chronicle*?"

Christopher retrieved his pen. "That's what I said, isn't it?" He gestured to Sara, ignoring Teddy's perplexed expression. "Sara, what do you suggest as talking points? It was my intention to have a general idea of what to mention, how to counter, et cetera, et cetera."

She offered him his prepared coffee. "Definitely ask why he felt he should 'suppose' rather than 'interview'."

Christopher's fingers caressed hers as he accepted the cup, an internal spark caused a clink of china. She clasped her hands in her lap. "So, be as polite as possible while giving him the benefit of the doubt?"

"I would no' want us to suppose, either."

Teddy set down his cup, a definite clatter resounding throughout the office. "Why wasn't I invited? Top, you know I wanted to go down there and ruffle some shirtfronts!"

Christopher laughed. "Now, Ted—"

"Don't patronize me, Top. Am I your friend or aren't I?"

"It isn't a matter of friends or partners. It's my responsibility—"

"I'm your partner, Top, so don't give me this balderdash about responsibilities not falling on both our shoulders. I demand to know why you didn't tell me you were going."

Christopher laughed. "Teddy, for God's sake. It isn't that hard to figure out the reason. We want to try and save our reputation, not make it worse."

Teddy scoffed. "Thanks for the vote of confidence. It's nice to see I'm involved in the gallery's inner workings, partner."

"Ted! I was teasing."

"It wasn't amusing. I don't appreciate being titled the irresponsible one. I'm as responsible as you are, Chris, and you damn well know it. Sorry," he cast as an aside to Sara.

"Of course you're right. I apologize. Let's not get up in arms about it."

"Fine."

"Did you wish to come along?"

"Why do you think I'm making an ass out of myself in the first place?"

Christopher laughed at the sheer ridiculousness of it all.

When Sara entered the *Chronicle*, she first noticed the unique smell.

It seemed a combination of scents, ink and long hours of hard work intermingled. It wasn't necessarily unpleasant. If anything, it gave Sara a hint at the amount of work a paper entailed behind the scenes. The atmosphere also held a combination of voices, machinery, and the creaking of office chairs.

There were only three rooms. The largest one held two

desks toward the back, two on the left toward an office, and then one single desk toward the front entrance where a lady of... colorful and... unique appearance typed something on what Sara had previously discovered to be a 'typewriter'.

The two desks on the left side of the main room were occupied by two men in shirt-sleeves and vests chatting together of varying subjects that Sara couldn't make out. The two desks toward the back were more like tables, and they held typesetting materials and templates for the initial master.

Beyond those stood the entry into a southern room, which Sara reasoned to hold the printing press. Several people could be heard talking and mulling about around it, but she couldn't tell if they still prepared the latest edition, or if it had already been finalized and sent out.

The office on the left side of the main room drew Sara's attention. The gentleman within didn't seem to be a harsh sort of man, unlike Mr. Brockle, but he did give an impression of... assurance and... Sara wasn't certain what else. He sported red hair similar to Teddy's, but the editor's had been neatly combed.

He wore shirt-sleeves and a vest, both clean and pressed, and his desk looked to be organized and very professional. In fact, the entire *Chronicle* seemed highly organized. Such gave Sara some hope that he might be reasoned with.

When Sara noticed Teddy approaching the colorful lady, she readied herself for the coming conflict.

"Do you have an appointment?" the lady asked in a somewhat nasal tone.

Teddy crossed his arms. "We've been trying to get an appointment for the past week, missy."

"There's no need to take that tone, sir. If you've no

appointment, then you've no appointment. Leave your card and someone will get back to you."

"Like hell I'm goin—"

Christopher stepped up beside him. "Miss, if you could at least tell the editor that we've arrived. Theodore Parker and Christopher Lake from the Richmond Gallery of Art."

The men at the desks outside the main office fell silent and shifted around in their seats. Sara clasped her hands in front of her.

The lady pressed her lips into a thin line before entering the editor's office beyond the two gentlemen. The editor made a single statement, which caused a bit of a fuss from the lady, and then he ushered her back out to the main room with a motion of his hand.

She returned, red-cheeked and eyes flashing, and slammed down her note pad. "Go right in."

"Thank you." Christopher silenced the snide remark from Teddy with a simple glance.

Sara was urged to precede them and kept her eyes strictly focused on either her clasped hands or the progress of her shoes toward the editor's office. Then the door was opened, three pairs of feet entered, and the door was closed again.

"Thank you for seeing us." Christopher spoke, tone polite. "This is Theodore Parker, my partner at the gallery, and I'm Christopher Lake."

"Good day, gentlemen. Barney Taylor. Editor. And you? Miss... ?"

Sara couldn't stop the twitch, and when she looked up, she clearly noticed both Teddy and Christopher's glances toward her. The editor produced a hand. "Miss Little," she introduced softly, accepting his hand in a gentle grip while praying hers didn't tremble. "Though I've also come to be known as Miss Kreyssler."

Mr. Taylor's right eyebrow twitched the same moment Teddy and Christopher exchanged glances.

"I am pleased to make your acquaintance, Mr. Taylor," Sara released his hand only after directing toward him a small and graceful curtsy. "You have a lovely establishment."

"Thank you." Suspicion slowed his response. He motioned toward the trio. "What can I do for you?"

"Let's not act so naive," Teddy retorted darkly. Sara restrained the twitch and felt a modicum of ease when Christopher touched her elbow.

"Good." The editor crossed his arms. "You've likely come regarding the articles."

"Is that what you're calling slander now?"

"Ted," Christopher warned.

"Don't make libelous accusations, Mr. Parker," Mr. Taylor warned. "I've the necessary facts to support the presented theories. And in case you hadn't noticed, this is a newspaper. We're in the business of publishing news, popular opinion or not."

"News involves facts beyond hearsay," Teddy reminded, his voice somewhat harsh while still exhibiting control. "To this point your newspaper only seems to publish those articles that either pose personal questions to the general public, or make assumptions based on circumstantial facts at best. In my experience, it's common practice to approach those involved before publishing the information, verification the main objective."

"Any attempts at interviews thus far, Mr. Parker, have resulted in nothing short of a rude refusal to comment."

"Your attempts were made after initial publication! You

expected a warmer welcome? Our refusals to comment were based on principle, of which you seem to be sadly lacking."

"My principle is based upon the fact that the public has a right to know information regarding those involved in the community."

"Including the slanderous assumptions regarding Miss Kreyssler?" Teddy pressed, hands fisting. "Personal matters don't affect Richmond, Mr. Taylor, and had you truly been sensitive to the repercussions to her blameless reputation, you would have made more of an effort to contact her before publishing that last article."

"Mr. Lake holds a position of respect and sway in Richmond. The public is interested in what interests him. I report that." Mr. Taylor motioned toward Sara with his arm. "Miss Kreyssler happened to be involved in that realm of—"

"Our gallery is that which holds sway over the public opinion, Mr. Taylor. Not Mr. Lake's friendship with Miss Kreyssler, nor mine with the same. If your goal was anything beyond sensationalism to sell more papers, you would have made more of an attempt to contact us regarding an appointment involving that business. Due to your lack of follow-through, what you've reported is not only hearsay and gossip, but near-slander. Any lawyer with half a mind will tell you the same."

Mr. Taylor's eyes narrowed. "Mr. Parker, I don't appreciate being threat–"

"You don't appreciate?" Teddy stepped forward, pressing his hands palm-down onto the desk. "You've deliberately put a negative light on our gallery's reputation and those people involved, publishing questions simply to get a reaction. If a retraction of your suppositions isn't printed within a week, with a personal apology included for Miss Kreyssler, my lawyer will be contacting you with a writ. Is that understood?"

Mr. Taylor clenched his jaw.

Teddy brusquely nodded. "Good."

Then the trio made their way out, very aware of the scrutiny of their progress. Once inside the carriage, Teddy grinned. "That was entertaining."

Both Sara and Christopher laughed. "Bravo!"

"Good job with your politeness, Sara. With all the nonsense he's printed, it really made him look the ass. Sorry I didn't let you two get a word in."

"I think the only reason neither of us said anything was that you shocked the living breath out of us."

"I told you I excel at confrontations. You've only never given me the opportunity."

"I resent that remark," Christopher protested. "The last time I let you have your blessed confrontation, I was banned from that hotel in New York City." Teddy laughed and Christopher pointed at him. "You only think it's hilarious because you stuck me with your penalty."

Sara's expression softened as she watched the two. Why she enjoyed watching them bicker she had no idea. She supposed the reason given before was true, the fact she hadn't ever had family to argue with before, but there seemed to be something more than that. Perhaps it was the fact she was trusted enough with their personal lives to be entrusted, also, with this aspect of their relationship.

"What time is it?" Teddy asked suddenly, retrieving his watch from his vest-pocket. "Drat! I've a meeting!" He nearly tumbled from the carriage. "Promise me you'll head over to Lake Manor and put together a small collection to display—even if only five pieces."

Sara noticed Christopher's more forced smile.

"Fair enough, Teddy. I've had enough of your nagging to last a lifetime. Plus, I had an earful from Gwyn the other day because I 'woke' some of my pictures without her."

"Good, but I'm checking up on you this evening. If I don't see progress, I'm picking them myself." Teddy scrutinized his surroundings and then rushed down the sidewalk. Christopher tapped the roof, signaling the driver to carry on. When he sat back in the seat with a deep breath to watch the passing scenery, Sara worried her lip.

"I'll be fine," he told her without meeting her gaze.

Sara could only pray it was the truth.

The carriage lurched to a stop outside Lake Manor.

Christopher stepped down and turned to receive Sara, who carefully set aside the rug and accepted his hand, cheeks flushed.

"Mind your step- Wait! Your heel!" Christopher caught Sara's waist and moved with her stumble.

She gasped his name, her hands resting against his chest as she looked up into his face with wide eyes. "Did I hurt you?" they asked simultaneously. Sara's rose lips parted with her quickened breath, which smelled of honey.

He forced his hands from her waist before he could draw her closer. "I'm fine. Did you twist your ankle?" He rubbed his tingling palms onto the sides of his trousers.

"I... I do no' believe so." She momentarily looked to her foot, lifting her skirts only enough to regard her ankle. "Should it hurt?"

"I would think so." Christopher noticed he continued to

rub his hands on his trousers. He clenched his hands behind his back. "Now I see why gentlemen are to help ladies from carriages."

Sara flushed and accepted his offered arm. He continued to fist his opposite hand behind him, and his stomach knotted. *God, I need your help.* He couldn't withstand close quarters with her after such an extended time in her presence. Not when she continued to support and encourage. To smile and laugh. To comfort.

Harold opened the door. "Good day, Mr. Christopher. Miss Sara. Coffee? Tea?"

"Not yet, Harold. Sara and I have a bit of work to do before dinner this evening."

"Certainly, Mr. Christopher."

Harold offered Sara a genuine and warm smile, which she returned, and then helped her from her coat. The duty had barely been completed when Christopher heard his daughter's running steps. Sara's face brightened.

Gwyn took hold of Sara's hands, blonde ringlets bouncing as she danced from one foot to the other. "Sara, Sara! We're waking Papa's pictures!"

Sara laughed and gathered Gwyn onto her hip. "And you have waited such a long time for this, have you now?" Gwyn nodded, eyes wide. "Did you want to help?"

"I'm not supposed to go up there," Gwyn reminded, her voice hushed.

"But both of us will be up there with you, poppet. You are invited." Sara looked to him for confirmation. He could only smile.

Gwyn squealed and hugged Sara's neck. "I get to see your picture!"

Christopher raised an eyebrow. "Gwyn, I haven't any

pictures of Sara."

"You drew them a long time ago. I'll show you!" She squirmed free and scurried ahead.

They followed more sedate behind her. "I'm afraid her imagination has run away with her. She'll be broken-hearted when we don't find the picture." He shook his head, brow furrowed. "I don't understand why she would think I had a picture of you."

"The little miss likely sees it more in her imagination than on paper. I remember being the same when her age."

Christopher watched Sara's profile with a growing smile. His step paused outside the now open door to the third-story staircase. Gwyn's cheerful giggles and excited steps could be heard from within. "And what dreams did your child's mind bring forth?"

Sara's cheeks flushed. "Just a child's wishes. A wish for family. For a home. A place to feel safe." She peeked at him from under her lashes and then passed to climb the stairs.

'A place to feel safe.' Something he attempted to offer her, aware his late wife would have wanted the same. Christopher scrubbed at his scalp and ascended the stairs after her. Gwyn sounded a mournful cry, and the staccato sounds of her approach preceded her appearance at the stair crest.

"Papa." A few loose sketches hung limp in her hands. "Your pictures were on the floor. Sara's picture has a wrinkle." Her lips drooped as she passed the disheveled ream to him. "I wanted it to be perfect."

Christopher glanced Sara's direction. She stood near the far window looking out at the snow-covered gardens and houses, her profile little more than a silhouette. The sunlight heightened the line of her profile and the reddish hue of her mahogany locks. "What picture, Gwyn? I haven't one of Sara."

Gwyn tugged the sketches from his grasp, the action drawing his attention. Once she cycled through half a dozen images, she handed them back again, her finger pointing to a charcoal on aged paper with tattered edges. "This one."

He stared at the sketch of a lady's profile near the window of an upstairs room, nonplussed. It was the same faceless lady he had seen throughout his formative years, especially during college. "Gwyn, Sara isn't in this picture. This is only the Lady of Charcoal. Remember when I told you about her? She was in my imagination."

"That's Sara," Gwyn insisted.

Christopher released a deep breath and looked up- He dropped the sketches and staggered back. Gwyn's gasp of despair attracted Sara's attention from the window. Her smile vanished when her eyes met his.

"Mr. Christopher? What's the matter?"

He continued to step back, mutely shaking his head as life and fantasy burned an image into his mind—He turned and fled, Sara's voice ringing in his ears.

TWENTY-SIX

The Pain of Perfect Timing

27 February 1894

Sara tapped her artistry pencil on the sketch paper as she stared out onto the whitened garden with unseeing eyes. Amy sat in the chair across from her within the observatory, stitching the hem of a gown of burgundy velvet while sparing an occasional glance to regard Sara's pale complexion. Gwyn hummed a child's melody as she played with a collection of blocks to make towers, bridges, and buildings.

"Gwyn." The girl paused mid-placement of a tower block to meet Amy's gaze. "Is your papa gonna let you sleep over tonight, too? Or is he gonna come and getcha?" A quick glance toward Sara revealed no change in complexion or posture. It was as if she didn't hear.

Gwyn shrugged and looked to her blocks. "I don't know. Sara said Papa had to go for a little while."

Amy lowered her stitching. "Go? Where? New York?"

Sara blinked and lowered her head. Still silent.

"I don't know. He didn't say 'good-bye'." Gwyn's lower lip quivered.

"That must've been some emergency for your papa to forget that!"

Amy heard the front door open and close, noticed Sara's quick look toward the front hall, and gave a blink of surprise when she excused herself from the room. Then hushed voices could be heard outside in the hall, one sounding more and more distraught.

"What in the world?" Amy asked in a hushed voice. She looked to Gwyn as she set aside her stitching. "I'll be right back, sweets." In the front hall, Teddy and Harold exited out the front door. Dix and Paul continued to speak to Sara in soothing tones.

Amy stepped forward. "What's happened?" She wrapped a comforting arm around Sara's quivering shoulders.

Dix sent Amy a reassuring smile. "Don't you worry your head, dear. Take your charge upstairs and get her some tea."

Amy curtsied and gently guided Sara to the stairs, doing her best to soothe her new friend.

Dix watched the two's progress with a vanishing smile. She lowered her head, pinching the bridge of her nose as she whispered, "Chris...."

"I'm sure he's fine, Sweet. He's come far since meeting her."

"Is it enough?"

"Enough to push him to the next step."

Dix took a firm hold of Paul's hand. "But... but it was Sara in those images, Paul. How will he move past that? You know how he is. Seeing this mysterious vision of a young woman before he even meets Carla? Before you and I even met Sara in England? How will he put logic to a miracle when it's his heart he needs to see it with?"

Paul placed a kiss on her forehead. "I'll let you know when I find him, Sweet."

Dix sighed. "Be careful, darling."

Paul sent her a wink and stepped out into the chill February air.

Christopher heard a deep sigh and lifted his focus to the window– color bled from his features. The Lady of Charcoal stood there, surrounded by muted tones of grays and black. The mists of colors drifted around her like whispers. Words wouldn't come as he stood there, and he was unable to approach for fear the dream would dissipate before he could see her face. He swallowed hard, but remained mute, lost within the conflict of color and muted white.

"I thought... I thought it would be a comfort for you," the Lady whispered. Though she faced away from him, the language of her body declared her desire to stay.

"You are a comfort, Lady," His voice rang tight, gruff.

She lowered her head, and shadows robbed the profile of her face from his sight. "I want to help, but...."

"You have." He approached with cautious, deliberate footfalls. "You have served as my inspiration for beauty and innocence. A desire God gave me. If you were to go...." It would be another agony of loss, one he couldn't bear.

She sighed. "Your Carla will always be with you."

"Of course, but God wouldn't let me forget your

inspiration even amidst my grief." He stepped forward, close enough now to hear the whisper of her breath, yet unable to see but the curve of her neck and the gentle waves of her hair. "I cannot let you go, Lady. The passion we shared together... I don't want to lose that again."

The Lady of Charcoal lowered her chin, it trembled. "May I... may I help?"

He reached out to enfold the supple warmth of her hand. "Yes. Be my Lady again. Be my inspiration."

The Lady of Charcoal sounded a soft sob. She tilted her face toward him, sapphire eyes glimmering with the tears that danced down rose-kissed cheeks.

His face paled as he stared down into the lovely face of—

"Sara!" Christopher choked out the strangled shout, fighting against the twisted covers to sit up. "No," he hissed. He kicked his feet over the side of the bed and gripped the sheet, squeezing his eyes tight as he shook his head. "It's impossible!"

The charcoals. The watercolors. The vivid impressions of the Lady who made him doubt she was simply 'fantasy'. And now, within his dream.... The overwhelming feeling of her presence. Her voice fit with her silhouette, tremulous and hesitant. Soft and gentle, as he had always sketched her—

Christopher shook his head again, fisting his hands into the fabric of the down mattress as tears burned his closed eyes. The laughter with Gwyn. The commonality of a passion for art. The comfort and the care taken with his grief for Carla– He fisted his hands in his hair. "Blast!"

She never wanted anything. She always gave. She always offered and listened. She never sought attention.

She never sought recognition. It was always others. Him. Gwyn. Dix. Paul. Teddy. Harold. Emily. Amy. Never herself. Never her future. Never. It was give; never get. It was offer; never receive. It was—

Christopher punched the softness of the bed, his head hanging. "It was supposed to be Carla," he choked out. Yet Carla had gone, to heaven with their son. But not before God made use of her to free a young woman with a broken heart.

He pushed away from the bed. *A friend. A surprising friend. Someone I trust. Someone I talk to. Someone who...* He hid his face in his hands. The silhouette. The profile. The line. The curve. The grace... It was supposed to be Carla, and yet....

Paul shut the door of the carriage house at Lake Manor. Patrick, one of the older drivers, worked on the rear axle of a closed carriage. "Hello, Patrick."

Patrick looked up and doffed his hat from his silver hair. "Mr. Paul. You need a carriage, sir?"

Paul noted the fresh travel stains on the carriage's chassis as he stepped further inside. "I think so. Are any of the larger available?"

Patrick cleared his throat, worrying the hat between his fingers. "I'm sorry, Mr. Paul, but I've got to hold onto it. Master Chris'll be needing it again."

Paul smirked. Patrick was the only one, other than the occasional slip from Harold and Emily, whom called Chris 'Master'. A remnant and very pleasant memory from earlier years. "It's fine. I can wait until he returns. I will only need to adjust some reservations. When will he be returning?"

The man rubbed at the back of his neck. "I'm not really sure, Mr. Paul. I just thought I should be ready in case he calls. It's a jaunt from Master Damon's in this weather."

"It certainly is that." Paul clapped the man on the back. "Thank you, Patrick. I'll see about getting a reservation at a closer location." Paul exited the carriage house with a slight smile. He enjoyed being right.

28 February 1894

The sun had long since risen from a sea of purple and orange. The haggard man slouched in the tattered chair didn't notice the new day. There in the attic of a college-friend's home, hiding within the cast-offs of previous years, he stared across from him at the old easel. Hazel eyes bloodshot. Face pale and shadowed with exhaustion and a day's growth of beard. Paint spattered clothing and body, the brush still between his fingers, spent.

The man raised a trembling hand to cover his eyes, choking out, "Oh my God" before his voice drifted to nothing. He ran a hand harshly down his face, doing his best to wipe the memory and inspiration away, even though he knew it was too late. The image had already escaped, from heart to mind to canvas.

A trio.

Carla. Gwyn... and Sara

Carla's image shadowed and ethereal, standing behind Sara with a supportive hand on the woman's shoulder—Christopher's throat tightened, but he couldn't look away. The wife. The surprising friend. The loving daughter. All such important strengths... And that trio of gentleness and laughter beckoned to him. Each glow of laughter experienced as if he himself had been present. Each rustling of fabric nearly heard, flirtatious yet timid.

Christopher sat forward, the brush dropping to the attic's dusty floor. He covered his face and choked another prayer, throat constricted on the tears of remorse. After all the rage he voiced, God continued to prepare the way to heal his heart. Through the screaming and the blame and hate, God worked to bring... *Sara.*

Sara dried another wave of tears from her cheeks. *Why did he run? Why did he look so... so....* Thoughts vanished with the rise of a sob as she covered her face with trembling and cold hands.

At a soft knock, Sara swiped the tears from her face. "Who is it?"

"It's Dix, love. May I come in?"

"Y-yes."

Dix entered, closing the door softly behind her. She drew Sara into a tender embrace. "All will be well, Sara love."

"N-no," Sara denied in a choked voice. "I... I did something."

"I hardly believe it could have been you. You wouldn't offend a soul, on pain of death."

"Then why d-did he go?"

"Dear Sara." Dix leaned back. "Please don't blame yourself. Chris doesn't. I promise you that."

"B-but...."

"I know, dearest." Dix drew Sara into another embrace. "You think you must have done something horribly wrong, because weren't you just standing there when he gawked at you like he did and then bolted? But it was something that's been a long time coming. Since he began his second-year classes at Richmond College when he was fifteen—Come along with me. Let me show you."

Dix took Sara by the hand and drew her down the hall to the master bedroom. She opened a dresser drawer and retrieved a leather-bound portfolio. Inside, a collection of finished and unfinished sketches. Curiosity drew Sara closer as Dix cycled through them, apparently seeking a particular—

"Here they are. Lovely, aren't they? A silhouette here. A back profile of a head there. A front profile here, but done in such a way to keep the face hidden by hair or shadow or flower.... This is a lady that Chris has seen in his dreams and on paper and canvas since his college days."

Sara looked up, confused, but Dix continued to stare down at the silhouettes and profiles. Finally, Dix lifted a single sketch of a lady's silhouette within a room. "This is a likeness of the image he saw when he bolted, Sara. An image he has seen in his mind for ages. A lady that, even after he fell in love with and married Carla, he still saw from behind: Faceless and turned away—it's you, Sara."

TWENTY-SEVEN

Lady of Charcoal

"W-what do you m-mean?" The words struggled and gasped from her soul. "I.... I have never met Mr. Christopher before coming here. I swear it!"

Dix set aside the sketches to take Sara's trembling hands. "Sara love, I'm not accusing you of a plot. Your coming has been nothing but a blessing. You've been a welcome addition to our family. A reason for Gwyn to laugh again. An accepting and thoughtful friend for Teddy. A bit of laughter and learning for myself and Paul." Dix brushed a tear from Sara's cheek. "And to Chris? You're a possible finish to the unfinished. A conceivable completion to his blank canvas—"

"No!" Sara wrenched her hands from the older woman's clasp and backed away. "Mr. Christopher deserves more than the likes of me. He should no' see me in beautiful pictures, dreaming about some lovely lady full of grace and poetry and... and...." She covered her face with cold hands, tears dripping. "N-no... not me."

Dix drew Sara close. "And why not? You let him be who he is. You encourage him to step outside of the agony. And you do it all with no expectation of anything in return. You give, selflessly, because that gives you joy."

Sara sobbed against the older woman as she choked out "B-but I do no' w-want him to think...."

"What, Sara love? He thinks of you as a friend. He sees you as an artist. Someone he can confide in regarding the gallery and his very passion: His art. What could he possibly believe could be wrong?"

But Sara didn't know. All these years she had done so well in keeping her emotional distance. Keeping her heart guarded. Keeping herself on the outside, safely ensconced within the arms of a God she knew she could trust.

Then she came to America.

Pushed outside her comfort to seek a new life. Shoved outside her caution and hesitation to a new way of thinking. Friends. Family. Acceptance. Belonging. Beauty. Things and thoughts she hadn't ever entertained. And amidst it all? One man who believed the best of her while pushing her to be her best. One man she came to trust and call friend. One man she had grown to—

Sara released a choked sob. "I love him, mum."

Christopher swiped the wetness from his face and lowered himself to sit on the floor, his back propped against his bed. He gathered up his leather-bound Bible from the floor beside him. He didn't understand. If the Lady of Charcoal was Sara, why... why Carla? He rested his head back against the bed and stared at the ceiling.

There came a soft tap and then the creak of the opening door. "Chris?"

"I'm sorry, Paulie. I had to... I...." Christopher shook his head. "I'm sorry."

Paul Donovan stepped farther into the room, closing the door behind him. "I know, Chris." He tossed his overcoat aside and sat beside Christopher's weary form. "Are you well?"

"I don't know. I'm confused. Why her? Why was it Sara in the images?" Christopher shifted his tired gaze to Paul. "Her friendship came when I felt myself slipping to the numbness. Her wide-eyed view of the world came when... when I stopped seeing anything beyond the agony. My smiles for Gwyn? Forced. The attention for supported artists? Stale at best. I lived each day in case there was a moment free of a reminder. Then Sara....

"She helped me face the reminders while showing that... that it was all right to miss someone. After all, hadn't she been without family or friend most of her life? She took away my excuses and she helped me grieve. To laugh. To mourn. To make more happy memories. Why her, Paul?"

Paul examined Christopher's haggard expression for a long moment. "Chris, God brought Sara to America for many reasons. Don't ask why this and why that. Be her friend. Accept her help. Accept the blessing she's been to you. Continue as you have, taking one day at a time. She doesn't expect more."

"But I don't know if I can continue to view her as simply a friend, Paul. Not after seeing her as...." The memory of the revelation still beat at his heart and mind, his pulse racing—He cleared his throat. "She's the first woman I've felt comfortable with since Carla's death. The first woman to share my passion for art and artist alike. A friend?" He groaned and dropped his head into his hands. "She's the woman from my images, Paul. The Lady of Charcoal. The internal personification of everything I desired...."

"I understand." Paul gripped his shoulder. "Two years without the comfort of a woman is a lifetime. No one would fault you for accepting Sara as the finish to your family."

"But I don't love Sara, Paul, and she deserves that much. I enjoy spending time with her. Teaching her. Learning from her.... I genuinely care about her, am attracted to her even, but I can't ask her to be the hostess of Lake Manor and mother to my daughter knowing that trying to love her might...." His spirit shuddered. "I don't want to resent her, Paul. Not her."

"Chris." Paul regarded his profile a moment. "Chris, considering your fondness and genuine concern, do you truly believe you would grow to resent her?"

"I...." But he didn't know. The roar of conflicting wants and needs overpowered any reason, making it impossible to discern the next step. She was a friend, but she was the Lady. He cared about her, but he didn't love her... and yet she was the Lady. How could he not love her?

Paul smiled. "Topper, don't burden your recovering heart with the questions. Simply enjoy your friendship. Sara may not be ready for anything beyond that. There is a lot of growing yet for her to stretch out beyond her rough history. Your friendship with her has made that possible. Step forth from that point in your view of her. Don't press yourself to anything more. Digest. Consider. Leave everything else where it is."

Christopher inclined his head, closing his eyes against

the onslaught of questions and possibilities. "I will try."

"Good. I will give you a moment or three to think on that while I see Damon about making a telephone call. Dix will want to know we haven't caught our death."

"Paul. Tell Sara...."

"Tell her it wasn't her fault?" Christopher nodded and Paul's features softened with an understand smile. "I will." Then he stepped into the hallway beyond, closing the door behind him.

Christopher lowered his head against the bed, blinking up at the ceiling as he picked at the nearby rug. "I needed some time, Sara," he whispered. "I only needed some time." But how much time would be enough when he saw the finish to a lifetime of images?

Sara caressed the tatted boutonniere finished earlier that day. Keeping her hands busy always helped her relax, and today had been no different. Even so, her mind continued to escape to thoughts of Christopher, praying for his peace. Lifting his spirit in a plea for grace and comfort. Life had been such a struggle for him, and to have this beat upon him, it tore at her heart.

"Sara love, you have that dreamy expression in your eyes again," Dix observed. She lowered the paper. "Thinking of Chris?"

Sara flushed.

"I thought so." Dix set the paper aside and thoughtfully regarded the woman sitting so timid and silent across from her. "Are you going to tell him how you feel?"

Sara paled, her imagination crafting his response and

the misery.... She shook her head.

"Why not? He genuinely cares for you, though he's convinced himself it halts at friendship." Dix scoffed. "Did the same thing for Carla, poor soul. I swear that boy is oblivious to all things but art."

Surprise widened Sara's eyes. "What?"

"Oh? I haven't told you this story?" Dix smirked. "It's by far the funniest. Let me see. Well, I know Gwyn told you Carla and Chris met at my 30th birthday party. It was our last month in England, so we decided to throw a grand affair at the gallery sponsoring Chris' exhibit. Carla was the younger sister of one of Paul's friends, who happened to be visiting a relative or something of the sort, and so she was invited to the party."

Dix laughed. "The poor dear; Chris I mean. He never was very elegant around ladies, due to his shyness mostly. That and he never gave much thought to them. Well, no thought to treating them differently than his other friends. Of which he didn't have many," Dix added as an afterthought. She arched an eyebrow at the revelation and then waved it away. "Never mind. Anyway. Somehow Chris was volunteered to gather Carla a glass of punch—it was likely a dare from Teddy—and promptly spilled it across the front of her gown. Not intentionally, mind you, though I do believe Teddy hoped for a less-than-glorious moment. Whether he did or not, Chris redeemed himself by—"

"Painting a picture over it," Sara finished excitedly.

Dix laughed. "My goodness, I still remember the roar of laughter as Carla very quickly became the center of attention, this young man kneeling at her feet painting a landscape or sunset or whatever it was on her gown. I don't know what made Chris think of it. I suppose it doesn't matter. During the romantic event, Carla talked to Chris of his painting and his display there at the gallery, what his goals were, somehow urged him to talk about his tentative plans to begin his own gallery.... I hadn't seen Chris so animated before in my life.

"It was much the same when Carla came to stay with Paul and myself while her parents toured Europe. Chris would come over to talk about art and architecture, and the time together gave them a firm and fast friendship. She loved hearing about his inspirations and commenting on his artwork just as much as she loved helping him and Teddy plan receptions and introductions to help the gallery gather its following.

"Chris was extremely comfortable with her and asked her opinion on practically everything. They would discuss the oddest things until the latest hours, and then he would be here early the next morning to escort her to the gallery, talking the entire way. Finally, Carla flat-out asked me if Chris would ever propose."

Dix laughed. "Believe me, I was floored. Chris hadn't ever mentioned romantic feelings for Carla, and he apparently hadn't mentioned them to her either. But all the attention and the activities they did together... she had fallen in love with him somewhere along the way, and I guess I don't blame her. Chris has always had a natural charm about him. Except when he loses his temper, of course."

Sara restrained a giggle.

"Anyway, I told her that if she loved him it would be in her best interest to sit him down and let him know. After all, she knew how shy he was due to how intensely he disliked the parties he would escort her to. So, the very next day Carla told him she loved him, and that she wanted to know how he felt about her.

"If I remember correctly," Dix said, frowning slightly, "Chris honestly said he didn't know if he loved her or not. He told her he liked spending time with her, that he liked her differently than he had liked anyone else, but he wasn't sure if he loved her because he hadn't ever been 'in love' before. Then, Chris told her he would need to take a day or two to think about it before telling her one way or the other."

Dix chuckled and shook her head. "Carla hadn't expected that honest of a reply, I don't think. She either expected a resounding 'yes' or an emphatic 'no'. But Chris has always been more thoughtful of decisions that affected his future. Just as he was more intense within his artwork rather than in his outward expressions. I think it was easier for him. Carla was the externally passionate one of the relationship, and I think he learned a great deal from knowing her.

"Enough of that, Dix," she murmured. "Let me think—Ah. On day three I believe, Chris confessed to Carla that he believed he loved her and he would like to talk to her father about beginning to court her, if it was all right with her. It was such an adorable conversation; Chris stuttered and stumbled throughout the entire thing."

Sara's expression softened as she sighed, "Poor Christopher."

Dix waved a hand. "It was good for him. So, Chris and Carla began courting, Chris grew even more fond, and then he proposed on their... nine-month anniversary? Or was it six? I can never remember that." Dix motioned toward Sara. "But the lesson to remember is that Carla had to confess her feelings to him in order to get him to reevaluate his feelings for her. Artwork he knows. Inspirations and presentations of artistic thoughts he understands. But his own feelings regarding women? I'm not so sure he understands that as well. He's decidedly better than he was before, but... I don't know. Once he believes he's set into a specific type of relationship, he has a tendency of tenaciously keeping it there."

Sara lowered her gaze to the carnation boutonniere. "You think... I might need to tell him first?"

"It's a possibility, Sara love. Just put that in your prayers and let the Lord lead you."

Absently nodding, Sara smoothed and delicately adjusted the petals of the tatted flower. A possibility of a first terrifying confession with two very different consequences. Sara sighed, using that to set the situation into the Lord's hands. She didn't know what would be best, just as she didn't know if she felt anything but a true love for Christopher. But she trusted God would do the best for everyone. She only needed to prepare her heart for the possibility.

The telephone under the stairs chirped. Both women moved their focus to the doorway as Gregory answered. "Why, Good day, Mr. Donovan."

"Paul!" Dix scurried from the room.

Sara lowered her gaze to her trembling fingers, love and concern overwhelming her. But she needed to continue as she had. Being a friend. A listening ear. An understanding yet guarded heart.

Such had never been a challenge before. But now? When she could feel herself growing more and more in love? What exactly did 'guarded heart' mean? Did it mean she didn't confess how much of a friend he was? Did it mean she was even more careful how she watched him? Or how she spoke to him? Or how... how she thought of him?

Sara released a deep breath. *Sweet Jesus.* Everything had changed.

"Paul?" she heard Dix call into the phone. "Is he...?"

Sara very slowly closed her eyes. *Please let him be –*

"Praise the Lord!"

Sara released a choked sob of relief.

"Of course, darling. We can make do by ourselves now we know he's with you. ... Certainly. Hold the line."

Sara vaguely heard the sound of Dix's approaching steps.

"Sara love? Paul would like to speak with you."

She took in a tremulous breath and wiped the tears from her cheeks as she made her way to the alcove. Then she took up the phone ear-piece with trembling fingers. "Yes, Mr. Paul?"

"Hello, my dear. I wanted to give you a specific message from Chris. He is sorry for worrying you, and expressly directed me to tell you it isn't your fault.

Sara closed her eyes, leaning hard against the phone as she nodded her head and tried to smile through the relief. "Thank you, Mr. Paul," she whispered, quickly wiping more tears from her cheeks.

"You're most welcome. We're visiting a friend of his from Richmond College. We'll try to be back before your lesson tomorrow."

"M-mister Christopher doesn't need to come back so soon just for my lesson," she whispered. "He should make a holiday of it. You know how much he needs one, Mr. Paul."

"Yes, I believe you're right, and I'll be certain to tell him. Tell Gwyn her papa sends his love and that we'll be home as soon as we're able."

"I will, Mr. Paul."

"Thank you, dear. Can I talk to Sweet again?"

Sara handed the ear-piece back to Dix and exited the alcove. Her knees collapsed as she reached the bench in the hall, the sobs of relief shuddering free.

TWENTY-EIGHT

Dreams of Home

1 March 1894

"Sara?"

Sara stretched under the down cover as the pit-pat of a child's step could be heard on the hardwood floor. Pushing herself up in bed, she gave Gwyn a sleepy smile as the little girl scurried up and then wriggled under the covers beside her. "Why, Gwyn. What's the matter? You have a dream again last night?"

"Is Papa home?" the girl whispered.

Sara smoothed the girls rumpled blonde ringlets. "Yes. Your papa and Uncle Paul came home last night."

"How come he didn't come to get me?"

Sara's lips drooped. "He likely did no' want to wake you, poppet. It was past your bedtime when your Uncle Paul got home." Sara wrapped her arms around the girl and kissed the crown of her head. "I bet he will come this morning for you." She hoped so. She prayed so.

"Sara?" Gwyn looked up at her, emerald eyes glimmering.

"Yes, poppet?"

"Why was Papa scared of your picture? Mamma says they made him happy. Like drawing a good dream."

A good dream. Sara kissed the girl's head. Maybe he didn't want her in that good dream? She was only someone his wife wanted to help. She was only.... "I do no' know, Gwyn. I wish I did." She was only Sara.

Gwyn sighed deep. "Sara?"

"Hm?"

"I think the picture was something he forgot."

Sara opened her eyes, her breath catching in her throat.

"Papa doesn't like forgetting. Maybe he was scared he remembered late. Like a birthday."

"What happens when a birthday is remembered late?"

"No party and no presents," Gwyn pulled back, gazing up at Sara with wide eyes. "You don't know?"

Sara flushed. "I have no' had a true birthday party, Gwyn. Just a bit of cake with my mum."

Gwyn gasped and sat up. Then she scurried from the bed and dashed from the room. "Auntie Dix! Uncle Paul!"

Sara surrendered to a soft laugh and threw back the covers. When she opened the door to the adjoining bath, Amy was already inside filling the tub with hot water.

"Good morning. Did you sleep better?"

"Yes, Amy. Thank you. The tea helped."

"Good. Are you having a lesson at the Manor today?"

"I…" Sara paled, and the want to see how he fared tore at her calm. "I do no' know." Would he want to see her so soon after his revelation?

"Well I'm sure we can find an excuse to get you over there." Amy helped Sara into the tub. "After all, Gwyn's still here. She'll be needing an escort over, and who better to do it than yourself?"

Sara lightly bit her lower lip. "I would no' want to make a nuisance of myself."

"Oh fiddle-diddle. After breakfast we'll pack you and Gwyn up and send you on your way. You've been getting right good with those watercolors of yours."

Sara stared at the soap suds on the water. She loved him, and on the cuff of the admittance there settled a terror. What if he found out and turned her away? She didn't want to lose this place that finally felt like home. "I... I do no' think I will."

Amy's hands halted mid-motion in Sara's soapy tresses. When she came around to face her, Sara couldn't meet her gaze. "But why not? You love the lessons. You come back brighter and happier each morning you have them!"

"I... I know. B-but Mr. Christopher only came back but last night. I think he should have some time to himself before starting again with me."

"But—But Mr. Christopher hasn't painted since his Carla went to the Lord. This is the first time he's—"

"Amy," Sara pressed, eyes wide and glimmering. "Amy, please."

The young woman sat back on her heels with a grunt. "Well I'll be. You've fallen for him." Sara's gaze retreated, cheeks crimson. Amy clutched the rim of the tub. "Then why in the world would you want to leave him to himself after he sent the house into such an uproar? Don't you want to be there for him?"

Sara choked back a sob. "I canno' go. I want to, but I...

I canno' do it."

"Why not?" Amy insisted. "He's been more his usual self since you came."

"He loves his wife, Amy." Her heart grew to an unbearable weight with the crushing realization. "It does no' matter if she's in heaven or here on earth. It does no' matter if my heart burns for him. He loves her. I-I canno' push him to go where he's not ready. I am his friend before anything else, and a friend would— "

"Go see if he's well. Any friend would do the same." Amy rested a hand on Sara's shoulder. "He had a shock, so you get yourself over there and make sure he's getting by. Certainly you don't press or prod about anything. You just go there. Like you did before." The young woman's grip tightened, drawing Sara's anguished gaze. "Like you want to now."

Christopher could sense Teddy regarding him over his coffee cup as he read through his mail. His friend had come that morning under the pretense of strong-arming him into a surrender of his art for the promised display at the gallery. No mention was made of the mysterious disappearance. No mention of Sara or whether or not she would be arriving for an art lesson that morning. But Christopher knew Teddy wouldn't be able to resist for too much longer.

The chink of china coffee-cup on saucer sounded the warning bell.

"So what in blazes happened? I should hook you on the jaw with what you did to everyone."

Christopher lowered the paper, uncertain how to

explain the situation. Even he was unsure where he stood in anything. "I apologize, Ted. I... I needed some time to myself."

"Time for what? No one will tell me a blasted thing about why you bolted. From Sara's reaction I thought maybe she said something—"

"No. Sara did nothing wrong." That she might attempt to shoulder the brunt of the guilt served as a spike to the heart.

"That's what I thought, but what else could set you off unless she said an innocent comment about Carla or some such thing?"

"It wasn't Carla." And that in itself was a confession of a multitude of things.

"Fine, so she didn't say anything about Car—"

"No, Teddy. You don't understand. The images. The silhouettes. The charcoals and pencils I've done for years.... They weren't Carla."

"Of course they weren't," Teddy said, his brow furrowing. "Her line wasn't right for those. Didn't you know that?"

Christopher blinked. "What?"

Teddy scoffed. "Oh for the love of—Chris, I've known for years Carla wasn't your mysterious Lady of Charcoal. You didn't start drawing Carla until after you began courting. The Lady of Charcoal came out a bit less then." Teddy shrugged. "I figured you were leaving fantasies behind for the real image."

"Not...." Christopher scratched at his scalp. "But I thought—Why didn't you tell me?"

Teddy's countenance twisted in confusion. "Tell you what? That Carla wasn't the Lady of Charcoal? Why? It didn't matter. You were falling in love with her. Anyone with a brain could see how she felt for you. The Lady of Charcoal was just a fantasy. We all have them."

"Sara is the Lady of Charcoal, Teddy!"

Teddy gave a snap of his fingers. "That's why she seemed so blasted familiar! I've been gawking at those images for ages—" He howled with laughter.

Christopher frowned. "This isn't funny." The doorbell chimed, and a few moments later Harold passed by the sitting room entrance to answer.

"Not funny, Top? Come on! Of all the craziness in life, this is the best."

"Fine. Laugh while you can, but your day is coming."

Teddy chuckled as he retrieved his coffee.

"Mr. Christopher?" Harold stood at the sitting room doorway.

"Yes?"

"Miss Sara has brought Miss Gwyn home from the Donovans."

Dread and eagerness battled as Christopher stood. "Oh."

Teddy regarded his friend, an amused smirk twisting his lips. With a shrug, he set aside his coffee and gathered his coat and hat from the floor beside him. "Well, I'm off. I never did contact those few who signed up for the children's classes." He paused long enough to cuff Christopher on the arm. Then he stepped into the hall and had a brief discourse with Sara before closing the front door behind him.

Harold cleared his throat, drawing Christopher's attention. "Miss Gwyn informs me she has already breakfasted and wishes to play with the fish and frogs in the conservatory. Only after saying 'Good morning' to yourself, of course. Miss Sara...." Harold cast a glance behind him. "Master Chris, the young lady doesn't look well."

"What?" Concern propelled him from the room with quick steps. Sara sat upon a chair outside the sitting room's entrance, her face white and her eyes dull. Gwyn stood beside her speaking in soothing whispers as one little hand stroked her cheek.

Christopher swallowed the rising lump and stepped forward, the sound of his shoes on the hardwood floor drawing his daughter's gaze. Sara's cheeks flushed before turning a concerning shade of yellow. Her eyes didn't stray from their regard of the gloves clasped in white-knuckled hands. He offered Gwyn a somewhat forced smile as she scurried forward with a delighted call of "Papa!" Sara's entire body grew taut.

He lifted Gwyn up into his arms. "Good morning, Angel Girl."

"Are you feeling better, Papa?" Her emerald eyes clouded with concern.

"Yes, I am, and I apologize for worrying you. I did a very bad thing running away without a 'Good bye'. I hope you can forgive me."

"Of course, Papa." Gwyn punctuated the statement with a kiss on his cheek.

Sara hadn't even yet offered a sidelong glance or a timid smile.

"Did you get mad that you forgot about Sara in your pictures?" Gwyn ventured.

Christopher paled, his eyes snapping to his daughter's innocent expression. "What?"

"The pictures. You hate forgetting. You thought Sara would be mad?"

Christopher cleared his throat and lowered Gwyn to her feet. "I wasn't necessarily mad, Gwyn. I was confused."

"Because you never met Sara before?"

A reluctant smile broke through the humiliation. "Gwyn, are you certain you're only five years old?"

Gwyn giggled. "Silly Papa."

"Then how did you become so smart?" She giggled again, inviting his kiss to each hand and then her forehead. "I hear from Harold you would like to go play with the fish and frogs. Go along. Try not to fall in, please."

Gwyn nodded and scampered off toward the conservatory.

The rustle of material behind him drew his quick attention. Sara moved toward the door. "Sara, wait."

She halted, her hand white-knuckled on the doorknob. Her back stiff.

He stood beside her, watching her cheeks alternately pale and flush. Her lips parted, her breathing rapid as she blinked down at her hand. "Sara...." But he couldn't say more. There was too much he didn't understand.

"It's fine, sir," she whispered. Sara released a slow breath before meeting his gaze. Her blue eyes... their blackened depths sparkled with the threat of tears. "We worried after you, certainly, but we knew God held you in His hands."

"I didn't mean for you to think you were at fault."

"I know." She lowered her gaze. "It's only a bit of a bad habit."

Mesmerized, Christopher watched the way she twisted her gloves in her hands. The slight flush of her cheeks—He swallowed hard and presented his hand, trying to reason why he hadn't seen the likeness before. "Forgiven?"

Sara's gaze was drawn to his reach. Then she smiled

and met his gaze, those eyes sparkling to life as she accepted his hand in a gentle grip. "Of course, sir."

The warmth of her clasp soothed the guilt. He motioned toward the sitting room entrance, he prompted "Coffee?" while continuing to hold her hand in his.

"Oh. I only came to bring Gwyn." Her cheeks flushed, but she didn't lower her eyes. "And to make certain you were well. You still need your holiday, and I do no' want to bother."

Christopher found he was unable to release her hand—He forced a release, enunciating his motion to the sitting room with a gentle hand to her back. "Come along, Sara. Stay a while... please?"

Her smile softened and she nodded.

Christopher guided her to the wingback chair across from his. He watched the light of the room dance in her hair as she prepared his coffee. The line of her nose. The natural color of her cheeks heightened by the delicate contour of her cheekbones. So much like what he would have imagined.

He accepted the offered cup and stared into the cream-lightened darkness. "How much did Dix tell you about the sketches?" His ears and face burned.

"A-a little."

"I...." Christopher cleared his throat. "I've been sketching and doodling with pencils since before I could remember. My mother once said that everywhere I went she would find at least three sketches, two dull pencils, and a multitude of smudges on her furniture."

Sara laughed, the soft melody welcome in the quiet of his home. He peeked at her as she toyed with the lip of her coffee cup. How long had he attempted to imagine a finish to the Lady of Charcoal? And now? Christopher's smile faded, and he swallowed hard. When Sara glanced up to catch his scrutiny, he dropped his gaze.

"My tutors complained I didn't focus on my studies, but they could never complain I slacked in my work. I kept up my marks, even when I spent a majority of my time sketching out the verbal images I studied of history. One tutor said I was better able to remember dates and facts when I put those studies to paper."

It was surprising, the feeling of relief that came with the telling of his history. Especially when Sara listened with such rapt attention. "When I went to study at Richmond College, my passion remained the same. I wanted to create beautiful imagery, to remind a country still reeling from a civil war that beauty could be found in the aftermath. That the future generations could remember a pain and learn from it to create better things. I felt... called to create things of family and beauty in creation. As if I were God's whisper to a grieving nation. A reminder of peace after what seemed an eternity of war."

She offered a timid smile, blue eyes glimmering as she softly whispered, "What a lovely gift to give."

Christopher looked down and released a slow breath. "Then the imagery began to change. I began to...." His hands tightened on the arms of the chair as he remembered the growing urge for a partner. Remembering a press on his heart to begin praying for what he wanted in a wife.

"Mr. Christopher?"

He blinked and looked up, noticing the fearful expression.

"Are you well, sir?" she whispered.

Christopher nodded. Then he noticed his right fist lightly pounding the arm of the chair. He halted the motion but couldn't drag his gaze from the scrutiny of his fisted hand. "I began to see the Lady of Charcoal in mind and canvas for ages. Ten years? Twelve? I don't remember anymore. I thought they would stop when Carla and I married. They didn't."

He heard the gentle rustle of her movement and felt her soft hold on his hand. His grip loosened, and he opened his eyes to meet hers. She knelt at his feet. "I thought it was some horrid joke," he confessed, his voice gruff. "I mean, my own wife brought you here, Sara. My own wife."

She inclined her head.

Christopher clenched his jaw, his eyes drifting to her hand covering his. Comfort. Support. Friendship. So many things he hadn't experienced in a woman since Carla. So many things he tried to deny he wanted. And now? His throat tightened.

Sara's hand tightened on his. "Is there... is there nothing I can do? I want to help, but.... You would tell me if I could do something to help?"

I've seen you most of my adult life. You've been an encouragement. A hope. A promise. "What more help could you be?"

"B-but it seems I push you into a bad way, even when I try no' to bother." Her voice quivered.

"Sara... you've been as much of a help as Paul or Dix. More even."

"But—Would it be easier if I had no' come?"

His insides recoiled. "Easier? Sara, my daily life has been easier with your coming. Listening to my grief without judgment. Offering another perspective without condemnation.... You gave me the push I needed to step past the grief which might have destroyed my family."

He enveloped her hand in a tight clasp, causing a flush of brilliant crimson. "If you were not here, my life would not be what it is now."

And those words settled into the very center of his being. An intensity of truth that smoldered and then sparked to a sudden burst of life. Giving him reason to struggle forward in his search to confess three simple words.

TWENTY-NINE

Moments in Time

3 March 1894

"Do you want to pick them out, or can Minnie-Gwynnie have the honors?"

Christopher, Gwyn, Sara, and Teddy stood in thoughtful consideration as they regarded the covered canvases on the far wall of the third story. Teddy wouldn't be swayed to wait another day for the unveiling of Christopher's art. To Sara's delight, he invited her to attend their own, more personal unveiling.

Gwyn scrambled to her father and took his hands in a tight clasp. "Please, Papa. Let Sara wake the first one!"

"Of course Sara can wake the first one. But no prompting from you. Take your turn the same as the rest of us."

Gwyn squealed her delight.

"Poppet." Sara caressed the girl's blonde curls. "Calm yourself down, or you will need a nap before the day is done."

Gwyn muffled the giggle, though she continued to bubble over with such youthful euphoria that she slightly bounced on the balls of both feet.

Sara laughed and embraced the girl. "Come along. You can stand close beside me as I unveil." She drew the girl along and they both knelt at the base of the daunting collection of hidden canvases. "Now, which one should I open?"

Gwyn hugged herself to keep silent.

A massive shape lured Sara's attention. She reached for it, expectation catching in her throat—

"Wait."

Sara twitched. Christopher stood beside her. To her surprise, boyish delight brightened his handsome face and very nearly mirrored that of his daughter.

"You gave me a fright," she scolded playfully.

"Did I? Sorry. I believe I know which one that is. I have a fancy to see your reaction." He crouched down beside her. "Go ahead."

Sara pulled aside the cover—Tears misted her eyes. "Oh Christopher." Her heart caught in her throat at the vivid imagery of the Thames of England. Stars and street lamps both glimmered upon the mirror surface of the water. Avenue life, peaceful and quiet. Buildings and houses in full color and radiance. A brighter reminder of home. "How wonderfully lovely."

Gwyn squealed. "I knew! I knew!"

"I painted this from a sketch done years earlier, and from my own memories of course." He chuckled. "I had forgotten this hid up here. I thought I sent it to Mother as a gift three Christmases ago." He cast her a sidelong smile.

"When's your birthday?"

"January second," she said, though her eyes and heart still absorbed the vivid image of a distant home.

Christopher snapped. "Drat." He drew the painting from the others. "I'll have this sent over and hung in your room. Happy Belated Birthday."

Sara blinked up at him. "But I could no' accept something so grand!"

"Don't be ridiculous," Teddy protested. "It didn't cost him a nickel. So, if anything, it's a poor gift. A cheap one, anyway."

"Oh no, Teddy. It is of himself, better than any one thing he could have purchased."

"Good point, Sara," Christopher said. He gave Teddy a firm nudge. "You could have reasoned that out for yourself. Thought is what counts in a gift given. Not the cost."

His friend smirked. "He says that now. Just wait until it comes time for you to give him his gift. That is something else entirely."

"Here now, Parker! Speak for yourself." Christopher shot Teddy a glare while setting the painting aside. "Which one is next?"

"How about this one?" Teddy pointed toward a mid-sized canvas on the right.

"I believe that—Well, I won't tell you. It's a bit of a kick to see Sara's reaction."

But Sara felt an aversion when her eyes fell upon the covered canvas, an impulse away that faded her smile. "Could we no'... could we open the portfolio?" She indicated a small leather folder leaning against one of the other covered canvases.

"Why? Those are just unfinished or unframed. Here."

Christopher stepped toward the previously mentioned canvas. "Let's unveil this one."

"Christopher, no." She caught at his arm. "Please."

He gaped at her. "Why, Sara, what is the matter?"

"Sara, Top never did an image of the war, if that has you worried."

"I...." She stared down at the cover shielding the canvas from their view. "I do no' want to unveil that one."

Christopher regarded her a moment before giving her hand a gentle clasp. "Fair enough. We'll rummage through the folder. It might make a good start for this time-line, don't you think, Teddy? Although it would be a good idea to open with the image of Richmond College. What do you think?"

He guided her toward the portfolio. Sara released a deep sigh and nodded as she followed beside, some part of her attention drawn to the canvas in the right corner.

Christopher was right. The portfolio held unfinished charcoals or watercolors, activities to perfect flowing lines and facial expressions, and a few sketches and watercolors of different types of flowers. Several of the sketches could be used for the beginning of the time-line, but the remaining would be filed away should Christopher wish to reminisce.

Then the unveiling began again, this time Christopher and Teddy doing more of the unveiling with Gwyn hovering over each revealed canvas. Sara watched the trio with a soft smile, sighing now and again as she saw his stress fade almost completely from his features.

The morning he admitted the importance of the Lady of Charcoal she noticed the difference to his expressions. That relieved her heart enough to feel right in keeping her confession of love to herself. There was still so much to learn of this man of calm, intense passion. She felt certain fear did not keep the words 'I love you' from being spoken. Instead, there was a press in her heart which made her believe he wasn't yet ready.

Or perhaps it was she who still needed to wait? Whatever the reason, the waiting seemed right, and Sara was willing to be patient for him. He had already suffered more than any man should, and if a pre-mature confession caused more pain....

Christopher suddenly laughed, and Sara's heart swelled. Yes. She would wait, for love was always worth the bittersweet pain of patience.

22 March 1894

"How are you doing, Sara love?"

Sara pulled her focus from the scenery so slowly changing from winter to spring. Concern and encouragement shadowed the older woman's expression. "I am fine, mum, thanks for the asking."

"His recent change of attitude had a hand in that, I'm certain."

Sara flushed. At times she believed him about to confess something she felt terrified to hope for. But then he would simply smile, give her hand a squeeze, and begin talking of something completely different. Each time it left Sara nearly breathless with her unspoken confession. In fact, the words began to ache within the depths of her soul.

"But why limit your lessons, Sara? They mean so much. To both of you."

"I...." Sara allowed a sigh. "I needed to do something, mum. It is so hard for him, being alone when he remembers naught but being with her. How could I continue to come when I knew how it goaded him?" She shook her head, the lush greens and peeking colors drawing her focus outside. "His heart is not ready for the tenderness of another woman, mum. Not yet."

Dix leaned forward to cover Sara's hands. She peeked to meet the older woman's brown gaze. "The time will come for the soothing, love. If I know my brother, it will come sooner than you think. You've but to remember one thing. Because you think of him before anything else, he'll come to love you the more for it."

Tears brimmed as Sara nodded, doing her best to wipe and blink away the wetness as the carriage pulled to a stop outside Lake Manor.

"One day at a time, Sara love. One day, and one day, and one day."

Sara choked back a sob as the driver opened the carriage door and offered her a hand down. Then Dix steadied Sara's ascent of the stairs with an arm around hers, offering occasional and continuous squeezes as Harold greeted their entry. As they stripped from their coat and scarves, however, Sara didn't hear Christopher's baritone voice, nor the tinkering of paint brushes against palette or water cup.

"Something is no' right," she whispered. The sounds of Lake Manor seemed heavy.

"Harold, where's Chris?"

"I'm not certain, madam. His bed hasn't been slept in, and he has not set foot in either studio or office. Miss Gwyn hasn't seen him, nor Em, and Thomas said he wasn't in the conservatory. He seemed a trifle bothered by a packet in the post, and a single canvas on the upper floor kept him up late with Master Theodore, but...."

Nausea made Sara's skin go cold.

"Sara love, see if he has hid himself away on the third floor. Perhaps he went in search of something?"

Sara nodded and turned away, doing her best to rush while not appearing as if she did so. *Oh Lord, please.* Sara ascended the stairs with care, the front of her skirt held within white-knuckled hands. "Christopher?"

"I'm here, Sara."

He sat at the far side of the room, his back against the wall as he stared down at a canvas held in a loose grip. The expected haggard expression wasn't there. He only seemed tired and thoughtful.

She tried to calm her approach, smoothing the front of her dress to hide the trembling of her hands. She knelt across from him. "Mister Harold said you had no' been to sleep last night."

Christopher head lifted in an absent nod, his gaze still arrested by the image in his hold. "I napped up here."

Sara peeked around her, giving a brief shiver at the chill in the room. "Are you well, sir?"

At that, he met her gaze and offered a slight smile. "I'm fine, Sara. I didn't mean to worry you."

His tender tone caressed her heart, causing a flutter that woke the flame of her cheeks.

"You were right to keep me from looking at this first. But now...." He motioned to the space beside him. "Now I think it's best you see it as well."

Sara adjusted her position, her heart racing when their arms brushed. Then he presented the canvas to her—Sara gasped at the stark image from her history, a girl standing alone, forlorn, by the maw of a shadowed grave.

"That's you, isn't it?" Christopher's arm enveloped her shoulders. "After your mother's funeral?"

"I-I do no'...." She stared up at him, tears blocking any view of his face. "H-how did…?"

"Paul and I were there," he confessed, his voice a hushed whisper. "Remember I said I had a display in London for three years? We explored the lesser-known areas and decided to visit the historical cemeteries that day. I saw the funeral from a distance, and so we made our way over."

Christopher lowered his focus to the canvas. "I prayed for that quiet girl all morning. Even after that day. I could tell a loved one had died, and I didn't want her to feel alone. So, I asked God to comfort her. To protect her. Provide for her. Love her." He turned his head to meet her gaze, his expression so tender the confession burned within her. "I was wrong before, Sara. God answers prayers, for mine have been answered for that young lady."

A sob broke free, and Christopher gathered her into his arms. The strength and warmth of his embrace hastened the tears, and she found herself caught up in a storm of grief. Each morsel of agony, all her lost loves and dreams, she released everything to soak the front of Christopher's paint-stained shirt.

Therein grew the ache. Even as he comforted her the way no one attempted before, she suffered the more for the knowledge she must love him in silence. Though she wanted to offer him passion and intimacy within the trust, she knew she must encourage only in friendship.

He yet grieved his first wife while venturing into the dangerous territory of a second.

That knowledge deepened the sobs, erasing the prayer she felt. It didn't seem fair she would love him so much when he wasn't ready. But God crafted a broader plan than what she could imagine. He always would. All He asked of her was trust and obedience. She followed before. She could again. It would simply be a harder journey, and therefore more of a blessing at the end.

"Blessings and miracles are odd things," Christopher admitted. "It seems they're harder to swallow. More of a challenge to accept. For me, it was easier to believe God took Carla and our son. Why?" He shook his head. "I don't know. Maybe I thought tragedies wouldn't happen because I had accepted Christ. I forgot that our belief is an additional strength. Peace against the hardship. A relationship of support. Instead, I expected... I expected a life without hardships.

"Life isn't fair. There are heartaches, miseries, and a multitude of other things. God is our strength to work through them. Unfortunately, I expected a guarantee against obstacles. I didn't see that I relied less on God for my strength. That was why Carla's death hit me so hard. I tried to control my life rather than trusting God with it, and death was the one thing I couldn't stop or control.

"So, instead of giving over the grief and confusion, I cut God out of my life. Whether it was to punish Him for letting a bad thing happen, or to protect me from having to confess my pride, I don't know. But He never gave up on me. Though I ignored Him, He made certain I had laughter, support, compassion.... All of my friends and family worked together to ready me for the next step: Letting Carla go to memories. Allowing myself to... live life rather than exist in it."

Christopher tugged Sara's arms from around him with a tender pull. When he looked down at her, his entire being smiled. Her throat closed around the words *I love you.*

"When I saw you as the Lady of Charcoal? Believe me, I let Him have it. I fumed and raged until there was nothing left to say. And when I saw this image?" He retrieved the canvas. "When I created this scene on that day so many years ago, there was no doubt in my mind this young lady would be blessed with happiness after the grief. That memory reminded me how much I loved God. It reminded me of the peace and inspiration I once accepted. That... that I had trusted Him with everything at one time. As Carla did. As you still do.

"That made me see what kind of man I had been, what kind of man I wanted to be, and what kind of man I became. Staring down at a maw of blackness that robbed me of my hope and future because of dwelling in a horrible past." He shook his head, and Sara watched his throat convulse with his hard swallow of grief. "And still He remained, doing His best to reach me."

Sara choked back a sob as she reached out to softly stroke his arm. "Because He loves you." *As I do. As I always will.*

Christopher nodded and drew in a ragged breath. "I know. I don't understand how you broke through the wall I built, Sara. I don't think I ever will. But thank you. For listening and praying and saying what God put on your heart to say. For pushing, even when I know you were terrified of what it could mean for you."

He cupped her cheek, tenderly brushing away a tear and then leaning in to kiss her there so softly.... Sara closed her eyes, biting back the whimper. When Christopher leaned back, Sara forced her eyes open.

He offered her another slight smile. "Thank you."

Summoning a return, she swallowed back the soft words pleading to be spoken.

THIRTY

Shifts of Waiting

27 March 1894

Christopher stared at the leather-bound portfolio, the tap of his fingers on the desk the only sound to break the silence. The entire morning images of Sara bombarded him, specifically the one of her waiting at the train station that first day. Remembering the vague change within the numbness. The shift that happened when she looked up to meet his gaze.

That first image always led to another. Of Sara and Gwyn together in the kitchen at the gallery. Then a third of them laughing together over art and colors. To a fourth of Sara delicately exploring the sophisticated scent of lilac. Then her face the evening of her first unveiling. Of her expression at their first painting lesson. Of so many others he feared he would never have enough time to sketch them.

Christopher fisted his hands, seeing again the visions of Sara with his daughter. Playing with her. Loving her.

Teaching her.... He smoothed his hand over the soft leather of the portfolio. The images pushed at him, a poignant reminder of the listlessness after Carla's death. Of the stark contrast after Sara came to them. He felt as if he had once more learned to breathe.

In college he completed page after page without realizing who graced the images with her presence. All dedicated to her silhouette. Her grace. Her elegance and innocence. His hold tightened on the portfolio. Each one acting as a prayer to find the one woman to share his life with.

Then he met Carla.

Christopher didn't want to believe he hadn't been guided to meet and love her. After all, Carla taught him to trust others with his opinion. She tendered the encouragement he had needed to venture into the risk of displaying his art to inspire others. She also taught him a deeper intensity of love, to trust someone with all of their being. Together they learned intimacy, and passion, and the joy that came with the struggle of loving another unique individual.

Christopher opened the portfolio to the first blank page. *This is what I felt when she died, Lord. Everything... gone. Empty.* He retrieved the pencil secured snugly within and gave his hand the freedom to move through memory, following a remembered line of a feminine silhouette. Recalling an elegant stance and inviting posture. But this time the Lady graced him with her smile. This image beckoned to him with startling clarity to her delicate features.

I know now why I gave a little twitch at your profile hidden from my view. You were the subtle reminder of a dream. The introduction, even, to a desire for the fulfillment of that wistfulness.

His gaze held hers, and he did his best to interpret the expression he saw. An expression he felt a slight reluctance to translate.

The pencil lowered, and Christopher released a quick breath. Then he smoothed the shadows of her face and neck with the caress of his finger. *Would I have been the man for your charcoal if Carla and I never met?* The question caused a hesitation before he softened the shading of her smiling lips.

"Mr. Lake, I might not be your sweet Carla, but I can listen if you need to talk about something..." her voice as gentle as he ever heard a woman's tone.

"Something. Everything. Nothing," he said softly, again caressing the line of her jaw and cheek.

"I just keep looking ahead to the blessing that might be waiting around the corner." Her voice choked with tears while her hand tightened in his. Soothing. Warm. Drawing him from the emptiness of his grief. *"Try to listen,"* she had whispered, as if her very heart and soul attempted to return his inspiration. *"Try to hear it."* As if her hushed voice, so soft, would help him into the light.

Christopher smoothed the hair near her forehead, remembering the softness and the scent. Remembering how it curled at her temples and behind her ear, tickling her and inviting a graceful movement of her hand.

The front door opened and closed, the entrant's steps approaching his studio. But Christopher couldn't tear his gaze from the smiling face of hope and welcome. The gem-like eyes twinkling with happiness and support.

The steps halted outside his studio. "Sara is delayed with Dix at home." Paul stepped farther inside, draping his overcoat over the arm of the nearest chair. "How are you doing?"

A long breath was Christopher's only ventured response at first. Then he closed the sketchbook and ran his charcoal-stained hand through his hair. "The inspiration would still be silent if not for her. She has always urged me beyond the fear." Such stark memories of shared laughter and tears. Eagerness and terror. Disappointment... and then the determination to try again. Christopher focused on Paul. "Do you recall the day you brought her for her lesson and we spoke mostly about her second display?"

Paul nodded and sat in the chair across from Christopher's desk. "She blossomed that day more than others, I believe."

"I agree. In fact, that may be the first day I truly saw Sara Ann Little. When she pressed me to leave my rage and grief on the paper, she was so gently forceful. Insightful into an artist's soul. Extremely open to God's healing whisper...." He lowered his attention to the front of the sketchbook. "I see her in an image, did I tell you? Her, Gwyn, Carla... myself so faint in the far corner. It isn't finished, I know, but I can't. Not until I know..." Christopher's chest tightened with the remembered vibrancy—and what it could mean for his future. "Not yet."

"Chris, take one day at a time."

"A day more to do what, Paul?" Christopher pressed, his tone resigned to the truth he could finally admit. "Acknowledge I have needs?"

"No. A day more to hear a question you haven't yet the courage to ask. A day more to be ready for the answer. Let it be."

"I can't, Paul. Her face has been burned into my mind, paired with an image seen since I was a lad barely able to sketch a leaf than a woman. Then there is the attraction I had begun to fight, the morning thoughts of her with Gwyn. The dreams—How can I let it be?" But why couldn't he be certain he loved her?

Christopher lowered his gaze to his paint-stained hands, turning them over, palms upward. But what he saw and felt were a different set of hands. Softness, warmth, comfort in a simple touch. "The care for her is unlike anything.... I talk to her of things I haven't since Carla's passing. Different aspects of my art, various styles, techniques, and assorted ideas for showings at the gallery. Yes, there's attraction, a constant, but...."

"Yet somehow different."

"Am I only attracted to her because she's a lovely woman with the same line as my fantasy Lady? Because—" His face flamed. "Because I need the touch of a woman?"

"Chris."

"Of course it is more than her appearance which appeals to me," Christopher admitted, looking away. "As I said, I'm fond of her because of how much time and care she's taken with me and my daughter. How much passion she shows for the gallery. Her innocence. Her intensity. Her tenacious faith which helped me through my grief and rage. Her inspiration that woke my own. But how do I know if I love her or if she's but a close friend? Carla was a close friend and I didn't realize I loved her until—"

"Chris, the only question you need ask yourself is 'Do I want to spend the rest of my life with her?' "

A life with a wife for his home and a mother for his child? A life with a woman who shared his same passions, who inspired and moved him? A life with a woman... like Sara? "Yes," Christopher admitted roughly.

"Fine then. Nothing else matters."

Christopher spluttered. "How can you say that? I should love her passionately if she's my wife!"

"Who says you don't?"

The question nearly sent him and his chair head over heels. "What?"

Paul's lips twitched upward. "Topper, all these things you've listed are proof of how much you care. Her opinion matters to you. Her reputation. Her safety. You treasure her trust and her insight. You seek her... perception." He motioned to Christopher. "You say you are attracted. Have you acted on that?"

Christopher frowned. "Of course not. Her reputati—"

"Exactly. Always have you been sensitive to what would hurt or encourage. Tenacious about supporting her and what was best for furthering the possibilities for her life. Yes, most of that was done out of responsibility as her sponsor at first, but when you confess these feelings?"

Paul chuckled "Chris, you are so much in love with her that you fear it may change your feelings for Carla and her memory. That is nonsense! I've never seen a man as much in love with his wife as you still are. I've also never before seen a man as completely comfortable and at ease with a woman as you are with Sara. This tells me one truth."

"I—" Christopher gulped down the confession, his gaze drawn to the potency of her likeness. Their eyes met and the sketchbook clattered to the floor. His head fell into his hands as the full intensity of the confession, "I love her," roared in his ears.

THIRTY-ONE

Pleasant Ventures

31 March 1894

Christopher placed the 'Trio of Life' onto the easel within his studio, eyes averted from the vague impression of the man at the corner of the canvas. *'He has something waiting for you.'* He must only journey through the shadows into the shifting colors of a completed picture. One full of heartache, happiness, anger, laughter, pain, joy....

Sighing deep, he finally looked to the man outside the Trio. The man who watched and smiled, knowing he was part of their joy. Welcoming their laughter. Accepting happiness.

The delicate aroma of lilacs and vanilla preceded Sara's soft sigh. "Oh Christopher"

Sara stood in the doorway draped in dusty rose and ivory, her mahogany hair aglow in the light of the sun. Christopher's chest tightened with the intensity of his adoration.

"It is...." Sara lifted those sapphire eyes to meet his gaze. "It is so wonderfully lovely."

"I—" *I love you, Sara.* He forced his eyes from her rose-kissed cheeks to the near mirror image of her on canvas. "I never thought to see anything again. The desire to create was a void."

Sara had recognized that loss in his expression when viewing a blank canvas. The restlessness as they looked to the scenery around him. How did such a timid woman find the courage to press him to change that blankness? To destroy the wall separating him from his inspiration. Urging him beyond the numbness to her friendship. Then beyond the friendship to the fondness. And finally....

She tucked her hand into his to give it a tight squeeze. An offering of encouragement. Of friendship and understanding. His insides burned with desire, a welcome intensity. An intensity God would help him control in order to encourage her trust.

Christopher gave her hand a gentle press and released it to take a step away. "I thought we might share a nature study walk of the conservatory today rather than a formal lesson."

Sara's eyes brightened, her lips parted in an eager smile. "Could we?"

"Maybe the colors will help you along with your inspirations? You seem to paint impressions rather than stark images, reminiscent of Monet, and intensely lovely." He guided her from his studio to the conservatory.

"I do love Monet. You... you believe I may learn to paint that way?"

"Certainly. If your oils reflect a combination of your

sketches and watercolor styles, I don't see why not." Christopher cleared his throat while casting her a sidelong glance. Her blue eyes sparkled with curiosity. "I could show you an example of entwining styles, if you like?"

"You... you will paint something for me?"

"In all honesty, I already did. " He cleared his throat again. "I interpreted one of your sketches."

"Did you?" Sara's face brightened, her blue eyes alight with pleasure. "Might I see it?"

Christopher motioned to a seldom used storage cubby beneath the second-story stairs. "I keep surprises and whatnot under here—Christmas presents or birthday paraphernalia—due to the fact Gwyn never seems to remember where the cubby is."

Sara giggled.

Concern overshadowed Christopher's eagerness to show her the image. "You don't mind?"

"Mind, sir? Mind what?"

"That I painted one of your sketches."

She blinked and tilted her head. "Why ever would I mind? Is it something not done?"

"Well, not without permission, generally."

"Oh." Her eyes crinkled at the corners. "I think it is wonderful, especially since your heart has been so sad with no' seeing the lovelies you painted once. Do you think you might interpret more? Would you mind if I watched when it's done?"

Christopher laughed and reached out to give her hand a collection of squeezes. "No, Sara. I wouldn't mind at all." It was a hope he would firmly hold to.

"Oh I am glad. I seem to learn so much more when I've but just come from viewing the lovelies at the gallery. And for you to have painted one of mine? What a... a...." She giggled and pressed his hand between hers. "I have no' a word for the wonder of it."

He laughed again, reluctantly releasing her hand to open the cubby beneath the stairs. "Well, don't commit yourself to showing wonder and amazement. You mightn't like what I've done with it." He stepped further inside. "Where in the world? I know I tucked it in h– Oh. Here it is." Christopher stepped back, bumping into Sara as he did so. "Sorry. Did I hurt you?"

She flushed and shook her head.

"You're an eager one, aren't you." Christopher chuckled. "Well, here it is."

As he presented the covered canvas to her he found himself almost hungrily watching her expressions. Waiting for the shocked gasp once she lifted the cover. Listening for the whispered "Oh my." followed quickly by the welcome "Christopher...." She looked up to meet his gaze, tears brimming. "I can hardly believe this was one of mine. You present it in a way more real and alive than my timid dream of something wanted once."

Red burned his ears as he self-consciously chuckled. "Oh come now. It's not as good as that."

"But it is." The painting drew her gaze. "It so is."

"I'm glad you like it." The statement drew a slight movement of her lips in a brighter smile. "I wasn't so certain one way or the other. I…" He lowered his gaze, absently rubbing at a paint stain on his fingernail when he felt her gaze. "I don't normally interpret others' work, so it isn't a strong suit of my... ability." Christopher glanced up in time to catch her continued soft smile.

Then she lowered her focus again to the canvas. "But

you are an artist." She slightly shook her head. "Such an artist."

Christopher's face flamed. "Fine, fine. Enough embarrassing the instructor. It's time to get to work." He touched her arm, drawing her attention and her smile before motioning to the canvas. "May I?"

Sara nodded, offering him back the canvas for its return to the cubby. When he turned again to face her, the smile of encouragement and softness on her countenance remained, her hands loosely clasped in front of her as she watched him. His chest tightened at that expression, somehow seeing a parallel with so many soft looks from his Carla—He set it aside, giving her a smile and then touching her elbow as he motioned toward the conservatory entrance.

"It has been an age since I have seen the colors of spring."

"A quiet walk was always my habit when I first began the challenge of watercolors," he told her. And the desire to walk with her to create new memories beckoned.

4 April 1894

"I think that's the best it's going to get," Teddy said, fists on hips as the trio regarded the penciled sketch of the intended display hanging upon the gallery's main exhibit wall.

They had worked non-stop on perfecting the impression of a time-line, one that would correctly display Christopher's artistic growth. It had been an interesting experience, and not too different from when the trio worked to perfect Sara's own art displays. Disagreements, discussions, laughter, and an experience of times Sara had previously never known: A collection of friends drawing closer while doing an enjoyed project.

For Sara, it was an extremely engaging idea and experience to be so intimately involved.

Christopher adjusted his crossed arms. "What do you think, Sara? Good enough?"

Sara continued to regard the charcoal, to watercolor, to oil progression with an absent frown of concentration as she nibbled the nail of her index finger, cheeks burning as Christopher's questioning glance became a somewhat boyish smirk. "Good enough."

"At last." Teddy turned away. "I'm going to head out and get the invitations. I ordered too few envelopes, but we've still got a stash in Minnie-Gwynnie's project room." Teddy shrugged into his overcoat. "Why don't you two start addressing those from the address list in the envelope box? I'll be back once I have the cards. Hopefully they have enough," he finished, mumbling while closing the gallery door behind him.

Christopher motioned behind him, down the hall toward the room where Sara had first seen Gwyn. "I hope you don't mind writing about one hundred invitations long-hand. Carla started me on the habit for those first displays. Said that it showed more care when they were handwritten rather than printed at a print-shop."

"So few people put such thought into things as simple as invitations."

"Teddy abhors the project, and with good reason." A smirk threatened as his hazel eyes twinkled. "His handwriting is atrocious. It looks as if a chicken stepped through an ink blot."

"It could no' be as bad as that!"

He ushered her inside to the adult-sized table and chairs in the opposite corner from Gwyn's. "I'll have him write one, just to prove it."

Sara laughed.

He retrieved a box of envelopes from the bookcase behind them and sat across from her. His knee brushed hers. "Pardon me," he said with an accompanying glance.

"That's fine, sir." She retrieved a handful of envelopes as Christopher arranged the pens on each side of the table, one for her and one for him. She readied her pen and the envelope. "Will you be sending an invitation to your parents?"

Christopher handed her the first few pages of the list and kept the remainder for himself. "I invite them to every display, though I know they won't be able to come each time. The trip from New York is a long one. They send me 'condolences' when they know they won't be able to make it."

Sara smiled as she watched him write the address, imagining him in the same position when he wrote the travel-itinerary letter to her so many months before.... "I hope they can make it to this one."

"I imagine so. They mentioned you in their last letter."

"Me?" Sara blinked at him.

"Dix and Paul write to them on a regular basis." He peeked at her. "And I've sent them a letter or two, along with a few pictures from Gwyn."

A flush colored her cheeks as she lowered her focus to the blank envelope. She didn't know why she felt surprise that he would have written his parents about her. Wasn't she under his care? His protection? Wasn't he doing his best to offer her a new beginning through his gallery? Of course he would write to them and keep them informed.

Christopher set aside the first addressed envelope and situated another, sending her yet another quick glance. "They can't wait to meet you."

Sara swiped away a hint of wetness. His parents. She leaned forward and did her best to focus on addressing her first envelope. The people responsible for teaching him to be the man he was. They wanted to meet her.

"Mother is much like Dix," Christopher warned. He fished out another envelope. "In other words, she'll instantly consider you part of the family and treat you as such."

"That's fine, sir," Sara whispered. It had been years since she experienced the nurturing tendencies of a mother. It would be heaven to have again. And Christopher's mother? Her heart soared.

Christopher smirked. "I guess Father is the same way, but where Mother is more subtle, Father will be a bit more forceful in his... suggestions. He takes initiatives that will more than likely give you a shock."

But he was a father. A figurehead of guidance she never experienced. One she craved and longed after for years. "I will no' mind," she whispered, and she could hear the hint of tears.

"No. I don't suppose you would." The softness in Christopher's tone made another tear brim, this time to tumble down her cheek. He reached across and covered her hand. "I wish you would let me search for your father, Sara."

The tone of his voice drew her gaze, and the expression on his handsome face brought her to the brink of her confession. She bit it back. "Mr. Christopher, he's gone. If he wanted to find me, he could have done so ages ago. Let him be."

"You deserve your family."

A soft smile caressed her lips. "I have one."

Their gazes held for a long moment before Christopher pulled his hand away and lowered his gaze to the partially addressed envelope in front of him. Concern began to rise, but before it took root she heard Christopher quietly say, "And you are welcome," as he again took up his pen.

Welcome.

Sara lowered her gaze to the pen in her hand. Since day one she felt welcomed and comforted, protected and included. Into his home. His family. His gallery. His way of life. Not once did she ever feel a bother, or an encumbrance, or an unwelcome guest. No. He welcomed her into a new life. A new family. Finally, a place to call home.

"Thank you."

THIRTY-TWO

Release to Breathe

13 April 1894

Sara stared at herself in the mirror with eyes twinkling in the soft luminance of the kerosene lanterns. Her face slightly flushed, enhancing the emotion which danced within her expression. The cornflower blue of her gown heightened her beauty, the simple line giving her an outward appearance of nobility. A sophisticate she hadn't known existed. A woman of stature and elegance. Desirable.

"Sara love?"

Sara blinked and looked to the door as it opened to reveal the elegantly beautiful face of Dix. "Yes, mum?"

"Chris is here." Dix closed the door behind her. "You look ravishing."

"Thank you, mum. I...." Sara flushed and looked again to the mirror. "I feel lovely. I never have before."

Dix gently rested her hands on each of Sara's bare

shoulders. "We women always feel beautiful when we're in love beyond anything we understand or know."

Sara lowered her gaze.

"Mother and Father are heart-broken they couldn't come, but I've a feeling there's a reason it didn't come about." The older woman met Sara's timid gaze in the mirror. "Chris has had a hard year, and I believe you're his end and beginning. I feel it in my heart and soul. Your spirit of tenderness will do his aching heart good. Hold that truth to you and don't let it get away."

"I won't."

Then Dix kissed Sara's cheek, giving her shoulders a brief press. "He's waiting in the observatory, dearest. Paul and I are going ahead."

"Of course."

She left the room, the sound of her steps moving away and down the stairs. Moments later, Sara heard the front door open and close and then the carriage as it rumbled down Monument Avenue toward the gallery. Sara blinked, a trembling hand lifting to finger the simple caged pearl dangling from the silver strand.

"Can you believe this, Mum?" she whispered to the reflection in the standing mirror. "A home and family. Friends. A place to be myself. I...." Her throat tightened around the words as her eyes burned. Her life had become a collection of blessings.

Wiping at her cheeks, Sara turned from the mirror to take up her white crocheted gloves from the dresser near the door and make her way out into the hall. At the thought of each happiness experienced thus far, her smile softened. Each one seemed greater and more poignant than the previous. And tonight? Surrounded by the wonders of

Christopher's art as well as the promise of revealing her identity to a public that loved her? She giggled as she made her way downstairs.

At the sound, Christopher stepped from the observatory to lean against the doorframe, crossing his arms as he watched her descend the remaining stairs. The dark charcoal three-piece suit he wore under his heavy woolen overcoat enhanced his good looks, even going so far as to remind Sara of an Italian Baron she met when thirteen. But Christopher's smile and the twinkle in his hazel eyes shined much brighter.

"I believe I may be in the wrong house," Christopher commented. One corner of his lips twitched upward. "I don't remember escorting a princess here."

Sara laughed, the melody echoing through the hall and heightening the brightness of the house. "And I only just thought as how you reminded me of a Baron I met once."

Christopher's left eyebrow rose. "A Baron?"

"Yes. You and your sister both have that European look about you. Did you no' know?"

"Had no idea." He winked. "Perhaps I will have our family lawyer do some ancestral investigating. I could be royalty."

Sara beamed up at him. To her, he was a prince among men.

Harold entered the side-room holding Sara's first display of art. "Mr. Christopher?"

"Yes, Harold?"

Harold motioned behind him toward the main hall.

"Everyone is beginning to gather in the main hall, as you requested."

"Ah. Is it that time already?" Christopher focused on Sara, whose soft expression hadn't wavered from its examination of his profile. He offered her his arm. "Your fame knocks, my dear. Shall we answer?"

Sara flushed and accepted, that her legs began to tremble as he led her forward. "I am so nervous," she admitted, breathless.

Christopher covered her hand with his. "Don't be. You'll be fine." One side of his lips twitched higher. "They'll fall over themselves to print rave reviews if you simply smile and look radiant."

Her cheeks burned a darker crimson, and Christopher chuckled. "You're doing that on purpose," she accused, though she couldn't repress the giggle.

"You can't prove that. Besides, I only said the truth."

Her lips twitched upward, but any further response vanished from mind when every pair of eyes focused on their entrance. Sara fidgeted with the pearl of her necklace as her hand tightened on Christopher's arm.

"Greetings, all." Christopher maneuvered her to a small platform erected at the far end of the main hall.

At the base of the steps to the wooden platform, Christopher stepped away, doing so only after giving her a comforting squeeze of the hand and a very slight wink. Then he stepped up onto the platform and faced the crowd.

"I'm glad to see a lot of new faces among the old ones. It means you've brought friends. Always a good sign for an artist, and not too bad for my gallery, either."

Chuckles rippled through the crowd, ushering a smile to Sara's face and relief to her spirit as she watched

Christopher charm the group.

"I know my exhibit isn't the only reason you've all put in an appearance, and I appreciate your self-control. I don't believe I've heard one question about the ever-mysterious new artist I discovered. Not even from the newspapers represented here today. So, I won't keep you waiting longer."

Hushed silence descended, and Sara caught Christopher's mischievous tilt of lip. She briefly arched an eyebrow. *What are you up to?*

"But first," the crowd released a collection of protests, "a little history, for the benefit of our newspapermen, of course."

Sara gave a slight shake of her head as she breathed, "Christopher Andrew…"

"S. A. L., we'll call the artist 'Sal' to save time," the crowd chuckled, "is a charming artist who hails from Richmond."

A wave of murmurs turned faces toward others with questions and confusion, apparently the exact reaction Christopher hoped for. Sara hid a smile. *Richmond Upon Thames, you imp.*

"Dix," Christopher continued, motioning toward his sister within the crowd, "and her husband invited Sal to contact me and my wife some time ago. Due to scheduling conflicts and responsibilities, the trip to our gallery wasn't taken until earlier this year." Christopher raised a hand. "And before you ask on specifics of the conflicts, answering will be up to Sal and not myself. Personal information, you understand."

The newspapermen standing in the front row near Sara nodded even as they scratched down shorthand notes.

Christopher nodded. "Fair enough. So, the artist arrived and agreed to be taken in as a 'sponsored artist' of my gallery. I agreed to keep their identity secret until they were ready to reveal themselves. After all, displaying artwork is much the same as opening one's very soul to criticism and encouragement alike. It requires quite a sum of courage."

Multitudes within the crowd vocalized agreements, including the newspapermen.

"As I knew it would be, their artwork was an instant sensation. An inspiration and intensity of innocence we haven't seen in a while."

"Not since you pulled your art," came a voice from the crowd.

Christopher smirked. "Yes, yes, Randall. Dix and Teddy have already hounded me about that."

The crowd laughed, and Sara giggled.

"At any rate, your acceptance and encouragement have helped them grow in confidence and ability, believe it or not. Encouraging them even to venture into new media, as you can see by the watercolors now on display. You have made them feel welcome, and because of that, Sal is ready to appear before you to accept your congratulations in person. So, I'm proud to present...."

Christopher stepped down and produced a hand to Sara. The action resulted in murmurs, chuckles and light applause. She flushed and accepted his hand and escort back to the platform. He turned her to face the cheering crowd. "Miss Sara Ann Little, known to many of you as Miss Ann Kreyssler."

The crowd's cheers of "Bravo!" and "Excellent!" drowned the remaining introduction.

"I told you so," he said, casting a wink her direction.

Sara smiled out at the acceptance and encouragement with glimmering blue eyes, unashamed of the tears coursing down her cheeks as she gripped Christopher's hand. When she finally focused on him, she could barely see his smile for the tears and euphoria.

"Congratulations."

When questions began, he focused back out at the crowd and lifted a hand. "One at a time. One at a time. We're all gentlemen and ladies here. No comment, Teddy."

The crowd roared with laughter.

"What do you propose to do about the articles in the *Chronicle*?" the newspaperman from *Harper's* asked.

Another collection of pressures was the result as Christopher answered. "A retraction and apology has already been printed in this evening's edition. And, contrary to what the *Chronicle* would have you believe, Sara and I have been acquaintances. Then I was her sponsor. Then her instructor, and somewhere within we became friends. There have been no trysts nor liaisons."

"What about you, Miss Little?"

Sara's focus shifted from Christopher to the older man in the front row with the thinning hair and the smart dark-brown suit. "Pardon?"

"What's your take on all this?"

That she felt like a princess from a fairytale. That she feared she still slept on the ship crossing the Atlantic. "I...." That, even worse, she would wake to hear the bellowing voice of Mr. Brockle shouting for his breakfast. Sara felt Christopher's firmer squeeze and forced a tremulous smile. "Could someone pinch me, please?"

THIRTY-THREE

Displays of Affection

30 April 1894

Sara clasped her hands in front of her with eager anticipation as she waited with Dix in the front hall of Lake Manor. As Paul kept Christopher away at a breakfast and luncheon with Damon Childers and his wife Maggie, Dix and Sara decorated the conservatory with hand-painted colored-paper lanterns and woven wreaths of flowers taken from the conservatory itself.

Hand-painted colored-paper lampshades had also been placed over each light, fully tested to make sure they wouldn't catch fire, with more woven garlands of flowers bordering the path from entry to dining hall, and from dining hall to conservatory. All other rooms, except for Christopher's studio where his presents were hidden, had been blocked by a garland of vines drooping across the doorway.

Hanging across the width of the front hall was also a carefully crafted and painted banner proclaiming 'Happy Thirtieth Birthday, Christopher'. A larger one hung in the conservatory, where Teddy and some of Christopher's friends from college hid away. Teddy had also arranged for a few of the gallery's featured artists and favorite patrons to attend. The grand total of company, including Christopher and Paul once they arrived, would be thirty.

Gwyn and Thomas hid at a corner street to watch for the carriage's approach. At the sound of running feet, Sara's hands tightened. Then the door flew open and Gwyn and Thomas hurried inside.

"He's coming!" Gwyn squealed, immediately dashing past to inform Teddy.

Thomas chuckled. "He'll be here in two shakes." Then he made his way to help the kitchen staff with final preparations.

Sara sent Dix a bright smile, unable to utter a word through the rising eagerness. The carriage rumbled to a stop outside.

Gwyn took a tight hold of both Sara and Dix's hands. "Oh goody, goody," she whispered.

Sara's skin tingled and her knees grew weak as she heard recognizable laughter and voices drawing closer. She tightened her hold on Gwyn's hand as the pair of men ascended the stairs, the subject of their conversation falling to the wayside beneath Sara's excitement.

The doorknob turned and the door slowly opened, Paul's voice recognized to say, "To England? Hm. You know, I think that would be fun," as he opened the door the remaining way and stepped inside.

Christopher immediately followed, turning to the

duty of closing the door and missing the view of gathered women. Paul sent the ladies a wink.

"I think so," Christopher was saying, nonchalant. "It would be a welcome escape from all the pressure here, for both you and Dix."

Sara and Gwyn exchanged quiet smiles and giggles, looking up in time to see Christopher's expression of shock.

"Happy birthday, Papa!" Gwyn squealed, scrambling forward to launch herself against his legs.

Christopher gaped at her for a long moment before the expression melted to a smile and he knelt to gather her into a one-armed hug. "And who thought and plotted this little surprise?" he asked, looking up at Paul and Dix. "One guess."

Paul laughed, shaking his head. "Guilty only in getting you out and back without suspicion. Everything else was the thought of these two lovelies."

Christopher stood, gathering Gwyn's hand in his as he stepped toward Sara. She held his gaze, cheeks aflame as she held herself in check. "Happy Birthday, Mr. Christopher."

"Well." Paul motioned down the hall. "I don't know about you, but I am in dire need of coffee and cake. Lead me, fair sweetness of the heart."

Dix laughed. "With pleasure, darling."

Christopher's focus didn't waver as he came to stand beside Sara. He presented her a leather-bound sketchbook. "This is for you."

"It is beautiful!"

He chuckled. "I am glad you like it, but I meant that what is inside is for you."

"Inside?" Sara opened the book, her voice catching in her throat at the first sketched image. "Oh Christopher." The image brought her back to her first days at Lake Manor, in the conservatory, when she first discovered the wonderful aroma of lilac.

"What is it, Papa? Did you get me one?" Gwyn squeezed his hand.

"It's for both of you, pictures sketched these past weeks."

"Pictures!" Gwyn danced around Sara, arms extended. "Is it you, Sara? Is it me? Can I see?"

Sara presented the leather book. "I will let you be the very first to see, poppet."

"Goody!" Then she scampered off toward the conservatory, clasping the book tightly against her chest.

Christopher offered Sara his arm. "That action was wiser than you know."

Sara laughed. "The dear. She will guard it diligently." His calm smile drew a peek. "You did very well at acting surprised."

The welcome sound of his baritone chuckle caused a tingle as Sara smiled up at him. "Because I was surprised. I had forgotten all about the party, to be honest."

"I am glad. Gwyn was so hoping Mr. Paul would no' confess the secret."

"Paul confess a secret? He would rather die than ruin a surprise. The more elaborate he needs to be, the better he likes it."

"Then this surprise must have made him see stars. All the intrigue and the tale-telling. Even getting your own chum mixed up into the scheme."

Christopher laughed. "I thought Damon seemed in a better mood than before. How long have you and Dix planned this party?"

"Since my second display."

"What?" He blinked down at her.

"It was such fun." She motioned to the colored lamps. "And see? We were able to do so many more creative things, and they took hardly any at all time to hang. It was worth the extra effort. After all, we only turn thirty once."

"Thank God."

"You know you do no' mind the extra attention."

"No, I suppose I don't." He leaned slightly toward her. "Which, of course, will prove Dix's point that I'm spoiled." Sara laughed. "That makes me think you don't believe me."

"I do," she said. "I only do no' mind doing it."

Because he never asked her for anything in return. He only gave when she was too afraid to ask, provided when she was uncertain where to go next, and supported and pushed when she was too scared to step forward.

"What was this about England?" Dix asked, her eyebrow arched as she regarded the handsome face of her husband.

Paul's lips twitched upward as he sipped his punch. "England, Sweet?"

"Don't give me that, Paul Michael Donovan. You and Chris are sharing a secret and you offered your expertise, didn't you, silly man?"

Paul kissed her hand again. "I did."

Releasing a deep breath, Dix rolled her eyes. "So we're away once more to England and adventure when we've only just become settled here again. Whatever will I do with you?"

"Come with me to England and leave your baby brother

and his inspiration to their own mischief," he proposed, winking.

Dix slightly smiled as she shifted her attention to watch Sara and Christopher. They spoke with a collection of friends and patrons of the gallery, a cluster of about eight people circled about the two.

"Her arrival couldn't have been more perfect," Paul said, drawing her focus. He smiled his usual boyish charm. "Chris was ready to struggle out of the grief and loss. He only needed a different... voice than what we offered."

"Now they need to make it through the next pain." Dix looked back to the pair as Mr. Jeffrey Stillwell approached the couple, patting Christopher on the back and drawing his attention.

Paul focused again on the laughing couple. "I've often said the Lord works in mysterious ways, and this shock of her being his 'Lady of Charcoal' was no different. It made him realize that his fondness and affection were more than what he thought."

"So... he loves her?"

"I truly believe he does," Paul agreed, nodding. "The only truth giving him problems is how much he loves her. The feelings are different than what he felt for Carla, and that makes him feel guilty. I think it will also be a continuing struggle for him, but one that he's willing to face with Sara."

Dix looked toward the couple when Teddy approached. "It looks as if presents are about to be unveiled. I can hardly wait to see Chris' reaction to one particular gift," she confessed.

"Do tell," Paul said, tone highly interested.

Dix laughed. "Oh darling."

"One more, Gwyn, and then you must go to bed."

The entire crowd complained in unison with Gwyn. But the girl was coaxed, as was the crowd gathered in the conservatory, and Christopher was offered one more present to open. The little girl scrambled back onto her father's lap to wait.

"And who is this one from?" Christopher read the affixed card and looked up to meet Sara's gaze. "From our lovely hostess."

Sara flushed. He began the duty of unwrapping the gift, the colorful paper joining its fellows that littered the area around him. Hostess of Lake Manor. *Oh if it could be so, Lord.* Sara peeked at him as the final bit of paper fell away, the unveiling drawing a hushed exclamation from the crowd. But Sara's eyes did not shift from Christopher's countenance, hungry for the approval and acceptance of this particular canvas.

An entwining of charcoal and watercolor depicting him and Gwyn together, as she had seen them so many times as a family. Gwyn the key to Christopher's smile, and he the foundation to Gwyn's loving personality.

"Oh Papa," Gwyn breathed.

Murmurings and soft exclamations of wonder began to rise within the gathered group, but Sara could only watch Christopher as he stared at the image. How his throat struggled with a hard swallow. How he blinked several times in succession to keep back the emotion. How his thumb caressed the specifically chosen frame.

Sara released a sigh of relief. *He loves it.*

A nudge at her elbow gathered her focus. Teddy winked

at her. He alone knew of her terror. Creating an image with such personal intensity fell well beyond what she ever risked before. Her heart soared with his acceptance.

Christopher met her gaze. "Thank you."

The gruffness of his voice sent her heart into her throat, allowing only a smile as she stepped forward to gather Gwyn from his lap. "Come along, Miss Gwyn."

"But, Sara."

"You promised you would go to bed when we said you were to go," Sara reminded. "That's why we let you stay up this late."

The chuckles of the crowd followed Sara and Gwyn as the two exited the conservatory.

"But it's Papa's birthday. I want to stay up with all of you."

"I know you do, poppet, but it's just too late for pretty girls like you." Sara adjusted Gwyn in her arms and onto her left hip as she navigated the hall and then up the stairs to the second story. "I'll be sure to have your papa draw lots of sketches of everyone dancing and laughing."

Gwyn picked at Sara's single silver strand necklace. Her lower lip protruded. "I suppose...."

Sara kissed the girl on the cheek. "Do no' fret. We can have another party for your papa tomorrow. This time you can be there for the entire event. It will be just us, and your Auntie Dix and Uncle Paul. Fine?"

Gwyn threw her arms around Sara's neck and kissed her. "Oh thank you!"

"But you must promise to go right to sleep. There will be no' sneaking out to watch."

Gwyn nodded, eyes wide. "I promise."

"Good girl."

Sara set Gwyn gently upon her bed, helping her from dress to nightgown and then brushing her hair and tying it into braids with ribbons.

"Where did you put the leather book your papa gave me?" Sara tucked the girl under the covers.

"I gave it to Harold so that it'd be safe."

"Good girl." Sara kissed Gwyn on the forehead. "Say your prayers."

Gwyn closed her eyes and folded her hands. "Dear Lord, thank you for papa. Please tell Mamma I love her. Thank you for bringing Sara. Please give me good dreams and... and..." Gwyn peeked at Sara from one eye. "And please make Sara my new mamma. Thank you. Amen."

Sara caressed the girl's blonde ringlets. "Good night, poppet. Sweet dreams." Once in the silent hall, she slumped against the closed door. "Amen, Lord. Amen."

Christopher finished his third navigation through the dancing couples in the dining hall of Lake Manor. "Have you seen Sara?" he asked Paul, stopping him on his way to Dix with a glass of punch.

"Not since she took Gwyn upstairs. Sorry, Topper." Paul gripped his shoulder. "Happy birthday."

"Thank you." Christopher turned from the main portion of the dining hall to make his way to the front foyer. "Harold." The older man exited the conservatory with a box of trash. "Have you seen Sara?"

"Yes, Mr. Christopher." He gestured back to the conservatory doors with a motion of his head. "She has wandered to the far portion of the conservatory. To the gazebo, in fact. I have taken her a glass of punch."

"Is she fine?"

"Oh yes, Mr. Christopher. She told me she wanted a moment to look through the book you gave her before going into the party."

"Ah." He glanced beyond to the etched glass doors. His eagerness to see her alone made him force his feet to remain still. He offered Harold a smile. "Did you need some help?"

"No, Master Chris. I can handle a few boxes of gift wrap. You enjoy your party."

Then he passed to places unknown, leaving Christopher to stare at the conservatory doors in silence and hesitation. It would be the first time in several hours he could be alone with her. A perfect time to make a confession of her worth to him. His hesitation centered on the fact he had no clue how to preface the admittance. Blurting didn't seem very romantic.

Christopher scrubbed at the back of his neck. "Oh why not?" He pushed through.

The gazebo came into view, and his steps slowed. Sara sat upon the lower steps, her burgundy gown fanned out around her as she viewed each image with silent intensity. If an easel and canvas stood beside him, her rapt attention to his sketchbook cradled in those delicate hands would have found itself immortalized in oils.

Christopher cleared his throat.

She flushed and smiled, swiping hints of wetness from her cheeks. "Hello."

"Hello, Sara."

She closed the sketchbook and repositioned it within her lap, her gaze not wavering from his. "I am no' avoiding the party. I promise. I only wanted a bit of time to see all the lovelies."

"I know. I met Harold just outside." He motioned to the sketchbook as he sat beside her. His eyes drank in the emotion of her face. "Do you like them?"

The book drew her gaze, and she smiled as she ran her fingertips along the cover. "I love them. They feel a little like re-living memories of my favorite moments with you. Thank you."

His gaze traced the lines of her cheek and jaw. The curls at her temples. The soft line of her neck. "It was my pleasure."

She flushed and lowered her gaze again to the book, silence descending. A silence Christopher dreaded at one time. Now? It was comfortable, simple, and oh so welcome.

Christopher pulled a bit of flower from the vine entwining the column to his left. "Thank you for the party, Sara."

"It was my pleasure to do for you, Christopher."

The caress of his name stood the hairs on the back of his neck and opened a door to a vision of a new future, but with a different silhouette. A different face. One that was welcome. One that... he felt he had seen his entire life.

"I am glad the party makes you smile like that," she whispered.

Christopher met her gaze. "Hm?"

She shook her head, cheeks flushed. "Nothing." Then her gaze retreated from his and she hugged the sketchbook to her chest.

Christopher watched her intense reverie as she stared away. Welcoming the desire to hold her, to show her just how much he cherished her presence in his life. His chest tightened with the possibilities. The opportunity to accept what she offered with such eagerness, and this time as more than 'friend.'

Sara released a soft breath. "Christopher, I...." Cheeks flushed, she cast a quick glance. "I do no' know how to thank you for all you have given me. You make me.... Even through your ache for your sweet wife you always made me feel welcome. I never knew such before coming here."

"I promised to protect you, Sara." He set aside the flower to take her hand in his. "With everything you offered to me and my Gwyn, such was easy enough to want for you."

When her presence helped him past the grief which held him back for so long? Yes. For now he could face the darkness to reach the light.

Clearing his throat, Christopher lowered his focus to that warmth in his, watching as his hand continued to envelop hers. A hold of support which rescued him from the emptiness. A tender touch that never demanded anything. How could he do anything except love her?

"Are you well, sir?"

He couldn't help but smile. "No. No, I don't think I am." Those beautiful eyes shone with brilliant clarity. He chuckled. "I don't think I've been 'well' since meeting you."

Sara's initial reaction was a blink.

Then those rose lips curved upward, and it was that smile which did an odd thing to Christopher. There, surrounded by the newness of spring and the soft scent of roses and lilacs, he found himself reaching out to caress a tendril of hair from her cheek. "Sara Ann Little, do you have any idea how much I love you?" The confession slipped forth as if it were the simplest of questions.

Again, Sara blinked, her quick intake of breath a momentary pause before a glimmer of tears. "What did you say?”

Christopher brought her hand to his lips, the caress lingering upon the velvet of those inspired fingers. “I love you, Sara Little.” A tear dripped down her cheek and Christopher leaned in to kiss it, closing his eyes at the warmth. “I don’t want to lose you ever again. Please, Sara. Be my wife.”

Sara choked a happy sob, drawing him close as she whispered “Yes, Christopher. Yes, yes, yes, forever and ever yes!” in a voice that sang.

He pressed his lips against her hair, reveling in her choked whisper of love as his arms finally embraced the woman from his dreams. God had presented a better tomorrow, giving Christopher a place to rest, supported and secure, within the arms of his Lady of Charcoal.

EPILOGUE

Sweet Dreams, Mamma

The woman stood misty and faded, vibrant green eyes twinkling with her smile as she kissed a young girl's forehead. The girl looked up, an expression of quiet knowing on her face. The woman offered her a soothing smile and brushed the blonde hair from her cherub-face with a somewhat trembling hand.

"You know I cannot come anymore, Gwyn?"

Gwyn nodded. "I know, Mamma. Sara's going to be mamma now. Like you said she would."

"That's right, sweet darling. You be her Angel Girl now."

Gwyn nodded again. Then she gave her mother's hand a tight squeeze. "I will always remember you, Mamma."

Carla Lake lowered herself onto the side of the bed again, enveloping Gwyn's little hand in both of hers. "As long as you live, Gwyn, you'll remember me. My face might not be bright in your mind, and my voice might not be clear in your ear, but you will remember me. Like a whisper. Or a bit of a favorite song." She leaned down to once more kiss her daughter's forehead. "You will always remember me."

Gwyn wrapped her arms tight around her mother, tears escaping. "I love you, Mamma."

Carla returned the embrace. "I know you do, Angel Girl. I love you, too."

Gwyn sniffed as she pulled back, tear-filled green eyes meeting her mother's. "Tell Baby Andrew I love him."

Carla touched her daughter's nose. "I will, darling." Then she urged Gwyn deeper under the covers and tucked them tightly around her. "Sweet dreams, Angel Girl."

"Sweet dreams, Mamma," the little girl whispered.

Carla offered her daughter another smile before standing from the bed and exiting the room, walking the halls and the stairs she remembered from another life.

Then, quiet and serene in expression, she paused outside her one-time escape; the room of flowers, scents, and blooms which held so many pleasant memories. Softly smiling, she rested her hand against the warmth of the glass. "May the Lord's blessings always be warm within your heart, may love never be far from this house, and may warmth and laughter always surround you."

Then she paused a moment more before turning to move away, fading to her new home within memories; his searching finally ended.

COMING IN 2014

Releasing Yesterday

Heart of the Blessed | Book Two

Christopher Lake accepted his hat and coat from the elderly gentleman who had been with him since before he could remember. "I'll be back later today, Harold. Likely with my father and mother in tow."

"Yes, Mister Christopher. Oh. A letter from a Mr. Conklin came in the post last night. I've put it into your overcoat pocket for reading on the way to Miss Sara."

Sara. Christopher smiled and nodded, hazel eyes twinkling with the welcome hiccup of expectation as he adjusted his overcoat and buttoned it up. "Thank you, Harold. If Roger Whitaker calls, give him the Donovans' number. Paul and Dix are leaving for England this next weekend, remember, and I need to touch base with Roger to inform him of the new plans."

"Yes, Mister Christopher."

Christopher took the armful of collected newspapers and quarterlies from Harold's hands and turned to step outside into the early morning dimness. He took in a deep breath and smiled heavenward. It felt ages since the last time he enjoyed a morning. Now he saw inspiration and brightness in everything around him. Teddy Parker, longtime friend from college, would have scoffed and made some sadistic remark about killing someone with sickeningly sweet sentiments of happiness.

Chuckling, Christopher boarded the carriage after bidding Patrick good morning. Then the carriage was off toward Monument Avenue and his sister's home. Christopher set his mound of papers beside him and searched within his pockets for the mentioned letter.

Chris,

I apologize, but an unexpected trip to England will make contact regarding the joint displays between our galleries impossible.

My business in England couldn't be put off. In fact, this particular trip has been several years in coming. When I return, I hope to plan a meeting between you and myself so that we can discuss details of the joint display, as well as the possibility of something on a grander scale. My own gallery hasn't had the influx of new material yours has been blessed with, but only due to a secondary issue that has demanded my attention. An issue soon to be resolved, prayerfully.

On another note, enclosed you will find a business card of a Mr. Leonard Johnson, Attorney at Law. I have contacted him with explicit instructions to give you whatever help is needed regarding the articles published in the 'Chronicle'. Correspondence has also been forwarded to the editor there, requesting a retraction of the slanderous suppositions as well as a formal apology to yourself and Miss Kreyssler, as well as S. A. L. If no retraction is posted by a set date, Mr. Johnson will be contacting you regarding further steps to be taken.

I have no tolerance for slander and suppositions that do nothing but encourage the idle wagging of gossip mongers' tongues. I have found both yourself and Miss Kreyssler to be charming individuals with a genuine care for each other as well as a passion for those you come into contact with. I will not stand idly by while those reputations are sullied and abused. Hence my forward action.

Once I return from England, I will immediately contact you, Miss Kreyssler, and Mr. Johnson regarding this issue and others.

With regard,

Joseph Conklin

Christopher smirked and tucked the letter away. *Again I see why Sara likes him.* Especially with the way he seemed to have adopted the two. Christopher laughed. "No one has ever taken me under their wing before. Well, not since Paul gave me the attention with the display in London when I was just out of college. Even now I wonder if it wasn't just to have a second honeymoon with Dix." Christopher chuckled while admitting it felt nice to have the added support.

The carriage rumbled to a stop outside the Donovan's home as Christopher again gathered the newspapers and quarterlies. "Patrick, can you hold these while I step down. I don't think Sara would appreciate a broken fiancé."

Patrick chuckled and accepted the armful of papers, giving Christopher the needed extra balance in order to step safely down from the carriage.

Christopher accepted back the articles. "Thank you, Patrick."

Patrick tipped his cap, revealing thinning silver hair. "You be needing me to stay around, Master Chris?"

"If you could. I'm sure Gregory won't mind you hanging around the kitchens for some cider or coffee."

Patrick grinned and tipped his cap again. "You have yourself a good morning, Master Chris."

"I will, Patrick. Thank you.

Christopher ascended the stairs, his expression softening to a different smile as the door opened to reveal Sara's bright face and slender form. She wore a blouse and skirt of ivory and cornflower blue, and the sunlight set her mahogany-brunette hair aflame. Each time he saw her he was amazed at her grace and beauty, as well as her welcome resemblance to his Lady of Charcoal. God's perfection of timing in revealing the fact still awed him.

He crested the stairs and returned her softly quiet welcome of "Good morning."

Once inside, she freed the papers from his grasp. "How are you this morning?" she asked, her voice wonderfully hushed.

Christopher shrugged out of his overcoat as he watched her watch him. "Good. You?"

If it was possible, the expression within her blue eyes softened. "Happy." The confession brought a flush.

One side of Christopher's lips tilted upward. "I see that." He tossed his hat onto the hall table and took the stack of papers back from her. "I'm glad to see I still have that affect."

Sara giggled, encouraging a wider smile from

Christopher, and then guided him farther into the house. "Are those the articles about your display?"

"About yours as well, and anything relating to the gallery. I thought we could go through them and make a scrapbook."

Sara gasped, her dark blue eyes wide.

Christopher chuckled along with the spark that lifted the hairs on the nape of his neck. "I hoped you would like the idea."

"My mum and I made scrapbooks all the time. We would use flowers from a walk, or bits of material or a program from a play. I loved making them. It was such an adventure."

Christopher watched the memories dance across her face as she spoke, wishing he could have seen some of those moments of her life. To try and understand a bit more how she could be so firmly grounded in a faith that he had turned from in his strongest time of need.

"I..." Sara's expression darkened. "I wish I could show you one," she confessed.

Christopher gave her arm a slight nudge with his elbow. "Stories will be enough. And with your sketches?" He nudged her again, and this time she flushed. "It will be as if they were done then and there. Better even than some of the photographs and tin-types I've seen."

"I have never had my photograph taken," she admitted. "It sounds as if it might be fun."

"It isn't. You must stand quite still." Christopher winked toward her, the sound of the staff setting breakfast onto the table in the breakfast nook growing in volume as the couple approached. "Gwin hasn't mastered it yet."

Sara giggled.

"We're determined to try again for Christmas this year. Hopefully being six this coming July will give her the needed... inspiration."

Sara muffled her louder giggle with a hand over her mouth as her eyes twinkled up at him, crinkling at the corners. A growing desire nearly choked him as he smiled down at her. He enjoyed the attraction and the pursuit of a more intimate knowledge of Sara and her past.

"Your childhood photographs were adorable," Sara was saying. "You looked so serious."

Christopher's ears reddened, and he looked away as he adjusted his hold on the papers in his arms. "Dix promised she wouldn't ever show those."

"But why not? They're wonderful."

When he glanced toward her, he noticed her expression blossomed from curiosity to a soft smile as she stared ahead.

"I love looking at them. It is like watching you grow up."

She sighed and lowered her gaze, and the action of wrapping her arm around his seemed almost... absent-minded. Natural. Christopher watched her profile as she continued forward, slowing their pace and deepening his examination. He wanted to understand why he had this almost instinctual friendship with her. Why they 'clicked' so much differently than he had with Carla. Why he began to feel as if he had known her for years rather than months.

"I did no' ever have a true childhood friend," she confessed. "Not one to grow with. My mum and I moved a bit too much for that, I suppose. But seeing so many in your photographs and paintings made me more able to know what it would have been like. I almost lived it with you." Sara released another breath, but this time she glanced toward him to meet his soft scrutiny. She flushed.

The pair came to a stop just shy of the entry to the breakfast nook, Christopher turning more to face her. His lips tilted higher. "Don't let those photographs and paintings fool you. I didn't have many friends growing up. Yes, I had a pack of fellows to run around with at church brunches and museum events or picnics, but they went home and so did I. Paul and Teddy are my only true friends." Christopher nudged her arm with the stack of papers and guided her into the breakfast nook. "And you."

The glow in her blue eyes shifted, settling into a calm smile that stole his breath. He pressed his lips lightly against her forehead, his ears reddening with the action. Then he took back the quarterlies and papers, giving her a wink that had her blue eyes twinkling. "These will wait for later. After breakfast, but before Dix and the rest get back from the station."

Handing them off to Gregory with a direction to put them safely into the front observatory, Christopher offered her his arm and escorted her to the table. "Do you realize this is the first meal we've had to ourselves since I proposed?"

"Is it?"

"Indeed." Christopher pulled out her chair. "I think Dix is getting back at me for something I don't know I've done."

Sara softly laughed. "Oh Christopher. Don't be ridiculous."

Christopher reached across the table to cover her hand with his and give a gentle pressure. When he did, her bare ring finger dragged his focus. His smile wavered as he gaped at it. *Chris! You didn't get her a ring?*

"Christopher? What's the matter?"

His face reddened as he met her gaze. "I just realized I didn't get you a ring." But he hadn't expected to propose at the time.

Sara's expression softened. "I do no' need a ring."

"You deserve a ring, Sara."

Pulling his hand from hers, he retrieved the chain from around his neck. Christopher stared down at the pair of rings dangling from the chain before undoing the clasp and dropping them to his palm. He retrieved one with a slow motion, looking within at the inscription before reaching out to take Sara's hand.

It fit as if fashioned for her.

He fingered the ring with his thumb, still holding her hand. "I suppose I shouldn't be surprised."

Sara stared down at it for a long moment before releasing a long breath. "Christopher." She slipped off the ring and tucked it into his palm, folding his fingers around it. "Christopher, I am not trying to replace your Carla. I am Sara, and I love you. And I love your Gwyn. And I will marry you, if you will have me as your wife." She clasped his hand within both of hers and very slightly shook her head. "But the good Lord would never ask me to try to be your Carla."

"Sara, I don't want anyone supposing anything as what the *Chronicle* did. A ring protects your reputation."

She brushed the hair at his temples with a gentle touch of her fingers. "Dear Christopher..." Then she again covered his hand with hers. "Carla's ring is Carla's ring, and I have no right to wear it. I love you the more for the reason behind the offer, but in my heart of hearts... I could no' do such a thing."

"Sara—"

Sara shook her head, giving his hand a gentle squeeze. "I can wait for the ring I am destined to wear, Christopher, just as I have waited for you."

Setting the rings and chain onto the table, he could only stare at her in shock as she continued to smile. Again and again she made her own place in his life, as well as in the lives of those around him. Again and yet again she never attempted to take Carla's place. She allowed him to love and remember his first wife without a reason to feel guilt because of it.

"Sara." But what else could he say to this woman that understood things he didn't know needed to be understood?

Giving his hand a gentle squeeze, she voiced a quiet, "I know," before focusing on the plate before her.

Lowering his gaze to his own breakfast, he could only stare down at it, his appetite suddenly lost. When he felt her sidelong glance, he cleared his throat and forced a smile as he met her somewhat dark blue eyes. "I love you," he found himself saying. He blinked and then laughed. "I'm sorry. That wasn't what I intended to say at all," he confessed while giving the back of his neck a scrub. *You what?* "Oh, erm, not that it isn't true. It was only... um... Well, I um—" *Blast it all, Chris!*

"Dear Christopher." Smiling, she motioned to his coffee cup. "You haven't yet had your coffee. Have some and settle your nerves."

Tension drained from his muscles and he rested an elbow onto the table, chin in hand. "I'd rather watch you eat breakfast," he heard himself informing her, immediately feeling the red reach his hairline as he kept himself from reacting to it. *You're making a fool of yourself.* But when she laughed, he found he didn't care.

Reviews are golden! Please consider leaving a review.

About the Author | Nona Mae King

Writing has been Nona Mae King's passion since childhood. She began writing young adult novels as a teen, graduating to inspirational and suspense romances in college. She also wrote and co-directed full-length plays for her home church, Canby New Life Foursquare.

In 2006, Nona moved to Washington State from her home in Oregon and married Michael King, a fellow writer, and continues to pursue a career in writing as an independent writing and editing professional for *Angel Breath Books*. She specializes on novels of romance and adventure. All the novels focus on faith, honor, respect, and the importance of communication in our relationships.

Connect with Nona Online:

Twitter: @nonamaeking
Facebook: facebook.com/NonaKing
Amazon: amazon.com/author/nonaking
Smashwords: smashwords.com/profile/view/nonaking
Book site: angelbreathbooks.com/

99003995R00234

Made in the USA
Middletown, DE
10 November 2018